HEARTS
OF
WAR

A NOVEL

HANNA WALKER

IMAGINEWE
Publishers™
ImagineWe Publishers
A Global Publisher

IMAGINEWE
Publishers™

Published by ImagineWe, LLC
ImagineWe Publishers
247 Market Street, Suite 201
Lockport, NY 14094
United States
www.imaginewepublishers.com

ISBN: 978-1-946512-94-9 (Paperback)
ISBN: 978-1-946512-95-6 (Hardback)
Library of Congress Control Number: 2024918801

For more information about publishing with IWP, please visit the website listed above. To shop our selection of books and merchandise you can visit: shop.imaginewepublishers.com

For my late grandmother, Susan.

It is because of you that a seven year old girl
dared to make sense of the worlds inside her head.
It is because of you that she still does.

You live within every word I write.

Contents

An Introductory Guide to the Greek Gods and Goddesses in Hearts of War

ZEUS: *The God of the Sky and Thunder. Also known as the king of the gods, and father to many of the minor deities. Zeus overthrows his father, the titan Cronos, and becomes the leader of the gods. He resides on Mount Olympus and is married to Hera, the Goddess of Marriage and Family. Zeus is known for the lightning bolt he wields, which he occasionally hurls from the sky like a spear.*

POSEIDON: *The God of the Sea. He is one of Zeus's brothers, and he rules over everything related to water. He is married to Amphitrite, and is known for having mood swings strong enough to cause shipwrecks.*

HADES: *The God of the Underworld. He is also one of Zeus's brothers. He is the ruler of the dead, and resides in the underworld with his queen, Persephone, and his three-headed dog named Cerberus. He is known for being cunning and manipulative, but merciful to those who deserve it.*

ATHENA: *The Goddess of Wisdom and Strategy. She is a daughter of Zeus, and as the myths say, she sprang from his head one day fully grown and clothed in armor. Historical and mythological sources paint her as the smartest and savviest of all the gods, with a love for mind games. She is perhaps best known for her role in Homer's epic poem The Odyssey, in which she helps to guide the* wayward Odysseus home to the island of Ithaca after the Trojan War. In Hearts of War, Athena does indeed embody the traits History has assigned to her, but she is also incredibly passionate, determined, and fiercely loyal. She can get stuck inside her head sometimes, and she can be terribly rigid, but she cares for the fate of humanity and believes deeply in the power of knowledge.

APHRODITE: The Goddess of Love, Beauty, and Passion. Her origins are somewhat vague, and vary a bit. Some ancient texts say she was born from seafoam–produced after the titan Cronos severed his father's genitals and threw them into the ocean. Other accounts say she is the daughter of Zeus. She is best known for her affiliation with lust and sexual desire, and her beauty has been revered for centuries. Her son, Eros (also known as Cupid), is also a god of love. It was decreed by Zeus that Aphrodite would marry the God of the Forge, Hephastus. Their marriage was largely an unhappy one, and Aphrodite had an affair with Ares, the God of War, with whom she had several children. In Hearts of War, Aphrodite's historical portrayal as a lustful and vengeful goddess is not as prevalent. She is incredibly kind, compassionate, and caring–she represents all forms of love, including romantic, platonic, familial, etc.

ARES: The God of War and Courage. He is the son of Zeus and Hera, and is the embodiment of a soldier in battle. He is opportunistic and strategic, but often lacks compassion and empathy for his fellow gods or the plight of humans. He is frequently depicted with a shield and sword. In Hearts of War, he is not a villain, but more of an antagonist. He often has a difference of opinion from his sisters, and he isn't afraid to let them know.

APOLLO: The God of the Sun, Prophecy, Healing, and Plagues. He is a son of Zeus, and has a twin sister named Artemis. He is also known for his love of music, dance, and archery. He is often described in myths carrying a bow and arrows, but in Hearts of War, he does not. He can be a bit of a trickster when he wants to be, and he takes a very neutral stance on death–he believes that prophecy decides when one's time to die is, and there is nothing to be done about it. It is not good or evil, only necessary. He has a soft spot for animals.

ARTEMIS: *The Goddess of the Hunt. She is a daughter of Zeus, and Apollo's twin sister. She is often depicted in the act of hunting on her horse, with her arrows ready to fire.*

AMPHITRITE: *The Goddess of the Sea. She is a sea nymph chosen by Poseidon to be his wife. She represents all things aquatic.*

HEPHAESTUS: *The God of the Forge and Metalworking. He is the son of Zeus and Hera, and he was born with a congenital impairment that resulted in lameness. He was cast off of Mount Olympus by Zeus for protecting his mother from Zeus's unwanted advances. He was betrothed to Aphrodite, although their marriage was not a happy one. After she had an affair with Ares, Hephaestus created a cursed necklace in his forge and presented it to Aphrodite's daughter as a wedding present. The necklace turned the girl into a snake, and as a result Zeus banned her to Elysium (the afterlife).*

OVERTURE
Athens, 2022

It is early evening on a balmy day in May. The setting sun lights up the sky in shades of amber and crimson, turning the streets of Athens warm and golden. People sit on crowded patios outside restaurants, smiling and laughing as they sip expensive wine. A young boy stands against a wall playing a violin, the mind of a composer long dead coming alive in his fingertips. Birds chirp; cars wobble down cobblestones never intended for their tires.

A woman crosses one of these streets, the heels of her red suede pumps clicking against the old stones in a steady, assured rhythm. She isn't in any particular hurry, although, of course, there is always somewhere to be. Her journey continues along the crowded sidewalk, and her presence garners more than a few stares as she passes by windowpanes and family dinners. This is to be expected—she has never gone unnoticed easily. Perhaps it's the perfume, the smell of rose and vanilla dancing in the air. Maybe it's her shoulder-length, perfectly wavy brunette hair—it frames a red-lipped, smokey-eyed face in such a way that you couldn't possibly imagine it looking better than it does right now. It is also quite probable that people—men and women alike—are noticing the way her black dress hugs her hips just right, like it was made for her and only her. But, then again, perhaps it's something different altogether. There is an air of mystery that surrounds this person like a shield. She is impossibly beautiful. The kind of woman poets write sonnets about.

Her journey ends at the door of an old tavern. The door opens seemingly by itself—as if by magic. This particular tavern is closed at this time of day, but if any passerby should think it strange that this woman gained such swift entry into a closed establishment, they will soon forget they ever saw such a thing. It's all in the perfume. Another woman—equally beautiful—sits alone at a table set for five. Good. She isn't early, but not late either. Just as she likes it. This once-yearly meeting serves as a chance to catch up and learn about everything new and exciting, which is a source of both excitement and dread. Things could turn sour fast. The other woman turns toward her, as if suddenly sensing her presence. A sharp contrast exists between these two. The seated woman is clad in a burgundy pantsuit and black heels, a pearl pendant hanging from a chain around her neck. Her hair, a lighter brown than her companion's, is swept up in a conservative and meticulous braided bun. With eyes shaped like almonds and high, defined cheekbones, this woman is all neat edges and sharp corners. The type prone to destroying pompous young men in ten words or less. The kind who thrives on intellect and strategy. Her smile feels almost cunning as she speaks.

"Hello, sister," her voice drips with curiosity, "It's been a while since I've sat across from you like this. I'm so glad you could take a break from…matchmaking. Or, is it lovemaking?"

The sister, taking a seat, grimaces ever so slightly. She hates petty judgment. Especially from those who do not understand her craft, nor try to. She crosses her right leg over her left in hopes it will make her look powerful. Her fingers push wavy locks away from her face as she replies in a sultry tone,

"Oh, how I've missed you, Athena. My perfect, radiant sister."

The comment elicits a chuckle from the Goddess of Wisdom, who snaps her fingers above her sister's glass. Instantly, sweet nectar fills it to the rim—the peach-colored liquid shimmering in the dimly lit room.

"I meant no harm, of course, my darling. Lighten up a bit before the others arrive."

Aphrodite picks up the glass and takes a long sip in response.

✳✳✳

The next time the tavern door opens, it does not do so calmly, but rather aggressively. Something reminiscent of a particular sort of smash. Aphrodite does not need to look to know it is Ares. Hulking, intimidating, *breathtaking* Ares. Athena hums in instant approval—she'll always be the Wisdom to his War. Aphrodite would be jealous if it weren't for the fact that she is the one in possession of Ares' affections. Goosebumps form on her skin as she thinks about the ways he's touched her, held her, in the dark—the way he's whispered in her ear how much he loves her. Of course he doesn't really love her—not in the way she wishes he did, anyway. She isn't sure if anyone has ever actually loved her the way she wants them to. How ironically pitiful. Damn these mortal disguises—she hates feeling emotions as intensely as humans do.

Ares selects the seat right next to her. His presence is strong, and not only because of his cologne. He practically smolders. She finally dares to look in his direction. He's wearing black pants and a white dress shirt, half unbuttoned. His dark, sun-kissed skin almost taunts her. She desperately wants to rip the shirt right off his back. She probably will later. She's always secretly wished they could have *more* though—a relationship that defined itself on something other than physicality. The problem is his personality. He's shiny and handsome on the outside, but dull and frequently rather ugly on the inside. On his best days, he's a good kisser with a knack for smooth talking. On his worst days, he's nothing short of an arrogant asshole. Aphrodite finds herself wondering which side of him she'll get tonight. His eyes seem to catch fire as he looks at her, a seductive grin across his face.

"The Goddess of Love is looking lovely tonight, as usual."

He reaches for her hand and brings it to his lips, kissing her knuckles first, then her palm. It sends shivers down Aphrodite's spine and leaves a fleeting, burning sensation in her fingers. Her voice is gentle as she replies,

"You flatter me."

Ares smiles at her, brilliantly, and opens his mouth to speak again. But, another voice from behind—familiar and mocking—fills the silence before he can think of the right words.

"I certainly would've declined attendance at this little meeting of the minds if I knew it would include such *nauseating* inclinations." There is a playfulness in the voice, "I thought you hated PDA, Aph."

Aphrodite can't help but smile as she shifts her gaze to the door, where the lithe and mischievous form of Apollo has cast a lean shadow on the floorboards. His usual East Asian disguise has altered slightly—his muscles are bigger, she can tell, even through his jacket. He's changed his hair as well, gone are the long, pin-straight locks.

In their place is a shorter, refined cut. It makes him look older and more mature, even though she knows that's technically impossible. Gods do not age. His style has taken an interesting turn as well. He is a monochrome daydream--wearing a cream-colored cotton blazer, collared shirt, and pants to match. A brooch resembling a golden sun sits clasped where the collar ends meet. If it weren't for his signature brown eyes that have always reminded her of a puppy, she'd hardly have recognized him. She tells him as much.

"You're experimenting, I see," her smile is genuine across her face, "How wonderful."

"I was bored, naturally," Apollo scoffs, "Had to change some things up."

"It's good to see you, brother. Where is your other half?"

"Artemis?"

"Obviously."

"She's all hung up over in Sweden. Some animal fiasco, I'm sure. She won't be attending our little get-together," Aphrodite sees a flicker of disappointment fly across Apollo's face briefly, but it is gone in a second, "Of course, I'll be sure to fill her in on everyone's dirty laundry, don't worry."

Aphrodite watches Athena smirk as the sun god makes his way to the table, taking a seat next to her. Considering Artemis's absence, there's no other god to wait for. The meeting can begin. The empty spot feels strange to Aphrodite, though, and she hears herself raise a question.

"Is there anyone else to include, seeing as Artemis will not be joining us?"

"Should we call on Persephone?" Athena muses.

"Good luck getting her out of Demeter's grasp," Apollo jokes, "She's only just arrived back from her winter stay *down under*."

"Perhaps Hephaestus would like to join?" Ares's voice is low next to her.

Aphrodite's heart rate shoots through the roof at the thought.

"I should think he has other things to do," her voice is as pointed as a knife, "Not to mention that I am sure his presence would cause nothing but trouble."

"I didn't mean to offend you. Forgive me."

She does not verbally reply, but feels herself nod in his direction. Her relationship with her husband is not one she likes to dwell on. Ares knows this, but of course, he likes the drama of it all. When Zeus first decreed that she and Hephaestus were to marry, she had been terrified. He was a very introverted, secluded god. She knew he had no patience for her and her line of work. She had been right in one sense, and he had surprised her in another. He was, on his best days, very thoughtful and considerate. Hephaestus was not a bad husband to her, even in the complete absence of Love. But he wasn't a very good one either, and she ached for the affection she knew he would never give her. Ares saw this, she's sure, as his best opportunity to sweep her off of the dirty forge floor and into his arms. She knows how wrong it was, to start an affair with Ares. She has a hard time believing Hephaestus's subsequent actions stemmed from any feelings for her, though. Aphrodite knows how gods work. Her husband was jealous. He felt fragile in the face of rejection. She wouldn't have cared if he had taken his anger out on her. In fact, she'd expected him to. They did eventually confront each other, and she let him have his moment of fury.

But then he took his revenge too far. He did something unspeakable. Something so cruel and unjust that thinking about it now makes her hands shake with rage. He took out his anger on her child, her daughter. Her sweet Harmonia.

Harmonia was a product of her affair, yes, but she had not asked to be. She hadn't asked to be conceived the way she was. She should've been kept out of it all. But her husband had to meddle—as he tends to do well. She should've known as soon as she saw that wedding gift from him—that horrible necklace with her baby's name etched on it—that it was cursed. She should have seen it, but she hadn't. She'd been too busy being happy that her daughter had found Love. The necklace did its job, and her daughter was cursed. Zeus had *no choice* but to transform her into a serpent and send her off to Elysium. Her sweet girl turned into a monster. Ever since, not a day has gone by without Aphrodite looking at her other children—sweet baby Eros especially—and wondering if they'll be next. If she'll somehow make him angry again and lose another child.

Aphrodite is pulled out of her thoughts by Athena's voice. She is taken aback by how gentle it sounds, now. Her sister certainly did not initially approve of the affair, but she knows how much Aphrodite loves her children.

"Do you have someone else in mind?"

It's in that moment that she realizes she does.

It does not take long for the Goddess of the Sea to appear in the tavern's doorway. She waits for nobody's greeting and no one's comment, but comes strutting to the table with the kind of nervous confidence only a beautiful, young nymph can have. Athena and Apollo share a knowing glance. Ares sighs, probably from having to share a room with another beautiful woman he shouldn't have for himself. Aphrodite knows she hasn't been particularly secretive about her budding friendship with Poseidon's wife. She isn't sure how it came to be, really. Perhaps it's her own origins that connect them so strongly. Aphrodite arose out of the Cyprian sea, the very same sea her companion lives and breathes. She notes the hair rings threaded through the goddess's hair and the barefoot sandals made of seashells adorning her feet. She is the embodiment of the seascape—and, therefore, the most daring in her human disguise. Her sepia-toned skin seems perfectly kissed by the Mumbai sun, and her dark, wild hair smells of salt water. Aphrodite smiles warmly in greeting.

"Thank you for coming on such short notice, Amphitrite."

"Well, it is certainly not every day one gets invited to dine with the gods."

"How are the dolphins," Apollo implores, not unlike a child, "Hopefully well?"

Oh, Apollo. Always so in love with the dolphins.

"They are wonderful," Amphitrite smiles brightly, "They're happy about all the sun you've been providing them lately."

Apollo smiles knowingly, as if he had planned the sunny weather specifically and exclusively for the dolphins. Athena cuts through the conversation then, a look of impatience on her face.

"May I suggest that we eat now? I have been waiting for what feels like an absurd amount of time, and I'm afraid you all run the risk of making me quite ornery if I am not fed soon."

Aphrodite rolls her eyes as Apollo laughs. He snaps his fingers in front of Athena's exasperated face, pointing dramatically at the ambrosia that appears on her plate.

"*Bon appétit*, mademoiselle."

Athena ignores the comment, and gets down to business in between bites.

"Let's discuss our endeavors. I'll go first, naturally. I don't know about all of you, but I feel as though I have more work cut out for me now than I have in years. Lots of intervening to prevent bad decisions, and certainly lots of war to attend to. It seems the mortals have a death wish, these days."

"I'll second that," Ares grunts, "But what is war if not human nature?"

"Speaking of human nature," Aphrodite perks up, "There has certainly not been a shortage of lovemaking among the humans. But I will say that, despite my best efforts, it is still quite hard to convince humans to love each other."

"Oh, come on, sis," Ares complains. "Why must you try to force that? Nobody should have to love everyone. It's irrational."

"What do you mean by that, Ares?"

"Well, if you truly need the clarification, all I meant was that war and conflict are ingrained parts of the human condition. It's in their blood to argue and disagree. Us gods are the same way, are we not?"

There was that condescending tone that always made her want to slap his perfect face.

"Well sure, War is part of the human condition," Aphrodite concedes, "But so is Love."

"Perhaps," Ares chuckles, "But it's not nearly as powerful. War is power."

"I disagree completely and vehemently. War is selfishness and cruelty."

Ares must have heard the passion in her voice, because he smiles mischievously. Another thing she has come to dislike about Ares—he loves getting a rise out of her.

"Is Love not cruel, my darling?"

If she was in her true goddess form, this comment would be easier to disregard. But this human form, this perfectly imperfect mortal disguise, means that words sting her sharper and emotions strike her harder. Maybe she's simply using that as an excuse for being so fickle. Either way, she feels her cheeks getting flushed in irritation.

"Don't you dare patronize me, you—"

"Perhaps there is a way to end this disagreement in a civil and godly manner," interrupts Athena hesitantly, "I propose a challenge to you, Aphrodite."

A challenge? That is simply her sister's strategic way of asking her to prove her position. As if the power of Love needed proof in the first place. Damned fools. But all four of them are looking at her expectantly, waiting for her answer. She knows saying no will make her look worse.

"What kind of challenge, sister?"

"One that would require you to put your storytelling abilities to practice," Athena's eyes sparkle like the pearl around her neck, "I want to hear—we want to hear—your best and most shining example of a time when Love proved more powerful than War, more enduring than Suffering. We'll judge your tale by how well you tell it."

Aphrodite thinks for a moment.

"Alright, I accept this challenge, but on one condition."

Ares sighs, "Of course, there's a condition."

Athena silences him with a wave of her hand, "What is it, sister?"

"Some of you may have integral parts in this story. All I ask is that if the story demands it, you speak truthfully about your perspective."

"I accept this condition," Athena agrees before Ares or Apollo can protest, "Now, begin."

PART ONE: ANNA

"To love or have loved, that is enough. Ask nothing further. There is no other pearl to be found in the dark folds of life."

-Victor Hugo

APHRODITE
October 4th, 1919

I was first acquainted with Anna Baumann on a dreary, cold October day. As you might be able to guess fairly easily, I prefer warmer weather, and thus, I was quite distracted by the cold and did not notice her at first. I had felt that familiar little feeling in my mind, *the goddess's intuition* if you will, as I was traipsing about the French Alps. Of course, I dropped everything immediately and ventured over to Germany to investigate once I confirmed that this moment of insight was indeed Love (or was it Fate?) directing me to my newest job. That is all I thought this tale was at the time, just another job. Another day of matchmaking for the Goddess of Passion and Beauty.

Love led me to a small town near the eastern border of Germany called Neu Zittau. I had been there once before, a very long time ago. I was pleased to see that even after all those years, it didn't seem to have changed much. But, of course, that's how it is in an old shipper's town. Neu Zittau is steeped in tradition, and I can imagine that the inhabitants of that place have always been grateful that no matter how much they might change, their hometown never will.

As I mentioned before, the temperature in this quaint little town was low, and I was frankly rather distraught about it. I was happy I had a warm coat. I quite literally almost walked right by Miss Anna; she was that good at blending into the crowd. But believe me, once my eyes landed on her petite form, she was nothing short of iridescent. She was, on the whole, very average-looking. A half-tamed mass of dark curls framed an oval face. She wore a white chemise, blue skirt, and a gray velour overcoat. A brooch sat perfectly positioned on the collar. Her eyes were what caught my attention— to this day, I think they were her best feature. They were brown in color, but with a particularly palatable hint of gold—a kaleidoscope of sunlight and cinnamon and honey. She embodied the sort of quiet humbleness of a young woman who does not yet know how strong she is—how strong she'll become. I was most intrigued by her, and naturally, I followed her.

It was a Tuesday, and just like every Tuesday of every week, Anna Baumann was making her way to the town bakery to pick up more bread for her father. The bakery was situated at the center of Neu Zittau, in the town square, and it served as a meeting place for many. It occurred to me that Anna was of a particular status among these people, judging by the amount of greetings and enthusiastic hand gestures she received and gave on our way to the boulangerie. The bell chimed as she opened the old door, and we stepped inside the establishment; both of our senses immediately overwhelmed with the smells of freshly baked goods. I can remember thinking it was a wonderful contrast to the cold weather outside. There has always

been a warm and inviting feeling about bakeries that I admire—
everything inside of them, including the people and food, are made
with plenty of care. It makes me happy to know there will always be
safe havens for Love to thrive and grow within.

The baker seemed to know Anna's order without even
asking her, and handed her a large, warm loaf with a gentle smile.
He inquired about her father, Albert Baumann, and my questions
about Anna's societal status were answered. I discovered he was a
shipper—a no-nonsense but immensely kind gentleman who did
business with practically everyone. It seemed that Anna's father
made friends wherever he went. The baker had a steady, jolly voice as
he asked after the rest of Miss Anna's family.

"How are those brothers of yours, Fräulein Baumann?"

"They are wonderful, sir. My sister, too."

"Oh goodness, how could I forget about your lovely twin,
Marta?" The baker laughed, "Good girls, the two of you are. I'm sure
you both have young gentlemen losing their heads trying to court
you."

"You are too kind, sir," Anna said as a rosy blush appeared
across her face, "If Marta had her way, she'd be engaged tomorrow.
But I'm afraid I am nothing but a lonesome maiden."

I noticed the way she said lonesome maiden as though she
had resigned herself to the idea that she was destined to the role
forevermore. Something crackled and popped inside of me.

"Your time will come, I am sure of it," the baker smiled,
"Send Albert my best wishes."

Of course," Anna said politely, "Have a wonderful rest of
your day."

I trailed behind Anna as she left the bakery and made her
way down the cold cobblestone streets toward her family's house.

The conversation with the baker had told me a few things about her, even though they hadn't really said much at all. I could tell by the way the baker implored about Anna's siblings that they, too, like their father, were the amicable sort. Lots of friends in lots of places. Anna's shy answers had given her away as someone much more prone to a watchful sort of solitude. There are benefits of quiet listening and learning, as my sister Athena would say. I got the sense that Anna and her twin sister, Marta, were especially different people—although naturally very close due to their bond. I did not need to see Marta to know she was most likely the talkative one, while Anna was the watchful one. The way Anna carried herself in public—hands in her pockets and nervous eyes on the path in front of her—also told me something even more relevant: she had yet to fall in love with someone. I was sure Anna fancied herself the type of girl who had no intention of falling in love with just anyone. No, she was too wise for that. She was waiting for someone who could make her heart sing. But I knew, just as Anna knew, that if she didn't settle soon, she'd have to live the rest of her life as an outcast. So it goes in a misogynistic society. It was clear that Anna had no intention of letting anyone down, but she wasn't going to rush Love, either. I smiled to myself, thinking about the way my senses had led me to her, despite this fact. It meant that things were about to change.

The Baumann residence sat on a small hill overlooking the docks and the river. I was surprised the house was not larger, honestly. It was not tiny, but it wasn't huge either. It was obvious that Albert Baumann was a saver, not a spender. He was probably the type to save money under the floorboards or invest it all back into his business. But size aside, the house looked well-kept and well-loved, the kind of place built on memories, dreams, and laughter.

Anna continued up the path to the front porch, me not far

behind her, when her gaze shifted to the window on her left. As my own eyes followed hers, I saw what it was she'd noticed. Her father was sitting at the dining room table smoking a cigar. I could deduce from the puzzled expression on his daughter's face that Albert was not accustomed to doing such things on Tuesday mornings. Usually, he was working on his boat. But there seemed to be someone else in the room with him, Anna and I noticed at the same time. Next to Albert—talking in an animated way with his hands—was another man, although much younger than Anna's father.

The two of us walked briskly through the front door into the foyer and then past the dining room to the kitchen, where Anna placed the bread in its seemingly designated basket near the window. As quiet as I know Anna tried to be, her father still noticed her. A brief flash of panic flew across her face as he called for her to come and say hello. Her nervousness delighted me in a strange way that I couldn't quite attribute to anything in particular. I just had the sense that things would soon be moving, changing, transforming. I watched as Anna swallowed the apprehension creeping up her throat and put on her best smile. I gave her a little push as her feet treaded ever so cautiously over the carpeted hallway, and although she couldn't see me, I knew she felt me. We stepped into the dim light of the dining room together, both of us keeping her previous comments to the baker in mind.

Albert stood from his chair at the sight of his daughter, and moved to put a strong hand on her shoulder. I heard him tell Anna to introduce herself, and for a moment, I was afraid her nerves had silenced her until her name formed effortlessly on her lips. Anna had surely introduced herself hundreds of times, to all kinds of people. I'd imagine she thought that none of them had ever given the name a second thought. What an innocent girl—almost humble to a fault.

She was foolishly wondering at the very moment if this mysterious man thought it a good name. Up until this point, I had been resisting the urge to allow myself entry into her conscience. I don't always like to intrude like that. But, you see, I was very interested in this girl and her curious disposition towards this newcomer. I could not resist. I entered her thoughts just as she was ruminating on the fact that her name had come from her late mother, someone she had always been most desperate to make proud, even after her death.

Her father began talking again about how old she was, and how dependable and good-hearted she was. There's no pride quite like that of a doting father. Both she and I took the moment to really look at the newcomer. The first thing that struck me about him was how handsome he was, and Anna's own thoughts indicated she agreed with me very much. A blush had crept its way onto her cheeks, turning them the color of roses. Anna, of course, felt such an observation was an improper thing to think of upon a first impression. I did not think it improper at all. Of course, a man is more than his looks, but I am the Goddess of Love. I know good genes when I see them. This gentleman was no ordinary handsome. He was tall, yes, with a distinct jawline and sandy hair combed just right. But there was something else, too. Something mysterious yet knowing, secretive yet open. There was a gentle sparkle in his eyes that accentuated their color—hazel like a sunlit forest. He was the kind of man featured in a history book, or perhaps an Edgar Burroughs novel.

Cliché, but oh so delicious.

He reached out an arm to Anna in greeting, his palms rough like a sailor's. Clearly, diligence and dedication ran through his veins. He took Anna's hand in his, and even I wasn't expecting what came next.

It only lasted for a moment, but I swear sparks flew between them—the kind only goddesses can see. His electricity seemed to light Anna on fire. The sheer lovesickness she felt in response made both of us giddy. The feeling was fleeting—but thrilling. Perhaps he felt something new and exciting too, because his expression blossomed from a smirk into a smile. When he finally broke his own silence, his voice had a low and steady cadence.

"It is a pleasure to make your acquaintance, Fräulein Baumann. My name is Otto Reinholdt."

"Oh, Herr Reinholdt, call me Anna."

"If it pleases you, of course. But then you must call me Otto."

"Alright," Anna felt herself smiling, too, "Otto it is."

"I truly owe you and your family a great deal—your father has just now given me work at his docks, for which I am most grateful," Otto continued, "I was in desperate need of employment, and it seems I've come at just the right time."

At this, Anna's father laughed and told Otto he was always welcome. So that's why he was at the house on Tuesday morning. Otto came to him asking for work. Of course, it made sense for her father to give it to him—he was always looking for a helping hand. Anna's cheeks still felt hot to her, and she hoped it wasn't too horribly obvious. She'd been raised in refinement—told over and over again in the two decades she'd been alive that she was the daughter of an important man in this town—she should know what was right and what was wrong to do in front of a stranger. Losing her composure over this young man's disposition felt like the wrong thing, certainly. She told herself the best thing to do was continue with her daily duties, as not to give Otto any ideas as to what she thought about him. I found myself rolling my eyes at the way she overthought things. Before I could nudge her in the direction of continued conversation, Anna found her voice again, although it seemed soft and nervous to her.

"Well, Otto, it is lovely to make your acquaintance; I am sure you will be a wonderful addition to my father's business. I hate to leave, but I must excuse myself."

"It was lovely to meet you, as well," Otto said with warmth in his voice. "I hope this won't be the last time I see you, Fräulein Anna."

"Surely not," she replied, silently cursing him for making her cheeks burn anew, "I look forward to seeing you around here, sometime."

Before he could say anything else, she turned and walked out of the room, toward the staircase that would lead to the safety of her bedroom. She could practically feel his eyes following her, and she hated that she liked it.

I can confirm they indeed were watching her every move.

This man was not here to court her; he was here to work on her father's boat. He was a sailor—hardly husband material.

I disagreed.

She'd never been a fan of the water; she couldn't even swim! But she'd be a fool to deny the feeling that her hand in his gave her. I made sure that thought filtered through her mind. I could tell it wasn't anything she'd expected, and it scared her to know just how his hands and his smile and his eyes made her heart race. She reassured herself that these feelings would pass and that would be the end of it. I almost burst with excitement in that moment as Love finally found her, and as I watched it soak into her skin like sunshine, I thought to myself,

Oh, my darling, this is just the beginning.

INTERLUDE
Athens, 2022

Aphrodite pauses as she reaches for her drink, draining the glass. Weaving stories is usually Athena's job, not hers. She isn't used to the way her throat parches, and her heart swells at the better bits. For a moment she's nervous she isn't telling it right, that perhaps someone else would narrate it better. But she's noticing the way Athena's eyes are glittering like diamonds, and the way Amphitrite has leaned closer to her, and she remembers that this is her story, she can tell it as she wishes.

But, of course, her brothers would not be themselves if they didn't have some sort of comment to make on her performance thus far.

"I'm assuming this next part is where things will actually happen." Apollo's expression is serpentine as he gifts her a playful grin, "I know telling stories isn't usually your thing, but this is supremely boring, Aphrodite."

"All great love stories have to start somewhere, brother," she retorts.

"If I was the kind of god prone to a good bet, I'd wager this silly little account of yours won't help you win any arguments," Ares chuckles in a way that infuriates her. "Just like Apollo said, Love is too boring—it's insignificant when you compare it to Suffering and War."

She decides it's better to bite her tongue. *Just wait; you'll prove it to them all in the end.*

She takes the moment of silence to reapply her lipstick; run her fingers through her hair. She needs to feel confident if she's going to tell the rest of her story. Her siblings feed on weak-minded thoughts, and she has a reputation for being, well, delicate. She knows that's the wrong idea entirely—she may be sensitive, yes, but not *delicate*. Not fragile and easily broken. The best personalities she's encountered—both people and gods alike—have a genuine and thoughtful sensitivity that allows them to understand others. She doesn't think her brothers and sisters—especially Ares and Apollo—could ever truly understand her. She doubts they even want to.

"I think this is a curious recounting," says Amphitrite with a genuine smile, "I think it's wonderful how Love works in such mysterious ways. It's almost intoxicating, is it not?"

"Mmm," Athena hums wisely, "the best things always are."

She doesn't know how, but Aphrodite senses the Goddess of Wisdom might actually be rooting for her. She doesn't know if that's ever happened before, and it leaves her feeling unexpectedly but soothingly warm. It makes her want to keep spinning her tale, if for no other reason than to prove to Athena she can. She clears her throat,

"On that note, shall we continue?"

APHRODITE
December 24th, 1919

After Anna and Otto's initial meeting, I left Anna alone for a bit. She needed the space to continue to develop her feelings on her own time. She was particular about relationships, and I didn't want my own excitement to get the best of both of us. Pushing her head first into something that she very much didn't want to rush into wouldn't have been wise at all. I lasted almost three months before it proved excruciating to keep my distance any longer. I was impressed I made it that long. You may call it nosy; but really I was just *invested*.

I re-entered Anna's universe at the end of December, just in time for holiday festivities. I have always loved this time of year. There's so much Love in so many different forms—romantic, familial, neighborly. I knew it would be the perfect time to check in. I found Anna in her bedroom, seated at her vanity. She looked much different than she had when I'd first been acquainted with her. She was wearing a lovely black frock complete with velvet buttons down the chest and an A-line waist. There was both powder and a bit of rouge on her cheeks. I watched as she wove a red satin ribbon through her hair, arranging the dark brown curls into a neat bundle at the base of her neck. With some fingerwork and slight pulling, she managed to create a bow. I slipped into her thoughts as the two of us admired her reflection in the mirror. She smiled to herself as she spritzed her wrist with the scent of flowers. She felt like a shiny new ornament on the tree. I was delighted. Nothing makes me smile quite like a girl recognizing her own beauty does, even if she only thinks so for a moment. All kinds of Love inspire me—that tends to happen when it's your reason for existing—but feminine self-love has always moved me in the kind of way you can't explain, you just feel.

Anna rose from her seat in front of the vanity, and slipped on her Mary Janes before making her way into the hallway and down the staircase, myself not far behind her. Her shoes squeaked a bit as she descended, and she remembered that she'd asked the housekeeper to shine them for that night's church service. Christmas Eve Mass had always been her favorite--everyone was happy, and the Christmas spirit never failed to take her breath away.

You might be wondering why I'm ruminating so much on a Christian holiday when I am a goddess of Mount Olympus. To that, I'll say this: Love moves in mysterious ways, and it chooses its stewards with a judgment none are truly privy to. Anna was raised Christian, so she celebrated Christmas. People get to choose what they believe in—nobody else has a say in it. It's possible to acknowledge my siblings and I while also choosing to follow the teachings of other higher powers, too. Nothing is ever as black and white as society says.

As we made our way into the kitchen, Anna stole a shortbread cookie from the jar in the hall. I smiled as she took a bite while simultaneously chastising herself for being unable to resist sweet things. Cookie crumbs fell onto her dress as she pushed open the kitchen door. She hastily wiped them away in embarrassment when she saw Otto standing there, nursing a steaming cup of coffee in his hands and staring at her with an amused expression on his face. Oh, how perfect.

"Ah, so the cookie thief has been you all along," he laughed melodically, "I can't say I'm too surprised, anyhow."

"Watch your words, or I'll make sure you never get one!"

"My darling Anna, where is your Christmas spirit? Don't tell me you've decided to become a Scrooge!"

She returned his laugh. She had grown comfortable with Otto since he arrived months ago, and they were rather close.

How delightful!

He had proven a great friend and confidant, contrary to Anna's initial feelings about him. She knew her father hoped she would marry him.

He was not the only one, of course.

Her father's health had not been the best lately—she could tell the many years in the shipping business had worn him down. She knew he wanted to see her find someone to marry so she'd have some kind of support. While Anna would've never considered Otto for that job when he first arrived, even she could admit that he had a strong and kind presence. He was certainly so much more than the electrifying figure she first encountered. He had all the right words, all the time. He brought her back to her center with just a look—especially when she got stuck in her own head. She had been shocked to discover that she was happiest in his company, and sad when he was gone. Marta told her that's how she knew she was in love, but she couldn't be sure. She'd always thought Love was supposed to feel like butterflies in her stomach or soaring through clouds. Otto didn't make her stomach flutter—her stomach had always fluttered for some reason or another. Otto made her heart steady itself. He was the calm after the storm—the steady rhythm of a song.

Anna decided to ask him about his plans for the evening. He mentioned to her the other day that his family lived far away, and he wouldn't be able to see them for the holidays. She had pried further, trying to discover more information about his mysterious childhood, but he wouldn't say anything else. She found the courage to ask him if he was coming to church:

"Will you be joining us at St. John's for Mass tonight?"

"I'm afraid not."

"What? But why not? Christmas Mass is so happy and wonderful!"

"I'm not sure I'd be welcome," he said while looking into his mug, "I'm Catholic."

She had not given thought to the idea that he might believe something different than her...but was it really all that different?

Nothing is ever truly that different, my dear.

"What does it matter, really? I think you should come with us tonight."

"Anna," his voice dipped low, "I wouldn't want to make the improper impression. Your father—"

"Vati won't mind at all! And as for everyone else, what they don't know won't hurt them. Please, Otto, I want you to accompany me."

After a few moments of silence, Otto nodded. It was all the confirmation she needed. She was surprised at how exciting it was to know Otto would be sitting next to her on such a magical night. She bounced over to him and wrapped him in a hug, telling him how happy she was that he agreed to come. He smiled at her enthusiasm and reached down to fix her necklace that had tangled itself somehow. His fingers lingered there, near her neck, for a moment like he was deciding if what he wanted to do was appropriate. He decided against it, whatever it was, but her heart raced all the same as he instead tucked a stray curl behind her ear gently.

Mon Dieu, je l'aime.

Although it was the first time he'd ever done it, it felt familiar. She was starting to wonder if she'd even be able to concentrate on tonight's service with Otto sitting right there with her. It would be a struggle for sure, we both thought.

✳✳✳

Just as both Anna and I knew it would, Mass began and ended without incident. While there were certainly stares and whispering from a few neighbors about the newcomer accompanying Anna, she could tell their musings were focused on a potential love affair and not religion in the slightest. She found herself feeling less embarrassed by those wonderings, and more proud to know people in this town thought she and Otto would be a good match. At one point during the service, Anna felt his hand rest on hers in the pew, and she didn't pull back. She liked how it felt, actually. After filing out of the church with the rest of the town, Vati pronounced that he had to get back to the house—why he didn't say—and suggested she and Otto take the long way back through town. I knew what he was trying to do, as did Anna. Surprisingly, Otto nodded, saying they'd be back at the house within the hour. My senses tingled like bubbles in a champagne glass.

Oh, this should be interesting.

It was then, walking through the lamplit, snowy streets of Neu Zittau, that Otto intertwined his fingers in Anna's. It felt so natural and innocent to her that his next move startled her. It certainly elicited quite the squeal from me. They were walking over a bridge—the Neisse flowing icy but calm under them—when Otto turned abruptly so they were face to face.

Before she could inquire about what was on his mind, his lips were on hers, and he was kissing her.

Time stopped.

Anna's thoughts, which before then had consisted of Christmas cookies and church hymns, were now consumed by him, and only him. He was equal parts confident and nervous, it seemed, because the kiss was as fleeting as it was passionate. He pulled away slowly, a soft smile on his lips and a glint in his eyes. Anna didn't trust herself to speak—afraid that if she did, the spell he'd cast over her would fall apart. Instead she looked up at him, dazed but also enamored, and returned a smile that blossomed into a laugh effortlessly. She knew he didn't need her to tell him that she thought she might love him. He knew. A couple more seconds passed in silence before he nearly whispered to her in a husky voice:

"Marry me."

Well, that was quite excitingly unexpected.

"Otto," Anna exclaimed nervously, "We barely know each other."

"And yet, somehow, it feels like I've known you for centuries."

"People will talk—"

"I don't care in the slightest about what anyone else has to say. I don't think you do either, Anna."

"I suppose you're right…have you even asked my father?"

"Of course I have. I would never dream of asking you without his blessing."

"He really said yes? Even though it's only been a few months?"

"He said he was confident I would be able to provide for you in all the ways you deserve. But please, darling, don't think of this as any sort of formal proposal—I know this is spontaneous and probably rather crazy, too. Think of it as a promise I'm making—a promise to you that whatever this life gives us, good or bad, I will always choose to navigate it with you."

"You have a way of taking a girl's breath away, you know that?" she inquired softly, "I can't even find words for you—you've made me a lovesick fool."

"All you have to say is yes."

"But why me, Otto? You are three years my senior—you've only just met me months ago! How can you be sure you care for me enough…to want to spend your life with me?"

"Anna, have you ever been in love?"

"I think I am right now."

"In order to love another person, you must feel it with every bone in your body. You must recognize the trust and strength that are essential to giving yourself to someone. I love you, there is no doubt. I trust you, and that in itself is proof that I care enough. I trust you, and now I'm asking you to trust me."

I should've known this intriguing young gentleman was as wise as he was attractive.

It occurred to Anna that she'd never seen him this vulnerable, this open. To know that her feelings were reciprocated brought a warm feeling to her whole body. She'd never done anything as spontaneous as what he wanted her to agree to. Truly, it made her rather nervous. But she knew she'd be a fool to tell herself she didn't want him. She wanted him more than she'd ever wanted anything.

It was in that moment she remembered something—a phrase she used to hear all the time growing up. She could hear her mother now, in her quiet but firm voice: *It is alright to be nervous about doing something, my love. It means it matters to you a great deal.* Her voice in Anna's mind gave her assurance, always her guardian angel. It was like she knew exactly what Anna needed to hear, when she needed to hear it. Otto was still looking at her attentively, trying to find an answer in her expression. I, too, was sitting on the very edge of my metaphorical seat in anticipation. Eventually, he asked her again.

"Anna, please...will you marry me?"

The answer came out easier than she expected.

"Yes, I'd like that. Very much."

If only Anna could have heard the way I screamed with joy.

APHRODITE
February 25th, 1920

A nna and Otto were married two months, almost to the day, after their engagement. I was rather surprised at first because I knew how much Anna preferred to think things through—how she usually liked taking her time. But I noticed a slight yet significant change in Anna after her betrothal to Otto. In the short time I'd known her, it had always been clear to me that Anna's every action was meticulously thought out—her nervous tendencies never allowing for anything too spontaneous or rash. Anything that might threaten her inner sense of security was automatically the wrong thing to do. Anna did things safely, or not at all.

But then Otto appeared in her life seemingly out of nowhere, and I'm quite positive he realigned her whole universe. Love can be like that, sometimes. Now Anna felt she could do things she wouldn't normally do—scarier things—as long as she had Otto with her. Luckily, I confirmed upon quick investigation that he wasn't some sort of shield she depended on for survival. It wasn't like that at all, thank the Gods. I hate it when a capable woman allows herself to be so consumed by her own self-consciousness that she becomes dependent on a man, usually the kind with a superiority complex. Anna wasn't that kind of woman, and Otto wasn't that kind of man. He didn't tell her how she should do things, and he didn't make decisions for her, either. Rather, he seemed to act as a sort of intermediary between Anna and her best intentions. He kept her anxiety at bay and, in doing so, encouraged her to live a little more fearlessly. I've come across so many humans (and a few gods) who are so sure that Love breeds regret and makes you crazy. They've got it all wrong. Love shouldn't make you foolish; it should make you brave.

On the day of her wedding, I found Anna flustered in her childhood bedroom. She was quite the vision, I must confess. My heart felt as though it might burst with happiness as I soaked her in. She was stunning. I slipped into her mind easily--it was starting to be a place I thoroughly enjoyed being. Her hands shook slightly as she clasped a string of pearls around her neck. She was beyond nervous, although not about the actual act of marrying Otto. That had been the only thing on her mind for weeks. Thinking about being his wife filled her with a sense of pride she'd never known before. She was truly preoccupied about all the pomp and circumstance that inevitably came with most weddings. Anna did not want much extravagance, mostly because she never did particularly well among lots of people, noise, or alcohol. Marta and her brothers, though, had insisted that it would be rude not to invite all the many aunts, uncles, cousins, and friends there were—especially because they all lived in Neu Zittau. Anna's father had been very quiet about all of it. She wasn't sure if it was because he didn't feel well, or if he knew she appreciated his steady—but silent—support most.

Marta burst into the room suddenly, back from her trip outside to find pine to put in Anna's bouquet. She was the type of woman tornadoes were named after, a maelstrom of exuberance and chaotic energy. She was indeed a very curious juxtaposition to Anna, but in a way that felt right, somehow. Marta and Anna were the last, most precious pieces to each other's puzzles. I could see that although Anna was a paragon of composure, there were hints of Marta's sparkling excitement in her eyes as she observed what her sister had found outside. Anna had told Marta countless times that her wedding bouquet didn't need to be fancy, but her sister had insisted pine would add a sort of charm to the ensemble. Anna had given up telling her no to that type of thing. She smiled at her sister's face, now rosy from the January cold. She was so terribly excited about this day, almost as much as Anna was. The two of them had been through everything together. This was a day they'd been dreaming about for years. Marta motioned for Anna to stand up and arranged the pine in the places she felt were best. Then, she pushed her sister in front of the mirror.

Anna found herself blinking back at a reflection she wasn't sure was her. She didn't know she could look like this, ever. It made me smile, to see her so blissfully ignorant—I knew just as Marta did that Anna had always been beautiful in a way that she never could see. I found myself wishing that a sliver of the spellbound feeling stirring in her heart would stay with her forever. Marta was right about the bouquet; the winter colors complimented Anna's brunette curls perfectly. But her attire really took Anna's breath away. The dress looked like it had come straight out of a fairytale; she felt different wearing it. The bodice was an intricate lace design, and she could feel the fabric hugging her hips just a bit. At the waist, it flared into layers of satin that stopped at her ankles, with tulle underneath to give the whole thing an A-line shape. Perfection, if I do say so myself. It was everything Anna had ever dreamed of in a wedding dress.

It was also her mother's. Anna wished she was there. She missed her in a way that made my heart ache. The late Mrs. Baumann would've loved Otto. She quickly pushed her late mother out of her mind then, because weddings were happy occasions, and she did not wish to be sad for her own. I agreed.

Instead, Anna thought about Otto again. She knew that any nervousness felt in the moment would evaporate seeing him standing there at the altar in his best suit--a flower on his lapel and a little boy grin on his face. She could not wait to start a life—*her life*—with him by her side. She couldn't wait to have babies with him, to grow old with him. After so many years of waiting, it finally felt like all the missing pieces of herself were coming together. Fate was building a precious little world for her.

Fate may have laid the foundation, yes, but Love took care of the rest.

I stood with the twins at the mirror as they both thought about how far Anna had come and the excitement she had to look forward to. A few more minutes passed, the silence between them conveying a million words, when the housekeeper knocked at the bedroom door, exclaiming that unless she wished to be late for her own wedding, Anna needed to leave for St. John's straight away. Marta hurriedly helped her into her heels, and the three of us made our merry way across town to the church, giddy with excitement.

I stood invisibly next to Anna as the organ began to play Canon in D. Her father stood at her other side, looking as dignified as he could. Anna shook like a leaf, the poor thing. This was surely the most nerve-wracking thing she'd ever done. I laid my hand on her shoulder in an attempt to infuse some love-fueled confidence into her bloodstream. I felt her relax a bit at my touch, and I smiled. I wished, just this once, she could see me. I'd done my hair so nicely, and I really did like the blue lace dress I'd found at one of the small stores in town. I hadn't been invisible when I bought it—the store workers had gushed over how perfect it fit me, not knowing that everything naturally fit me perfectly because I was, in fact, a goddess. But I could not allow Anna to see me. She couldn't know how I was interfering in her life. I, of course, didn't think of it as interfering at all. More like mentoring, or coaching. I coaxed her to make all the decisions she wanted to make but didn't think she had the guts—heart—to follow through with. I had every intention of being her biggest supporter in life, and especially love. That was precisely the reason I so desperately wished I could show myself to her. I wanted her to know she had someone cheering for her, helping her along. That's all someone like me ever really wants, isn't it? To know that her efforts are felt, appreciated, and returned? Nothing gives me greater joy than Love does, and I've always hoped that the affection I give away finds itself welcome and cherished by the people who deserve it most. Anna was one of those people; I could feel it. Love wouldn't have led me to her if she hadn't been worthy of it or me.

I slipped back into her thoughts as the ushers opened the doors to the chapel. The way Anna's mind flipped from anxious to awestruck in a second made me smile so wide my cheeks hurt. Each pew was covered in pine garland and ivy with a twinkling candle, and rose petals decorated the aisle. It all felt quite magical to Anna. Standing at the end of the aisle next to the officiant was, of course, Otto. She smiled at the carnation sitting on the lapel of his suit coat. He'd combed his hair just right, and she could see he had shaved, too. He looked exceedingly handsome and charmingly stoic, like a knight or a prince.

The walk down the aisle felt like the longest minute of her life, with so many people staring at her. Anna gripped her father's hand the same way she used to when he'd take her out to sea with him, and the waves made her stomach lurch. She did her best to focus on nothing but Otto. He seemed so happy, even though none of the guests in attendance were members of his family. He had made up the excuse that they lived too far away to be able to come to the wedding, and Anna had tried to argue until he shut her down. She knew there was so much more to say on the subject, but she also knew he didn't want to talk about it. She had given him the benefit of the doubt.

She felt much better after reaching the altar. Otto's hands intertwined with her own steadied her in a comforting way, and he never took his eyes off of her even for a second. He mouthed the words, *you look beautiful,* and naturally, her cheeks blushed furiously. She really could not concentrate on a single thing the officiant said—she was busy looking at her soon-to-be husband— until it was time for the vows, and she registered that she would have to speak out loud in front of everyone. She had decided to keep them short and sweet, because she was terrified of messing them up and because she knew Otto knew how she felt without her needing to explain it. Her voice sounded quiet as she started speaking, but as her confidence grew, she heard herself more clearly.

"Otto, my goodness, how I love you. I love you like I love the birdsong on a spring morning, like I love the way wind whistles through the trees. I love your smile, and your heart, and your mind, and I always will. For better or for worse, in sickness and in death."

That bit about the birdsong was quite good, if I do say so myself.

She gifted him a smile as she finished, marveling at the way his eyes twinkled like stars in the candlelight. She felt him run his thumbs across her knuckles gently as he cleared his throat.

"My darling Anna. I barely have words for you, because if I'm being quite frank, there are very few that would adequately describe the way I feel about you, about us."

He'd barely started speaking, but she could feel the tears in her eyes already. He was just the slightest bit blurry around the edges. *Love's got a good grip on this one.* He continued,

"Up until a few short months ago, I did not believe in true love, or love at first sight. Call it whatever you'd like, but I didn't think I was destined to find it. But then I laid my eyes on you for the first time, and I felt something bloom in my heart like a rose. It was like divine intervention had led me straight to you."

Oh, how deliciously ironic.

"I love you, my darling, and I promise to choose you and cherish you over all else for every day forward. There will never be another. For better or worse, in sickness and in death. I will be there for you always and forever."

Anna felt the tears move down her cheeks as he finished, but she didn't care. She couldn't describe the feelings inside of her if she tried. How did she get so lucky? She hadn't done anything particularly noble or exceedingly kind—yet she'd somehow been gifted this wonderful and loving man to share her life with. What had she done to deserve someone like him?

My darling, you don't have to do something heroic to be deserving of love.

I found myself stepping out of Anna's thoughts as Otto was told he could kiss his bride. There are certain lines I don't cross, certain things even I know are better kept private. The kiss was magical enough from an outsider's perspective. I didn't need proof that Anna's heart rate nearly doubled as Otto held her face in his hands and kissed her so thoughtfully and passionately it felt as if Time itself had stopped to savor the moment. I didn't need to confirm that she loved the way his cheeks dimpled when he pulled away from her lips and grinned like a child who'd just scored his first football goal. The picture was clearly painted with facial expressions alone. I felt victorious in a sense. The hardest part; getting them to fall in love, was over. Now, I just had to make sure they stayed in love, which I wasn't worried about.

In another sense, though, watching Love work its magic was bittersweet. The feeling came with every job I took on, but it was particularly strong as I registered the melody of Anna's laugh and the magnitude of Otto's passion. My susceptible human skin tingled, and my chest tightened observing his arm around her waist and her hands on his chest, and even as I tried my hardest to keep Love and only Love in my heart, I couldn't deny the other, subtler feeling ever-present in every nook and cranny. It proved a feeling I was all too familiar with, an emotion I had come to loathe with every fiber of my being due to the way it impeded my divine purpose and muddled my mind. You see, my job as a goddess situates me as a conduit for Love—the channel that allows it to find its way to the people it's destined for. Love meanders through my bloodstream and interacts with every part of me. It flows in through my red lips and my olive skin and flows out through my manicured fingernails.

But the love in my veins is not mine. It does not belong to me but rather to everyone else. You'd be surprised at how debilitating that can be, sometimes—how haunting it can feel to remember every human I've given the gift of romantic love, knowing that I've never felt its effects the way they have, and not knowing if I ever will.

It's why I am so terribly protective of my children. When I look at them, I do feel something that I think might be Love, but not the same kind that I so often bestow on unknowing couples. It is a deep and profound feeling that is hard to describe. It's something like an ache, except it hurts in such an agreeable and fascinating way that you never want it to stop. I hope Anna gets the chance to know what it feels like—motherhood. I hope she someday knows the feeling of holding her child for the first time and seeing the future in its eyes. I suspect that the universe might just realign itself when that happens. Any child of Anna Baumann is destined for great things.

INTERLUDE
Athens, 2022

"Alright, stop right there for a second," Ares interrupts. "Did I just understand you correctly?"

Aphrodite huffs in slight annoyance. She had hoped nobody would say anything, and that she could continue on with the story, as if she hadn't detailed any of her inner thoughts at all. Ares's incredulous expression almost makes her laugh, except she knows what he's about to say next.

"You say you've never felt the Love you give away for yourself," he fumbles his speech, not wanting to dare to believe what he's thinking could be true. "What am I, then? Does our relationship serve no purpose to you?"

"Oh, it certainly serves a very pleasurable purpose, Ares. Don't fret," Aphrodite explains with more than a hint of sarcasm. "But you don't love me. You never have, and you never will."

"Of course I do!"

Athena's voice lilts to the surface of the short silence that follows, filling in words where Aphrodite can't find any.

"Lust is not the same thing as Love."

Ares looks at her with fire in his eyes, hating that she's not taking his side. She continues.

"You look at Aphrodite and you see the source of your sexual desires, something to be conquered perhaps, or someone you go to when you're feeling unsatisfied with yourself and need someone to gently stroke your ego. That is not what it means to love someone, Ares."

Aphrodite has never felt more thankful for her sister than she does now. Ares opens his mouth to speak again, but Athena cuts him off.

"Maybe, if you're feeling ambitious, you could pay closer attention to Aphrodite's words as she continues her story. I think you'll find it is a tale of significant intrigue and importance."

The look Athena gifts her from across the table is one she very rarely sees. Her sister is beaming—a delicate but genuine smile devoid of any sort of malicious intent. Her eyes are not gleaming as usual, but sparkling. It informs her that Athena remembers, now, how the rest of the story unfolds. Aphrodite hoped she would—she plays a significant part in it.

Having sufficiently shut Ares up, Aphrodite takes another deserved sip of nectar and a small bite of ambrosia. She's about to continue when she realizes the next part of the story is not for her to tell.

Apollo jolts out of his boredom-induced doze as she barks his name, nearly falling off his chair. Such an endearing little asshole. She's sure to make her voice sound perfectly sugary as she offers her request to him.

"Apollo, I think I'm just about ready to take a break from speaking for a while, and I think that, perhaps, you might be interested in narrating this next part of the story for us."

"Wh—what?" He looks suspicious. "Me? How am I supposed to tell your tale?"

"Well, I should think you'd like to take credit where it's due."

She fixes her gaze on him intensely until she feels her own thoughts transfer from her mind into his. His eyes widen as he remembers the details of a particular set of circumstances, a series of events that only he—the god of prophecy and knowledge, healing and plagues—could have been responsible for.

"I do suppose," he responds with mischief in his voice, "that I'll bask in my own brilliance for a short while."

Aphrodite sits back in her chair and folds her hands in her lap.

"The stage is yours, brother."

APOLLO
September 23rd, 1920

I t wasn't that I didn't remember this part of the story, as Aphrodite thought. The memory was there in my head; it was just a bit hidden. An old trinket sitting on the highest shelf of an old closet. I am not like my sisters—who feel a duty to take diligent note of everything and everyone they encounter amidst their godly duties. One could say I'm a bit more like Ares in that regard, except I'm much funnier and, frankly, more emotionally secure. My brother's masculinity is so fragile. I have always been comfortable with my own sexuality, my own manhood. It's a good thing too—I simply do not have time for that kind of existential questioning—not when the whole of humanity needs me.

As I was saying, I do not get as attached to the humans I manipulate as my sisters do, which is why I often forget about most of them. There are so many to keep track of, and my job often entails humbling them at best, *extinguishing* them at worst. A living, breathing human being has exciting moments, sure. But a dead one? If I allowed myself to get hung up on every human I ever paid a visit, I'd be a foolish and ineffective god indeed. Humans are the pieces on the chessboard of the gods. Some of higher mortal importance might have rook status, or even royalty status, among us. But that doesn't make them immune. Most humans are nothing more than pawns to me. That daring boy Icarus was the only mortal I ever felt anything towards. Watching him soar through the sky on his way down to the sea produced a magnificent, powerful ache in my calloused heart. Most humans are so concerned with security and well-being that death seems like a punishment. Not Icarus. He knew the secret—death is not a punishment, it is the price one must pay for true freedom. I watched that boy twist and tumble his way into the domain of the dead, and I knew deep in my soul that although he was plummeting into the depths of the dark ocean, his heart would forever be soaring in the clouds.

Alas, I am veering in the wrong narrative direction. My apologies.

I have since taken the particular memory Aphrodite reminded me of from its shelf inside my head. I have wiped the dust away so it shines.

This particular recollection starts, naturally, with a proposition.

It was one of those early autumn days where the air crackled with a sweet freshness, and the meadows bloomed with cornflowers and chrysanthemums. My shoes clicked against the cobblestone pathway that led up to the Baumann residence, which bustled with activity. Marta came flying out the front door, holding a rucksack in her left hand while clutching a straw sunhat in her right. She was dressed for traveling—a long wheat-colored overcoat draped around her shoulders stylishly, and she'd substituted her usual summer sandals for sensible laced boots. There was a rosy hue on her cheeks and sunlight in her hair. Had Aphrodite been there with me, I'm sure her heart would've pinched looking at Marta then. She seemed like a summer dream. Old Albert Baumann followed his daughter onto the porch, decked in a suit coat, pants, and dress shoes. Wherever the two of them were going, it was important. Of course, right at their heels was Anna, with the usual preoccupied expression on her face. She was dressed in a simple linen blouse with a wool skirt, which led me to understand that wherever her father and sister were going, Anna would not be accompanying them. Their voices became a mélange of pitches and emotions.

"Might one of you explain to me again where you're going?" Anna questioned breathlessly. "As of last night, there were no plans for traveling."

"Anna, stop being ridiculous," Marta said in an impatient tone. "I've told you already. A man who does business with Vati, Herr Steiner, has asked him to meet to discuss some things, and this man happens to have a very handsome son to whom he'd like to betroth me."

"So you're just going to go meet him? Just like that? What if you don't like him?"

"I am keeping a positive outlook, Anna. Something I know can be hard for you. It's going to be wonderful, you'll see. Right, Vati?"

Marta and Anna both looked expectantly at their father, who shrugged.

"I would say it's worth the trip to Berlin to find out. I've been meaning to get there to have a conversation with Herr Stiner about the shipping business. I'd like to tell him about your husband." He nodded towards the figure of Otto standing in the doorframe. "He should know when such a diligent, up-and-coming shipper has made his debut in the business."

Anna's apprehension was overshadowed briefly by a feeling of pride in her husband. She knew her father had been thinking about bequeathing a boat to him soon, as a gift for helping him so much. Her mind switched back to Marta as another question formed in her mind.

"How do you plan on getting to Berlin? Are you taking the auto?"

"No, silly. That would take too long," Marta explained, "Vati got us tickets for the train. That's why we have to hurry; we're due to leave in thirty minutes. Perhaps you could tend to my garden while I'm gone. I wouldn't want all my pretty flowers to die of thirst."

Anna rolled her eyes as Marta turned and started down the path I was standing on, the scent of flowers floating past my nose as she passed my invisible form. Albert turned to Anna and placed a gentle hand on her shoulder.

"Don't worry about us, my darling. Berlin is not too far away, and I think this trip will be good for Marta. We'll only be gone for a couple of days, I promise."

Silly humans, they'll never understand how dangerous promises can be.

"You'll ring me when you arrive?"

"Of course."

"Alright. Have a safe trip."

I moved to stand next to Anna as she watched the two of them make their way down the path to the main road that led into town. She waited until they had rounded the corner out of sight before traipsing her way back up to the house. Otto opened his arms for her, and they stood in a loving embrace in the doorway. Gross, if I did say so myself. I followed the two of them into the house. It was a tidy abode—rather large but not too grand. I spied the housekeeper as she flashed by the staircase on the second floor, a duster in one hand and a cleaning cloth in the other. She was an older woman, probably around sixty, with the kind of disposition that exuded warmth.

Otto led Anna through the front lobby and into the kitchen at the rear of the house, his fingers intertwined in hers as he guided her into a seat at the old wooden table. He had a certain presence about him that I found most intriguing. He was, on the surface, exactly what most men strive to be—handsome, strong, *masculine*. His hair appeared perfect in a wonderfully imperfect way; the locks of flaxen hair falling in his eyes seemed to have been strategically placed there. His slightly sunburnt skin and his calloused hands gave him away as a hard worker and dedicated craftsman. But something strange pervaded his aura, too. Something that seemed to contradict his ultra masculine attributes—a softer, gentler side that conveyed reverence and patience as well as placidity and a hint of secrecy. I could see why someone like Anna was drawn to him. There was something about the way he looked at her, as if he could see straight through every façade and wall she'd built up around herself. He was a very rare man indeed. I wondered to myself what it might be like to lie with a man like that. In all of the many lifetimes I'd endured, I had not come across anyone like Otto Reinholdt in a long while. In a sense, it made me a little jealous—it made me want to, perhaps, show Anna that he did have some flaws. I could tell that within the hazel of his eyes, there were secrets blended with the sagacity. Behind that gentle smile, I was sure there was pain, too. We all harbor pain in some form, even gods. I decided to hop into Anna's mind. It would be the easiest way to get what I wanted out of this mysterious man—

if I could convince Anna to ask Otto certain questions, then perhaps I'd get the answers I sought.

Anna's mind was much more enjoyable to be poking around in than I initially thought it would be. I had expected a jumbled mess to go along with her nervous habits and knack for overthinking, but her thoughts were precise, considerate, and quite imaginative. There was a pleasing order to the chaos in her head, and I recalled my sister Athena whispering her tidbits of information to me from some forgotten time ago: *Remember Apollo, not all chaos is bad; it creates just as easily as it destroys.* Sometimes, I wish my sisters had given me bad advice so I'd have a reason to be annoyed at their constant presence in my head.

Currently, Anna's thoughts focused on her sister, which made perfect sense considering Marta's recent exit from the house. She missed her already. It wasn't exactly what I'd hoped for, but I could work with it. I gently pushed at the edges of her conscience, prodding her gently enough in an attempt to get her to share her feelings with Otto. I was pleased when my efforts were quickly rewarded. Her quiet voice lilted to the surface of their shared silence.

"It feels too quiet without Marta here."

"You miss her already, hmm?" Otto's face lifted in sympathetic amusement, "She's only just left, you know."

"Yes, I know. It's silly, but it's true. I just…I have a strange feeling about this trip she and Vati have embarked on. It just seems so spontaneous."

Ah, yes. Fate often masquerades as Abnormality.

"When has your sister ever not been spontaneous?" Otto inquired with a chuckle.

Anna did not respond. She supposed he was right. For a few moments, the chirping of the birds outside the window was the only sound throughout the whole house. I took this stretch of silence as my cue to push a bit harder, further, towards what I wanted. I sent a pulse of doubt down Anna's spine at the same time I planted inquiry in her brain.

"Speaking of family, how is your brother? Surely he is feeling better?"

Otto's face contorted in confusion. This was too fun.

"What are you talking about?"

"Your brother, darling. Your family couldn't come to the wedding because your brother was ill...you told me he was advised not to travel."

The expression that came very suddenly over Otto's face was arresting, if I do say so myself. I had never seen such an exquisite combination of confusion, fear, and regret. I had planned on planting the possibility of dishonesty in Anna's mind, but Otto did the job for me.

"Your brother was ill," Anna questioned with a dangerously curious strain in her voice, "Wasn't he?"

Instead of answering her, Otto took a slow sip from the coffee mug in his hands. My senses tingled in anticipation, and I could feel Anna's starting to burn. Her voice went up in octave and intensity.

"Answer me, Otto."

A long sigh escaped him as he replied.

"I have no idea what the status of my brother's health is. I have not known for a while."

"So what I'm gathering," Anna's voice pricked and prodded, "Is that you either knew he was ill and for some unknown reason have not reached out to him in the last nine months, or you lied to me."

The air almost fizzled in the silence that followed. Otto's face was hardening into stone, and Anna's looked as if it would crumble any second.

"Why would you lie to me about your family?" Anna asked as calmly as she could, "Why wouldn't you want them at our wedding?"

"It's complicated, Anna—"

"I don't give a damn how complicated it is, Otto. You've barely breathed a single word about them for as long as I've known you. I've assumed you were just private about them, and for a while I felt like it was none of my business. My mind is changing now, quickly."

"I won't be discussing this with you right now."

Anna looked at him incredulously. Had he really just shut her down like that?

"Yes, you *will*." She could feel the blood pumping through her head.

"Perhaps you did not understand," Otto's words were clipped and aggravated, "We are done with this conversation. I have work to do."

Before she could get another word past her lips, Otto had deposited the coffee mug on the counter and was moving past her. She did not turn to see him leave, but heard the door slam shut behind him. Confusion melded with the anger inside of her. Why on Earth would he lie to her about such a thing as his family? She had told him everything about hers, including the terribly personal feelings she harbored surrounding her mother's death. It hurt her to know that she had been so willingly vulnerable with him, yet he refused to give her even the smallest detail about himself and the family he'd grown up with.

Some people run from their pasts.

As soon as I thought it, Anna did too. It hadn't been intentional, but I was glad all the same. She was wallowing in her own self-pity instead of thinking logically about the situation. Her anger seemed to dissipate in a second, and what replaced it was something more akin to shame. Perhaps, she thought, it was too painful for him to talk openly about his family, for whatever reason. She knew exactly what it felt like to talk about things that were just too painful to bear. She knew that helpless feeling—like there was lead in her stomach and a stone in her throat. She wondered if Otto had felt that way moments ago. Surely, he must've felt something unpleasant, because he had to physically remove himself from her presence. She vowed that later, she would make it up to him. She couldn't push him to talk about things he didn't want to, no matter how much she wanted to know.

Frankly, I thought a little pushing wouldn't hurt him.

✳✳✳

The rest of the day transpired without any sort of incident, to my displeasure. I wanted, in a stubborn and inexplicable way, to *rile* Otto Reinholdt. It was like a little itch that wouldn't go away, no matter how hard I scratched. I am no trickster like my brother, Hermes, so this was a development for which I had no justification. After his small outburst earlier in the day, it seemed that Otto had strongly re-fortified his emotions into his usual calm and content demeanor. I couldn't seem to get past it. I encouraged Anna to answer a few of his questions in a snarky way, and I even forced his dinner plate to clash to the floor just as he was about to wash it. After these small failures, I started to realize that perhaps I did not want to rile him, per se, but simply prove there were dents in his armor. I wanted to show Anna that nobody was perfect, not even her daring knight.

Aphrodite had played a part in romanticizing him to the point of nausea. I suppose that's what is expected from the Goddess of Love.

I stayed with the two of them late into the evening. I certainly had other business to be attending to, but I was curious to see if Otto's family would come up in conversation. There seemed to be a need for apologies and explanations. Anna had retired to the bedroom, and I had settled in a chair in the corner of the room. I was getting exceedingly bored and desperate for some excitement. I looked down at my watch. It wasn't quite time for that, yet.

Soon enough.

I heard Otto as he opened the door as quietly as he could, making his way over to the bed. I watched as he crawled in next to her, laying on his back and staring up at the ceiling. Surely, that was my cue to leave. I felt frustrated that I hadn't gotten what I wanted. My invisible form stood and turned towards the door when I heard the sheets rustle. Otto had turned to face the curve of Anna's back. I was about to dismiss the movement when his voice broke the silence, low and hesitant.

"Anna, are you asleep?"

There was no response for a moment, but then her voice, resigned and sleepy.

"No, not yet."

"I am sorry," Otto started, "I should not have lied to you."

"I forgive you," she whispered into the darkness. "I am also sorry. I shouldn't have pried the way I did. I thought if you'd want to tell anyone, you'd want to tell me. I see now that was foolish to assume."

There was silence for a quarter of a minute, and Anna was nervous she'd said the wrong thing. But eventually, he spoke again. His voice sounded cautious, like he wasn't too sure what to say.

"I suppose, now that we're married, you ought to know about them."

Oh, now we're getting somewhere.

He took a long pause before continuing, "My father died when I was eighteen. It was wintertime, and he fell off one of the docks in my hometown and died. I'm not sure if he hit his head on the ice, or if he drowned...but I suppose it doesn't matter. The outcome was the same."

Anna flipped over to face him in the bed, her expression stricken. I almost wanted to laugh. What had she expected to hear? She reached out and took his hand in hers, moving closer to him so their foreheads almost touched.

"Oh Otto, I'm so sorry."

"It is what it is. I had a...complicated relationship with him. He was not a nice man."

I could see Anna swallow hard, even in the dark.

"My mother was left with twelve children to feed," Otto continued. "I was the oldest, so I had to find work and provide for my brothers and sisters. The youngest two were six weeks old."

"I can't imagine how your mother felt," Anna murmured.

"My mother is the strongest woman I know."

There was pride in his voice as he said this, and Anna could tell his relationship with his mother was one he cherished deeply.

"She sounds like a wonderful woman."

"Yes, very much so."

She had promised herself she wouldn't pry. I smiled as she revoked that vow in hopes of opening him up a bit more.

"I would love to meet her someday."

"I wish you could," Otto's eyes reflected sadness and regret, "But I am not allowed to see her anymore. I am not permitted to see any of them."

Ah, finally. What I'd been looking for.

"What? Why not?"

Otto sighed gently, and brushed a lock of hair out of his wife's face before answering.

"You see, Anna, I've never agreed with war. It turns good men evil. When the Great War broke out, my country wanted me to fight, but I refused. They blacklisted me."

"What does that mean?"

"It means that nobody in my town was allowed to hire me for work. I had to leave, and leave I did. But I didn't depart calmly or easily, as much as I hate to admit it. I am not proud of the way I acted. I ended up finding under-the-table work on a boat. I started sending money back to my mother regularly, but then the war ended."

"But isn't it a good thing the war ended? Didn't you go back?"

A hesitation.

"I could not. The treaty all the countries signed…it required Germany to give my hometown to Poland as part of the necessary reparations. Nothing happened right away, but by the time I found out about it and tried to go home, everything I'd ever known was already starting to become Polish, not German. It just so happened that I had angered members of the local government when I left after defying the draft. They still harbored anger towards me—especially because they were being essentially forced into a new culture. They must've blamed me, in some disillusioned way. They informed me that I could either return, denounce everything I'd previously said, and become a Polish citizen--or stay in Germany and never go back to the place I'd grown up."

Otto's voice faltered a bit, like he was nervous to speak the next bits out loud. I got the sense that he'd never told anyone this story before, and he was afraid of how it would be received. He must've decided that Anna deserved to know and make the judgment for herself, because he soldiered on.

"That kind of ultimatum infuriated me. I had no interest in appeasing any government officials, especially those particular ones. I told them just that. I realize now that I made my decision angrily and selfishly. I wasn't thinking straight, and I should've been. I now have to live with it for the rest of my life."

He stopped talking then, waiting for Anna to say something. In truth, it was hard to know what to say. She couldn't imagine having to leave her father and her siblings, and then be told she wasn't allowed to see them ever again. She could sense Otto held a lot of pain and guilt in his heart over his decision to stay in Germany. He probably worried about them all the time. But Anna knew his pride was as strong as black coffee, and as unwavering as a maple tree in a storm.

"What about letters? You could write to your mother, surely."

"I've tried, but she stopped answering. Eventually, she'll write in Polish anyway, and I would not understand her anymore."

The finality with which he said it told Anna that he did not wish to talk about it anymore. She didn't blame him. She wouldn't want to talk about such things either. She planted a tender kiss on his forehead and squeezed his hand firmly, in a hopeful attempt to let him know that she loved him and that she was glad he told her something so personal. She wanted more than anything to be the kind of wife who was gentle and loving, but also strong and reliable—a steady ship with sturdy sails. As she drifted off to sleep, she told herself that she would give Otto a big and wonderful family to make up for the one he loved and lost.

APOLLO
September 25th, 1920

Naturally, I had to come back to see the real masterpiece come to fruition. My sisters would tell you that if it really was a masterpiece, as I've chosen to call it, it was a dark and twisted one indeed. I have no qualms with that label. That is often the nature of Prophecy, and I must deliver it no matter its intent or consequence, just as Aphrodite must deliver Love, and Athena must deliver Wisdom. It had been two days since I'd left Anna and Otto—both of them in a state of relief and contentment with themselves and their situation. There was a small part of me—nothing more than an inkling—that pitied them. I was, after all, about to burst that bubble of happiness. It was a feeling that proved easy to tuck away into the back of my mind. I had a job to do, and it didn't matter whether or not I felt that job was immoral or painful or undeserving. I don't have a say in what Prophecy decides. I am a messenger—the necessary intermediary within a universal system. I hadn't gone to see it happen.

I set events in motion, but I choose to not see them through to their end. I do not have as prominent a taste for blood and…wreckage quite like Ares does.

The Baumann residence was dark as I walked up the same cobblestone path as two days before, it was fifteen minutes past midnight, after all. The house was shrouded in an eerie sort of silence— the kind that immediately precedes chaos. I adjusted the wool blazer around my shoulders, smoothing the collar and adjusting the small sun-shaped pin attached to it as I waited for things to begin. I found myself pacing the length of the front porch. I wasn't sure why I got so anxious about jobs happening on time. I supposed it had something to do with the fragility of it—everything could go sideways very fast if I wasn't careful.

I heard it just as I looked down to check my watch. The shrill sound of a telephone.

The smile crept onto my face slowly and then all at once. I wasn't happy about what was about to take place. I'm not that callous. I just couldn't help but acknowledge the beauty of Fate. It never failed to amaze me. The sound of the telephone was an adrenaline rush in itself. The Baumann residence of course had one of those most interesting devices, many well-to-do families did those days, but using one was expensive. Telegrams were cheaper, which meant the ring of the telephone coming from the second floor signified urgency. I heard the housekeeper silence the ring through the open bedroom window—heard the sleep and confusion in her voice. I reveled in the brief silence that followed. As the poor old woman's quiet voice transformed into cries of horror, I let myself in through the front door.

The housekeeper—her name was Jane—ran straight to the room Anna and Otto shared. She slammed on the door once, twice, three times.

"Fräulein Anna! You must wake up now, something terrible has happened—oh, it is terrible...terrible!"

It was Otto who opened the door—Otto who saw Jane shaking like a leaf in the hallway with tears streaming down her face, wringing her hands. I saw in his eyes how he knew exactly what she was about to say. That was his best trait, in my godly opinion. He always knew. Anna appeared behind his right shoulder and I felt the panic flood her senses, the confusion overtake her brain. She moved in front of Otto to grip Jane's shoulders.

"Jane, what on Earth is the matter? Are you okay?"

A resigned sort of look crossed Jane's face as she croaked out the devastating words.

"Oh my sweet Anna, there's been an accident."

✳✳✳

Within a week, every flower in the garden was shriveled. The watering can sat in the corner on the front porch, completely untouchable. Anna could not bring herself to so much as glance at it. She didn't know if she'd ever be able to grow a garden again. Look at a flower the same way again. She had promised to water those flowers, but she hadn't. The withered remnants laid like crippled skeletons against the dirt, the pretty blues and pinks and yellows washed away into the mud. They looked the same way she felt. I pitied her more than I should have. I, too, had a twin. I knew what it felt like to be tethered to someone else by an invisible string—a thread of gold that signified a cosmic sort of connection that was irrevocable. It was hard for me to imagine what it felt like to have that connection severed. I imagine it felt devastating.

In the days that followed the news of the accident, Anna replayed that midnight conversation over and over in her mind like a broken record. It was all so clear in her memory: the confusion, the panic, the tears. Jane's voice splintering with emotion. *They are gone, my child. Gone forever.* She remembered very little after that, though, only the feeling of Otto's arms around her shoulders and his lips against her forehead. She's sure she probably did not believe it, not at first. But then she must've cried, must've screamed. She's sure she would still be in denial, had she not been forcing herself to think the terrible words every hour.

Her sister was dead.

Her father was dead, too.

The man who'd called on the telephone to deliver the news had called again the next morning. He said they should expect the bodies within two weeks. The police were having a hard time identifying people—so it goes with train wrecks, he said. Anna had promptly thrown up onto the hard pine floors of the front entry. It made her lightheaded to think about her sweet sister, her other half, her *Marta*, ripped and crushed to pieces like a paper doll. Never again would she get to see her sister's sunshine smile, or hear her musical laugh. Anna could practically feel the way Marta's absence burned a hole in her heart and left stains on her soul. The only form of solace she allowed herself was hoping that wherever her sister and father had gone away to, they were together with her mother again. It still stung like a slap to the face, though, thinking about how someone as good as Marta, who overflowed with love and light and goodness, was doomed to the cruelest of fates. She did not deserve that kind of ending. Neither of them did.

Every time Anna closed her eyes, she replayed her last exchange with her sister in her mind. She heard the excitement in Marta's voice that she hadn't picked up on in the moment, and she heard herself, too. Heard the way she complained and worried in a clipped, annoyed tone. Why couldn't she have just been happy for Marta? Why had she been so bitter? Otto tried every night without fail to comfort her. He whispered soothing words in her ear, and held onto her throughout the night like she might disappear if he didn't. He reminded her that it wasn't her fault, that her cynicism hadn't caused the accident to happen. She didn't have the heart to tell him that his efforts were in vain. She knew it wasn't her fault, it wasn't anybody's fault.

That didn't make it hurt any less.

INTERLUDE
Athens, 2022

Tears blur Aphrodite's vision as Apollo's voice fizzles out. She hates this part of the story. She hates hearing about the way Anna suffered, but she especially hates knowing that she hadn't been there to comfort Anna when she needed it the most. Apollo would say that even if she had been present when Anna received the news, she wouldn't have even known a goddess was there. That's beside the point. Aphrodite could've comforted her in smaller, invisible ways—leaving a soothing warmth inside of her in the middle of the night, or giving her painless jolts of courage when she felt as if she might break down. Aphrodite is happy that Anna at least had Otto there with her. It would not be the last time his steady support would be needed in the years to come.

She is brought out of her thoughts by Amphitrite's sing-song voice, now laced with concern.

"Are you okay?"

"Yes, I certainly am," she smiles as she conjures a tissue and wipes the tears away. "Nothing to worry about, I promise."

Although she can't see his face, she can tell by Athena's exasperated expression that Ares is probably rolling his eyes, maybe even making a face. He doesn't understand emotions. Aphrodite expected nothing less. She's surprised when Athena's voice filters through her thoughts, connecting to her own telepathically.

You're sure everything is alright?

It makes Aphrodite smile.

Yes, I promise. That part just makes me sad is all. I'm fine, now.

She expects to see Athena relax and cut off their connection, but she continues.

Don't let Ares make you feel bad about yourself, or make you want to stop telling your story. He has the emotional intelligence of a flea, or an eel perhaps.

Aphrodite stifles a laugh.

I can't stop weaving our tale now, sister. The best is yet to come.

She almost doesn't catch the way Athena's mouth quirks up, the way her eyes lose some of their hardness. Even though she closes the curtain on her emotions again a second later, it's clear how much Athena cares about this story—how much she has invested in it. She's sure that Athena assumes Aphrodite will be telling the whole story. She can't wait to tell her she's wrong when the time is right. For now, though, the Goddess of Love is very much still *le raconteuse*, and there certainly is so much excitement to be recounted still.

APHRODITE
November 14th, 1920

She noticed it exactly fifty days after the accident. Her reflection in the mirror left no room for doubt. If I had been in her presence before that day, I would've known instantly. The Goddess of Love just *knows* about that kind of thing—that kind of change. Anna radiated with a new and subtle light that I knew she couldn't see in the depths of her sadness. It was Love reflected in heat, filling her body with new life.

Anna was pregnant. She had been since June.

The realization left Anna feeling a few different ways at once. Disbelief mixed with happiness in a way that brought tears to her eyes. She'd always wanted to be a mother. To become one now, after so much had been taken from her? It felt like the universe was giving her just what she needed. This baby growing in her stomach suddenly felt like solace and comfort—a tiny green shoot growing up out of the dirt where nothing but dead flowers had been before.

The relief was indescribable.

I felt Anna's gratitude for the universe surge through me, warm and lovely.

I moved to stand over Anna's shoulder so my reflection joined her own in the mirror, although only I could tell. I suspected in that moment that even if I hadn't been invisible, Anna would have hardly noticed me there. She rubbed her stomach with gentle hands as she let herself get lost in her thoughts—thoughts about the future, no doubt. A lazy, effortless smile painted itself across her face as she moved sideways to get a better angle of her bump, and I swear—in that moment—I don't know if she'd ever seemed more beautiful to me.

She turned suddenly towards the door, seemingly remembering her present reality as she called gently to her husband in the next room.

"Otto, darling, come in here."

Her voice betrayed no sense of urgency or harm, but nonetheless Otto was next to her in no time at all. At first, he most certainly did not understand, because Anna didn't verbally say anything, just stood smiling at him in a starstruck kind of way. But then, eventually, his gaze moved to their reflections in the mirror, and then to her stomach. His eyes widened as he realized what he was looking at, and for several moments, he just stared at Anna. I sensed it took a lot to rob words away from a man like Otto Reinholdt, but here he was, speechless. Eventually, he moved to wrap his arms around his wife from behind (I stepped out of the way, of course) before leaning into her and placing a gentle kiss on her temple as he murmured,

"Does this mean what I think it means?"

"Yes," replied Anna, excitedly.

Otto responded with another kiss, this time on Anna's cheek. "We've finally done it..."

Another kiss, on the jawline, and a bit more searing than the last.

"We made a baby..."

His lips found the crook of Anna's neck before moving to her shoulder.

"We did," she nearly whispered. "So I take it you're happy with this news?"

"Very," he mumbled as his fingers came to rest on Anna's chin. He pulled her face towards his own before landing one last kiss on her lips. He held it for a few seconds, savoring it, before pulling back to look her in the eyes. "I love you, you know."

"I do know, and I love you, too."

"I can't wait to meet our baby."

"You're going to be the best father."

"You'll be an even better mother."

Their lips met again, this time upon Anna's initiation—although she giggled the whole way through it. She hadn't felt this happy in a long time.

How delightfully domestic.

"How exciting it will be," Otto said once they'd broken apart once more, "For our child to be born on the water?"

The thought made Anna's brain stutter for a moment.

"What do you mean, darling?"

"We'll be setting sail any day now, remember? That means you'll give birth on the boat! I wonder which port we'll be in—it's sure to be on the birth certificate."

"Surely, I should have the baby in a hospital, don't you think?"

"It would be much cheaper—not to mention easier on you— if we call a midwife on board when the time comes."

Anna could not for the life of her imagine what it would be like to bring a child into the world as her surroundings rocked with the waves all around her. Frankly, I did not like the idea either. But there are certain battles that should be waged in the moment, and others that are best left alone. This was, for the time being, one of the latter.

"I suppose we'll just have to see what happens when the baby decides to come," Anna sighed as she endeavored to change the subject, "We still have a long wait ahead of us."

"Indeed, we do," Otto murmured as he played gently with a stray lock of her hair, "And until then, we will work to make sure our new floating home is in tip-top shape."

Anna smiled in response. She still wasn't quite sure how she felt about living full-time on the rivers pulling barges. She'd willingly agreed to the proposition—there was something about boat life that felt rather interesting and exciting, despite the prospect of endless hard work and potential hardships.

She allowed her mind to wander back to the day they'd acquired the boat—a gift from her father. Thinking about him caused a lump to form in the back of Anna's throat, but she'd become rather acquainted with sadness in the last month and a half, and she'd learned to exist within it--despite it.

It had happened about two weeks after the accident. Anna's brothers—Max, Fritz, and Hermann—had been looking for their father's will. Anna had been the one to find it hidden in the desk in his study. It had been odd to look at it, she remembered, because it had seemed so new, like Albert had recently redone it. She'd made her way out of the study and back to the dining room table, where Otto and her brothers were looking through Vati's financial paperwork. She'd handed the will to her oldest brother, Max, and had watched as he inspected each page. He'd nodded at certain things and uttered an interested "hmm" at others. Once he'd finished his reading, the document had been surprisingly laid in front of Otto on the table. Max's voice was surprised but sincere, as if the document contained information he hadn't expected, but he was happy about it all.

"Well, Otto, it looks like my father saw great promise in you."

"Such praise is greatly appreciated," Otto had surmised, *"But I wonder what you mean by it?"*

"It seems he's left you his best boat," A cheeky smile had appeared under Max's mustache, *"The one you've been working on… he has made it clear that he wishes for you to have it for growing your future shipping business."*

Otto's expression had changed all at once from one of serious confusion to burning pride. Anna knew at that moment that he must be elated, and her father saw enough in him to bequeath such a prized possession. Otto had, of course, been the captain of someone else's ship before--climbing ranks back when he was working under the table the previous year, but he'd never captained a boat he owned. Anna recalled with a smile the way his voice had rung with excitement and disbelief as he'd answered her brother:

"I am deeply honored your father saw such potential in me, and I will take great care of this boat. But, what about the three of you? I should think he would give a boat to his own blood before me."

"You married our sister, which made you something of a son to him," Max explained, *"Besides, none of us have plans to continue the shipping business. We are not too naturally inclined on the water. Just promise us that by taking care of this boat, you will in turn also take good care of Anna. She is not too fond of the water—I'm afraid she'd*

probably flounder if told she had to swim."

There'd been a mischievous grin flashed in Anna's direction that made Otto laugh, and her blush. It was certainly true that she didn't know how to swim—water scared her a bit. But oddly enough, the thought of sailing off with Otto hadn't frightened her in the moment, and didn't frighten her now—not like she thought it would. Traveling from port to port, soaking in the sights and sounds of new cities, it all seemed sort of dazzling to her. Of course, she knew ship life was hardly glamorous, but Otto had a knack for making any situation seem exciting. It would be an adventure, if nothing else.

Later that night, as they'd laid in bed, Otto had turned to her with a question:

"What are we going to name it?"

"Name what?"

"Our boat! It needs a name, of course."

"Oh, for goodness' sake, name it whatever you like."

"But Anna," she'd been able to tell his expression was incredulous even in the dark, *"You must have a say in this. It will be as much your home as it will be mine and our children's."*

"It's funny, isn't it?" she'd sighed, *"Did you ever imagine we'd raise a family on the water? We'll have to have some sort of lodging on land, of course, but I'd imagine we'll spend a great deal of time on the boat...perhaps it is too dangerous a lifestyle for small babies? What if we cannot have a baby right away?"*

"Of course we'll have a baby soon, Anna, you can't lose faith after we've only just started trying! We'll have a whole hoard of babies, and they will have a life full of adventure! They'll be tiny sailors— warriors of the sea...that's it! We should name the boat after the warrior of the sea!"

"And who would that be, exactly?"

"Poseidon, of course!"

"Poseidon...I like it. There's a nice ring to it."

"Then it's decided. That's the name."

Lodged within Anna's thoughts as I was, I absorbed this particular memory with her. I wish she could have heard the way I cackled at that name choice for the boat. It only made sense, considering the sea life they were about to embark on, but there was a part of me that half expected Zeus to hurl a lightning bolt in Otto's direction out of jealously. There must've been a part of Otto that hoped he was favored by the God of the Sea. Why else would you name your livelihood after him? I like to think at the end of it all, the man truly was held in high esteem by my mighty uncle. He deserved it, in any case.

Coming out of her thoughts, Anna couldn't help but smile at how the universe worked—she'd been with child during that conversation, and neither of them had realized it. This child was a product of their love in the making.

A love in the making, thanks to making love.

Am I the only one who just adores a play on words? I am? Right, I'll stop.

I must have accidentally planted my own musings about the more biological explanation for her pregnancy into her head, because suddenly Anna's thoughts were exploding with an impatient yearning to have Otto as close as possible, if for no other reason than to thank him for his service.

That hadn't been my intention, but who am I to stop that kind of thing? If Otto Reinholdt was anything, he was *dutiful* in more ways than one.

Sometimes, thinking about her husband left Anna feeling reckless, like she'd do anything just to feel him against her--reminding her that his kind soul wasn't the only thing she was attracted to. Luckily for her, he'd begun planting kisses all over her again, and she could tell by the urgency hidden within each one that the moment would escalate if she wanted it to.

She found that she did, in fact, want it to.

He started slowly, he always liked taking his time when it came to pleasuring her. She felt his lips press against the bare skin at the base of her neck as his hands mapped their way slowly down her torso, as if he didn't already know every dip and curve by heart. He groaned softly as he pressed himself against her from behind, and as she turned in her arms to face him, she could see the lust in his eyes. He used to try and hide that desire for whatever reason, at the start of their marriage. She guessed he'd grown tired of that by now.

The two of them stood so close to each other that Anna could feel the heat radiating off of Otto's skin, their lips mere inches apart. He hesitated there—right at the edge of his restraint—for a long moment, just to watch the ache in her eyes as she burned for him. Always one for the chase, wasn't he?

Anna didn't let him hold out long. She closed the distance between them as she rested her hands against his face and pulled him to her. He tasted like coffee and mint.

"Will it hurt the baby," he whispered against her mouth, "If I take you to bed right now?"

"No," she choked out as his hands continued to wander dangerously, "I think we'll be just fine."

"Good," He murmured as he laid her down against the pillows.

Later on, the two of them lay tangled in the sheets, basking in each other's company—Otto twirling one of Anna's curls through his fingers as she traced the muscles on his arm.

"I never asked you," she pronounced quietly, "If you know what exactly we'll be pulling up and down the rivers on this barge of ours?"

"Iron ore and coal, most likely," Otto answered as his thumb caressed her temple, "Perhaps more if it is asked of us."

"What if there is another conflict? Will the country ask us to help support the war effort?"

"Don't think such things, my love," Otto quickly replied, "After the destruction of the Great War, there won't be another war for at least fifty years."

"Good, I would hate to bring children into that kind of world."

It was almost too ironic to acknowledge the way the man was so incredibly wrong. Otto always had a knack for optimism. He would be bitterly disappointed in his country down the road, of that I was sure.

INTERLUDE
Athens, 2022

As she takes a moment to clear her throat, Aphrodite glances at Athena across the table from her. While her sister gives the outward appearance of nonchalance, Aphrodite knows her well enough to understand where to look to find the opposite emotion. A glint of something—is it mirth?—flashes through her eyes like lightning, and the quirk at the corner of her mouth suggests it's taking everything in her not to smile.

Of course, Aphrodite also knows why Athena wants to smile, but they're not at that point in the story quite yet, are they? All in due time.

"Not that it really matters," Amphitrite mentions, "But my husband was honored that Otto would see it fit to name the boat after him."

"Are you sure he didn't just want to see Zeus jealous?" Ares replies.

"It is rather fun to get Father all riled up, sometimes." Apollo smirks.

Athena sighs and pinches the bridge of her nose.

"Boys, you should know by now that upsetting Zeus only makes things worse for you in the long run."

"It's totally worth it," Apollo answers, "When you see him all hot and bothered because of something so insignificant."

"I think," Aphrodite chimes in, "That the reason Poseidon liked having a boat named after him had more to do with what boats mean to him rather than any desire of his to upset his brother."

"That logic isn't very fun, sis," Apollo drawls, "Leave that stuff to Athena. You're supposed to be excited about drama and jealousy."

There was a time, centuries ago, when that might have been true. She wasn't proud of all the humans she'd *enchanted* in the name of dramatics. But she'd grown sick of that. That kind of thing wasn't what Love stood for, so she didn't want to stand for it either. Ignoring Apollo's comment, she endeavored to explain further.

"I'll be the first to admit that boats are rather boring literally, but they're very interesting symbolically. They represent a spiritual journey on the sea of life—a crossing, an adventure, an exploration. They're also cradles; the place where the journey begins as well as the safe haven during a storm."

"It makes a lot of sense then, that Otto would want to raise his children on a boat," Amphitrite nodded, "He wants to protect them, but he also wants to encourage them not to be afraid of the unknown—to seek opportunities and live life to the fullest."

A contemplative "hmm" from Athena confirms the truth in the nymph's words, and Aphrodite takes it as a sign to continue.

APHRODITE
March 20th, 1921

The last months of Anna's first pregnancy proved much more difficult than she imagined they would be. The back pain felt constant, and her stomach seemed so heavy that she wondered some days if she'd be able to hoist herself out of bed. I wish I could've provided her with some sort of reassurance, or at least a sense of solidarity. I had, of course, been pregnant several times myself—and although a goddess's pregnancy window is much shorter and smoother than a human one, it is still a bothersome and painful experience. Many of those days consisted of Anna not being able to move around very well, and me filling her mind with happy baby thoughts to remind her that the payoff at the end would be more than worth it.

Living on the water, of course, was certainly not helpful in alleviating Anna's discomfort. She and Otto had set sail on *Poseidon* roughly three weeks ago, and although she would never say anything to her husband, I could tell that it was taking my girl a while to adjust to waves in constant motion and rooms that rocked. Anna had wanted to stay on land until the baby came. If I had been given the opportunity to be seen and give an opinion, I would have agreed with her, but alas, I was not, and Otto had a convincing way about him that almost drove me crazy. He reasoned that once the baby was ready to come out, they'd call a midwife aboard, and Anna could easily give birth on the boat. Psh, listen to that human man talk of ease as if he understands what it's like to give birth to a living, breathing baby. Men exhaust me sometimes. Anna was obviously and rightfully uneasy about this plan. I did my best to inspire a sense of safety in her mind. I knew everything would work out; it always did if I could help it. I knew this baby would make an appearance any day now. It's something you're just naturally attuned to when you're a goddess. Anna was also so swollen and huge that she looked as though she might just burst soon. She wanted to finally be done with the pregnancy part of having a child and get to the much more exciting part of raising him or her.

When the baby finally decided it was ready to meet the world, it was early morning.

I knew it was about to happen as soon as my mind melded with Anna's. There was a nervous sort of buzz among her neurons and bubbling energy in her bloodstream. Her body knew what was to come, and it was *excited*. As desperately as I wanted to somehow tell Anna about this turn of events, I kept the knowledge to myself. Instead, I let Love loose inside my own body until my human fingers tingled with joy and my head felt like a glass of champagne. Oh, how I just adore surprises.

Anna could hear Otto in the galley, making her breakfast, judging by the sound of clanking pots and the wonderful smells. She smiled to herself—as she had many times lately—thinking about Otto as a father. She just knew he would be so patient and kind, and he'd teach their child all there was to know about life. Seeing her smile like that made me smile, too. While it took her a few tries and a mental boost from me to get out of bed, Anna eventually made it up and out of the cabin. Otto must have heard her, because there was a cup of coffee waiting at the table. He came over as she sat down, setting her breakfast in front of her with a forehead kiss.

"Good morning, darling," His smile was sincere and perfect, "How did you sleep? Hopefully better than the other night."

"Last night was much better. I'm so hungry. Well, I suppose the baby is hungry, too."

"Well then it's a good thing I made you some food, now, isn't it?"

"Yes, but you didn't have to. You shouldn't have to do everything around here. I feel bad. I usually do these things, you know."

"Anna dearest, I don't mind doing it. I want to do it. Now eat before it all gets cold."

She sighed softly to herself but picked up the fork anyway. It wasn't surprising to me that Anna felt guilty about her inability to function at full capacity. She'd grown up in a household where she'd been expected to contribute her share to the best of her ability, all the time. That happened when you became motherless at an early age.

As she finished her food, I watched from across the room as Anna collected her plate and silverware and stood up, with the obvious intention of doing the dishes. She was going to clean up her mess today, I heard her think to herself, she wasn't an invalid. Anna bent down slowly, reaching for the soap and the rag under the sink. She started to straighten herself out again when she felt it. Something wet, trailing down her leg. Her eyes narrowed in utter confusion at the same time mine popped open in anticipation. After a few seconds, it dawned on her.

Her water had broken. Right there in the galley.

Anna heard herself call to Otto, and the frenetic tone in her voice had him next to her in what felt like mere seconds. He stared at the water on the floor and then up at her, a smile about to break across his face. It was finally happening. She would have smiled back if it weren't for the contraction she felt next. Her face twisted in pain as she gripped the counter, trying not to double over onto the floor.

Everything after that was quite the whirlwind, I must confess. Otto immediately called for the midwife and helped Anna back into their bed. I sat next to her, invisible fingers carding through dark curls. I didn't even know if she could feel it in the physical sense, but I know she felt it instinctively. I was only concerned about comfort, not touch. The midwife arrived after what felt like too long to both Anna and myself, the local doctor at her heels. I could feel the anxiety creeping into Anna's brain. She had no idea what to expect next. The pain had doubled since her water broke, and she found herself wondering if it was normal. She hoped the baby was okay. The midwife asked her if she knew how many minutes were in between each contraction, and she wasn't sure. She heard herself say that it felt like they were coming once every minute or two, and the midwife checked to see how dilated she was. Another contraction came faster than expected, and this time, it hurt so badly Anna cried out. Through the pain, she could hear both the midwife and the doctor telling her to push, and she wondered how they expected her to be able to do anything at that moment. Her head was fuzzy, and the room was slightly spinning. There was a dense humidity in the air that made her hair stick to her forehead, and the smell of her blood and her insides made her think that if she moved a bit too much, she'd throw up.

Through all the heat and nausea, she could feel her baby coming—violently and impatiently squeezing its way out of her body and into the world. The pain was too much to bear. Anna's thoughts came in panicked flashes in between the waves of hurt. *I'm going to die giving birth, this baby is going to kill me.* I tried my best to reassure her that the opposite was true, this baby was going to breathe life into her like she'd never dreamed before. I'm not sure how much help I was. She could barely even register Otto's presence next to her on the bed. She knew he had a cloth on her sweaty forehead, but she couldn't feel it at all. She could barely see his face through her tears. Every sound was fuzzy to her ears except the midwife's commands--she rang crystal clear in Anna's head like she was a soldier and the midwife a drill sergeant. She kept telling Anna to push, push, *push*. Anna tried her very hardest to obey her commands, but she couldn't tell how hard she was pushing, or even if she was doing so at all. She didn't know if she'd last much longer. She was so tired she could hardly think. Seeing her in such agony felt like a dagger twisting itself into my heart, even though I knew she'd be just fine.

After a few more minutes that felt, to Anna, like hours there was an excited exclamation from the midwife followed by the sound of small but mighty cries. Her body immediately went from tense back to a somewhat relaxed state, and it felt like she'd been run over by the auto. She looked over to her husband and found a grin on his face from ear to ear—a smile so happy and genuine that her eyes filled with tears again. This time, they were happy, though. If she'd been able to see me, she would've found tears in my eyes, as well. I could taste salt as I tried to hold them back. The midwife exclaimed that the child was a girl, and she placed the tiny human in Anna's arms. All at once, she was struck by how strange yet lovely the child was: in her experience all newborns looked just that—newly born. Her daughter was no different. She was covered in blood—her skin an angry purple color. Her body shook with every cry as her tiny fingers curled into fists. But somehow, she was the most beautiful little creature Anna had ever laid her eyes on. Anna created her—this wonderous being. She was all hers, and she loved her more than anything.

All of those feelings, so pure and genuine and new, just made me cry harder. My girl had a girl of her own. I nearly choked as memories assaulted me like missiles—this child in Anna's embrace looked so much like my Harmonia had looked in her first moments. She had the same tiny nose and faint glow about her that nearly made my heart seize with emotion. There was nothing more lovely, nothing more sacred, than motherhood. It was a calling of the highest order—one with the power to alter one's DNA. I knew that from this day forward, Anna would never be the same. Never again would she live for herself or even for Otto. From now on, this tiny human would be the embodiment of life and the bright source of light in Anna's universe. That's how it should be. It pains me, sometimes, to see such beacons of hope brought into a world full of such chaos and darkness. It hurts to look at someone else's daughter and hope she'll get the chance to lead a life she's proud of. It hurts even more to know my own will never get the chance to.

I probably would have lost myself completely in the bittersweetness of the moment had the aura in the cabin not changed. There was suddenly a sort of hum throughout the room, like the particles in the air had been charged with electricity. It was gone as soon as it arrived, replaced by the unmistakable smell of citrus wrapped in vanilla.

What is she doing here?

I watched as my sister materialized in the corner of the room, her demeanor the paragon of control and her coiffure as perfect as ever. I would've asked her right then and there why she felt the need to intrude on my assignment, my Anna, so unexpectedly if I'd thought she'd register my words at all. But it was clear, really, My questions would've been ignored. Upon closer inspection of Athena, I could see that her eyes were fixated on the child—tracking it's every cry and movement with the attention of a doctor or, well, a mother. I would've laughed at the absurdity of Athena being maternal in any sense had I not noticed the way those eyes of hers also shined liked diamonds as she beheld the small girl against Anna's chest. It was obvious she could see something I couldn't.

All at once, Athena was in my head.

Isn't she beautiful, sister?

Of course she is.

I sensed her the second she took her first breath. Wisdom...it drips off of her like honey.

It was suddenly very clear to me why Athena was there. This child, Anna's first daughter, was her newest assignment. Before I could decide what to think about this, my sister continued.

And to be born on such a special day, at that.

What do you mean?

Oh Aphrodite, use your brain for once. Today is the Vernal Equinox.

I hadn't realized. I chose to ignore the mocking undertones of the comment as I mulled it over in my head. A child born on the Vernal Equinox. No wonder Athena was so enchanted by her. This day, of all days, was particularly telling. It represented rebirth and new beginnings. It meant that this small girl was destined for great things. Just as I predicted all those years ago at her parents' wedding. This child, in her own way, would help change the world.

My mind jumped back to Anna's thoughts as I realized what she'd logically been considering the past few minutes as I'd been ruminating on things: a name. Anna sifted through all the names she and Otto had gone over in the past nine months until she landed on the one she'd loved since the day she found out she was pregnant. She knew just looking at her daughter that it would be hers. A first name all her own, and a middle name to live up to.

Helene Marta Reinholdt.

A smile cracked briefly across Athena's face, brighter than the sun itself. Then she was gone as fast as she'd arrived.

INTERLUDE
Athens, 2022

As she finishes her thought, Aphrodite notices there is an expression on Athena's face that she's never seen before. It's as if hearing about the birth of Helene has reignited some long dead flame inside of her. In a way, it throws her off a bit. Her sister has always been the definition of reserved, private, unemotional. Aphrodite isn't sure any of them are used to seeing even a morsel of feeling from Athena. Talking about Helene seems to bring attention to the holes in Athena's armor, but she is just now realizing they are holes Athena has created herself, just for Helene. There aren't many mortals that have had that kind of grip on her sister before—the Grecian wanderer Odysseus was the only one Aphrodite could think of. He hadn't been that special at the end of the day, had he? Better that Athena had coached him home to Ithaca—he had been much too manipulative and cunning for her to handle.

"So," Ares interrupts her thoughts, "Are either of you going to tell us why and how exactly this baby is going to change the world?"

"If I told you now it would spoil things, wouldn't it?" She answers with only a hint of playfulness in her voice.

"I don't know if you noticed, but Athena is short-circuiting at the mention of the kid's name, so I feel like, just maybe, it's an important part of the plot."

"Well, brother," Athena says, staring out the tavern window with a strange look on her face. I suppose you'll just have to be patient."

Ares grunts but says nothing in return. All the gods sitting around the table know he might be the least patient of all of them. Aphrodite pours herself another cup of nectar as Amphitrite speaks up.

"I cannot wait to see what Anna is like as a mother, I'm sure she'll be just amazing."

The sea goddess practically vibrates with positivity. It makes Aphrodite smile into her glass before setting it gently on the grooved wood of the table in front of her. She snaps her fingers and a gold-embossed hand mirror appears in her left hand. As she reapplies her makeup and runs her fingers through her dark curls, she feels a small but not insignificant tug in her chest at Amphitrite's comment. Anna's experience as a mother—really anyone's experience as a mother—always makes her feel proud and envious in equal measure. She quickly swallows the lump forming in her throat.

"Oh, yes indeed. This is a happy time in Anna's life," She replies quietly. "But you'll find her journey is more complicated than you think."

"Makes sense," Apollo pipes up, "Motherhood is fickle."

"Fickle in circumstance, perhaps, but hardly ever in affection. That's precisely what makes it so sacred, brother. A mother's love—"

"Knows no bounds, is the strongest force in the world. Blah, blah, blah. I get it. Just remember that while every child has a mother, they aren't always good ones."

She chooses not to ruminate on that subject. It made her very angry. Instead, she clears her throat and prepares for another round of storytelling. Athena flashes through her mind in a split second with a reminder in her voice.

Your words are magic, sister. Let them forge a path to enlightenment, not ignorance. Show these gods what it feels like to wear your rose-tinted glasses, and victory will be yours.

She feels the thrill in her chest as Love signals its agreement.

"Let us continue, *viva voce.*"

APHRODITE
March 30th, 1927

I must confess that after Anna gave birth to Helene, I was not able to see her for quite some time. I originally decided to keep my distance for a short while, simply because I wanted to give Anna and Otto the privacy they deserved. Becoming a mother is no small feat, and I felt that Anna needed to discover what that looked like for her without intervention or guidance from me. I know, I could've just stood there and observed without interfering in any way. I did not trust myself enough to do that; I cared too much about Anna's feelings. I would have jumped at the slightest sense of doubt or self-deprecating thought.

I wish I could say that was the only reason I stayed away from Anna for so long, but alas, it was not. The 1920s proved to be quite the interesting little decade, especially across the Atlantic in that roaring spectacle of America. Lots of beauty wars to moderate and lustful inclinations to...*entangle*. I'll confess it was all quite fun, watching Love move in flashes and bursts like that. I encountered a most interesting young man who had written a riveting story for his lover about the highs and lows of lust and obsession among the Long Island elite, only to drown himself in alcohol when his muse proved too similar to her misguided fictional counterpart. A pity, but oh so dramatic. I digress.

By the time I made my way back to Germany for a check-in with my dearest Anna, it had been six years. I arrived on the sunlit deck of *Poseidon* at the precise moment the boat's horn gave a low proclamation. It was almost as if Anna's universe was welcoming me back into its midst. Distant pitter-patter of small feet gave way to a sight that made my heart swell: two little girls in matching floral dresses and dark braids bounded across the wooden boards in a spirited game of tag. The older one was obviously Helene, and I could clearly see the same powerful aura that had encircled her at her birth reflected now in the fierce green of her eyes. She looked so much like Anna and Marta. The smaller of the two girls was new to me, but I sensed quickly that her name was Margarethe, and she was two years younger than Helene. Children are always more attuned to supernatural presences like myself, and they tend to be much more open to mental communication. Most of the time, they have no idea they're even giving it, which was certainly the case for little Margarethe.

I made my way past the girls to the lower deck of the boat in search of Anna. I found her in the main cabin that served as her and Otto's bedroom. The clock next to her on the nightstand read 7:00 am, and she was dressed accordingly in a plain nightgown with her hair loose against her back. I registered what I thought were baby noises coming from across the small room, and I turned my invisible form around to find a small cradle belonging to the most recent Reinholdt addition. This child was small and sensitive, with a cry not unlike a puppy's. Adorned in nothing but a linen diaper, it was clear to me that this third baby was a boy. His tiny hands clutched his blanket with a grip of iron as he cooed incessantly, having recently discovered his own voice for the first time. He reminded me of my sweet Eros.

I was certain, without a doubt, that the arrival of this baby boy, the first for the family, had been nothing short of miraculous for his parents, especially Otto. It was clear to me, just as it was clear to Anna, that he wished to keep shipping in the family—to make a true business out of it. I thought if given the opportunity, Otto would surely pass on all his knowledge of boats and economics to his son with the passion and dedication of a natural-born teacher.

I combed through Anna's thoughts until I discovered that she'd named the baby Ernst, and even though he hadn't even been alive for more than three months, Anna could tell he was sensitive and even-tempered. His older sisters would give him a run for his money in a few years. They were all so similar, yet so different.

Helene, being the oldest, carried with her an air of responsibility and reason—very quiet, but always thinking and always caring. Wary of everything and everyone until they proved to be trustworthy, she was whip-smart and never missed a beat.

Sounds like someone else I know, naturally.

Margarethe was their wild child, to put it simply. Otto called her his "firecracker," and she certainly lived up to the nickname. The child embodied a sense of fearlessness that was foreign to her older sister. She'd only just celebrated her fourth birthday, but Anna could tell that once she was older, any younger siblings would have to listen and behave, or risk their sister's bossiness. Anna was interested to see how her girls reacted to having a brother. Margarethe was closest in age to Ernst, and already he enamored her. It was quite possible she thought he'd arrived for the sole purpose of becoming her constant companion. She did not leave him alone easily. Helene was ever so curious about him as well—she was at the age where she wanted to know how things (including humans) worked. Anna would catch Helene watching intently when she breastfed him, and when he cried, she always wanted to know exactly why. Anna didn't mind explaining— something about her eldest daughter's knack for questioning reminded Anna of herself at the same age. Her parents had often been more dismissive than explanatory, and she didn't want to be like that, too. She wanted her daughter to feel comfortable asking her anything she was curious about.

It's funny, isn't it—how setting examples can be so defining for a child?

I made myself comfortable amidst Anna's thoughts as she swung her legs over the side of the bed and moved to the narrow closet that held her dresses. She pulled out the same style of cotton housedress she'd been wearing for years. Boat life was hardly glamorous, and while she liked not having to constantly worry about her appearance, there were days when she missed the hair ribbons and tulle of her youth. Otto always told her that she looked just as beautiful in a old, stained dress as she ever did in any of her expensive dresses from back home. She knew he genuinely believed that, but she did not.

I agreed with Otto about that, and I always would. As the Goddess of Love, I am required to admit that beauty is in the eye of the beholder, and that it was entirely possible for Otto to see beauty when Anna saw the opposite. But if that idea is true, then another one must also be: there is more to the word beauty than meets the eye. A woman with a perfect face but an ugly soul is not beautiful. The only thing that matters, truly, is what's on the inside, and once a woman learns how much her power is worth—once she realizes she has power at all and chooses to step into it with grace and forgiveness—that is when she becomes so beautiful it's blinding. I could see that Anna had acknowledged that power in some ways, but not others. She had lots of feelings about the way life was imprinting itself onto her—whether it be through her looks, her clothes, or her duties. Anna was almost twenty-eight years old now, and although she looked the same as she had at twenty, she felt the significant weight of the past eight years.

There was a part of Anna that would always be twenty years old in my mind—and not because she physically looked that way. A goddess doesn't associate with age often—why would we? We are immortal. Anna's physical age was very nearly twenty-eight, but her heart was and always would be much younger. There was a reason I was assigned to Anna when I was, and it is the same reason I will always look at the woman in front of me and see the girl she was before.

As it was, Ernst needed a changing. So, Anna traveled to the head with him as she continued to dwell on how fast things had changed in just a few short years. I got the sense she dwelled on the subject quite often. The baby's tiny fingers grabbed at Anna's curls as she laid him down on the makeshift changing table, his eyes—so much like her own—staring up at her with wonder. Oh, how she wished she could see the world through his little eyes. She couldn't remember what it was like to wake up each day curious about everything, to marvel at all the sights and smells. Those times were long gone.

Were they? I disagreed. A woman's life doesn't have to stop when her child's starts.

It was easy for Anna not to think about the passing of time from day to day, because she was so busy making sure babies were fed and not falling off the boat's deck. But there were moments like the present one, looking at her son, when she couldn't help but feel like her life was passing before her eyes. It was 1927—in July, she'd be another year closer to being alive for three decades. Some might say that twenty-eight was still very young, and she knew that it was in all reality. But it felt like just yesterday she was only eighteen years old, and her whole life was in front of her. She and Otto had been married seven years already, and soon, they'll have known each other an entire decade. Her sister and father had been gone for almost as long.

She pushed that specific and intruding thought out of her mind as she left the head and made her way up the narrow, metal stairs to the main deck—a freshly-changed and very content Ernst on her hip.

It was time to focus on being a mother.

The girls seemed to be playing with their dolls animatedly closer to the front of the boat. They were so invested that they did not notice Anna as she arrived. Good, she would have a few more minutes of peace. She found Otto sitting at the wheel smoking a cigar, slowly and surely directing the boat along the Oder. He seemed distracted, like he was thinking too hard about something. She murmured a greeting as she kissed the top of his head.

"Good morning, darling. Thank you for letting me sleep in a bit."

"Of course," he answered absentmindedly, "You should get time to yourself sometimes."

"You seem...preoccupied. Is everything alright?"

"Yes, everything is fine," he proclaimed, "I'm just thinking about the state of things."

"The state of which things?

"The state of the country. I was talking with a gentleman at port the other day—he says we're headed for a depression."

"And you believe him?" Anna had never known Otto to take such opinions to heart.

"Any other time, I wouldn't. But the thing about it is, Anna, I've noticed changes...in prices, in supply, everything. Germany is having a hard time finding money."

"What do you think is the reason?" she asked nervously. How could the country be out of money?"

"I reckon that damn treaty, the one they signed up in Versailles, is the reason. We must pay for the Great War...and have you seen the state of our cities? They need rebuilding after all that fighting. It's putting us in debt."

It was hard for Anna's brain to comprehend how an entire country could run out of money, and truly the prospect made her nervous. What would happen to the people in the country if the government had no money? What would happen to her family? Surely, there would be hundreds, thousands, of citizens without work. Otto was right, a depression seemed to be on the horizon. Anna responded with the only thing she could think of, the thing that brought her the most comfort.

"Well, whatever the case, I have hope the government will figure this mess out. I am sure the Reichstag will be able to come up with some solution."

"The Reichstag can't even figure itself out...all those greedy and selfish politicians. I'm not sure they'd know what was right for the people who truly run this country—us working citizens--if their lives depended on it."

"What do you think needs to happen, then? Who could possibly help Germany, if not the Reichstag?"

"The Reichstag will help in the end, I think, but what we really need is a new leader—a good leader. Someone to pick this country up off its knees and raise it to new heights."

"You talk as if you have someone in mind."

"There's that Hitler fellow--of the National Socialist German Worker's Party. I don't know much about him yet; I have to do some more research," he paused briefly, then continued, "But that party is going places; I can feel it. Hitler has a way with words I haven't seen from any politician in a long time. I think if anyone could bring this country back to prosperity, it would be him."

"I hope, for the country's sake, that Mr. Hitler lives up to your expectations for him."

That's how it always starts, isn't it? Desperate hope. It was true that the country was being propelled headfirst into a chaotic decade. There would be many people without jobs and even more people without food or adequate shelter. What was also true was the way Hitler was giving people a reason to go on despite all that. At the very start, he truly was saying all the right things—making all the right promises. Hitler certainly possessed an uncanny ability to shape words in his favor until they did his bidding for him. What wasn't clear at the start, but became very apparent once he became chancellor, was the magnitude of the prejudice that fueled those words.

Otto and Anna would support Hitler's plan to bring Germans together during a dismal period in German history, that is, until he would inevitably go too far.

INTERLUDE
Athens, 2022

Aphrodite is forced to stop briefly to take a long sip of her drink. Her throat feels so dry—she isn't used to talking this much at once.

"The way Anna feels about motherhood, and the loss of her girlhood, is really interesting," Amphitrite mentions, "I've always thought becoming a mother was all celebrating."

"Please don't read too far into Anna's ideas," Aphrodite rushes to explain, "Motherhood is certainly a celebration—of new life, and, of course, love."

Ares grunts again next to her. The thought of elbowing him in the stomach flits through her mind, but she refrains. Knowing him, he uses some sort of spell to give himself rock-hard abs—literally. She isn't about to hurt herself just to goad him.

"You don't have to justify motherhood, sister," Athena declares, "We all know it's special, don't worry."

"You don't have to be sarcastic about it."

Athena blinks mutely and looks taken aback, as if she hadn't realized what she'd just said was sarcastic. Sometimes Aphrodite wonders if the lack of tact amidst all that intelligence is a purposeful flaw in Athena's design, meant to test her and keep her on her toes.

"I'm sorry, the words didn't come out the way I wanted them to. All I mean is that Anna's feelings surrounding the shift from daughter to mother—girl to woman—do remind us of something important."

At least she apologized. She doesn't do that often. Aphrodite decides to count it as a win.

"What would that something be, sister?" Ares questions with a hint of disdain.

"That life is all about balance," Athena holds her palm towards the ceiling, and an image of the divine scales appears in a shimmer of magic before disappearing into thin air. "Where there is a give, there is also a take. Every gain has an equal loss. Anna is recognizing that in order to be the mother she's always wanted to be, she must be willing to give up her girlhood. She must choose to leave the past alone before she can look ahead into the future."

"But," Aphrodite shakes her head in confusion, "I don't think Anna should feel required to abandon everything she is just because she brought a child into the world."

"Of course not," Athena agrees, "That's not quite what I'm getting at. All I'm saying is that the innocence that defines childhood isn't something that can last forever—it's not meant to. Anna is dealing with the fallout of watching that innocence disappear. There is a kind of maturity that mothers must possess if they wish to be successful. It is from that maturity that women understand how to teach their children about acknowledging the pretty parts of life while protecting them from the ugly parts."

That made more sense when Aphrodite really thought about it. Growing up is unavoidable. Always has been, and always will be. There is inherent loss in it—a pain that persists for some time because of it—but that is simply the way of things. It's the kind of hurt that makes one stronger, and smarter.

"Let's jump a few years in time," she cleared her throat. "We'll see just how much those growing pains paid off."

APHRODITE
April 30th, 1934

The end of April was a time that most German children waited in anticipation for—because of Hexennacht, of course. Many call it Walpurgis Night these days, but I think the former sounds more palatable, does it not? I can't say it was my favorite of the human celebrations per se, but it always proved interesting to observe. Similar to the English celebration of All Hallow's Eve (or is it called Halloween, now? I might be a few centuries off), there is lots of costuming, dancing, singing, and lighting bonfires to keep the evil spirits away. Human superstitions can be so charming.

Imagine the surprise and disgust I felt in my heart upon discovering that the leader of Germany had subverted the celebration to benefit his agenda.

It seemed Hitler had somehow gotten the message about his plans for the celebration out to the entire city of Hamburg, and it was rather clear that participation was not only encouraged but expected. Massive bonfires were lit throughout the city, and it was still unclear what exactly everyone would do at each one. Many assumed it would be similar to years past, with some sort of speech sanctioned by Hitler to further glorify the Reich.

That assumption was very wrong.

✳✳✳

Anna felt the fire before she saw it, which gave her a good idea of just how big it was. She wasn't sure what all of this was about, but she had an unidentifiable feeling in her stomach that she didn't like as she continued down the cobblestones in the direction of the heat–Helene trailing behind her. She'd known that Otto would not want to attend with her due to his distaste for Hitler, who had become the chancellor last year, but two of the children being sick proved a sounder excuse. Her husband had already been half peer-pressured, half forced to join the Nazi Party the year prior, and Anna knew he was only biding his time before rescinding that membership. She didn't want to think about what could happen to them when he finally did so. Any attention from the government was not the attention she wanted, and the thought of going against a mandatory participation order became terrifying if she let it.

The closer they moved towards the bonfire, the more the street seemed to faintly glow. The firelight reflected off the street lamps and moved across the ground as if the spirits they were supposed to be fending off had already been let in, and were now dancing around with glee. Anna debated for what wasn't the first time in her almost thirty-five years of life if these spirits were actually evil or not. She'd noticed over the years that evil had become a synonym for unknown, for different. One couldn't control something they didn't understand, and that tended to scare people. But evil, true evil, was something else entirely.

As they rounded a corner, the bonfire came into view. Its size, as predicted, was massive. Was it safe to have something so large burning in the middle of a city square? Surely not. As they found a spot to stand in the crowd, Anna watched as her daughter took in the scene around her with critical eyes. At thirteen years old, Helene tended to prefer an existence built on observing others rather than actually interacting with them. Anna could hardly blame her, she herself had been the same way at that age. Helene was a thinker, always looking to learn something. But unlike Anna, the girl wasn't afraid to tell other people exactly what she thought when asked. She didn't care to keep quiet for the sake of others, and she seemed to almost desire a debate just so she could prove the other person wrong. Even then, Helene was never rude, never demeaning. She lit up every room she walked into. She could make anyone laugh, especially her siblings, when they didn't think they wanted to.

It was in those moments, when her girl was challenging assumptions or smiling other people's sorrows away, that Anna swore she saw Marta—alive and well after all. It nearly broke her heart every time, seeing her beloved sister reflected in her eldest daughter's face.

There is a reason Helene was named the way she was. Destiny is a funny little thing.

Anna forced herself to stop thinking about her sister before she got herself swept away in a gust of sadness. Tonight was about singing and dancing—having fun. At least, that was what usually happened on Hexennacht. Now that she thought about it, though, nobody around her was dressed up, and there was no music at all. A peculiar smell permeated through the air, though. What was it?

Anna couldn't seem to place it. Something was burning, surely, which made sense considering the bonfire in front of her. But it didn't smell like a usual bonfire–the musky scent of wood seemed to be unpleasant and mixed with...chemicals? She could detect the faintest presence of something close to vanilla, as well. What on Earth was that smell—

Paper, darling. That's the smell of burning paper.

Within seconds of my mental correspondence with her, Anna's head swiveled to her left, then to her right, trying to pinpoint where and why someone would have decided to burn paper.

Listening will help you more than looking, if you do so carefully.

It was unlike me to speak to Anna twice in such short succession, but it was obvious there were too many people crowded in front of her for her efforts to yield anything useful. To my delight, Anna stopped and listened to me, straining her ears to catch anything that might give clarity. Slowly, Anna focused on one particular sound resonating above the commotion of the crowd–a voice shouting the same phrase over and over, like he'd been told by someone important to say it until his throat bled. Anna felt her mouth go dry upon realizing what it was.

"Verbrennt die Bücher! Burn the books!"

Burn. The. Books.

She wasn't just smelling paper, she was smelling books, and they were on *fire*. The Reich was using Hexennacht as an excuse to burn books. What was perhaps worse was the ease with which the people around her were complying. She felt Helene push against her as she spoke close to her ear.

"Why are we burning all the books? What is wrong with them?"

Anna did not endeavor to respond, because there wasn't a good answer. She felt herself start moving through the crowd in front of her instead, startling Helene.

"Mutti, where are you going?"

She needed a better view of whatever this horrible excuse of a nationalistic show was. It felt like she was barely moving her feet, and rather being lifted to the front by everyone else surging forward in a mad rush to have their turn throwing literature into the flames. She felt Helene grab her hand from behind, but before she could endeavor to turn her head and reassure her daughter, someone thrusted something into her other hand and shouted at her to throw it in turn.

She looked down to find a thick volume, already covered in ash and coming apart at the spine. The book's title stood at attention in half-worn gold letters across the front cover: *Les Misérables*. One of her favorites.

Before Anna could dwell on the novel any longer, her surroundings caught up to her. There was a great shove, and her feet slipped from under her. She heard Helene shriek behind her as she landed face-down on the cobblestones. For a long moment, all she could hear was the sound of shoes scuffing the ground, keeping time with her own frantic heartbeat. All around her, people continued to push past her towards the front of the crowd, not bothering to help her up or ask if she was hurt. The book, which had slightly cushioned her fall at first, was now pressing against her stomach in a rather uncomfortable way. A young boy, no more than ten, nearly stepped on her as he streaked past, his immature voice trying to sound older than it was as he chanted "Verbrennt die Bücher!" as if it was the sweet refrain to a poem Hitler had written himself. Seeing such an innocent and naive mind corrupted into believing books deserved such a fiery fate made Anna so angry she felt tears spot her vision. She supposed the rumors about Hexennacht were true–some things were evil, after all.

Those things weren't spirits, though. They were humans. They were leaders.

The book pressed to her chest felt especially heavy as Anna's world slowed to a halt. Victor Hugo's words appeared from the dark corridors of her conscience, the sentences leaping from the depths of her mind to wrap themselves instead around her heart as she silently recited them from memory.

If the soul is left in darkness, sins will be committed. The guilty one is not he who commits the sin, but he who causes the darkness.

Victor always did have a way with words, didn't he? A charming fellow, and a wise one, too. It did not escape my notice that Anna had memorized that particular quote of his. It is seldom the case that people are born evil. Most of the time, they are turned into monsters by the society they live in.

Hitler had already turned that little boy into one, just as he surely had many other children. Anna would be damned before she let him touch her own. She'd nearly let him succeed, bringing her girl–her Helene–with her into this insanity; she refused to give him anything more.

Ah, finally. A decision.

Time resumed its chaotic tempo as Anna slid the novel beneath the fabric of her coat before endeavoring to stand. Everyone around her was in too much of a frenzy to notice she'd made it back on her feet, let alone that she was empty-handed. Well, everyone except Helene.

"Mutti, where is the book?"

"Quiet, meine *Hummel*," Anna whispered frantically, as she

took Helene's trembling hand in her own once again, "We must go, follow me."

As the two of them made their way back through the Hamburg streets towards the docks, Anna didn't let them stop once, nor did she look behind her to see if they'd been followed. To look would have given them away. It felt as though the book was surely burning a hole through her clothes and into her chest—the illegality of what she'd just done threatening to bring her to her knees if she stopped moving for even a moment. She felt silly, in a sense. It wasn't like she'd stood up to the SS officers or threatened anybody. So why did this small act feel so big?

The smallest acts are often most significant, precisely because they go unnoticed.

Anna had never done anything like this before; she'd never fancied herself the rebellious type. But she'd taken a book—one deemed irreverent and sanctioned by the government to be destroyed in contempt. Her whole life, Anna had always felt she didn't have the right kind of courage to ever do such a thing, and yet, she had.

Courage doesn't distinguish between right and wrong, it is subjective. To have courage is one thing. To choose what you do with that courage is quite another thing entirely.

✳✳✳

The door creaked on its hinges as Anna slipped into the cabin Helene and Margarethe shared. They'd been back from the disastrous Hexennacht celebration—if it could even be called that—for nearly two hours, and Anna felt more like herself again. She knew it would be foolish to not speak about it with Helene—Anna needed her to know why she'd stolen the book when she'd been told to destroy it.

So, Anna had waited until she knew Helene would be alone in her room–Margarethe always played cards with her father before she went to bed–to sneak a few moments with her. As expected, Helene was furiously scribbling in her cloth-bound journal when Anna knocked.

"May I come in?"

"Of course," Helene smiled softly as she looked up at her mother, "Are you feeling better?"

"Who said I was feeling poorly?"

"Mutti, please. You were a mess when we got back earlier."

Anna chuckled at the way Helene spoke, as if she herself hadn't been trembling.

"I have something for you, darling."

Helene's eyes seemed to double in size as Anna pulled the worn copy of *Les Misérables* from behind her back. She set it gently in her daughter's lap, watching in amusement as Helene ran her fingers over the cover carefully.

"I can't believe you really stole it, Mutti."

"Well, the Reich had no right to burn it. It's a classic, one of my favorites."

"What is it about?"

"War and bravery. Love, too."

"It's so big," Helene giggled, "I wonder why they wanted to burn it."

"Words are power, Helene," Anna sighed, "And when a book contains so many, that kind of power can be seen as a threat. A danger."

"What do you mean?"

"Words...they are like swords. The way we choose to use them dictates their power, but they always have the ability to wound—even kill," Anna paused, trying to find the right words to make her daughter understand, "We must be careful of how we handle that kind of weapon."

"I've never thought about words like that," Helene said thoughtfully, "Like weapons."

"Words can hurt more than actions, if we want them to."

"Like when Margarethe tells me I ought to stop eating so many pastries."

"Or when you tell Margarethe her dress looks ugly."

Helene had enough humility to look sheepishly into her lap. Anna continued.

"People like the Führer, they tend to misuse words."

"How do you know?"

"If you listen to the words he chooses, he often twists them in ways that help him but hurt others. But when you strip Hitler of his words, he has nothing."

Helene sat quietly for a moment, deciding what she thought about Anna's comments. It always made Anna smile to see her concentrate—her brow furrowed so endearingly. Eventually, Helene spoke up once more.

"You say books are like weapons..." she started hesitantly, "But you wouldn't have saved a gun or a knife from a bonfire."

Oh, I see why Athena likes this one so much.

"I said that words are weapons, not books. They are parts to a whole," Anna explained, "Books are something wonderful, something special."

Humans and gods alike are so quick to assume that Love only connects someone with someone else. This is not true, not at all. How could anyone see the way talking about literature made Anna's eyes glow—how could someone feel such passion—and not believe in the power of Love?

"Books are words with magic breathed into them. When you take your pen and let a word loose on the page, and then you add another, and another—you recreate them, give them a reason to be. Those words, once they have a home and a purpose, let you see the magic they hold hidden inside. Suddenly, what was nothing more than a collection of letters moments ago is now a whole new constellation of meaning—they will make you, and break you, and they'll show you exactly who you're meant to be if you let them. Helene, if you only let them, books will give you more truth than anything else in this world."

"But Mutti, you said words—books—are magic. Magic isn't truth, it's...illusion."

"Is it? Books often tell us lies, that is the point of works of fiction especially, but they do so to show us the truth. There is nothing more magical than that."

"So, that means that the reason Hitler wants to take books away..." There was the furrowed brow again, "Is exactly why we need to keep reading them. They're magic, but not in an impossible fairytale kind of way—in a way that makes our minds strong."

"Exactly," Anna beamed, "Nothing is more important than a strong mind. Never forget that."

My senses hummed happily as Love signaled its agreement. I wished every human could see books in the same way my Anna did. I wish they could know what it's like to love something with that kind of conviction. I think the world would be a better place—a more forgiving place.

I watched as Anna kissed Helene on the forehead before making her way out of the cabin. I lingered a bit longer, just so I could watch Helene tentatively crack the spine of Hugo's masterpiece, bringing it to her nose and inhaling the musty scent of all those revolutionary ideas.

The twinkle in her eyes as she did so did not escape my notice. I was sure that, had my hand mirror been present, the same shine would've been reflected in my own.

INTERLUDE
Athens, 2022

"How poignant," Apollo surmises into the silence as Aphrodite pauses, "There's nothing quite like bonding over the power of words."

Aphrodite wishes she could tell if he's being facetious or not. What he said was true all the same—mother and daughter had found something that connected them, not only to each other but to every person in the world. Words were power, as Anna had so simply put it. Aphrodite agrees with that sentiment, just as she knows Athena feels the same way. In fact, her sister understands the weight of words better than any god at this table; she's made it her purpose to serve as their keeper—the one who holds their secrets and honors their truth.

At the moment, Athena is looking down into her cup contemplatively, as if she's turning the story over in her head in order to decide what she thinks about it. She always makes Aphrodite nervous when she does that—it always feels like there's some sort of criticism coming.

"I don't know if I buy the whole 'books are magic' argument," Ares debates, "Us gods are magic, clearly, and it implies that books are just as powerful as we are. That's impossible."

"No, it's not," Athena's voice is sharp in retort. "Magic is magic, its host doesn't denote its power. It flows through every worthy thing—living or not—with the same ability and the same control. That power may feel different from one perspective to another, but make no mistake, it is less subjective than you think."

"The Wisdom that hides between the letters on a page is the same Wisdom that lives in you," Aphrodite clarifies, "It transforms its appearance to fit the purpose at hand, but it's not different."

"Yes," Athena's eyes soften as she relaxes, "Just as the Love that breathes meaning into a kiss is the very Love that breathes life into you."

Aphrodite smiles at the comparison. It's almost overwhelming to her sometimes—the knowledge that the magic chose her, of all the gods, to fulfill the important role of the guardian of Love. There could be no higher honor, in her eyes. There is nothing she believes in with a greater conviction.

She also believes that it's possible for magic to serve two purposes at once. Athena knows books hold magic in the form of Wisdom, and she isn't wrong, but books are mighty deliverers of Love, too. They are companions for the lonely, and comforters of the sick. They teach and they embrace in equal measure.

"Well," Apollo cuts through her thoughts, "I'm sure Anna's circumstances only get more complicated from here. I want to see some more action."

"We will continue when Aphrodite is ready, Apollo," Athena chastises.

"I'm ready," she clears her throat, "Now where were we?"

APHRODITE
September 16th, 1935

The Monday afternoon air felt crisp against her face as Anna made her way through the streets of Hamburg. She was on her way back to the boat, having just picked up some things at a small street market. Soon enough, she and the children would move to the apartment for the winter, but the warm weather seemed to be sticking around for now. Holding onto her arm was the newest member of the Reinholdt family—and one I personally hadn't been acquainted with yet. Her name was Anneliese, and as she walked beside her mother, her braids swung back and forth in a way that made me laugh. At three years old, she was a beautiful little creature. Multiple older women had already stopped mother and daughter on their journey to and from the market to exclaim about how darling Anneliese was. Anna loved to tease Otto about how the compliments would only increase in frequency as the children got older. Having so many daughters had certainly given Otto a run for his money. He'd started telling Helene and Margarethe that they were not allowed to ever kiss a boy under any circumstances, which, of course, always resulted in lots of blushing and giggling and proclamations that they'd never love anyone like they loved him.

Anna didn't think they had anything to worry about with Helene, at least not for a while. Although she was the oldest at fourteen, she preferred spending her time alone with her books and her knitting needles. Anna wasn't sure if Helene had actually ever endeavored to speak to a boy, and if she had, Anna never heard about it—which probably meant it didn't go well.

Margarethe, on the other hand, had dared a boy to kiss her at five years old.

She glanced down at the watch on her wrist. The girls would be home soon, and she'd be able to leave Anneliese with them while she went to pick up Ernst from his primary school not too far from the docks. Otto had been trying to convince her to let Ernst walk home by himself ever since he turned eight in May, but she wasn't ready to allow it yet. Her only son was very shy, and didn't stand up for himself easily. She could only imagine what would happen if someone tried to speak with him on his journey and he didn't know what to do. She also just loved seeing his perfect little face light up when he found her in the crowd of parents waiting in the pick-up queue. She loved all of her children with every fiber of her being, but there was something about Ernst's gentle soul that made her melt. She hoped he never lost that tenderness.

I was deeply familiar with the way Anna felt towards her son, I hold the same emotions in my heart for my own.

Anna picked up Anneliese as they approached the dock, balanced her on her hip while carrying the bag from the market in her opposite hand. The girl was certainly capable of walking the entire way, but the dock boards could be very slippery, and the last thing she needed was her three year old screaming in the water.

As it turned out, having a higher vantage point allowed Anneliese to see the visitor before she did.

"Mama, look," she exclaimed as she pointed a grubby finger in the direction of the boat. Margo has a friend!"

Sure enough, as Anna squinted in the sun to get a better look, she could make out Helene and Margarethe standing on the foredeck with a boy she'd never seen before. He stood awkwardly next to Margarethe, and as she approached the gangway, she could see a look of mild distress in his expression, although he seemed to be trying to hide it. What on Earth could be going on? Did Margo think, at twelve years old, that she was allowed to have a beau? Heavens help them if she did.

I knew immediately that the stress radiating from this child had nothing to do with romantic feelings for either of the eldest Reinholdt girls. I wished his troubles could have been chalked up to something trivial like that—perhaps in a different universe, they would have. But this boy had bigger things to worry about, as Anna would soon discover.

Margo started speaking a mile a minute as soon as Anna's feet touched the deck.

"Mutti, I'm so glad you're here. Helene and I brought our friend home with us. His name is Simon," she gestured towards the boy without looking back at him. "His parents own a bakery downtown that's on our route home, but when we arrived there today, the police were there, and they were painting big yellow stars all over the windows and Simon's mother was standing outside on the sidewalk crying. She didn't want Simon to be there, so we told her he could come with us for a while until the police left."

She paused to catch her breath, and Anna interjected before she could continue.

"Slow down, my darling. Why don't you let your friend explain things, hmm?"

Four sets of eyes swiveled to look at Simon. Up close, Anna could see he wore round glasses and a tweed jacket. For a boy the same age as her daughters, he had a bit of a baby face, and his hair seemed to be combed and parted just right. His voice was timid as he started to speak.

"I'm sorry to intrude, Frau Reinholdt. Let me start by saying that my family and I are *Juden*, so if you are uncomfortable with that, I can leave now."

The boy was Jewish. It was suddenly a bit clearer to Anna what was happening.

"We don't have a problem with that in this family," she rushed to say, "You are more than welcome here. Tell me what's happened."

"Well, you know how the government feels about us, right?"

"Unfortunately, yes. I do. Have they done something?"

"They took away our citizenship."

"What?" Anna's mind couldn't compute what he'd said, "What do you mean, they took it away? They cannot do such a thing."

"They can, Frau Reinholdt. My mother told me so when I saw her just now. She said the Führer has created a new law that strips us of our citizenship and says we cannot marry non-Jewish people. They came and marked my parent's store with the Star of David so people will be less likely to want to buy from us."

Anna found herself at a loss of words for this poor boy. The antisemitism movement had undoubtedly grown since Hitler became chancellor two years prior, but she'd hoped that it wouldn't grow into such a horrible display of hatred. Had the government truly sanctioned this? What kind of leader did such a thing? That man was surely mentally unwell—he'd made her ill at ease ever since his platform had transformed from focusing on unifying the country to dividing it. Not to mention his absolutely vile campaign to censor everything publicly consumed, whether it be books, newspapers, or music.

She knew her husband thought Hitler was positively out of his mind for his dreams of creating an Aryan state. Such a thing wasn't reasonable, nor was it moral. There were many non-Jewish citizens of the Reich that did not have blond hair and blue eyes. Any rule that stated brown-haired, brown-eyed people didn't deserve basic human rights was blasphemous. It was outrageous.

As she stood there trying to come up with something to say that even came close to conveying those feelings, she heard Otto come up behind her—having just realized they had company. She glanced at him briefly to find an angry look on his face that suggested he had heard everything Simon had just said.

"We're sorry to hear this," her husband's voice declared, "What can we do to help? Have they said the bakery cannot stay open?"

"No, at least not yet," Simon pushed his glasses up the bridge of his nose nervously. "They probably just want people to stop buying from us. I'm sure many people will."

"Consider us regular customers, then, from now on. Anna can stop in and get bread, can't you dear?"

"Of course," Anna agreed as she tried to plaster a smile onto her lips, "We'd love to support your family, Simon."

The boy seemed to relax a bit at her words, and Anna felt better knowing she'd reassured him in some small way.

"Thank you both. I cannot tell you how much it means to my family. I know my father is trying to move us away from the city, but my mother doesn't want to leave yet."

"If you ever need it, this boat will take you to the countryside, no questions asked," Otto proclaimed.

"I will tell my parents about the offer, although they are sometimes too proud for their own good."

"Nothing wrong with being proud—without it, we wouldn't have much left."

A smile cracked across Simon's face for a second at the comment. Anna could tell that he was very proud of both his parents and his culture, and would be forever.

"Feel free to stay as long as you want, Simon," she chimed in, "And please, let me give you some food—you must be starving."

✶✶✶

Simon stayed at the boat for about an hour before he became restless about being away from his parents. Anna encouraged him to leave with enough food for a few days and promised she'd stop by the bakery next time she ventured into the city. She walked him all the way down the dock, too, just to make sure he went off in the right direction. Anna waited until he turned a corner out of her sight before she started the walk back up the dock. She passed their neighbor, an older gentleman named Fritz, who moored his boat near theirs and waved to him just as she always did. Today, it seemed, he was in the mood to chat.

"Who was that boy with you, Frau Reinholdt?" His voice carried a sharpness to it that Anna didn't like very much. He'd never spoken to her like that before.

"Good afternoon, Fritz. The boy is a friend of my daughter's. He was just visiting."

"Is he a Jew?"

Such straightforwardness felt almost rude to Anna, but she answered him kindly, albeit deceitfully. His tone put her on edge.

"I have no idea, not that it would be of much consequence."

"I'd be wary of helping those folk; nothing good will come of it."

"Whatever do you mean? He's just a boy."

"There are pure boys, and there are dirty boys," the man drawled as if he knew everything there was to know about the world, "Associating with the dirty ones will get you into trouble if the Führer finds out about it. If I were you, I'd do what's best for you and your family, and let other people figure themselves out."

Hearing someone call that innocent child *dirty* made her grit her teeth in angry silence. She found she couldn't give Fritz an answer—she didn't want to. She felt herself nod towards him and smile mechanically before hurrying herself down the rest of the dock and back onto *Poseidon*. She rushed to relate the exchange to Otto, not realizing at first that Helene was very obviously listening to the conversation. As she told her husband about what the man had called Simon, Helene's face contorted in a combination of surprise and rage, as if she couldn't believe someone would dare to say such a thing about another human being.

I got the godly sense that Helene had never seen such blatant and ugly prejudice firsthand before. It hurt me to know just how much of it she would see from now on, from friends, teachers, strangers, and leaders. But there comes a time when children must realize that life can be very unfair and very unjust. Within the world Helene and her siblings were growing up in, the success of one man usually meant the demise of dozens. It was important to me, just as I knew it was important to my sister, that Helene saw such ugliness. She needed to see it, and react to it. She needed to be upset by it, if she wanted to endeavor to change it someday.

I'm sorry; I've gotten ahead of myself. Back to the scene at hand.

"There is nothing wrong with helping people," Otto surmised once Anna finished.

"I know, but what will we do if this escalates? Will we be under suspicion?"

"I don't give a damn about anybody's suspicion, especially Hitler's. Everyone deserves someone in their corner."

I always loved that about Otto Reinholdt—his willingness to advocate for people when they couldn't do it for themselves. If only there were more people like that. The Hitlers of the world wouldn't stand a chance, would they?

APHRODITE
November 9th-10th, 1938

Anna opened her eyes with a sigh as the sound of baby cries filled the small apartment bedroom. Little Klara (known by her siblings as Kitty) had made her grand entrance into the world about a month prior, and just like all newborns, she liked to proclaim her hunger for breastmilk every few hours.

A glance at the clock on the bedside table informed her it was nearly midnight as she swung herself out of bed. Otto was out on the river, seeing as it was the middle of the week, and she chastised herself yet again for not accompanying him. Nights with an infant were so much easier when there were two of them, but she hadn't wanted to leave Helene to deal with the apartment by herself–she was incredibly responsible, but still only seventeen. So, Anna stayed while Otto went, and cared for the children by herself.

As she took Klara out of her crib and moved into the sitting room to breastfeed, she noticed movement in the kitchen out of the corner of her eye. Upon investigation, Anna found her eldest daughter sitting at the table.

"Darling, what are you doing up? It's so late," Anna inquired as she approached the outline of her daughter in the dark.

"I was thirsty," came Helene's quick reply as she held up a glass of water, "I could ask the same of you."

"Klara was whining to be fed. I thought I'd take a walk with her before I tried to get her to go back to sleep again."

Helene nodded, and Anna was sure she would've said more had she not been prevented by an awful shattering sound coming from outside. Anna liked keeping a window or two open at night to let the fresh air in, and now, through one of those open windows, she could make out the sound of voices, too.

Immediately, Helene flew to the glass, her eyebrows knit in confusion as she tried to make sense of what she could see happening on the street. More sounds floated upwards as Anna came to stand beside her: a cacophony of footsteps running, people shouting, and glass breaking. Surely, Anna thought, she was witnessing a robbery gone wrong.

How I wish it was only a robbery. This is much worse than that.

Anna was about to move towards the telephone to call the police when she noticed Helene's eyes widen incomprehensibly and stopped in her tracks.

"What is it? What do you see out there?"

"Mutti, there are boys from my school out there breaking windows."

"What? How?"

"And look, there are two SS officers just standing there, not stopping them."

Before Anna could ask her why on Earth school children would be smashing windows, Margarethe flew from the bedroom she shared with her older sister–her face painted in various hues of anger.

"I swear to the heavens, that piece of absolute *shit* Harald Kranz is about to get his ass whooped for waking me up in the middle of the *night vandalizing the city with his friends!*"

Anna didn't know whether to be more surprised by the expletive or the threat.

"I didn't believe they were actually serious about it," Helene whispered with surprise, seemingly knowledgeable about something Anna was not, "I didn't think they'd do it."

"Do what? What is happening?" Anna asked for clarification as she shifted Klara nervously to her other hip.

Margarethe answered as she swung a coat over her shoulders.

"Those disgusting boys would rather do exactly as they're told than think for themselves for once in their stupid lives," she spat as she spun around the kitchen in a whirlwind of fury, "They're like actual sheep."

"The boys in Hitler Youth were talking at school today about starting a riot against the Jews tonight," Helene explained nervously, "They kept boasting about it–saying the Führer was counting on them to destroy anything Jewish they could find."

The explanation made Anna pale with anxiety. The government was constantly discriminating against Jews, and had been stripping them of their rights steadily since Hitler had taken power five years ago. But this–this was new. If what Helene and Margo were saying was true, they were calling on children–*children*–to commit heinous crimes against their neighbors–against good people who hadn't done a thing wrong.

Anna, darling, the children aren't committing any crimes if the police have sanctioned it.

The thought made her positively sick to her stomach.

She came back to the moment at hand upon hearing the apartment door open.

"Margarethe, you are absolutely not leaving," she started to say.

Her daughter either didn't hear her or chose not to, because she stormed through the doorway anyway, hellbent on inserting herself into the chaos to...what? Grab some boy by his collar and scream at him to stop?

I think that was probably exactly what that lovely, tempestuous girl wanted to do.

"Margo, please be sensible for once," Helene shouted after her in a way that reminded me so much of Athena, and also Anna. When it became more than obvious that there wasn't much that would stop her sister, Helene sighed.

"I'll go after her, Mutti."

"No, I don't want either of you out there alone."

"Then come with us," she said over her shoulder as she followed Margarethe. Bring Klara if you must."

And then she, too, was gone out the door. Anna felt as though she might explode in frustration as she slid a pair of shoes on hastily and stumbled out of doors after her daughters. She hoped none of the other children woke to find her gone.

She instantly regretted her decision when her shoes hit the sidewalk at the exact moment a horrific scream sliced through the night air, sending shivers down her arms. She looked around wildly, first for Helene and Margarethe, and then for the source of such an awful sound. She found both only a few feet in front of her.

Helene had pulled Margarethe back by her coat, and the two of them stumbled against the brick wall next to them as several Hitler Youth boys ran out of a building less than a block away, laughing and shouting profanities. Following them out were two SS officers in uniform with a man caught up in their arms and a woman trailing behind them. Anna swore the ground started glittering oddly as the officers dragged the man into the middle of the street and forced him onto his knees.

It's all the shattered windows, dear. This is a night of broken glass and broken dreams.

The woman, who Anna presumed was the man's wife, also fell to her knees in front of their now-demolished store. Blood bloomed against her shins and her palms as the glass cut into her skin, but she didn't seem to even notice.

It was then that one of the officers shoved the man to the ground, hard.

Anna heard Helene breathe in sharply—or was it her that gasped?--as the poor man's face hit the cold cobblestones, and both officers began taking turns kicking him everywhere they could think to. Margarethe made a move to stop what was happening, taking several steps in the direction of the street, but the sight of a military pistol being flashed in warning stopped her in her tracks. The man's wife was still crouched on the ground, her screams having been transformed into heart-wrenching sobs as she watched her husband be half beaten to death. Anna wondered if she would've tried to help Otto, had they been in this situation. Surely, she would have. She couldn't imagine being so paralyzed.

If that woman tried to help her husband, both of them would be shot dead.

My comment sent a chill of terror through Anna. She felt like she might be suffocating as the officers continued to beat the man senseless and his poor wife continued to cry. With every sickening kick, it became harder to think properly, as if she could feel each blow herself. She clutched Klara, who had started whimpering, against her chest as tears blurred her vision. One glance to her left confirmed Helene was very upset as well. Margarethe looked as if she wanted to throw up her dinner. Anna hated that her daughters lived in a place where this kind of thing was allowed to happen— where the police were allowed to beat people for unjust reasons, and the leader of the country had turned his people against each other in the name of some kind of twisted unity.

Eventually, the kicks slowed, and then stopped completely as the officers decided the poor man had been through enough. Or perhaps they grew bored. Either way, they handcuffed him—as if he could've run away in his half-conscious state—and stuffed him in a car. His wife watched from her place on the pavement as they drove him away. Her sobs had quieted to whimpers, due in part to the new presence of a young man next to her who seemed to be trying his best to soothe her despite the tears falling in crooked lines down his own face. Anna's heart ached for them, and she wanted to approach them—ask how she could help them—but before she could say anything, Helene broke through the stillness of the moment, shouting down the sidewalk towards the two figures.

"Simon Frier?" Her voice sounded as if it might break at any moment, "Is that you?"

The young man's head shot up at the sound of Helene's call, and when his gaze found the three of them standing in their nightgowns, a mix of relief and anguish clouded his eyes. Sure enough, Anna could recall seeing this boy before—he'd come to the boat with the girls one day years ago. He and his parents had just lost their citizenship due to some asinine law of Hitler's creation. Anna still remembered the warning she'd received from their neighbor, Fritz, about staying away from Jews after the boy had gone home.

"My goodness," Margarethe gasped, "That is Simon."

Both girls remembered how to move at the same time, careening down the street towards their friend. Margo instantly engulfed him in a bone-crushing hug, while Helene knelt down to inspect his mother's bloodied hands. By the time Anna caught up with them, Simon's mother was back on her feet and clutching her son's arm like he would disappear if she didn't. There was surely a part of her that truly believed it to, after watching her husband be ripped away from her. Anna wasn't sure exactly what to say at first but eventually decided to address her daughters.

"Girls, let's bring Simon and his mother back to the apartment," she instructed, "We'll get them cleaned up and figure out what's happened."

"Yes, alright," Helene agreed, "Simon, you remember my mother, don't you?"

"Of course, I would never forget your kindness when I visited your boat, Frau Reinholdt," the boy's weary eyes met hers as he tried to give her a smile and failed. He leaned close to his mother and whispered something in her ear. Whatever it was filled the woman's pale face with gratitude, and she allowed herself to be walked down the street and up a flight of stairs into the apartment. Once her hands and knees had been washed of blood, Anna brought her to the kitchen. Helene placed a steaming cup of tea in her hands with a question.

"Frau Frier, how are you feeling? Can you tell us what happened?"

The woman took a long sip from her mug before she endeavored to answer.

"We'd heard rumblings about a riot happening tonight," she started, "And while I cannot say I truly believed one would happen, my husband wanted to stay up to make sure the store would be safe."

"We live above the store," Simon interjected.

"Yes," his mother continued, "Which is worse than if we didn't. When the SS came with that group of Hitler Youth boys, they stormed straight into the house looking for my husband."

Anna almost gasped at the image the words conjured in her mind.

"They took my father by the arms and practically carried him out," Simon added, "And then they started ransacking the entire store. It is completely ruined."

"I am afraid to stay here without my husband," Frau Frier admitted as fresh tears filled her eyes, "But where will we go? How will we get away?"

Here was something Anna could help with, finally.

"We can help with that," she proclaimed, "My husband is out on our boat as we speak. When he comes to port to pick up supplies tomorrow, he can take you to the countryside. I don't know how far away from Hamburg you'll be able to get, but if you can make it to Brunsbüttel, you should be able to find passage out of Germany if you so choose to."

"We will make it," Simon exclaimed, "I will make sure of it."

✳✳✳

Anna refused to let Simon and his mother go back to their destroyed home for the night, and so they settled in the sitting room until morning. There wasn't much else that could be done, which frustrated her to no end. The night's events seemed to have caught up to her girls, but Helene especially. While Margo stayed and comforted Simon, Anna found Helene curled in a ball on her bed, her cheeks wet and her hands shaking. Helene lived in an almost constant state of nervousness, and it broke Anna's heart to watch her struggle due largely to the fact that she understood exactly what it felt like. She knew that watching her friend's father get arrested had shocked her to her core. Helene was probably wondering what the man had done to deserve such treatment. She was probably wondering if the same thing might happen to her father if he didn't do as he was told. She was wondering if the same thing might happen to her, someday.

At that moment, as she rubbed her girl's back and whispered comforting words, Anna wondered what kind of mother she was, to willingly bring children into a world full of such chaos and suffering. How was it fair to them, to have to endure such madness? How was it fair not only to her children, but all German children? How was it fair to *Jewish* children, who must watch the people they love get beaten and ridiculed for simply being who they are—who must watch the life they love be ripped from them because of things they can't control? How was any of this fair to any child? It made her positively sick. What kind of world was this?

I didn't know how to answer her in a way that felt adequate. What kind of world was it? A misguided one. A scared one. A damaged one. It was a world in need of transformation, a world in need of Love.

I understood Anna's disgust at how her country had allowed itself to fall so far from grace. For the entire rest of that night, from November 9th into November 10th, thousands of Jewish businesses, homes, and places of worship would be defiled and destroyed in the name of the Reich. Jews would be displaced, arrested, and killed. And what would the non-Jewish public do? Not much. Some would cheer and shout praises, and those people belong in the worst parts of the Underworld. Others—the majority—would hide behind their curtains or watch the events unfold from street corners and cry silently as they watched neighbors and friends be stripped of their humanity. Hitler had created a situation that forced people to rewire themselves away from empathy and towards survival. Helping someone meant hurting yourself, and when that help was so often retaliated against in horrible acts of violence, it was safer to focus on survival—getting through the day. It was a horrible predicament, and Anna felt its implications severely. She wanted to help, but what would happen to her children if she did? Would they be targeted? Bullied? Assaulted? Everything felt incredibly terrifying.

I also understood how Anna could question raising a child in such a volatile environment—such questioning only ever comes from a desire to protect and care for others. It is my staunch belief that children are so often like fireflies—little beams lighting up the darkness; stars illuminating the night sky. One star might not shine bright enough to wash the dark away, but a constellation of them is enough to lead sailors home. Children are the future, and always have been. We all grow up. They are like little prophecies—as my brother Apollo might like to put it—omens that the bad times won't last forever, that they cannot last forever if civilization is meant to go on.

So when Hitler came along and corrupted the children, I started to get very frustrated. I started sympathizing with the idea of not having babies at all.

But then, of course, I shifted my gaze from the mother to the child herself. I saw the tears of empathy shining in Anna's eyes reflected in Helene's. I saw how living in this hellscape called life had made the girl see things a little differently—she trod carefully and thought incessantly. She wanted to clean up her world until it shined again. She hoped that she could be the one who fixed the good things in the name of destroying the bad ones.

More than anything, when I looked at Anna's eldest daughter, I saw Love molded in Reason, and that would surely make all the difference, wouldn't it?

INTERLUDE
Athens, 2022

Aphrodite takes a moment to catch her breath as she finishes what can only be described as a bit of a rant. She registers how quiet it is and looks around the table at the faces of her brothers and sisters. Ares looks angry, but then again, he always does. Apollo looks uninterested, while in contrast Amphitrite looks so engrossed that she's struck a pensive pose without meaning to. All of them are trying their very best not to meet her eye, all except Athena. Of course. Her sister's feline features hold her in an intellectual death grip—it is obvious that she's hanging on to every word Aphrodite has just said, and turning it over in her mind again, and again, and again.

Aphrodite wants to tell her it's usually seen as rather rude to stare at someone so intensely, but before she can, Athena's face morphs into an expression she has never seen before—at least not on this particular sister. Aphrodite can count on her fingers the amount of times Athena has looked truly happy. Those instances usually involve toying with the fates of mortals or verbally destroying immortals. She's never seen Athena look so delighted in this sort of circumstance, but it's clear as crystal: a sparkly glow in her ocean eyes and a smile in full bloom across her face that exudes light and love and pride. Aphrodite feels her cheeks blush at the realization. *Athena is proud of her.* Never in her long existence has she believed that her sister—her magical, sagacious, exquisite sister—would ever feel truly proud of her. Athena has always thought Aphrodite's line of work is superficial, her passions too lustful—hasn't she? Or has she understood her more than Aphrodite thinks she has, all this time? This is new, uncharted territory.

She feels a few different ways all at once, but one feeling she is all too familiar with sends pulses of heat down her spine and through her fingers. It feels as though there must be glitter in her bloodstream as Love pulls at her heartstrings tenderly—playing a melody she memorized a long time ago, but this time adding a harmony infused with something uniquely Athena. Bergamot and vanilla fill her senses, and she has a sudden desire to pick up a book and inhale the words within it like they are a life-saving drug. In an instant, she knows what it's time for; she's waited long enough.

This story isn't Aphrodite's anymore.

Her own cognac eyes meet her sister's sapphire gaze with a confidence she hasn't felt in a long time. Athena notices the slight change, she is sure, because her demeanor shifts. There are questions hidden in her posture—in the way she clasps her hands together and tilts her head to the left. Aphrodite's voice is as soft as rose petals as she makes her newest intention known.

"I think," she starts nonchalantly, "This is where my time as storyteller comes to a halt."

"What do you mean? You can't leave it like that. You'll lose the challenge!" Amphitrite exclaims from somewhere off to her right.

"Oh, my darling, not to worry," Aphrodite smiles at the young nymph's concern, "I have no intention of losing this challenge. I only mean that from this point forward, this tale requires a new muse, a new keeper of its precious words."

She stresses the last syllable in a way that makes her intentions obvious. Athena's face flashes in surprise for a brief moment before she tucks the feeling into the back of her mind and tries to replace it with a smirk—although she is only half-successful. Aphrodite can't help but keep smiling at her. She can see how hard it is for Athena to keep her mask intact at the moment. She lets it sink in for five glorious seconds more before taking pity on her sister and filling in the silence.

"I suppose I should've asked you if you'd even be interested in helping me tell—"

"I am," Athena cuts her off. "I am interested. I'd love to."

"I'm glad," Aphrodite answers, "I know how much you care about Helene."

There is silence for a moment.

"Yes," her sister murmurs. Gone is the edge in her voice, replaced by a softer, whimsical tone that washes over Aphrodite the way a beloved memory might, "My brave girl."

"Whenever you like, you can start."

Athena slowly brings her hands to her hair, making sure each pin is in its rightful place before moving to adjust the pearl around her neck. She snaps her fingers towards the table in front of her, and instantly, another glass of nectar appears. She takes her time taking the first sip, as if she needs the extra moments to decide how she wants to begin Helene's story. Telling it will be no easy task.

Eventually, the goddess's deep, melodic voice takes flight, and the story begins again.

PART TWO: HELENE

"The sincere wish to be good is half the battle."

-Louisa May Alcott

ATHENA
September 10th, 1941

My goodness, where to begin? I suppose I could commence my contribution to this exposé in a few ways—it's simply a matter of deciding what period in Helene's timeline feels like the most logical place to start. I think that, perhaps, we can skip over the girl's early years. They are rather boring compared to her later ones. Helene was a child similar to others her age, living in Germany in her 20sand 30s. It was undoubtedly a tumultuous time in the country's history, but not nearly as treacherous as it would be later on, and German children like Helene remained blissfully unaware of the dangers arising all around them. Were her parents worried about the depression that overtook their country due to war reparations? Of course. Did they desperately miss what it felt like to be at peace? Yes, again. Were they as hopeful as any other citizen of the Deutschland when, in 1933, a particular charismatic psychopath promised he would give them that peace they longed for? Certainly. Luckily, that sentiment did not last long for Otto Reinholdt—that most interesting and clever man lost trust in Adolf Hitler almost as fast as my sister Artemis could shoot a deer. As one might imagine, he passed on that sense of distrust to his eldest child—his pride and joy—Helene. There's just something about the oldest child in any family, isn't there? It's quite the peculiar phenomenon. Helene Reinholdt was no exception: she was wonderfully goal-driven and independent, which also made her perfectionistic and rather stubborn. To her mother's dislike, she was never afraid to be outspoken--although it's important to note that her outspokenness was not uncontrolled. She reserved it only for instances that deserved her utmost attention and respect; things she cared deeply about.

Obviously, I loved that about her.

Allow me to flip through the pages of this epic tale to a very specific day in 1941. September 10th, to be exact. I had not seen Helene for many years when I arrived at the family's tugboat on this particular day. I had kept tabs on the girl her entire life, but that period in history proved to be rather *busy* for me. The previous two years alone had been ever so tiresome, thanks to Hitler's choice to invade land that didn't belong to him and make it his own. There's nothing quite like plunging the entire world into war with one horrible decision.

All that considered, it was no surprise that I had neglected my yearly check-ins. I was delighted to find my girl had truly grown into herself. At twenty years old, Helene was the paragon of beauty. Of course, I do not refer to beauty the same way my sister Aphrodite does. No, to me, beauty is much more enduring than looks. Helene was the type to carry a book with her at all times, along with a compact little journal to write down her thoughts at any given point during her day. Her eyes sparkled constantly—her gaze nothing short of investigative. Helene liked knowing things, and she liked forming opinions on them in turn.

I, of course, had known she would possess such a character the second she was born—perhaps even before that. When Wisdom tugs at my intuition, I listen and do its bidding. As soon as I caught a glimpse of the first Reinholdt child in the earliest minutes of the Vernal Equinox in 1921, I knew she was destined for powerful, worthy things. She came into the world clothed in Wisdom.

On this particular late summer day, my invisible form stepped onto the Reinholdt tugboat to discover a scene I could only describe as adoring chaos. Within seconds, I understood what had occurred: the latest baby had been born. I sensed, too, that this baby was the last for Anna and Otto. I can't say I blamed Anna for wanting, finally, to stop giving birth. I would've stopped way before she did—actually, I would never have a child at all. I can grasp the nobility of motherhood, of course. At its core, being a mother means giving up yourself in order to give someone else your world. I just do not think every woman's ultimate wish should be to have a child. A woman is more than the sum of her biological parts—more than a machine with only one purpose. It is simply preposterous to waste a vibrant life like that.

Anna Reinholdt had given birth six times now. Helene, of course, was first, in 1921. Then came Margarethe in 1923, Ernst in 1927, Anneliese in 1932, Ingrid in 1936, Klara in 1938, and now Werner in 1941. It was no small thing that this final and youngest baby was only the second son in the entire brood. Standing invisible in the middle of the boat, I saw that this birth was a very joyous event indeed. Otto was grinning from ear to ear, showing off his newest son to the other children. Helene sat off to the side, separated from the baby's coos and commotion. Her nose, unsurprisingly, was stuck in a book, but I could plainly see she wasn't reading at all. She was watching the events unfolding in front of her with a look of slight amusement. I sensed frustration and listlessness in her expression, too.

I stepped into the girl's mind with ease—almost as if she was an old friend inviting me in for a cup of tea. Helene's mind was fascinating, to say the least. Had been from the start. She'd been withdrawing into her imagination for years in order to make up for the loneliness she felt in her real life. It made me sad, knowing my girl felt that way, but it wasn't something I hadn't been expecting. Helene was special, and although nobody had ever told her as much, I felt there had to be a part of her that knew it, deep down. Helene would rather spend all day in her head than in reality, and it wasn't because of anything her parents did or didn't do, necessarily. They clothed her and fed her, and made sure she received a good education. But eldest daughters always have the highest expectations placed upon their shoulders, don't they? Since the day she was born, her parents had grand dreams for Helene—she would be the one with the best job of all of them, the best prospects. Otto Reinholdt showed off his eldest to anyone who would listen.

And then there was Anna.

Helene's relationship with her mother was founded on a deep and enduring love, but it was also very complicated. There were many days when Helene was convinced that her mother looked at her, but couldn't quite seem to see her the way Helene hoped she would. She saw a daughter who had come of age—a young woman whose most important duty was not spending her days with her nose in a book and her head in the clouds, but rather with a sibling on her hip and another at her skirts. It wasn't that Helene did not understand the lucky position she was in. She knew there were other families who were struggling to make ends meet, or worse. The least she could do was help take care of her brothers and sisters. It wasn't like they had asked to be born, and they needed guidance and love just as much as anyone. She was smart enough to know what the world was like, and her own place in it.

That didn't stop Helene from dreaming of the kind of person she wanted to become: a woman defined by her brains before her beauty. A woman of substance who dared to make her reality look like her dreams, instead of hiding away in imaginary worlds, she could only pretend she was changing. It was all rather confusing for Helene—these hopes she housed in her head. But it was clear to me what Helene desired. She wanted to be somebody. Not just anybody, *somebody*. She wanted the time she spent walking around on this planet to mean something. She wanted to be important to other people, not for what her body could do but for what her mind and heart could do.

I wished I could have leaned in close to her ear and whispered the truth—that she was destined to be all of that and more. I could not, though. Instead, I watched as Helene reluctantly set aside her book to make room for the tiny body of her baby brother. He was a squirmy one, that Werner, with fire in his veins and diamonds in his gaze. Not so different from his eldest sister, if I did say so myself. It's funny to me, sometimes, how life repeats itself. Time has never been linear like all the modern scientists say it is. The ancients had it right all along. What goes around comes back around. The snake will only ever eat its own tail.

I watched as Helene ran her fingers gently through Werner's soft curls on the top of his head. I could tell she loved him, just as she loved the rest of her siblings. It was not lost on her how far

apart in age they were. Not many other twenty-year-olds she knew
had baby brothers.

It was as if the thought of others her own age reminded her
of her other duties. She glanced quickly at the watch on her wrist as
a hint of panic swept across her expression. It was gone in a flash,
and replaced by a look of determination. Helene deposited the baby
back into his mother's arms in one swift motion, and yanked on her
new Oxford shoes at the same time she wrapped a sweater around
her shoulders. Her father gave a low chuckle in her direction, while
Anna called out in exasperation.

"Where could you possibly be going in such a hurry, darling?
Stay and sit with your brother for a bit longer, won't you?"

"I can't," Helene answered over her shoulder as she shoved
books into her bag, "I just remembered I have class in thirty
minutes. I have to go now, or I'll be dreadfully late."

"Class, again? My goodness, it feels like you've only just
arrived back from that university, and now you're off again!" Anna
looked tiredly in her daughter's direction. "I'm sure it wouldn't be
a problem if you missed a lecture, just this one time."

"You want me to miss class? On purpose?"

Helene shot a glance at her father. Otto gave a hardly
perceptible nod that must have told Helene not to worry—they'd
be able to handle things just fine without her. She directed her gaze
back to her mother before continuing with a slight huff.

"I'm sorry, Mutti, but I can't. How will I ever learn all there
is to know if I'm not even in class? I'll be back before you even have
a chance to miss me, I promise."

Before Anna had a chance to say anything else, Helene bolted
for the stairs that led to the upper deck of *Poseidon*. Margarethe,
two years her junior, called after her from down the hall.

"Why is it that you always get to leave? I'd like to get off this god-forsaken boat every once in a while, too!"

Helene's laugh was melodic as she shouted an answer from the top of the stairs.

"I suppose you can go to my comparative literature class in my place, if you'd prefer it."

"Oh, piss off Helene. You know I'd rather jump into the Elbe stark naked than listen to some sour-faced professor—"

Otto's stern reproach silenced Margarethe before she could finish her sentence, giving Helene permission to dash up the rest of the stairs and out onto the foredeck. Her brother Ernst was on his knees scrubbing at the deck boards as she all but skipped past him. A grunt was all she received in acknowledgement as she shouted goodbye over her shoulder at him. The blue bicycle kept in one of the storage lockers was taken from its home and maneuvered down the gangway—the wheels harmonizing with eager footsteps against the old wood of the dock.

I followed Helene as she made her way through the streets of Hamburg. Do not ask me how I kept pace with her whilst she flew across the cobblestones on her bike. A goddess never gives away her secrets. I assumed by the heat that this was only just the beginning of the school term—the hallmarks of summertime hadn't even begun to fade away yet. The sounds of the boat horns and the pungent smell of seafood native to the Speicherstadt district faded the farther away from it we went. Helene's father loved docking Poseidon there, near the warehouses. It was the easiest place to exchange the goods the boat carried up and down the Elbe every day. He claimed there was never a shortage of people to talk to and interesting things to see. Helene did not particularly agree with him. She preferred the hustle and bustle of the inner districts of

Hamburg—where the smell of bread and automotives replaced the smell of fish and dirty boardwalks. She loved watching old men read the newspaper on park benches and young mothers buy *süßigkeiten* from street vendors as their little children waited with eyes the size of Reichsmark coins. She loved the way people called out to each other in greeting, and how the trees that lined the canals seemed to whisper their secrets whenever the wind blew.

Helene's ride through the city ended in the Rotherbaum district—exactly thirteen minutes and twenty-eight seconds later as the bike screeched to a halt at the front steps of the *Universität Hamburg*. The flag of the Reich blew rather ominously just to the right of the tall oak doors. Hundreds of years ago, the swastika was a symbol of peace. It makes me mad even now, years after the events of the 1930s and 40s, to think about the way the Nazis appropriated it. To them, it meant power and vengeance, a far cry from the original intent. I noticed that while most students making their way into the building hardly gave that flag a second thought, Helene seemed unable to ignore its existence in her line of sight. It was like a stain on what I sensed would have been the perfect image of intellectual progress, otherwise. This interested me, because, up until this point, I had not been quite able to tell what exactly would drive my girl to fulfill the destiny I knew she possessed. I had little inclination of how she'd discover it, either. But this was ever so interesting to me—this silent but obvious distaste for something that had become mainstream and rather popular. Popular is not quite the right word, though, is it? Most German citizens either went along with Hitler's completely asinine view of what the world should be because they agreed with him, or they were too scared not to agree with him. There were certainly people who loved the way Hitler justified their conspiracies and played up their fears as if they were founded in anything logical. There were also the whispers about the ghettos, of course. Those rumors were enough to silence even the proudest of men, the kindest of women. If people were being sent into horrible conditions for simply being themselves, what would happen to someone who purposely disobeyed the authority?

It seemed Helene couldn't be categorized like that. She did not like Hitler; that much was obvious to me and probably others, too. That in itself was dangerous. Dislike often leads to many different feelings that, in turn, elicit many different decisions. The most important? Change. Helene hated what Germany stood for, which made her want to change things.

That made my senses tingle.

Of course, her father was her biggest role model in that regard. Otto, like many German men, became a member of Hitler's party at its inception—it became more of a requirement than a choice eventually—but back in the early 30s, that man didn't need force quite yet; he was rather charismatic. By 1935, though, Otto had rescinded his membership. He refused to support a party and a campaign that so blatantly used good intentions to mask the desire for power. That decision reeked of danger—Anna had fretted over it for a week—but Otto did it anyway. That flaming defiance burned so brightly within his eldest daughter, it was almost blinding.

Isn't it just *wonderful* when the universe puts the puzzle together for you?

I followed Helene through long hallways and up winding stairs until we arrived at room 302, where her Comparative Literature class was about to start. It was a good-sized classroom, not too big that one would have to shout, but not so small that it felt like anyone was sitting on top of someone else. The professor was scribbling something on the board with endearing intensity—there was a cloud of chalk dust surrounding him like a bubble.

The boy arrived as Helene was fishing her notebook out of her bag.

A full head of red hair plopped down right next to her, making her go rigid. Oh, my sweet Helene, never very good at social interactions back then. The young man twirled his pencil between his fingers for a moment before leaning close enough to Helene that she could smell his cologne.

"You're in my Antiquities class, aren't you?"

"Y-yes," Helene stuttered at his straightforwardness, "I believe I am."

"Wasn't it you who wrote that piece about Aristotle's *Poetics*? That was brilliant."

His voice was soft and deceptive, as if there was always the possibility he had a secret agenda and he was biding his time before acting upon it.

"I'm glad you enjoyed it," Helene replied hesitantly, "Aristotle's work has always interested me."

"I especially liked what you said about Aristotle missing the point of art being progressive," the boy's words came out slow and deliberate, "He was so rational and strict that he couldn't see that the best kind of art is rather rebellious."

I could see Helene was falling for the bait, even though she told herself to be wary.

"Exactly," she conceded, "If the creation of art is supposed to adhere to a set of strict rules, then naturally, the only way for an artist to create something new and powerful is by explicitly breaking those rules. Otherwise, every new piece of art would be the same as every other, and therefore not actually novel at all."

She looked a bit flustered as she finished her sentence, as if she hadn't been expecting to say quite as much as she had. It made me smile. The boy smiled, too—rather genuinely—before turning in his seat so he faced the professor once more. This most interesting young man did not say another word to Helene for the rest of the class, but I could see by the way his eyes kept darting to look at her, only to dart back to the board a second later, that he had something on his mind.

I was beginning to doubt that he would say anything at all when the professor dismissed the class. Helene walked out ahead of him, knowing she really should be getting back to the boat as quickly as she could. At the last possible second, he seemed to work up some kind of courage.

"Hey, wait!"

Helene turned around, looking flustered again, as he caught up to her in the hallway. To both of our surprise, he practically pushed Helene against the wall as he started speaking in a low voice.

"You really do believe that, right?" His eyes had excitement in them, "All that stuff about progress only happening when someone dares to do something new?"

"Wh—what are you talking about?"

"Just tell me, do you believe that? Do you think novelty creates change?"

"I—yes, I think I do believe that," Helene said, starting to look a bit panicked at the close proximity of this man's face to hers. "Why are you whispering?"

"Because I don't want the wrong kind of person to hear us, obviously."

He continued, talking faster than before.

"I saw you the other day, looking at the pamphlets."

Helene's face lost all color.

"I don't know what you mean."

"Oh, but you do," He smiled, "You picked one up off the ground, and while you threw it away, you looked through it first. It was right after that prick Hans bragged about treating his family's Jewish housekeeper like shit. I know you remember."

She swallowed the lump in her throat.

"I remember."

"I help make those pamphlets, you know."

It was in that moment that I understood who this boy was, and what he intended to ask Helene. I almost laughed out loud at the way Fate works. Helene now had a decision in front of her, she could either tell someone about this (he had just confessed to participating in something very illegal), or she could say nothing. She chose her next words carefully.

"You know that is wildly against the law."

"Yes, obviously."

"But you just admitted that you do it."

"Sometimes, the only way to achieve something good is by doing something bad. You said it yourself. Change doesn't just happen on its own."

What a lovely specimen you are, philosopher.

"I've never done anything illegal in my life!"

"Now is a great time to start, I'd say. It's not as if the man we're aiming to piss off is a god or anything."

"I know some people who would probably try to refute that point."

"Exactly why our pamphlets are important."

That comment seemed to halt any comeback Helene might

have had in its tracks. She knew he was right. He must have seen something shift in her gaze, because he smiled and backed away from her.

"Meet me at the café on the corner of Rappstraße and Grindelhof at 10:00 am, in two days' time. Make sure nobody knows where you're going."

He started to walk away, seemingly not expecting a response, when Helene remembered something rather important.

"Wait, I don't even know your name!"

He turned back briefly to flash a smile at her as he continued walking down the hall, shouting over his shoulder as he turned the corner.

"Arthur, but you didn't hear it from me!"

✳✳✳

Helene rode back to the boat in a state of contemplative disarray. Bold of this boy to assume she would simply drop everything to become a member of some illegal student organization dedicated to taking down Hitler. That was too far. It was where she drew the line. She couldn't possibly do anything as reckless as that. What if her parents found out? She'd never be allowed off the boat again.

Call me a bad influence, but I felt the need to step in. I knew this could be Helene's ticket to fulfilling her destiny, as cliché as it sounds. By the time she arrived back at *Poseidon's* dock, she was not feeling quite as vehemently against the idea as she had when she left the school. Call me manipulative, I do not care.

Helene let the proposition utterly consume her. She couldn't read, couldn't write, couldn't hold a conversation without thinking about it. She had never seen herself as someone capable of acting on her opinions. It wasn't a matter of caring enough. There was plenty of caring to go around–she hated Hitler. Despised the way he brainwashed people. She especially hated the way he used words— the most sacred form of power and knowledge—as a weapon to hurt people with. But it scared her to think about acting on any of that.

It was a good thing Wisdom and I was there to give some advice. As Helene lay down in the bed she shared with Margarethe that night, I planted some wisdom into her thoughts:

Remember, the Führer is a manipulator, not a leader. When you strip him of his words and give them to others, he has no podium to stand on--no fortress to hide in. His greatest asset can also be his greatest detriment, as long as you play your cards right.

It was clear to both of us the next morning what Helene had decided.

ATHENA
September 12th, 1941

Helene left the boat two mornings later under the guise of needing to attend class. She knew this excuse would work on her mother, who did not know her schedule all that well. Her father, though, had almost certainly memorized it. She was sure that he knew she wasn't being entirely truthful when, after waiting for her mother to become preoccupied with baby Werner, she told him she was off to the university. She didn't know why he chose not to mention the obvious deceit—perhaps he saw the pleading gleam in her eyes—but he simply smiled softly and nodded his assent.

I was ever so pleased with this, of course. I had always hoped the ever-present sense of adventure that permeated throughout Otto would present itself in Helene, someday.

So now, Helene's shoes were clicking hurriedly against the cobblestones of Hamburg. She opted to leave her bike on the boat.

She wasn't sure why, but she liked the opportunity to appreciate the city at a slower pace. The warm sunshine on her skin reminded her to breathe, and the bustle of late morning activity proved a wonderful distraction from the obvious breach of morals she was about to partake in.

The café on the corner of Rappstraße and Grindelhof was rather busy, which Helene supposed was better. It always surprised her how, even with a war on, so many people went about their daily business as usual. She supposed it did make sense—why would anyone want to stay shut up in their homes? What was the point of living in such a curious and exciting place if one did not have plans to enjoy it? She had wondered before if a place like Hamburg would ever be in danger, if the war grew even more intense and the Allies marched nearer. There had been air raids in other places before, and sirens had been installed to sound throughout the city if there was potential for an attack. But Helene could not, for the life of her, imagine any army targeting a city like Hamburg. There were more women and children living in the city than any soldiers, and besides, it wasn't even the capital. Hitler lived in Berlin, hundreds of miles away. Surely, any logical military would focus their efforts on destroying Hitler himself, and not an entire city of innocents.

I had seen enough wars in my time to know that nothing about them was logical. Helene would have to find that out the hard way.

The young man from Helene's class, Arthur, was seated at a small table on the outside patio. Helene wasn't sure why he'd choose to sit outside—it seemed safer to sit in a forgotten corner where nobody would care about their conversation—but then she noticed the two SS officers enjoying their cappuccinos in the window, and of course, it made sense why he'd chosen the patio. She noticed, too, that Arthur was sitting with his back facing the officers, which meant she would be the one they saw if they glanced out. She was sure that had been on purpose, too. A young woman was much less likely to engage in things she shouldn't be—at least, that's what most men Helene knew thought. She calculated in her head how she would school her expressions to appear as aloof and unbothered as possible no matter where this conversation with Arthur led.

Yes, my darling. Use that brain of yours.

The boy wore a white collared shirt under a light sweater, accompanied by a hat that made him look like a newspaper boy. I quite liked that hat, if I'm being honest. A briefcase stood at his feet, but I could tell it was mostly for show. He sipped a steaming latte as if he didn't have a care in the world. I knew in that moment I would grow fond of this boy, almost as fond as I was of Helene, although not quite. Nobody compared to my Helene.

The late summer sun became less inviting and much more unbearable as Helene took a seat in front of Arthur, opting not to speak as she nervously played with a button on her dress. She figured he would do most of the talking during this rendezvous, and she proved herself correct a few moments later when his voice skewered the silence between them.

"I am happy you came. Part of me didn't think you would."

"Why is that?"

"Well," he took a moment to look her up and down. "If you'd like my honesty, I thought I might have scared you off with my rather bold approach the other day."

"Boys like you do not often scare me."

Only Helene and I needed to know that was very much a lie.

"Hmm," He smirked at her confidence, "Good to know."

"I would suggest you say whatever it is you wanted to tell me, I certainly do not have much time. I barely made it past my parents without arousing suspicion."

"I understand. Thank you for coming anyway, despite the risk."

Arthur leaned forward and took her hand. The sudden physical touch jolted Helene nearly out of her seat, but she did not retreat. Something inside of her believed it was meant as a decoy. Just a young couple having coffee together as they discussed things lovers do—certainly nothing related to treason. She had to lean even closer as Arthur started speaking in a very soft and secretive tone.

"As I mentioned before, I help produce the pamphlets at the university."

"Yes," Helene said facetiously, "I do recall that most interesting bit of information."

A smile pulled at the corner of Arthur's mouth.

"I've been watching you, these past few weeks."

"I'm starting to think you really have no clue how to talk to women, Arthur."

"I'm a bit rusty, forgive me."

"I'll let it slide this time."

He took a sip of his coffee before continuing.

"The pamphlets, they're just a very small part of a much bigger operation. Think of it as one piece of a large puzzle. We do many different things, really. Whatever is needed."

"Arthur, please just speak plainly about how I fit into this."

"Well, I think you know what it is that I want to ask you."

"You want me to help you with your pamphlets."

"Not just the pamphlets, Helene. The whole operation."

That rendered her silent for a long moment. I was nearly bursting at the seams.

"So," Helene spoke slowly, almost afraid to speak, "You want me to help with this operation. What kind of operation is it, exactly?"

"It's a group dedicated to taking down the Führer; resisting him and his efforts. We're called Blackthorn. Pretty neat name, if you ask me."

"According to the government, the existence of such a group is rather blasphemous."

Arthur looked like he wanted to giggle.

"Yes, indeed."

"What would I be doing, if I were to say yes and join this Blackthorn group?"

"Whatever my superiors want."

"Your superiors?"

"The founders. The leaders. They started in Berlin, but the network has since spread throughout Germany. Like I said before, Blackthorn is responsible for more than just creating and distributing pamphlets. There's much work to be done."

Helene waited before responding. Arthur could call the group by any name he wanted, but the truth of the matter was clear: this was the resistance he was talking about. The actual resistance, not just a bunch of school kids making jokes about the Führer in a newsletter. Her stomach churned at the thought of doing something so unbelievably illegal. I felt it was time to step in.

Don't think about how illegal it is, my darling. Think about how daring it is, how brave. Think about the people you could help. This war isn't exactly what you think it is. It's much bigger than you know—much more sinister. There is someone out there who needs you.

Helene visibly gulped before saying what she felt was the most logical thing. Was it really logical? Well no, but as I mentioned before, these kinds of things never are.

"I'd like to speak with these superiors of yours before I make any kind of decision."

"Wonderful," Arthur's eyes glittered, "I was hoping you'd say that."

✳✳✳

Not once in her twenty years of life had Helene ever entertained the thought of sneaking off the boat. It was something that seemed so unfathomable to her, so stupid, that it never crossed her mind as something she'd ever want to do. Her father used to say she was his only daughter who had her head screwed on perfectly straight. Margarethe usually just called her a prude and a kiss-ass. She wondered what her sister would think of her now as she walked silently down the dock towards the shore. The watch on her wrist read 12:35 am. She hoped this meeting would be short-lived and she could be back in her bed by 2:00 am, at the latest.

It hadn't been Arthur who'd requested a meeting in the middle of the night. His boss had, and because she was looking to make a good impression, despite the fact that these people were technically criminals in the eyes of the state, she'd agreed to a 1:00 am meeting. Arthur had explained that his superior did not often show face during the day—for obvious reasons, he said—but that as long as they were careful not to arouse the suspicions of an SS officer on night patrol, they'd be fine. Helene had no idea how exactly to purposefully evade someone on the street, especially if she was the only one on it, but she would endeavor to do her best.

I think that was one of the things I came to love most about my girl. She always did her best, even when she was unsure.

Helene had never seen a city so quiet in her life. She supposed that was in part because she had never been out at this time of night before. But a part of her knew that many people were wary of going out at night now that there was a war on. She supposed it was easier and safer to just stay inside. Her father had stories from when he was younger than she was now—tales of drunkenness and teenage debauchery in the local taverns and through the streets. She supposed nobody really did that kind of thing these days. It was such a shame, how it wasn't just the big and obvious things in life that war tended to destroy.

She made it to the designated meeting place with hardly any trouble. She'd only had to hide against the darkened broad side of a building once when she heard the monotonous tap of shoes against cobblestone and knew it was an SS officer on patrol. He had strolled right past her—a lonely watchman on sentinel—and she'd allowed herself a moment to remember how to take air into her lungs before hurrying the rest of the way to her destination. Upon reaching it, Helene glanced down at the ripped piece of paper in her hand, where Arthur had scribbled the address in crooked handwriting. She was at the correct location, she was sure.

She looked up at the shuttered building in front of her. It seemed to Helene that it had once been a restaurant of some kind but was now very much closed and run down. She noticed there were lighter spots imprinted on the building's front, just above the door. Upon inspection, she could see the outlines of letters where a sign must have once proclaimed the establishment's name. In the center of the grouping of letters, she saw, with a sinking feeling in her stomach, the fading imprint of the Star of David. A Jewish business, then. One that Helene was sure had been well-liked before the Nazis closed it down. She wondered where the people who'd owned it were now. How were they able to make a living anymore?

Arthur's note instructed her to walk around to the back of the building, which she promptly did. She noticed her hands slightly shaking as she knocked on the door in just the way he had instructed her to do: two taps, followed by a pause and three more taps. As she waited for someone to answer the door, she could feel the beginning of intense trepidation taking over her mind, and there was a split second where she wanted nothing more than to run away as fast as she could, not stopping until she was back safe in her bed next to Margarethe. She probably would have, too, if the door hadn't opened.

She couldn't see him very well in the dark, but she knew it was Arthur. He wore cream-colored slacks and a white buttoned shirt, the top two buttons not clasped together. He held a glass of what looked like whiskey in his hand. A warm smile greeted her as she stepped into the building—Arthur closing the door and locking it behind her. When he spoke, his voice still held that same playful tone it had at the café, but it was clear he felt no need to whisper in this place.

"Helene, you're here right on time."

"Did you expect me to be late?"

"No," he leveled her with a teasing look. "I took you to be the type who arrives to everything much too early."

She ignored the implication of his comment as she followed him down a dimly-lit hallway. She could see a brighter light in a room beyond, and she assumed that was where they were headed. As they approached, Arthur took another swig from his glass. Curiosity got the best of her.

"Don't you think it's perhaps the wrong time to be drinking hard liquor, Arthur?"

"No, it's certainly not the wrong time to drink hard liquor, *Helene*."

She was about to serve him some kind of retort when a new, very refined, very English voice chimed in.

"Is there ever really a *right* time to drink it?"

Helene looked to her left, following the voice. She discovered they'd made it to what could only be described as a sort of hybrid of a parlor and an office. Interestingly, there wasn't much furniture save a large desk and three chairs—one behind said desk and two in front of it. Most interesting, though, were the two people Helene found occupying the room. The man was standing with his hands in his pockets. He was rather plain, with blond hair and light eyes that ensured most people of any importance (or threat) would glance at him and then move on without much thought at all. He wore a suit coat and dress pants, even at this late of an hour, and had an expression on his face that told Helene he wanted to be at home sleeping.

The woman—the one whose voice Helene had heard—was seated with her feet propped up on the desk. She seemed to be the opposite of her counterpart in every way. Helene guessed she was in her mid-twenties, not much older than she was. She wasn't nearly as pale as the man. There was a richness to her that Helene found hard to describe—she seemed almost golden, like sunshine had melted into the sepia tones of her skin and the brown in her eyes to make her faintly glow. Her hair, dark as midnight, flowed long and wavy past her shoulders. Helene found herself wondering if she always kept her hair loose. Most women, her mother had told her, kept their hair in tidy braids and knots, at least in public settings. It was more sensible that way. Helene was smart enough to see that the woman seated in front of her was not like most women.

Nor is she the tidy, sensible type, I suspect.

As Helene and Arthur sat down in the two remaining chairs, there was a stretch of silence that made Helene want to crawl into a corner. She could feel this woman's eyes on her—analyzing her, judging her. Helene found herself desperate to know what she was thinking, which felt inexplicable. She didn't even know this woman. Why did she care what she thought of her?

Arthur broke through the silence, finally, with an introduction.

"Helene, these are the people I answer to. Wilheim Krause," He nodded towards the man before directing his attention to the woman, "And Genevieve Harrison."

Before she could add any sort of introduction for herself, Genevieve spoke again.

"Why are you here?"

The question was pointedly directed at her, she realized. She hadn't been expecting the territorial tone. It made her very nervous.

"I, uh...I want to help."

She knew it sounded pathetic, but she wasn't sure what else to say. Genevieve didn't miss a beat.

"Lots of people say they want to help, but when it comes down to it, they don't," She moved to take her feet off the desk, sitting up and leaning towards Helene with a look of impertinence in her eyes, "What do you have that those people don't?"

"Well, I hate Hitler."

The laugh that erupted from Genevieve's lips made Helene blanch.

"Of course you do, he's a fucking psychopath."

Helene nearly flinched at the sound of someone saying such harsh words so easily, about the leader of Germany no less. It was clear this woman had no fear and no regard for authority either. She supposed that, being English, Genevieve didn't need to have regard for authority she didn't answer to. This was all starting to feel like a game of chess she'd been set up to lose. Genevieve didn't even let Helene make the next move.

"Hating Hitler isn't enough. Hate isn't enough, not in this line of work. You have to have a real reason, Helene, or else you'll crumble at the first taste of danger," Her voice lowered an octave as she leaned even closer so her body was practically covering the desk that separated them, "So I'll ask you again, *why are you here?*"

It was clear to Helene in this moment, just as it was clear to me, that this was not a woman to be trifled with. That feeling that my sister Aphrodite is always talking about—that bubbling, popping sensation in the bloodstream—I'd never felt it until that moment. I understand how someone could get intoxicated by that feeling if they weren't careful. I gave Helene the invisible nudge she needed to answer the question honestly.

"I'm here because I love my life and the people in it." She urged herself to continue even though her chest felt too tight, "My father always says that actions speak louder than words—that if you want to have integrity, you have to be willing to do as you say. I'm here because I have spent my whole life thinking but never doing, and I'm sick of it. I am *tired* of sitting around while he runs his mouth, burns books, and hurts people. Is that the answer you're looking for?"

At first, Genevieve's expression remained stony, and Helene was afraid she'd said the wrong thing. Even Arthur looked unsure. But then, Helene noticed the way Genevieve's mouth quirked up at the corners, almost imperceptible but certainly there. She schooled her expression a second later, but it didn't stop Helene from feeling a

small morsel of pride. I could plainly see that Helene was expecting
Genevieve to congratulate her in some way, to validate her answer
and tell her that yes, she did have a purpose after all. Instead, after
a moment, she stood with a flourish and poured herself a drink.

"Your father seems like a smart man."

Helene chose not to say anything and was rewarded a
moment later.

"Where did you and Arthur meet?"

It was Arthur's turn to speak.

"We attend classes together at the university. Helene's by far
the smartest in the class."

"Let her speak for herself, Arthur. She isn't mute," Genevieve
pinned his gaze with her own before glancing back to Helene,
"Intelligence is only half the battle. You seem too soft."

"Pardon?" Helene had never once been called out so plainly.

"I said that you seem too soft. Like you'd crumble if an SS
officer looked at you the wrong way," Genevieve smirked as she
took a small sip of the water in her hand, "How do you plan to fix
it?"

"You tell me."

The smirk bloomed into a cheeky half-smile.

"Good answer."

A moment went by in which they stared at each other—one
of them eager to prove herself capable and the other seemingly eager
to watch her fail. Finally, Genevieve broke away from Helene's gaze,
setting the glass of water down on the table with more aggression
than perhaps was necessary.

"I think we're done here."

As she made her way towards the door, Helene's mind
clouded with confusion, and she heard herself speak up,

"Wait, what am I supposed to do now? Am I allowed to join? Did I pass the test?"

Genevieve turned around with a playful expression on her face.

"Oh, Helene, the test hasn't even started yet." She paused, seemingly for effect, before continuing, "Meet me after your last class for your training. Arthur will tell you where to go."

And with that, she was gone.

✳✳✳

As Helene crept back into her bed, having made it back to the boat with no trouble, she turned the words Genevieve said to her over and over in her head. She'd said that hate wasn't enough to succeed in the resistance, but then she'd told her she was too soft. How did any of that make sense? Helene was starting to think that the older she got, the more puzzling people became. Genevieve seemed like the hardest kind of puzzle, the kind with over a thousand pieces where you never know if one could be missing until you get to the last part and realize the whole thing is unsolvable.

As Helene drifted off to sleep, I gently placed a new thought into her head.

Genevieve Harrison isn't missing any pieces, nor are there all that many of them. She is simply the kind of puzzle that nobody has ever bothered to try and solve. But, then again, there's a first for everything, isn't there?

INTERLUDE
Athens, 2022

The Goddess of Wisdom takes this moment to collect both her breath and her thoughts. Her brothers and sisters are all wearing expressions of relative intrigue. She knows it isn't often that they hear her tell this kind of story, perhaps because she doesn't particularly like telling them. She has made an exception in this case, for Helene. Helene deserves to have her story told in a way that does her justice. Athena wouldn't trust anyone else to tell it.

Naturally, Ares is the first to speak up—to complain, of course.

"I don't understand why hate isn't enough of a reason for Helene to join this group...it's the resistance, for the love of Zeus!"

Athena has to hold back a smile as Aphrodite sends a scathing response back.

"No, Ares, I wouldn't think you'd be able to understand what it means to have a purpose beyond fucking anything with a pretty face and nice tits, and blowing up people you don't like."

"Well, do you understand what in the Underworld it means, *all-honored goddess?*"

"In fact, I do," Aphrodite says as she forces herself to calm down. "I'm sure it will become clear to you as Athena continues."

Amphitrite speaks up then, going on about her love for the story thus far. Athena finds herself tuning the nymph out, and instead focusing her attention on Aphrodite, as she's found herself doing quite a bit in the past few hours. She doesn't know how she's never noticed it before, but it feels like she's seeing her sister's true self for the first time in her very long life. Her first reaction, earlier, had been jealousy. She'd seen the way Aphrodite cares for humans, how she reveres and respects Love so thoroughly and completely, and had felt a pang of longing to be like that—to be better than that. But now, having taken over telling this tale from her sister, it is clear to Athena that nobody could ever rival Aphrodite's ability to embody Love. It is embroidered into the fabric of her sister's heart in the same way that Wisdom walks the corridors of her own mind. Love makes her whole; it completes her. Something about that kind of dedication feels deeply admirable. Even looking at her sister now, Athena can see it plainly on Aphrodite's face. How has she never noticed it before? She supposes she had never bothered to look for it. She'd seen what she wanted to see—a lustful and shallow goddess who took pleasure in watching Love bring people up and tear them back down.

Perhaps it's this human disguise that is allowing her to see it differently now. Her sister hasn't been wearing it for too long—only a handful of decades. To gods and goddesses, that's nothing.

Yes, it surely is her human form that adds to this magic Athena can now see so clearly. She's gone for something a bit more subtle this time. There have been times centuries ago when Aphrodite preferred bolder, more extravagant looks. But not this time. She could easily be mistaken for a local, with the olive tone of her skin and the dark waves of her hair. But it isn't the physicality of it all that's giving Athena pause at the moment. Her beauty is striking, it always is, but not in the usual distant yet ethereal manner. The beauty hidden in this particular version of her sister is the kind that makes others feel welcomed and at ease in her presence.

Aphrodite laughs then, at something Apollo says, and Athena's breath catches looking at the lines of laughter and kindness etched delicately around her eyes. Her smile is infectious, capable of melting the hardest hearts and soothing the deepest wounds, Athena is sure. She finds herself truly, inexplicably touched by Aphrodite's sensitivity to Helene's story. Yes, this part is Athena's to tell, but her sister has given her the space to tell it—on her own terms. This challenge is between Aphrodite and Ares; she doesn't have to let Athena tell any part of it. But she had, and now Athena feels almost silly for the way she's treated her sister for centuries. They really have been striving for the same goal all this time, haven't they? They just use different tools to obtain it. The ancient philosophers would say that matters of the head are nothing like matters of the heart. Athena can think of so many old adages from humans who believed themselves enlightened—lessons about listening to your head instead of your heart, and warnings against letting love blind reason. But was Wisdom all that different from Love? Athena had always thought it was, but now she isn't so sure.

She comes out of her head as Apollo makes a prediction.

"I get the whole wanting to join the resistance to make a difference idea, but it seems to me that Helene is just yearning to be remembered in some way."

"Is that a bad thing, Apollo?" Athena asks in response. "You would know better than most how intoxicating it feels to be remembered; we all do. People have worshipped us for centuries—left us offerings and even sacrifices. Who would we be without someone remembering us?"

"I think it's not just about memory, in this case," Aphrodite muses, "But legacy, too."

"They're basically the same thing, sis," Apollo says as he shoots her a smirk.

"Hardly! Memory is collective consciousness. Legacy is proof that memory means something."

"She's right," Athena adds, "Memory refers to representations of the past. Legacy, though, has everything to do with how we use memories to shape the future. The memories any human may choose to represent them will directly affect the way others perceive them after they're gone."

"I think Helene wants to have a different legacy than Hitler, surely," Apollo concedes.

Aphrodite scoffs.

"Who wouldn't?"

"You'd be surprised," Ares says with a dark tone, "At what humans are capable of when they feel threatened—what they deem right and just in the face of fear. They do crazy shit. They hurt a lot of people to make themselves feel better, stronger."

"That sounds like cowardice disguised as fearlessness, to me."

"You're right, it is. I'm convinced that by the end, everyone who mattered knew Hitler was a coward, everyone except himself. Must've been the narcissism."

While Athena doesn't really think Ares is one to talk about the faults of narcissism, he isn't wrong. Hitler was a coward. Helene had certainly been smart enough to see that, and Athena had seen the burning desire in her eyes to prove herself better than that. Athena's heart swells with pride, thinking about how well Helene *did* prove that, in the end. Even after all these years—not long for gods, but an entire human lifetime—Athena still cannot fathom why exactly she became so attached to Helene. Just thinking about the young woman fills her with a warm feeling she hasn't found often in her long existence. There were so many women like her throughout history, and there certainly will be more in the future. Helene was special, certainly, but she wasn't a queen, a famous politician, or a magical enchantress bent on saving the world. She was just a girl. *Maybe that's the point*, she thinks. Helene was an ordinary girl with an extraordinary vision for the future. She cared about others and wanted to help those in need—of a savior, of a teacher, of a friend. Perhaps, Athena realizes, it's not about succeeding in the end. She believes Helene succeeded when all was said and done, but she knows a few of her brothers and sisters might not agree with her once she's finished.

Maybe, it's less about succeeding and more about believing. It's about finding hope in all the places where everyone else sees demise and loss. It's about finding all the dark, desolate corners of abandoned lives and working to let the sunshine back in. If Helene was good at anything, surely it was being hopeful. That must count for something, right?

Yes, of course it does.

She feels herself touch the pearl sitting at the base of her throat—an old habit that she doesn't even realize she's doing most of the time. The gemstone is infused with Wisdom and just a touch of Love (something Aphrodite will never know about). It gives her the reassurance she needs to push ahead with this little tale she's been tasked with telling.

The other gods and goddesses surrounding her halt their conversation as she clears her throat, intent on beginning again. Once she is sure that all eyes and ears are upon her, she allows her voice to carry over their collective silence like a song.

ATHENA
November 20th, 1941

I left Helene to her own devices for about two months—I was needed in England as a temporary advisor for Churchill (and invisibility wasn't required! How freeing it felt to see and be seen in return. I've come to love this current human disguise—obviously he didn't know my real identity and he never will). When I arrived back in her sphere of existence, I thought I'd find her on *Poseidon* or attending classes. She wasn't at either place, but rather training with Genevieve. Oh, how my heart soared. I'm starting to sound like my sister.

The two young women were back at the abandoned restaurant that had, at this point, become their primary meeting place. Genevieve was seated casually on top of the large, mahogany desk facing Helene, who had perched on one of the armchairs with her legs crossed and hands clasped together. Every so often, she would reach for her wrist and fiddle with her watch as if she hadn't already checked the time at four previous moments. I chuckled at how different they were, even in their body language. Genevieve's hair was in its usual free-flowing state, with dark makeup that complemented her skin tone. If Helene looked like an inquisitive owl, Genevieve surely resembled an elegant raven. Although, in this particular story, there was no tormenting while perched upon a bust of Pallas. This raven preferred stalking around in heels and overcoats.

Not to mention Pallas does not appear in bust form, this time around.

It seemed that this rendezvous was less of a training session, and more of a lesson. There were no weapons in sight. I knew that Genevieve was bidding her time in that regard—introducing Helene to weapons too early ran the risk of giving her second thoughts, and I could tell that Genevieve couldn't afford to lose her, not when she'd lost so many resistance fighters already. In the month I'd been away, they'd surely talked about weapons—Genevieve wasn't stupid. She would make sure that Helene understood how a gun worked, down to all the little nuts and bolts, before she'd be allowed to even hold one, let alone fire one.

Helene had a notebook positioned in her lap, and I couldn't hold back a smile at the thought of her taking vigorous notes and then studying them when she was supposed to be studying for her university classes. Oh, how her mother would positively howl if she knew.

She opened the journal to a fresh page as she uncapped her fountain pen. It had been a gift from her father when she started university, and Helene never went anywhere without it.

Seeing that Helene was ready, Genevieve began.

"Alright, let's get started. As you know, due to your...

thorough notetaking," a ghost of a smile flashed across her face as she spoke, "Our first few meetings focused on learning about weapons, how they're made, and how to handle them."

I knew it. A goddess always knows.

"Today, I'd like to talk more about what will be expected of you as a member of this branch of Blackthorn."

"Oh good," Helene spoke with her eyes still focused on the paper in front of her, "I've been wondering when we'd talk about that."

"What has Arthur already told you?"

"Not much, just that you do a lot more than create pamphlets."

"What we also focus on—what you'll be focusing on soon— is reconnaissance."

I watched as Helene swallowed hard at the implication.

"Can you elaborate on that?"

"You'll be going into occupied territory and doing any number of things—picking up sensitive information, meeting other agents at checkpoints, moving Jews to safehouses..."

"That seems rather dangerous."

"Oh, it is," Genevieve smiled in a way that felt unsettling to Helene, "That's the fun of it though, isn't it?"

Helene did not think it sounded fun at all. I thought it sounded quite exciting. I'd have to work on infusing Helene with some of that excitement.

Genevieve continued her lecture as Helene furiously scribbled words onto the next blank page in her notebook.

"France is a hot spot for activity right now, especially because only part of the country is Nazi-occupied. Many Jews moved south from the bigger northern cities to avoid being sent away. I suspect

Hitler will move to take the south of the country soon, though. We need to move fast."

"Do I....will I be sent there?"

"Don't look so spooked. You aren't even close to ready for that yet."

Helene's shoulders visibly sagged in relief.

"Since Arthur says you do quite well in your classes," Genevieve persisted, "I think you'd be best suited for helping make pamphlets. You write well, yes?"

"I try."

There was a pause that saw Genevieve pinch the bridge of her nose in what felt to Helene like irritation.

"Goodness, Helene, it's okay to think you're good at something."

"Sorry," she mumbled as her face flushed hot. She hadn't meant to say something wrong.

Genevieve waltzed toward her, stopping mere inches away from Helene's face.

"Here's something to write down in that journal of yours," she began in a low voice, "Genevieve Harrison's first rule for becoming successful: *never* say you're sorry."

Music to my ancient ears.

"Anyway," she continued as if the interlude hadn't happened, "I think you'd make rather thought-provoking content for the pamphlets. You'll work with Arthur on your first one, and then once you have the hang of it, you can try one by yourself."

Helene nodded her assent in silence. If there was anything she was truly proud of, it was her writing ability. Her father always proclaimed she could write speeches for the king of England if she wanted to. She wasn't so sure she was *that* good, per se, but there was something about the way Genevieve had shut down the slightest notion that she couldn't do it that made Helene feel warm in a way she was unfamiliar with.

She still didn't know what it was about this woman in front of her that piqued her interest. What she *did* know was that she was usually very capable of reading people—analyzing them—and yet Genevieve eluded her in practically every way. She had an air about her that exuded the kind of mystery that grabbed people's interest, and just when they got close enough to think they could figure her out, she'd change the locks and create new riddles to ensure she was always a step ahead. Genevieve's heart was the labyrinth, but she herself was both the minotaur and the craftsman. Helene felt like the sacrifice—wandering around like a lost tourist before being devoured.

That imagery made me laugh. It wasn't too far from the truth. I could sense the way Genevieve held herself at a distance from others, and I saw how she preferred leaving people in the dust after toying with their hearts—it meant hers would never be the one broken in the end.

I suddenly had an itch for information. A desire for knowledge. I wanted to know how far Genevieve would let Helene push her way through her walls. A thought Helene had pondered on when she first met Genevieve, but had since disappeared from her psyche, now made a glorious and divinely prompted comeback. Watching Helene blurt a question out of her mouth before she could think to reserve herself proved rather entertaining.

"Where in England are you from?"

Genevieve shot her an inquisitive look, obviously not expecting Helene to ask anything so off-topic. Judging by the way Helene's cheeks flamed, she hadn't been expecting it either.

"I was not aware you were familiar with English geography."

"Only a bit," Helene gulped, "I was mostly just curious. If you don't want to—"

"County Sussex. It's southeast of London, along the coast. My father's family has lived there for generations."

"And what of your mother's family? Are they from London?"

Genevieve gave her a dubious look, as if to say *I know you aren't that stupid*.

"Surely you can tell by the way I look that I'm not a purebred English lass, Helene."

I didn't think someone's face could flush even deeper red than Helene's already had, but I was wrong.

"I would never assume something like that."

"No, of course you wouldn't," Genevieve gave her a reassuring but sad smile, "My mother was born in India. She travelled to France looking for work, and she met and fell in love with my father—who was in the country for business at the time. I was born in France, actually, but we moved back to England when I was four years old."

"Do you have any siblings?"

"No, it's just me."

"That must be nice. I have an exceptional amount."

"It has its nice moments, but it's mostly just lonely."

The two young women descended into silence, Genevieve silently cursing herself for saying something too vulnerable, and Helene at a loss of how to respond to it. At this point, my divine hunch had been proven correct, and I relished in knowing I was right. Genevieve had told Helene more about herself in under one minute than she had anyone else, perhaps ever. An interesting development, if I do say so myself.

It hadn't escaped Genevieve's notice, either, it seemed. There was a look in her eyes as she stared intently at everything that was not Helene: a look composed of questions and longings. A look that acknowledged--finally, after so very long—a worthy opponent.

No, a worthwhile companion.

No. Both.

It took me a moment to realize I had unknowingly pushed my way out of Helene's mind and into Genevieve's—which hadn't been the plan but was something I could work with, surely. I registered that from within Genevieve's psyche the room was starting to feel too hot; too cramped. A distinct feeling of insecurity intertwined itself with interest, and everything began to feel overwhelming. She needed some air, or perhaps some liquor. She needed time by herself. She needed to be away from this place.

Helene broke the stillness first.

"This pamphlet you'd like me to put together is there anything in particular you want me to write about?"

Genevieve took a deep breath before turning back to face her.

"No, just make sure it's something you care about. If you don't want to write about it, it won't be good. It needs to be good."

"I'll think on it for the next few days, and have something written by next week."

All Genevieve could think to do was nod. Another second passed, where neither woman could find it in themselves to say anything before Genevieve's body pushed her towards the door.

"Let's end for today. I want to give you time to think this afternoon, and I'm sure you have classes to attend." She continued with her back facing Helene as she put on her coat, "Let's meet here in one week. Same time."

She didn't wait for Helene's response; she was too nervous about saying something she shouldn't. She knew the rule—better than anyone. She'd created the damned thing herself.

Genevieve Harrison's *actual* first rule for being successful: The less people know about you, the less they have to hurt you with. The moment you allow someone to see the real you, you've already lost.

What a silly little rule. I was sure Genevieve thought she was rather wise for creating such a thing. I was also sure she was very wrong. I'm the Goddess of Wisdom. Trust me, I know. I had high hopes after discovering Genevieve walked around with this worldview, though.

It meant that Helene and I could endeavor to change her mind.

INTERLUDE
Athens, 2022

"Ah yes, Athena's favorite pastime," Apollo's voice filters through the collective divine consciousness with a taunting cadence, "Playing with the minds of mortals."

"Only when they're lying to themselves," Athena shoots back at him with a knowing look, "I'm only guiding Genevieve and Helene towards destiny, after all."

Ares furrows his eyebrows together as he takes a swig of nectar.

"So your pet's destiny is to...what? Have a little dalliance with her female superior? Who happens to be the head of the Hamburg branch of the anti-Nazi resistance movement?"

"That will be the last time you refer to Helene Reinholdt as *my pet*," she hisses.

"And you will most certainly never refer to their relationship as simply a dalliance ever again," Aphrodite says with an expression of distaste, "It was much more exquisite than that."

Ares huffs into his glass, as if he regrets saying anything at all.

Good, Athena thinks. *That means he's learning how to keep his mouth shut.*

She knows how it must look to him—to all of them. The way Athena feels towards Helene isn't the way she feels about most humans. She doesn't feel this way about most gods. She can't help the protectiveness that washes over her whenever Helene is brought into conversation. She'll never let anyone, god or man alike, paint Helene as anything other than brave, and smart, and true. She feels almost like a mentor to Helene—the one who saw the girl through so many trials, so much hardship. The one who gave her recognition and peace in the end when she needed it the most.

After everything, that's what Helene deserved—still deserves—more than anything.

She finds herself glancing at her sister. Aphrodite's eyes are warm, like gently glowing embers, as they meet her own. She knows just what it is that Athena feels—she feels it herself in a much more intimate way all the time. Athena is sure that if she found herself so acquainted with Love the way Aphrodite is—if she could recognize it in every person and place, and watch it weave its way through every little thing—she would surely be overwhelmed. Overstimulated. She has limited her affections to just Helene, and even that, sometimes, is difficult for Athena to come to terms with. She's never been one to embrace her emotions, or the emotions of others, openly. For as wise and strategic as she knows she is, when it comes to things that can't be formulated into a concise plan or understood through purposeful analysis, Athena proves to be...rather ineffective. That's why each of the gods has their own specialty anyway. She was created for a specific purpose. Wisdom is her domain and Love is Aphrodite's. This new realization that the two can and do exist together like an invisible machine is positively mind-boggling to her. She does not feel adequately prepared to tell the rest of their story—does not feel adequately prepared to interact so completely with both Love and Wisdom.

Her face must be betraying her thoughts because suddenly Aphrodite's voice echoes against the walls of her mind.

Don't be afraid, Athena. There is nobody more capable of telling this tale than you.

I should think you would tell it well enough, sister. You understand Love.

Don't underestimate your ability to understand anything, Goddess of Wisdom. That's not who you are. Helene would be proud to know her life was held in such learned hands.

Aphrodite retreats back into her own head before Athena can respond. She supposes her sister is right. Perhaps she doesn't fully understand now, but that's not to say she never will.

The Goddess of Wisdom knows many things, and if she doesn't know something, she doesn't let it stop her. She endeavors to change it.

She endeavors to learn.

Athena takes a long, steadying breath. There is a *clink* of fingernails against chalice, followed by silence. She continues.

ATHENA
December 15th, 1941

Helene pondered for days over what to write about in the pamphlet. Arthur had provided her with a number of ideas she could work with, but she'd rejected all of them. So many people had already written about them. She wanted to write about something nobody had thought of before. *Just write about the economy*, Arthur had said rather flippantly, *how all the Jewish businesses have closed*. Helene was surprised at his dismissiveness. The closing of all Jewish businesses had been going on for some time; there were many pamphlets already written about the subject, many authored by Arthur himself.

Helene didn't want to write about things people already knew of. She wanted to open people's eyes. She wanted something new. A quick perusal of some of Arthur's previous work told her that he often wrote about the same three things, and with a formulaic approach that made it very clear the same person had written all of them. That struck Helene as rather dangerous—weren't he and Genevieve concerned the Nazis would catch on to them? Surely they weren't stupid. They hanged anyone they could catch who opposed them.

She decided she didn't need Arthur's help to write anything, even if Genevieve wanted them to work together on her first attempt. Arthur acted like an annoying child when she informed him she wouldn't need his assistance, and she felt compelled to compromise by telling him he could read everything she wrote before it was published and spread. The only problem seemed to be her own inability to find a worthy subject to write about.

The only thing I could do, naturally, was place a very big issue at her feet.

✳✳✳

She wasn't sure why she'd been so adamant about accompanying her mother into the city today. Perhaps it had something to do with the fact that she knew Anna was nervous about going herself, even though she'd never say it out loud.

Or perhaps it was divine intervention.

Today was the day one of Helene's littlest sisters, Ingrid, was allowed to come home from the hospital. She'd been cooped up in Kinderkrankenhaus Rothenburgsort for an entire month due to a complication with her hip. One day, she'd been running along Poseidon's deck, chasing after Kitty, and she'd tripped and fallen rather hard. They'd discovered that her hip had completely dislocated once they arrived at the clinic. Seeing Ingrid in that hospital bed—which looked so big due to the fact that she was so small—broke both Helene's and Anna's hearts. She had been terrified, of course, she was only five years old. The doctor explained that surgery was needed in order to fix the problem. Helene's stomach had churned at the thought of her little sister going under a surgical knife so young, but she swallowed her apprehension for her mother's sake. It was her job to be the strong one in times like these. Worrying wouldn't help anything. The doctor had also explained that it was highly likely Ingrid had been born with a hip deformity of some kind—one that had remained dormant until she fell and hit it the wrong way. Helene just couldn't help but worry about the after-effects of it all. She hated the idea that her sister could have problems getting around for the rest of her life. It was obvious Anna was very anxious today for that same reason.

She knew her mother had prayed and prayed that this surgery worked, and that Ingrid would be able to walk again. Helene didn't want to think about Ingrid being stuck in a wheelchair for her whole life. She'd hate to see her confined to such an awful, and certainly painful, existence. She was thankful Ingrid would not be wheelchair-bound aboard Poseidon, at least. Anna had convinced Otto to buy an apartment in Hamburg recently, and Helene was rather enjoying not having to live on a boat. It was a much shorter commute to her classes and also proved much easier to sneak away from when she trained with Genevieve.

As they approached the clinic, Helene couldn't help but notice how utterly gloomy it looked, for a children's hospital. Shouldn't such places be bright and happy? This was foreboding and dark–there was a cold and sterile feeling that surrounded the campus that made Helene want to leave as soon as she arrived.

Appearance often reflects intention, or so I've noticed over the centuries.

Ingrid's doctor met them in the front lobby. A taciturn gentleman with round glasses and a rather unfriendly demeanor, Dr. Fuchs exuded an energy that meant business. Helene was sure he possessed a rather terrible bedside manner without having to experience it herself. For what was now the second time in only a few minutes, Helene wondered why a children's hospital did not have gentle and kind-looking doctors. Surely, this man did nothing but scare the children under his care.

Dr. Fuchs led Helene and Anna down several maze-like corridors to the specific ward Ingrid was staying in. The dim lighting and the exceedingly sterile smell of the entire place reminded Helene of dying more than they did healing. It surely couldn't be healthy for the hundreds of children residing within the walls of the hospital. In Helene's experience, although she supposed it was limited, children came alive with the right amount of sunlight and clean air. Her heart broke for the children who didn't get to go home yet, and she knew the really sick ones might never get the chance to.

Eventually, Dr. Fuchs finally stopped. He instructed them to wait in the hallway while the nurses got Ingrid ready, saying she'd be prepared to leave in just a few minutes. While her mother stood and patiently waited by the door, Helene found herself pacing the length of the hallway. When she was feeling impatient, she tended to pace.

Thank goodness our girl possessed this habit—she would've missed something rather concerning had she not.

Had she been turned the other way, she would never have noticed it. But she was facing just the right way, looking in just the right direction at just the right time, to catch a flash of movement from down a different corridor—beyond a door that was closed and locked, but made of glass. Her attention caught, Helene turned to get a better view, her gaze sharpening on a little boy—he couldn't have been more than four years old—being led—no, dragged—away by an unsympathetic nurse. The boy was sobbing, that much was clear by the way his face contorted, and he moved in an abnormal way– like his legs didn't work the way they were supposed to. As Helene watched them from behind the door, she became convinced the boy must be disabled in some way–which explained why he couldn't stay solidly on his feet. The condition felt familiar to her, and she racked her brain for anything she might have learned in her classes at school until she remembered: *cerebral palsy*. This poor little boy must be afflicted with it, or something similar. Her heart ached for him. She was grateful that Ingrid's hip problem was curable, and she was sure the same could not be said for this boy.

She continued to watch as the nurse forced the child down the rest of the hallway, a feat that took some time, before they both disappeared behind another door, which presumably led to some other ward. Helene was about to turn back when her eyes caught the inscription painted above the frame of the door the boy had just been led through.

In bright, bold letters: *Kinderfachabteilungen*.

Special Children's Ward.

Helene didn't like the way the word made her feel, although she knew it was unfounded. She had no idea what went on in this hospital–she had no idea how sick any of these children were. "Special" seemed to imply that children occupying that ward had a disability of some kind. Perhaps they needed to be kept separate for safety reasons? She supposed it was rather plausible that a young disabled child could be at a greater risk of injury, especially if they didn't have the same capabilities as other children. But there was something unsettling about the way that little boy had screamed at being dragged there–like he was afraid. She had too many younger siblings to not be able to distinguish between hungry cries, sleepy cries, and fearful cries. That boy had been terrified. She would have to ask Arthur, or Genevieve, about these special wards. Perhaps they could give her clarity.

She was brought out of her thoughts on the matter when her sister emerged in a wheelchair, her little face pale but so full of excitement. Helene found herself grinning at that happiness. She watched as Anna knelt so she was eye level with Ingrid, clasping small hands in her bigger ones.

"Hello, lovely," Anna said in a soft voice.

"Hi Mutti," Ingrid nearly whispered in response, "Am I allowed to go home now?"

"You are indeed," Anna stroked her curls gently, "Vati and I are so happy that you are. We missed you so much."

"Will Kitty be there when we get home? I learned a new game that I think she's really going to like. You need marbles to play," the girl exclaimed breathlessly before continuing, "I think baby Werner would like it too, but he's too little to play. I just know he'd try to eat the marbles."

Helene couldn't help but laugh at her sister's thoughtfulness. After Kitty was born two years ago, Ingrid took quite the liking to her. Helene was sure it was because they were so close in age. They were the best of friends. She answered instead of Anna.

"Yes, Kitty has been waiting ever so patiently for you, and I'm sure she will love learning a new game."

Ingrid looked up at her with stars in her eyes.

"Do you learn fun games when you go to school, Helli?"

There was that nickname she hated. She didn't have a cruel enough heart to ever tell Ingrid she didn't like it—it sounded too sincere whenever she said it.

"Nothing nearly as interesting as a marble game," Helene replied.

The nurses suggested that they bring the wheelchair with them—Ingrid shouldn't be walking on the uneven cobblestone streets quite yet—and Anna could deliver the wheelchair back to the hospital within the week.

Back at the apartment, Ingrid was delighted to find her father had come three days early to see her—Otto and Ernst usually spent the week on Poseidon pulling barges, and joined the rest of the family every weekend. It seemed he had made an exception for his girl. He proclaimed that his daughter was finally released from the hospital, and that was cause for celebration—he wouldn't have missed it for anything. He even picked up a cake on his way, which, of course, made Ingrid ever so excited. After dinner, Anna, Otto, Helene, and Ingrid were sitting in the living room when Otto turned his attention to his second youngest daughter.

"Ingrid, darling, how long did the doctor tell you to use the wheelchair for?

"He said whenever I was ready, I could stop using it."

"Well then," a smile lit up Otto's face, "Do you reckon you're just about ready?"

"I don't know, Vati..." Ingrid's voice had suddenly become hesitant.

"Well, don't sound so nervous! You've been training for this for a whole month!" Otto's voice boomed with excitement, "What do you say you try walking over to me, hmm? It's not too far away. I want to see your new and improved hip in action."

Ingrid, still looking a bit more hesitant than Helene liked, nodded slowly, and she moved to stand up ever so gently. Helene wasn't sure why she was so nervous, but she supposed she would be too if she had just spent a month in the hospital. Her stomach dropped, though, when Ingrid put weight on her legs, and her face twisted into an expression of pain.

Dr. Fuchs said she shouldn't be in any pain anymore.

Ingrid immediately sat back down in the wheelchair, having seemingly made the decision to not attempt a walk across the room. There was a cloudy look in Otto's eyes that Helene knew had made Ingrid upset, because she started crying.

"I'm sorry, Vati," she lamented through her tears, "I can't—I can't do it, not without anything. I bet I could do it if I put the brace on, maybe—"

"Did the doctor say you would need the brace?" Helene interrupted gently. She was not expecting her to need her brace anymore. Judging by her mother's pale complexion across the room, she hadn't either.

"Well, no..."

Otto looked at her with a defeated sort of expression. Helene knew what he was thinking, because she was thinking the same thing.

It hadn't worked.

The operation did not work like it was supposed to.

"Well, there's no use in being upset about it," Otto proclaimed, breaking the silence, "We'll wait a few days, and if nothing has improved, we'll go back to the hospital and see if there's anything more they can do to help us."

With the verdict drawn, Anna ushered Ingrid away to get ready for bed, leaving Helene alone with her father. She found she couldn't contain her distaste.

"That stupid hospital didn't do anything to help Ingrid."

"Come now, Helene," Otto reproached, "The doctors and nurses surely did everything they could–it just didn't seem to be enough."

"You didn't see the place, Vati. It's dark and depressing and scary. I wouldn't be surprised if they purposely didn't fix Ingrid just so we'd have to go back and give them more money."

"Not everyone is a swindler, Helene."

"No, but not everyone is a saint, either."

"What do you suppose I do? Rothenburgsort is the closest children's hospital around."

"Put her in a private clinic, one that isn't funded by the government. No special interest."

"What does it matter if it's funded by the government? Surely Hitler couldn't use a children's hospital to peddle his lunatic ideas."

Helene chose to keep her mouth shut. It was obvious that her father didn't want to believe Hitler would stoop so low as to use sick children to fund the Reich. She had no trouble believing it. In fact, she'd had a sinking feeling in her stomach for hours, ever since she watched the little disabled boy disappear into the Special Children's Ward. She knew–she just knew–that something more sinister was at play within the walls of that hospital.

She'd be damned if she wasn't going to find out what it was.

Anna was tucking Ingrid into her bed–Kitty already asleep next to her–when Helene knocked gently on the door. Ingrid's eyes lit up at the sight of her eldest sister coming to say goodnight to her, which made Helene feel guilty for having stopped the routine last year. Anna left the room upon noticing her, saying she needed to make sure Anneleise was getting ready for bed.

Once Helene was alone with her sister, she came to kneel next to the bed, tucking a stray curl behind Ingrid's ear before whispering to her, so as not to wake Kitty.

"Ingrid, can I ask you a question?"

"What is it, Helli?"

"Did anything scary or bad happen while you were at the hospital? Were the doctors or nurses ever mean to you?"

Ingrid shook her head against the pillow.

"No, nobody was ever mean to me."

"That's very good, Inga. That makes me happy."

"They didn't like Heidi very much, though."

Something about the way Ingrid's voice sounded sad gave Helene pause.

"What do you mean, was she very naughty?"

"No, I don't think she was naughty; she never spoke. I don't know how you could be naughty when you don't say anything."

"Why didn't she speak?"

"She couldn't."

Helene didn't like this at all.

"What do you mean, she couldn't speak?"

"The nurses said she was born like that. They said she wasn't normal," Ingrid started picking at a loose stitch on her nightgown as she spoke, "But, I liked her just fine. Her bed was right next to mine until they moved her."

"Moved her?"

"Yes, one day, the nurses took her away. They said she had to have some tests done because she didn't speak," Ingrid's words started coming faster, "I waited for her to come back, but she never did. The nurses said she had to go to a different hospital. But...I don't think she left."

"You don't? Why not?"

"Because one day, when I was doing my walking exercises up and down the hallway, I found her stuffed bear in the closet."

"Why were you in the closet, silly?"

"The nurses kept candy there. They said I could have a piece every time I walked down the entire hallway."

"I see. Was it strange seeing the stuffed bear in the closet?"

"Yes! Heidi never went anywhere without her bear. She wouldn't have left without it," Ingrid's face was contemplative as she continued, "So, I think she must still be at the hospital. But why wouldn't they let her have her bear, Helli? She's probably very scared without it."

At this point, Helene could feel her heart beating a little too fast. Something wasn't adding up. She wasn't stupid—she knew Heidi's disappearance had to be connected somehow to the boys'.

Of course they were connected. There is no such thing as a coincidence.

ATHENA
December 16th, 1941

The winter air bit at Helene's cheeks as she hastened down the sidewalks of the Winterhude quarter. She'd taken the newly-electric S-Bahn from the university—about a twenty-four-minute ride. The train hadn't dropped her off at her destination, but rather a few blocks away from it. She'd had to plan this trip in between her classes, and she'd gone to great lengths to hide the ticket from her parents, which hadn't proved hard in the least. She knew Otto wouldn't have cared, but her mother certainly would have. Helene wasn't sure why—her mother never talked about it—but Anna hated trains. Helene was sure it was less of a hatred and more of a fear, but she had enough sense to know Anna would probably have a hemorrhage if she knew her daughter was riding one, and one run by electricity at that. Leave it to her mother to be irrationally afraid of anything new.

How I wish I could have told Helene why her mother feared trains. It had nothing to do with novelty—nothing to do with Anna being stuck in her ways. Memories, especially of horrible things, have the power to paralyze.

Hamburg's massive public green space, the Stadtpark, came into view as Helene rounded a corner. Genevieve had agreed to meet her there at 11:00 a.m. sharp. She'd sensed surprise and a bit of concern in Genevieve's voice when she'd called her at home. Helene had disguised her intent with an invitation to a walk in the park with tea to follow, but she knew Genevieve had gotten the hidden message: she needed to speak with her about something urgent. Genevieve had suggested the Stadtpark herself, presumably because she lived near it but also because the crowds of people would aid in distracting any SS officers from their conversation.

It was obvious to spot Genevieve as soon as Helene reached the park entrance. She was seated on a bench with her legs crossed, wearing a plaid scarf and a long black coat. Her hair blew in the wind, as did the pages of the book in her lap. Certain thoughts that threatened to consume her whole floated to the surface of Helene's mind, and she pushed them back stubbornly. Why did Genevieve have to be so pretty, just sitting there on a bench? It was hardly fair.

Genevieve looked up from her reading as Helene approached.

"There you are; let's walk for a bit. It's much too cold to sit still."

Helene followed her in silence as they started down the nearest path. She could see Genevieve studying her intently.

"Are you alright?"

Helene smiled at the nervousness in Genevieve's voice.

"Yes, of course, I'm perfectly fine. Don't worry about me."

"What is it that couldn't wait until our next training session?"

"What do you know about the Special Children's Wards? At the hospitals?"

Genevieve's face darkened, "I've heard rumors. Nothing more."

"Are the rumors as bad as I think they are?"

"How do you know about these wards? I hear Hitler is not hiding them, but he isn't speaking about them at length either."

As Helene related everything she'd seen at Kinderkrankenhaus Rothenburgsort, along with what Ingrid had told her, Genevieve's posture progressively became quite rigid. Once Helene finished her recounting, she was silent for a few moments before giving any sort of reaction. Helene could tell she was choosing her words carefully.

"I'm assuming you plan to write your pamphlet about this topic, yes?

"If you think it would be worth writing about. I didn't want to start writing until I had more information. I figured you might have it."

"I have heard a few things, none of them good."

"Tell me."

"Well, first of all, Rothenburgsort is not the only children's hospital with this ward. All of the government-funded hospitals have one," she started hesitantly, "You are right to have a bad feeling about it. My sources have told me the Special Children's Wards are part of a plan Hitler created himself."

"Created for what purpose, though?"

"He wants to euthanize disabled children," Genevieve whispered, like saying it out loud would alert an officer, "After using them for experiments first."

Of all the possible explanations Helene had conceived of, the truth was the one she'd desperately hoped wasn't true. It meant that her sister's friend Heidi was probably dead. The little boy, too. Helene felt positively sick, willing herself to keep her breakfast in her stomach.

"That's...*murder*. He's murdering children."

"Yes. He is."

"How on Earth is he allowed to do that? Does no one care that the leader of the country is a killer? Of *children*?"

"Helene, use that beautiful brain of yours. He's been doing the same thing to the Jews—many of them also children—for years. What does Hitler want more than anything?"

"Well, the purification of Germany, whatever that means." The words felt sour on her tongue as she said them, "That's why he doesn't like the Jews. He doesn't think they're pure."

"That's why he's sending them in hoards to the ghettos to work until they die, yes. He's killing disabled children for the same reason, Helene. It doesn't matter if children have blond hair and blue eyes. If they also can't walk on their own, they're nothing to Hitler. He doesn't think they're *genetically good enough*."

The way Genevieve emphasized her point drew Helene's thoughts immediately to Ingrid. Her sweet baby sister. She had a hip defect, one she was born with. Did Hitler think she wasn't genetically good enough? Would he experiment on *her*, if he could? Would he kill *her*? She felt light-headed thinking about that possibility. She must have swayed, because she felt an arm wrap around her shoulders as they continued their walk, supporting her.

"I-I can't let my father put Ingrid back in that hospital," she stuttered, "They'd surely do something horrible to her if they knew the surgery hadn't done a thing."

Genevieve had a look of sympathy—or was it empathy—reflected in her gaze as Helene's eyes met hers. Gloved fingers squeezed her arm gently, and although it only lasted for a brief moment, it did not escape my notice. Genevieve didn't seem like the type who was quick to comfort, and yet, she'd comforted Helene almost immediately, as if seeing her companion even the slightest bit stressed had caused the same feeling to fester in her own chest. This was an interesting, new piece to the human puzzle Helene and I were endeavoring to solve. Genevieve's involvement in the resistance made more sense to me, now that she'd let this side of her slip from behind the mask.

Genevieve hated seeing other people suffer—hated the idea that someone might be suffering—because she was all too familiar with the feeling.

I had been acquainted with Genevieve for a few months now. I could clearly see her desire to make the world a better place—the same passion Helene possessed, only much stronger. The ease with which Genevieve willingly gave herself to other people was a direct result of her desire to help them—to love them. Many people may feel the same way, but they are not capable of the self-sacrifice it takes to turn thought into action. The ones who can, people like Genevieve Harrison, are able to precisely because they know what it's like to not get the help and love they once needed—*deserved*. Genevieve's life purpose hinged on giving to others what she believed she'd never receive.

Looking at Genevieve right then was like staring at an edgier, more rebellious version of my sister. Oh, for the love of Zeus.

The unexpected tenderness from her companion did not escape Helene's notice either. Sharing in the warmth of Genevieve's coat combined with the knowledge that they were touching each other—however innocently—caused Helene's cheeks to redden so fast she might as well have fallen flat on her face into the snowbank.

There was now a very light and airy feeling blooming in the middle of her chest. It seemed to be mixing in a very strange way, with the dread filling her head with visions of her sister dying in the hospital. It proved a combination that felt very wrong for many reasons. She stuffed her hands in her pockets, not knowing what else to do with them.

What a pair the two of them made.

Genevieve eventually put a stop to the awkwardness as she moved to adjust the scarf around her neck and thus removed her arm from it's place around Helene's shoulders. Her voice sounded deceptively nonchalant as she continued the conversation.

"I would put her into a private clinic. They're more expensive, but safer."

It took Helene a moment to pivot back to the topic at hand. We can't all be as skilled in acting as Genevieve, I suppose.

"I mentioned that possibility the other night. I hope my father takes it seriously."

"I know I've never met him, but from what I've heard, he is a smart man. He'll do the right thing," Genevieve gifted Helene with a gentle smile, "Of course, if he sees the pamphlet you're going to write about it, he'll be more easily persuaded."

"He can't know I wrote it."

"Did I say you should tell him you did?"

Silence fell over the two of them as they continued their walk.

"I think you should write the article, and give it to Arthur to print. You can help him distribute it," Genevieve's voice had taken on a determined tone as she continued, "I can't guarantee they'll be posted for long—pamphlets are usually ripped and trashed pretty quickly—but hopefully the right people will see it and question some things."

"Alright, yes. I'll write it up tomorrow. I'd like to do some... research tonight."

That made Genevieve halt in the middle of the walkway, her eyes luminescent with curiosity. Only I could detect the worry also present in the stare she gifted Helene.

"Please don't do anything stupid."

"Did I say I would?"

I smiled in spite of myself. Helene was certainly about to do something she shouldn't. Would it be stupid? No, nothing important is stupid. Would it be dangerous? Most certainly.

✳✳✳

The constellations that speckled the night sky were conveniently missing as Helene journeyed through the empty streets of Hamburg yet again. Perhaps they weren't missing, per se, but hiding—conspiring with her. The thought proved comforting. She'd made sure to wear a pair of shoes that would make minimal noise—the best option proved to be her slippers—and she relished in the way even she could barely hear her footsteps on the cobblestones. Nobody could know what she planned to do under the cover of darkness—and there was certainly a chance she could get caught. It wasn't the SS officers on night watch whom she was worried about. No, she wasn't planning on wandering the streets or meeting anyone at a secret location. She was on her way to a very public place—at least during the day—and she was much more attuned to the possibility of being caught by the occupants of said public location if she wasn't careful.

Genevieve had all but begged her to explain what she planned to do, but Helene remained strong. She knew if Genevieve uncovered her plan, she'd want to come with her, and that wouldn't do. Not at all.

Trespassing on park grounds after hours or surveying someone's house by the light of the moon—that was one thing, and a thing she would have gladly wanted Genevieve's company for.

Breaking onto the grounds of a Nazi-funded hospital for children? In order to find proof of the rumored murders taking place there? Quite another thing entirely.

As Kinderkrankenhaus Rothenburgsort came into view, Helene surveyed the wrought iron gate that outlined the entire perimeter of the campus. The metal was old enough that it had started to rust in certain spots—something she'd noticed the other day when she and her mother had arrived to bring Ingrid home. It did not take long to find a small section of the gate that had come under such disrepair that someone, bless them, had decided it needed to be replaced. Several metal bars had been taken out of a section along the eastern side of the lawn, and the opening they left was just big enough for Helene to squeeze herself through. Once on the opposite side of the gate, she tied a red hair ribbon she'd brought with her around the nearest iron post. Once her task was complete, the ribbon would guide her back to the opening.

Now, for the task at hand.

The building itself was almost completely shrouded in darkness, save a handful of windows at the rear of the building. Helene decided those windows were as good a spot as any to start her search. She wasn't stupid enough to try and break into the building—surely it was locked at night—so gazing through as many windows as she could would have to do.

I had a suspicion the windows would provide Helene with everything she needed.

The first two sets Helene peeked through looked in on the same bathroom—and to her disappointment, there was nothing of note within it. A toilet sat against one wall, and a sink against the other. There was a sterile look to the room that suggested it was either not frequently used or very frequently cleaned.

The next lit window Helene came upon belonged to a much bigger room. It was situated at the back of the building on a corner. Helene could see that a door had been opened leading to the courtyard that was now only mere feet away. If she rounded the corner, she'd surely see it. As she surveyed the rest of the room, she noticed a long metal table situated in the center. It was surrounded by bright lights and chairs, and Helene could make out the shapes of a variety of medical instruments placed haphazardly on top of it. There was a sink in the corner, as well as a showerhead attached to the wall next to it. A mysterious dark substance splattered the floor, the color of rust.

Helene wondered what exactly she was looking at until I nudged her mind in the direction of the only logical solution. This was surely where surgeries were conducted: an operating room. Perhaps even the same operating room where they'd worked on Ingrid's hip. While it wasn't a sight that was, how should I say it, *pleasing to the eye*, the room wasn't any kind of anomaly, especially considering the kind of establishment it resided within. Hospitals had operating rooms, and they were not generally thought to be pretty.

I was about to step into Helene's mind once again, to tell her to move on, when both of us heard a noise that during the day wouldn't be cause for concern, but in the middle of the night certainly was not comforting.

Voices. Around the corner. Mere feet away.

Helene froze immediately.

Well don't just stand there, darling. They'll surely see you.

She crouched against the building a second later, palms pressed against the bricks to steady herself. Her hands shook, and not because of the winter air. I felt that perhaps she needed more guidance from me to distract her from the obvious danger she was in.

Focus on figuring out who these voices belong to, and what they're doing.

She refocused under my instruction, although hesitantly. Truly, I wasn't sure if listening to the voices would prove all that helpful. I just wanted to distract Helene from panicking.

As Fate would have it, eavesdropping was exactly the thing to do.

Once Helene steadied her breathing enough to hear properly again, she concentrated on the sounds floating through the air around her: there were two distinct voices, one male and one female. The man sounded older, and he spoke with an air of pretentiousness that suggested he was the female's superior. Helene strained her ears to catch the words flying between them.

"You grab that end, and I'll take the other."

"Where are we taking him, Dr. Fuchs?"

Dr. Fuchs. The head doctor. The one who performed Ingrid's surgery.

"Do not associate it with a gender, nurse. That only leads to attachment, and that won't do. Not anymore. We must move the cadaver to the crematorium. Once it's there, we won't trouble ourselves with it anymore."

"What will I tell the parents? Won't they wonder what happened?"

"Let me handle that. As far as they are concerned, the death occurred by natural cause."

"You think they'll believe that?"

"Of course they'll believe it. I'm the doctor; they aren't," Dr. Fuchs's voice took on a dismissive tone, "Besides, this cadaver was impure, which made it useless to society at large."

"Not useless for scientific purposes."

"No, this one proved quite intriguing. The Führer will be pleased."

Despite having the sudden urge to throw up her supper, Helene silently inched sideways along the wall until she was close enough to the corner of the building to see around it without being seen herself.

What she saw made the blood freeze in her veins.

Dr Fuchs—aided by an older nurse—carried something large across the courtyard. No, *not something. Someone.* They were transporting a body from the hospital's morgue to the crematorium, where they were presumably going to burn it out of existence. Helene tried to glimpse the possible identity of the dead person, but the body was meticulously tied up in a sheet. Clearly evident, though, to Helene's utter disgust, was the age of the deceased. The body was too small to be anything other than a young child. It was so small, in fact, that Helene guessed this child couldn't have lived longer than seven, maybe eight years. Helene never wished she had a camera on her person as badly as she did in that moment.

This was it. This horrifying scene in front of her was exactly the proof she needed to write the pamphlet. There had been a part of her that had come to the hospital hoping she'd be wrong, and that the doctors would not be murdering children. But now that she did have the proof, now that she knew they were monsters, she had everything she needed.

The match was lit, and she was ready to burn this place to the ground.

ATHENA
January 23rd, 1942

By the time the new year rolled around, the pages-long pamphlet accusing the renowned Kinderkrankenhaus Rothenburgsort of murdering its patients was a topic of conversation in every household in Hamburg. Some were outraged. Some didn't believe it, despite the unknown author swearing to have caught the esteemed Dr. Leon Fuchs disposing of a child's body in the dead of night. There were many who did not concern themselves with it—people who did not question the Reich because they didn't care enough to. If Hitler thought the country was better off without disabled people in it, so be it.

As much as I'd like to think that latter group of Germans was motivated to support Hitler because they were scared not to, or because they'd given up on life altogether, I do not believe it. I've been around for centuries. No matter how many times humans will tell themselves otherwise, *some people are just bad*. In the absence of Love, there is Hate. Conversely, and perhaps more frighteningly, in the absence of Empathy there is Apathy. Hitler brainwashed so many Germans into thinking Hate would save them—that they were running some existential race and the only way to win was to push others down and run them over. He created in the minds of his people the sense that it was them against everybody else, and only the strongest deserved to survive. He said it was only natural instinct.

It wasn't natural. It was selfish. It was dangerous. But alas, I digress.

Arthur hadn't said much of anything when Helene showed him the finished product, other than that he was sure Genevieve would find it *satisfactory*. She figured he was still sulking over the fact that she hadn't let him help write it. Thankfully, he helped with the distribution across the city. The prospect of doing it alone terrified Helene. He had his own pocket-sized, hand-drawn map detailing all the usual spots Blackthorn posted pamphlets, and they'd spent several hours in the dead of night tacking Helene's words to walls and telephone poles, tree trunks, and bulletin boards. Arthur also reminded Helene of something Genevieve had mentioned to her once before: that it was likely every single pamphlet would be taken down and thrown away within a day. It was the game they had to play if they wanted to get any information out at all, he said.

This proved to be an illogical justification to Helene. Surely, the SS officers were able to find and get rid of every pamphlet so quickly precisely because they were posted in the same spots every time. It made sense that, if put in new locations, it would take longer for each pamphlet to be destroyed. She'd relayed her thoughts to Arthur, of course.

"Don't you think they'd be posted longer if they weren't hung in such obvious places?"

"The locations on my map are the ones most visible to the public for the most time. Even if they do get ripped down in a day, think of how many people still have the chance to read the information because it's been placed right in their faces? It's what makes the most sense."

Helene hadn't thought a response necessary. She knew she wouldn't change his mind. She supposed she agreed with Arthur when it came to specific locations. Posting in the Stadtpark, for instance, was certainly a good choice. She supposed the bulletins at the university saw many intrigued eyes every day as well. But there was something about the way Arthur spoke of the inevitability of her work being so easily destroyed that bothered her. She'd worked hard on this pamphlet. She'd stayed up through several nights making sure it was perfect and said everything she wanted to but couldn't say out loud. She was proud of it, and she loathed the thought of every copy being torn down before anyone had a chance to digest her words and form their own opinions.

She didn't want people to simply look at her pamphlet; she wanted them to read it.

So naturally, she decided to take matters into her own hands, for what was now the second time. I thoroughly approved of this, of course. Helene was her own person with her own ideas and opinions. It was about time she started acting on them. After all, she'd be doing Blackthorn a favor by ensuring a wider audience.

And so that was how—on one cold January morning—families across the city, the Reinholdts included, woke to find a curious and very well-written leaflet stuffed in their mailboxes. Surely, whoever had done this should not have—only government officials could put things in mailboxes—but nobody could figure out who the author was. It wasn't written like any other pamphlet they'd seen. This one was so compelling and passionate and *persuasive*.

By the middle of the month, Otto had Ingrid placed on a waiting list for a private clinic in the suburbs. It proved an expensive one, but after reading the condemnation of Rothenburgsort and Dr. Fuchs, he refused to bring his daughter back there. Helene felt more relieved than she had in months. She felt like her sister was safe, now, and thanks to her efforts. Now that the news had been out for several weeks, people had stopped wondering about the identity of the pamphlet writer. She was sure nobody had even an inkling of the idea that she had anything to do with it all.

I was sure Helene thought herself quite enchantingly mysterious for pulling off such a stunt successfully. Well, *almost* successfully.

✳✳✳

The night of January 23rd was especially cold. The winter wind whipped against the windows of the Reinholdt apartment with a rattle that made Helene want to crawl into her bed and hide under the covers, even though it was only six o'clock. Her father was out pulling barges in this weather. She didn't know how he did it, year after year. His business had boomed now that there was a war on. The Reich needed materials, and they needed them often. Helene didn't particularly like knowing her father's business aided the war effort, but the thought of him losing work and her siblings going hungry wasn't a pleasant thought either.

She was about to open her current read in an attempt to get a few chapters in when her mother called from the other room, wondering if she'd help prepare supper. She groaned but made her way to the kitchen anyway. No sense in arguing with Anna over things like supper. She knew she'd lose in the end.

Luckily, Anna's only request was that she cut vegetables. Easy enough. The two of them settled into a quiet rhythm—Anna stirring a broth of some kind and Helene peeling potatoes. These moments were the ones Helene found most calming, just her and her mother doing their domestic duties in busy silence.

That silence didn't last very long. Anna's voice rose out of the quiet as she struck up a conversation with her eldest daughter.

"Your father has heard a rumor about a new tactic of Hitler's. Apparently, he is referring to it as the 'Final Solution.' Have you heard about this?"

Of course Helene had heard about it. Genevieve had gotten wind of a meeting in the Berlin suburb of Wannsee—a meeting attended by all the high-ranking government officials. Her sources confirmed that the meeting had concluded with the decision to implement the "Final Solution to the Jewish Question" immediately. The solution, apparently, involved every Jew in Europe being rounded up and sent to camps in Nazi-occupied space, where the German government planned to kill every last one of them. There was a part of Helene that didn't want to believe such a thing could ever be true, that any government in the modern world would be allowed to do something—to even think something—so heinous and evil. And yet, despite everything, she did believe it. Without a doubt, she believed that the Chancellor of Germany had sat himself down at a conference table surrounded by his generals and declared his intention to completely wipe an entire group of people off the face of the earth. It made her so positively sick that she didn't know what to do with the knowledge of it. She felt her expression contort as she answered her mother.

"Yes, I've heard of it. The Führer plans to murder every Jewish person in Europe."

"He's lost his damn mind," Anna exclaimed as she shook her head. "What kind of lunatic would think such a thing was moral?"

"I don't know. I don't think he's concerned with morality, and if he is, he's got it wrong."

"Something's not right in his head, that's for sure."

There was a pause where neither of them said anything. Helene went back to focusing on the task in front of her, now cutting the peeled potatoes into cubes. She was halfway through the second potato when Anna's voice broke through her concentration.

"Surely, that will be the topic of your next pamphlet, yes?"

The knife froze in mid-air as Helene's stomach bottomed out.

Oh, how perfect.

"I have no idea what you're talking about, Mutti."

"I'm not stupid, Helene. Please don't patronize me."

The silence was almost excruciating as Helene struggled to find something to say. Anna seemed to recognize that, and chuckled.

"Did you really think I wouldn't notice your light on through the crack in the door three nights in a row? Or the way your eyes lit up when you saw your father reading it? You've wanted Ingrid moved to a private clinic since the day she came home, and that pamphlet did the trick."

"There is no name on the pamphlet; anyone could have written it."

"No, not just anyone," Anna glanced up with a dubious look, "I've read your stories, and the essays you write for school. There is a flair to your writing—a certain persuasion. Nobody writes better than you do, darling. I knew as soon as I read that pamphlet that you composed every word of it, and now I'm stuck between wanting to be proud of you and wanting to slap you until you're cross-eyed."

A look of terror flashed across Helene's expression. I was really starting to enjoy myself.

"I am an adult now," Helene said as she tried to muster some kind of childish bravery, "I can do what I want."

Anna seemed to disregard the statement altogether.

"It is unlikely that you accomplished this all on your own, so I'm inclined to believe you've joined some sort of group. Is that correct?"

"Mutti—"

"Don't you dare even consider lying to me, Helene Reinholdt."

"I…," Helene's face was now bright red, and she looked as though she might burst into tears at any moment, "…yes."

Anna was quiet for a moment. She did not make a scene, as Helene thought she might. She didn't do much of anything—just chuckled again as she shook her head. There was no malice or even disappointment in her voice as she nearly whispered,

"You have more of your father in you than I thought."

The way her words came out, with a distinct air of inevitability, made Helene inexplicably angry.

"I am not my father; I am myself. I chose to do this all on my own."

"Yes," Anna's words were sharp to reflect her tone, "I can see that clearly."

"I'm sorry if you don't like it, but it is what it is."

"I just did not expect this from you, of all my children. Margarethe, perhaps. But surely not you."

Helene swore she saw red as her mother's words hit her square in the chest. Of course she hadn't *expected this from her.* Hadn't expected her precious Helene to break the rules. Hadn't expected the golden child to waste her potential so assuredly. She wanted to punch a hole in the wall thinking about her mother lamenting to anyone who'd listen over her daughter not being the good girl who stayed at home and watched her siblings all day and never had a single thought of a different kind of life. Anna wanted Helene to be just like her, didn't she? She wanted her to sit around and play house while the world moved on without her. But Helene didn't want that—she refused to become that. She could feel her words dripping off her tongue like venom as she endeavored to respond.

"You just want me to be like you, Mutti," she said as her voice rose an octave every passing second, "That's all you've ever wanted for me—to stay away from danger, to do everything the way everyone else does it. I refuse to be such a *coward*."

Anna's expression changed slightly as Helene spoke, and I could see the way her daughter's words had struck some kind of nerve. Her voice now carried a sadder undertone.

"That's not true, Helene," she started, "I have never expected you to do everything the way I have. Truly, since the day you were born I've hoped you would be more than I am. So much more."

"Then why would you spend my entire life telling me how things should be done and what is proper and what is not? Why would you make me feel like a failure because I didn't turn out the way you expected?" Helene's field of vision became blurry as hot tears gathered in her eyes, "Why would you tell me, however subtly, how I should live, if you didn't want me to follow what you said?"

"I would never demand that you follow in my steps," Anna whispered as she endeavored to clarify, "But Helene, what kind of mother would I be if I didn't at least leave footprints for you to follow if you so chose?"

There it is. There's the truth of the matter.

Helene was not the only one with tears in her eyes, now.

"I've never…" Anna started, her voice made of eggshells, "I've never wanted you to feel so trapped, so misunderstood. Please know my intention has always been the opposite."

She continued before Helene could interrupt.

"I had so many expectations placed on me as a child. Everyone in my life seemed to know what I should do and what I should be—and it was suffocating at times. The day you were born, I remember the way you looked at me with those fresh little eyes of yours, so new but so full of curiosity and light already. I decided at that moment that you would never know what it felt like to not have a say in how you lived your life—I would raise you in a world of choices and teach you how to weigh them in your mind and make the best decision for yourself."

There is no better lesson for a girl to learn.

"Someone else might tell you that a mother's role is to protect, but it's so much more than that, Helene. A mother's most important duty—her highest calling—is to love her children. That means protecting them, of course, but it also means teaching them and guiding them. I wanted to give you one path already formed—my own path—while also letting you create your own. I wanted your choice to come down to whether or not you wanted to take my already-formed one, or the one of your own making. Knowing that you would always have two options reassured me that you'd be alright out in the world—that if there ever came a time when you found yourself scared or doubtful of the path you'd made, you'd always have mine to follow. You'd always be able to find your way back to me. But Helene, for what it's worth to you, my pride in you would have surpassed lifetimes no matter what path you chose in the end."

Helene was quiet for a few moments as she searched for the words she needed.

"I think I understand," Her voice sounded so much smaller than she wanted it to, "But if you say you'd be proud of me either way, why does it feel like my decision to join the resistance effort has upset you? I don't want that."

"I am upset you kept it from me, yes, but I could never be upset with you for caring about the world enough to want to change it. That is what I meant when I said there was more of your father inside of you than I thought."

"Does he...know?"

"What? That you wrote the pamphlet? Of course he does. He didn't want to confront you—wanted to wait for you to tell us all by yourself," Anna smirked, "I told him pigs would fly before my firstborn gave away her secrets freely."

"Is he angry with me?"

"No, I don't think so. You know your father—if he could waltz into government headquarters and give Hitler a piece of his mind, he would."

I knew Anna was right about that. He surely would do exactly that if the consequence for doing so wasn't jail or death. Otto Reinholdt knew what it felt like to be blinded with passion to the point of action, but he also knew exactly what it felt like to pay a hefty price because of it. The man had already lost his family once because of a rash decision, many years ago. He wouldn't make the same mistake again.

By now, Anna's tears had dried, and she'd slid her delicate mask back into place. Her daughter wouldn't see her cry again any time soon. Helene, on the other hand, found herself consumed by anxious tears that contradicted her mother's reassurances.

"Mutti do you…do you think I should tell Vati? Is he waiting for me to tell him?"

"Only if you want to," Anna replied with a gentle smile, "He trusts that you know what you're doing, and that you'll be careful. That's all we care about, that you're as careful as you can be."

"I am being careful, I swear."

"Good. Now don't tell me any more, or I'll just worry myself sick, alright? Not another word about it as long as I'm in the room."

"I promise, Mutti."

"That's my good girl. Now go fetch Margarethe and tell her to set the table for supper. We'll be eating shortly."

And with that, the conversation surrounding Helene's involvement in Blackthorn was over, at least for the time being.

INTERLUDE
Athens, 2022

As Athena paused to take a bite of ambrosia, a very perplexed look flashed across Amphitrite's face.

"It seems to me that Anna doesn't know the extent of Helene's involvement with Blackthorn. I expected her to be angrier—well, no—I suppose I just expected her to have more reservations about Helene joining the resistance."

Athena would let Aphrodite answer that.

"You're not wrong," her sister acknowledges with a sugary voice, "At this point in the story, Anna understands the illegal nature of what Helene's doing, but the real danger of it is hard to grasp for her."

"She must believe that Blackthorn is nothing more than a small group of students," Apollo adds, "And not a legitimate operation with hubs across the country."

"She's in for a treat then, isn't she?" Ares chuckles. It isn't hard for him to see where the story is headed—which isn't the case for Amphitrite, it seems.

"But truly, how dangerous can writing pamphlets get?"

Four sets of eyes stare at her with incredulity. After a few moments, Amphitrite groans with realization.

"She's not just going to write pamphlets, is she?"

"I'm afraid not," Athena smiles gently, "She's proved herself quite capable after successfully breaking onto the grounds of a hospital and writing a scathing review of what she found there. Genevieve was quite impressed."

"I'm pretty sure Helene could've smeared dogshit onto a piece of paper and Genevieve Harrison still would've been impressed," Ares sneers.

Athena ignores the comment and continues with her previous thought.

"It is important to note Amphitrite's concern, though. At this point in the story, Anna understands that Helene has made a decision, but she doesn't know the full implications of that decision. Of course, she will find out eventually, and it won't be easy for her."

"I'm wondering," Apollo pipes up, "If Helene feels like writing that pamphlet was worth her parents finding out about her secret? Anna seemed rather perturbed at the thought of Helene lying to her, but when pressed about it, Helene still didn't tell the whole truth—only confirmed the parts of it that her mother had caught on to. It just seems like this might cause a problem later."

"I won't give anything away," Athena quips, "But Helene's involvement with Blackthorn will only grow from here, and just like anything worth mentioning, it's bound to get messier."

"So more drama," Apollo grins in satisfaction, "Just what I love the most."

ATHENA
March 14th, 1942

I f Helene had known that today's training session would involve handling weapons, she probably would've feigned illness, but by the time she noticed the target hung on the wall of the abandoned restaurant with several bullet holes ripped through it, it was too late to leave. She knew this day was going to come eventually–she certainly couldn't go into her first mission without knowledge of how to defend herself–but she was dreading the way Genevieve would inevitably look at her after she failed again, and again, and again. She'd gained Genevieve's respect on the school smarts front–at least she thought she might have–but street smarts? Absolutely not. Helene hadn't forgotten what Genevieve told her during their first meeting. She knew intelligence could only go so far–and it certainly wouldn't save her if there was an SS officer waving a gun in her face.

I didn't totally agree with Helene on this, but it was the kind of thing that can't really be learned until a kind of situation arises where the only thing standing between you and death is a riddle, or a password. I digress.

Genevieve had her back to the doorway, and Helene was thankful her instructor couldn't see the way her face lost all of its color as Genevieve expertly disassembled a handgun sitting on the desk in front of her. To her dismay, Helene only managed to take her coat off before Genevieve launched into what was sure to be a lengthy training—her long, black tresses flying through the air as she spun around.

"Helene, you're here. Good. We're doing something a bit different today if it wasn't already clear. Do you know what this is?"

"That's a gun."

"Not just any gun, Helene. This is a P38 pistol. Standard issue for most German soldiers. If you're going to go out on any kind of mission, you have to know how this pistol works inside and out."

"Can I ask how you acquired this pistol? I can't imagine a German officer just giving it to you willingly."

"I stole it, obviously."

"How could you have managed that?"

"A resistance fighter never gives up her secrets," Genevieve scoffed, "But if you must know, I took it on my way out of his place the morning after a night of very mediocre sex."

"Oh, right...okay."

Helene squirmed slightly at the mention of sex. Nobody in her family had ever really talked to her about it. She knew her parents surely had any possible answer she could be looking for—they had too many kids not to—but she'd never thought to ask, and they'd never told. If she lived in an alternate universe where she was engaged to someone dashing, she supposed her mother would've sat her down by now and told her the ins and outs of it. But alas, she was just herself–just Helene–and there were no men of any kind asking for her hand in anything.

She almost envied Genevieve for the way she could engage in promiscuous behavior so freely. Helene supposed it was rather easy to do so when one looked like a deity incarnate. She was sure Genevieve could have anyone she wanted at any time, man or woman alike.

I chuckled at the way Helene's cheeks turned the color of roses at the thought.

She forced herself to focus on the moment at hand when Genevieve motioned for her to step up to the desk.

"We've talked about how you would theoretically assemble a gun. Now I want you to actually do it."

"Right now?"

"No Helene, next fucking week," Genevieve rolled her eyes, "Obviously now."

As Helene surveyed the parts in front of her, she noticed Genevieve hadn't fully disassembled the gun–she'd field-stripped it. It meant that Helene wouldn't have to worry about all the tiny springs and pins that had to interlock onto levers, locks, and slides. She almost sighed out loud in relief. Now, she knew from her past lessons, she'd only have to concern herself with assembling the frame, barrel, slide, and magazine. Not too difficult.

"I can see that brain of yours firing up," Genevieve interrupted her thoughts, "Talk me through your process. What's the first step?"

"Fitting the barrel assembly into the slide, making sure to push the locking block up so it fits securely."

"Good. What's next?"

"The slide fits onto the frame, but the takedown latch has to be rotated down. Then, I'm pretty sure I have to pull the slide far enough back so I can rotate the latch back into a locked position."

Genevieve's silence urged her to continue.

"Once the latch is locked, I can let the slide move forward, and then all that's left is the magazine."

There was a part of her that reveled in the sound of the magazine slamming into place. She snuck a glance to her right and felt her chest swell with pride when she saw the upward pull at the corners of Genevieve's mouth. She had dimples when she smiled–Helene had never seen them before–and added to the sparkle in her eyes, they rendered Helene completely distracted. Her face was just so perfect, and Helene's chest nearly ached, thinking about what it would be like to be that beautiful. She knew she wasn't ugly herself, but she was nothing compared to Genevieve. There was a part of her–buried so deep in the corridors of her mind that she could barely sense it–that instinctually wondered what Genevieve did to make her lips look so pink and full.

Helene, darling, try your best not to get too ahead of yourself.

If my remarks didn't pull Helene out of her reverie, the sound of metal *unsheathing* certainly did. For a split second, she thought Genevieve had decided to get rid of her, but upon fully turning around, she saw that wouldn't be the case. Her dark-haired companion was holding a dagger in each hand. It was clear that she'd be keeping one of them, but the other was being extended in Helene's direction.

"Don't look so spooked, please. It's a knife," Genevieve huffed, "Guns are easy to handle; you just aim and shoot. Knives are much more complicated to wield with accuracy in a heated moment, so we need to practice."

"You want me to throw this dagger at the target?"

"I want you to fight me with it."

It took a moment for Helene to mentally compute the request. If she'd been able to see me, she would have noticed the grin plastered nearly from ear to ear across my face. I do not often smile as such, but I can't help my love for a good knife fight.

"I d-don't," Helene stuttered, "I don't think I can do that."

"You can, and you will. It's just a training exercise."

"But—"

"Helene, you are perfectly safe." Her chestnut eyes softened slightly as she spoke, "You know I'd never dream of hurting you."

Perhaps she'd dreamed of doing other things to Helene, but certainly not hurting her.

Before Helene could protest any further, Genevieve placed the outstretched knife into her hand. She knew that compared to the gun she'd just held, this knife was compact and light. But it felt heavy to her all the same as she stared at the curve of the blade.

"Is this a military issue, too?" She inquired in a whisper.

"No," Genevieve pronounced as she pulled her hair up into a bun, "I couldn't get my hands on one. But it doesn't matter; all knives work the same way. If you can get close enough to your opponent, you stab them."

Helene didn't respond, and Genevieve continued in a voice that reminded Helene of a grade school teacher.

"The most important thing to know about fighting with a knife is that you must always hold onto it with a firm grip."

"That seems rather obvious, doesn't it?"

"It's not, especially for untrained people like you," Genevieve leveled her with a slightly condescending look. "If you let the knife slip, you could slice your hand, or your thigh, or the knife could go flying. You want the knife to hit your intended target, and nothing else."

The smell of lavender and vanilla filled Helene's senses as Genevieve stepped closer.

"Let's pretend I'm an SS officer, and I've stopped you on the street because you seem suspicious to me. Let's say you've tried all the verbal tactics you can think of, and now the only thing left to do is *fight*."

She finished the sentence with a hiss, and Helene felt the hairs on her arms stand straight up. She couldn't imagine standing up to an SS officer like that; she would surely die.

"You will not let me kill you like this," Genevieve continued, seeming to read her mind. "You take out your knife as I take out mine. The first thing to do is size me up."

"So I know exactly what I'm dealing with."

"Exactly," she smiled, "You'll want to take into consideration my height, my weight—all of that. You can assume I have fast reflexes and that I know how to wield with accuracy. I have been meticulously trained to do so."

"So, that means I have to focus more on blocking—and making sure I'm able to deflect or move out of your knife's path."

"Yes, precisely. It's like a dance, in a way. Whatever you have to do to keep yourself on your feet with your knife in your hand—you do it."

Before Helene could even think to respond, Genevieve moved. Closed fist met stomach. There was a flurry of papers as her backside crashed into the desk behind her, and in less than three seconds, Helene lay crumpled to the floor. Pain flooded her senses, and it took her a moment to overcome it as she squeezed her eyes closed. When she opened them again, she saw Genevieve towering over her, arms above her head, and the knife poised to strike her straight in the chest. Anger and embarrassment flooded through Helene's veins so fast it was nearly blinding. I had personally never seen Helene angry. I suspected Genevieve had knocked her down on purpose in an attempt to coax the emotion to the surface of Helene's psyche. I'll admit it was a good tactic.

"Always expect the unexpected, Helene," she smirked, "You'd be dead right now if I was actually an officer."

Helene's legs shook pitifully as she got back up. She hoped it wasn't noticeable.

"Okay," she said, trying desperately to swallow her desire to run back to her parents' boat and hide, "I understand."

"Let's try something else. Come at me. I know you're pissed, I just—"

Helene didn't let her finish her sentence. It wasn't like Genevieve ever let her finish her own. She launched herself at her opponent, and the element of surprise saw them both crash to the floor—Helene sprawled on top of Genevieve as her fists clenched onto the older woman's blouse.

Naturally, Genevieve just laughed.

Helene had never heard her laugh like this. Sure, she'd snickered and smirked before, but she'd never laughed so genuinely like this—like sunshine breaking through a storm cloud. It was a beautiful, rare sound. It made Helene's blood boil.

"That's much better than before," Genevieve praised once she'd grown tired of laughing at Helene's expense, "But you've forgotten something rather important, haven't you?"

Dismay flowed through Helene as Genevieve waved her knife around in the air. She had, indeed, forgotten the most important thing—the goddamn knives they were supposed to be fighting with.

Had she pulled that impassioned stunt on an SS officer, he would've simply stabbed her straight through the heart without batting an eyelash. She'd made herself vulnerable in the midst of her frenzied reaction.

Genevieve was waiting for this precise moment—the second just after Helene realized what she'd done wrong, but just before she could think to remedy it. Ankles intertwined, the ceiling moved sideways with a rush of air, and the two women switched places. Now Genevieve crouched on top of Helene—their faces mere centimeters away from each other. Helene could feel steel pressed with gentle pressure against her throat, which surely meant that whatever this challenge was, she just lost. But it was hard to feel as though she'd lost anything, not with a pair of golden brown eyes staring straight into her own. Studying her. Learning her. They glowed in a way Helene couldn't describe in simple terms--sunlight shining through a glass of whiskey; sweet sap against pine bark. She had to squeeze her own shut, had to block out that brightness.

Genevieve's breath was warm against Helene's ear as she leaned impossibly closer. Her lips moved in a whisper as the knife's cold edge danced against Helene's jawline. Her velvet voice caused goosebumps to form along Helene's forearms.

"Better luck next time, love."

The promise hidden within those five little words awakened something inside of Helene, something wild and mesmerizing and dangerous. In that moment, there was nothing in the entire universe that she wanted more than to hear that voice over and over again.

It didn't take a goddess's intuition to understand what had occurred. Helene had realized that she was not envious of Genevieve's beauty and never had been. She was in awe of it.

She didn't want to *be* Genevieve. She wanted to be Genevieve's.

Genevieve's...what? Her friend. Her lover. Her reason for letting her guard down.

Her everything.

It was surprising that Aphrodite didn't appear in a cloud of glitter as soon as the words formed in Helene's mind. I was happy she'd finally come to realize what I had seen from the start—never mind that the more in love she felt, the more out of my depth I felt.

Helene clenched her teeth hard as desire ran through her, to preserve her silence if nothing else. She didn't trust herself not to say something exceptionally stupid while Genevieve was still lying on top of her. It proved a rather...compromising position.

Loaded silence lasted for another ten seconds before Genevieve rolled off of Helene in one swift, graceful motion. By the time Helene felt it safe enough to open her eyes, her companion was already on her feet and sheathing both knives with a look of passivity on her face, like they hadn't been sprawled on the floor staring into each other's eyes mere moments ago.

How lovely and infuriating Genevieve was. Did she feel the same way about Helene, or was it all in her head?

Trust me, it's not only in your head.

It was then Helene realized she probably looked quite peculiar still lying on the ground and hastily jumped to her feet. She busied herself with cleaning up the space around her, trying her best not to look at Genevieve across the room. Still, Helene could see her in the peripheral–draping her coat over her shoulders stylishly, shaking her hair loose from the bun she'd kept it up in to train. Before she could stop it, the thought of touching that hair flew through Helene's mind. She forced it back out as quickly as it came, afraid somehow that Genevieve could read her mind.

Even if she had been able to read Helene's mind, I was positive there wouldn't be anything to fear.

Genevieve broke their silence first.

"Good work today...have a good night."

"You too, Genevieve."

She wanted to say more, anything else, but her tongue felt huge and heavy against the roof of her mouth, and the moment passed. Genevieve made her way towards the door, and it seemed to Helene that she wasn't going to say another word, either. It was probably better that way, considering how training had gone. Helene forced herself into a crouch in order to pick up the papers she had knocked off the desk earlier. She waited and counted Genevieve's footsteps as they made their way across the floorboards, her heeled boots making clicks in time with Helene's heart. She had counted to ten when the footsteps suddenly stopped.

"Helene?"

A beat.

"Yes?"

"It's becoming exhausting to hear you use my full name every time you speak to me," she said in an exasperated way, "We've passed the pleasantries stage at this point, haven't we?"

Helene felt like she might be suffocating.

"Um, I—yes, I...suppose we have, yes."

"Please, just call me Eve."

Now, she was absolutely sure she wasn't breathing correctly.

"But," Helene started, unsure, "Arthur says only your close friends are allowed to call you that."

"Did he? Hmm."

She paused in contemplation, and even with her back to the door, Helene knew Genevieve was smiling. She imagined what it

246

looked like blooming across her face, making her eyes sparkle with delight. Her voice, playful as ever, confirmed Helene was right.

"Well, he would know that kind of thing, so I'm not surprised."

She left the room then, not deigning it necessary to say anything else. I found myself chuckling at the way Helene broke into a sweat. Everything was shaping up to be so much more than I had initially expected it would be, and these new implications were nothing short of dramatic.

But drama, for a goddess, is positively delicious.

INTERLUDE
Athens, 2022

Athena is sure that the smile spread across Aphrodite's face upon hearing of Helene and Eve's *escapade* could most certainly win over the hardest of hearts. She understood, now, how Aphrodite got so excited when she talked about romance. It was indeed quite exhilarating to describe the moment someone falls in love for the first time.

"I never pinned you down as a romantic, Athena," Apollo chuckles, "Has Aphrodite poisoned your drink, by any chance?"

"Of course she hasn't," she chuckles as Aphrodite shoots him a dirty look, "I just know how to tell a good story; you know this."

"Sure," Amphitrite jokes, "Whatever you say."

"Either way, I'm done discussing romance in great detail for a short while," she adds, "Which will hopefully give you enough time to remember how stone-cold and reasonable I am."

Aphrodite immediately takes a sip of nectar in response to

Athena's sarcasm, and although it does distract from the smirk on her lips, it doesn't hide the mischievous twinkle in her eyes.

Her siblings think a training session is too romantic for her? Oh, how they are mistaken. Athena is just getting started.

ATHENA
July 20th, 1942

Helene awoke to Margarethe giggling in her ear, exclaiming that there was a dashing young man there to see her. Her still half-asleep brain could barely comprehend what her sister could be talking about—considering she didn't know many dashing men. It took a few moments, but once she did realize the only logical explanation, she flew from under the covers faster than should have been humanly possible.

Margarethe, naturally, saw the way her sister hastily threw her robe over her shoulders and jumped to conclusions. She saw how haphazardly Helene ran a comb through her curls and assumed the only thing a younger sister could: the man must be an admirer.

The irony of it gave me quite the chuckle. If only Margarethe knew who really held Helene's affections.

"Helene, how could you not tell me you had a beau?"

"He is certainly not my beau and never will be."

"He's so handsome, though! With such nicely pressed shirts!"

"Did he say why he's here?"

"Well, he told Vati he had a school question, but it's July, so obviously that's just what he's saying so he can see you," Margarethe giggled again incessantly, "I'm sure he really wants to kiss you."

"Margo, I will not be kissing anyone, but especially not him."

"We'll see about that, won't we?"

Helene wanted to send a retort over her shoulder as she reached the top of the stairs but decided there wasn't much of a point. It was probably best if her sister thought she had a crush. It was better than her knowing the truth.

She nearly tripped over Kitty playing with her dolls on the floor as she rounded a corner a little too hastily. She couldn't imagine what he needed to tell her this early on a Saturday morning. Surely, it could have waited until Monday afternoon when she saw him for class.

Her heart nearly skipped with anxiety as she made it to the foredeck. There stood Arthur—adorned in khaki trousers and a white linen shirt—talking about the economy with her father. He gave her a dazzling smile once he noticed her, and she knew she'd never live down meeting him in her nightgown. Her father excused himself after giving her a look she'd never seen him gift her before, and then she was alone with Arthur. His voice was ever so playful as he spoke.

"That's a nice robe you have, Helene."

"You're an ass for coming here on a Saturday morning."

"I didn't know you lived on a boat. It's charming."

She'd had enough of his small talk.

"Why, exactly, are you here?"

"I come bearing information."

"Information that couldn't wait until a more suitable time?"

"Genevieve asked me to tell you in person as soon as possible. She didn't want a telegram being intercepted."

"Alright, fine. What is it?"

"Wilheim has decided you and I are ready for our first mission. I'll be going to Poland, you to France."

The color slowly began draining from Helene's face. She hoped it wasn't noticeable.

"When?"

"Not in the near future, at least not for you. I'll probably ship out sometime next month, but from the way he and Genevieve were speaking about it, you wouldn't be going for a few months, at least. Eve said something about wanting to train with you a bit longer."

Helene was silent as she tried to wrap her head around what Arthur was saying. Was she ready to go to France? By herself? She supposed she was, logically speaking. She knew how to defend herself, and she knew how to blend into crowds.

No one is ever truly ready for a task of such importance.

Arthur seemed to be reading her mind.

"For what it's worth, you're one of the smartest people I know. You'll do just fine out there in the field."

"Thanks," she mumbled in response. "What should I do in the meantime?"

"While I know Eve doesn't want you leaving yet, the final decision is Wilheim's. Make sure you have a bag packed, just in case he changes his mind."

Helene nodded silently. She didn't know what one took with them on a covert operation into a foreign country. She supposed she'd have to make an educated guess. Upon seeing her consent, Arthur turned to the gangway, seemingly having no intention of overstaying his welcome. He stopped as his feet hit the dock boards, calling up to her with another brilliant smile plastered across his face.

"If I don't see you again before I leave, have fun in France!"

She did not give him the pleasure of a verbal response, but she found herself waving at the last second. She hoped he'd be especially careful in Poland. She didn't want to think about what would happen to him if he got caught in the middle of his op.

✳✳✳

After watching Arthur's silhouette disappear into the distance, Helene made her way back down the stairs and into the galley in search of breakfast. Luckily, her mother had a plate of eggs and toast waiting for her. Anna did not mention anything about Helene's early morning visitor, although the smirk on her face told Helene that Margarethe had already gotten to her.

"Hi, Mutti."

"Good morning, darling. Did you have a nice sleep?"

Before Helene could respond, Ingrid came flying into the room, her eyes alight with curiosity. She seemed to be practically bursting at the seams, and Helene marveled at the way Margo must have told anyone she could about her suspicions about Helene's love life.

To her chagrin, that wasn't exactly what Ingrid had in mind.

"Helli is it true? Are you really going to France soon?"

Oh, goodness. Won't this be interesting?

Helene hadn't even thought to make sure she and Arthur were alone on the foredeck when he'd given her the news. She hadn't assumed anyone would think to listen. Obviously, she'd been wrong. Ingrid had eavesdropped rather intently, it seemed, and now not only did she have to find some sort of excuse for her sister, but she had to explain herself to her mother.

How she wished she'd stayed in bed and sent Arthur away.

"Well, Inga," she started hesitantly, "It is true. I'm going to France...on a holiday."

"A holiday?" Ingrid's expression was incredulous, "Is that man going with you?"

"Well—"

"Is he your boyfriend?"

As much as she hated the thought of being romantically paired with Arthur, it was the only lie she could guarantee her family would believe.

"He...is, yes."

"Is he going to be your husband someday?"

Absolutely not.

"I don't know, maybe. Now enough with these questions, go find Kitty. She's playing all by herself, and I'm sure she'd like some company."

That seemed to satisfy Ingrid, and she skipped off as she hummed some tune Helene couldn't remember the name of. Excruciating silence descended on the galley as she waited for what was surely about to be a hellish conversation with her mother. When Anna still hadn't said a word after several minutes, Helene found herself speaking up.

"At this point, I would prefer a lecture to this silence."

Anna's all-knowing gaze finally met her own, and she instantly wished she'd bitten her tongue.

"You shouldn't lie to your sister, you know."

"I didn't," Helene proclaimed as she mustered up the small bit of courage she could find, "I will be going to France. Not yet, but soon."

"But you said that boy was your beau. That's not true, is it?"

"No, but I knew she'd believe it."

"I suspect they'll all believe it."

Several moments passed before Anna continued, moving to wash the dishes as she spoke.

"When I asked you, months ago, if you'd joined a group, you admitted that you were writing pamphlets."

"Yes, because I was."

"It seems you omitted several details in that conversation."

The steely tone in her mother's voice put Helene on edge.

"I'd only written a pamphlet. Nothing else."

"You were also training at the same time, were you not?"

Helene's lack of an answer was enough proof for Anna that she had, in fact, been training at the time.

"I'm worried that you're in over your head with this, Helene," Anna turned, so her back faced the sink, "Writing a pamphlet is one thing, but going to another country for what I presume is an illegal and dangerous reason? I can't help but think this is getting out of hand and out of your character."

The same feeling she'd felt the first time they'd talked about her involvement in the resistance threatened to once again take hold of Helene's insides and squeeze until she burst apart. So what if this was *out of character* for her? So what if it was dangerous? She didn't give a damn about any of that; she wanted to do her part—she wanted to make the monsters running the country pay for what they were doing—what they were creating.

"I don't care if it's illegal or dangerous," she managed to get out through gritted teeth, "I want to make them pay for what they've done."

It was clear who *they* were. How bloodthirsty my girl sounded. Even I'll admit that it didn't sound like the Helene I had come to know, but we all say things we don't fully understand when we're angry.

"Some battles are not yours to fight," Anna replied, "I'm not sure you're thinking straight about this whole thing."

That accusation—one that implied she *hadn't* spent countless nights lying awake overthinking every part of her involvement in Blackthorn—was enough to make Helene lose her grip on the self-control she had left.

"*Not thinking straight*? Are you serious? Of course you are. How could you say that to me, when you know it's not true?"

"All I meant is that I am nervous you don't understand what it is you've signed up for."

"I have a perfectly clear understanding," There were now frustrated tears spotting her vision. She hated the way her mother could make her cry when no one else ever did. "I know what's really going on here. You don't think I should be doing this. You don't like that I joined in the first place."

"Darling—"

"Let me finish, please. You think it's fine for me to think whatever I want, but now that I'm acting on those thoughts, now that I'm capable and willing to fight, you don't like it. That's it, isn't it?"

"No, Helene. That's not it."

"But it is! That's how it feels, at least. Where is your integrity? You have all of these thoughts, too! I know you feel the same way I do about Hitler, about *everything*! But you never do anything to change the things you don't like! What kind of life is that? How can you look at the injustice in the world and not do something about it?"

"Resistance means so much more than killing the enemy, does it not?"

In the space where there had been many words a moment previous, there was now a void in which Helene found herself lost in. Her mother continued in a tone much softer than Helene expected after she herself had spoken so harshly.

"I am not made of knives and explosives, Helene. That's not who I am. I think war turns people evil."

"But surely, there is courage in choosing to fight a war," Helene sputtered, "It is brave."

"Yes, of course it's brave to walk through a minefield, and it's brave to hold a gun in your hand and know you will shoot it if you must. But when you make the conscious choice to help the victim rather than defeat the enemy? That is braver. That is choosing life over death. That is resistance. It is the only way love wins, when it's all said and done."

Aphrodite told me once that Anna could easily run an entire kingdom on her own if she so desired. I never completely understood why until that moment. I watched with a rare tenderness in my heart as Helene struggled to grasp the weight of her mother's words.

"So, are you going to tell me I can't go to France, then? Because I'm going to help in defeating the enemy?"

"No, you will go to France. I cannot imagine anything I say would stop you. But please, my darling, don't forget why you chose to resist in the first place. At the end of the day, it's not because you hate the Führer, and it's not because you want to make anyone pay for their sins, either. I have seen the desire to help others burning inside of you since you were small, Helene. Fuel that fire. Stoke those flames until they threaten to devour you whole. When you burn for others, you burn for love."

I wish Aphrodite could have heard her say that. She would've been so proud.

In the quiet moments that followed, it became clear to both Anna and Helene that the conversation was as good as over. There wasn't anything else to be said, was there? Because Anna was right— Helene had allowed other people's actions to, in an almost invisible way, dictate her own. She'd very nearly let herself get caught up in all the horrible rhetoric behind Hitler's campaign and then the campaigns against him in turn.

Wasn't that what she hated the most about the way the people around her—neighbors, classmates—acted towards Hitler's ideas? Wasn't it sad they way they all blindly agreed to hate things without any desire to acknowledge and support the good things? This wasn't about hurting people. It was about helping them. Killing someone, even if out of necessity, wasn't something to brag about, even if that person was horrible on all accounts. She wouldn't be happy if she found herself in a situation where the only way out was to kill or be killed. Had she truly thought she would be?

Shame consumed her as she stood facing her mother—her smart, thoughtful mother. Her words allowed Helene to think about a moment years ago when Anna had saved a book from a bonfire. She'd been so curious about that book, and when her mother had given it to her after sheltering it from the flames? She'd read the whole thing before immediately going back to the beginning and starting again. She couldn't have been older than fifteen or sixteen years old—but she hadn't forgotten the determination written across Anna's face that night, nor had she forgotten the bravery such a choice must have demanded. Helene knew she couldn't have been thinking about herself in that moment, which only made the act seem braver, in hindsight.

The bravest acts of all are uniquely selfless.
When you burn for others, you burn for love.

✳✳✳

Eve sent her a telegram later, just as Helene knew she would, asking if she like to have tea in her sitting room. This, of course, was code for a training session.

At least, that's what Helene assumed.

Within a minute of arriving at their usual meeting spot, Helene sensed something wasn't quite right. There were no weapons waiting to be handled, and Eve wasn't perched elegantly on top of the desk waiting to give her another lecture. Instead, Helene's dark-haired companion was curled into an armchair reading a book. She looked up when Helene entered the room but made no move to stand or say anything at all.

"Hi," Helene spoke warmly, "What shall we be training with today?"

There was a weariness in Eve's stare as she replied.

"There won't be any training today, I'm afraid. I just...I wanted some company, I suppose. Someone to talk to."

"Oh, alright," Helene was surprised, "I don't suppose you actually have tea?"

"There's some around here somewhere, although I don't have any sugar. There's some old biscuits, too."

"What are you reading?"

Eve held up the cover for Helene to see. *A Tale of Two Cities.*

" 'Tell the Wind and Fire where to stop—' " Helene quoted.

" 'But don't tell me.' " Eve finished.

"I didn't think you were the type to like Dickens."

"Do I dare ask who you thought I did like?"

"Someone unabashed, like Louisa May Alcott or Virginia Woolf. Perhaps Daphne du Maurier."

"I did like *Rebecca* very much."

A hush fell between them as Eve set the book down and sat up in the chair. There seemed to be a thousand thoughts running wild through her head—at least, it seemed that way to Helene. Was she preoccupied? Perhaps the uneasy set of her jaw could be chalked up to fatigue, but likely not. There was obviously something Eve wished to discuss, something that seemed to be bothering her enough to want to speak with Helene face to face. The tension was palpable. It concerned Helene.

Her words were careful once Eve finally decided to speak again, although they weren't anything Helene expected to hear.

"I am considering going to France in your place."

"What?" Confusion quickly spread through Helene as she looked at Eve incredulously, "No, I'm going to France. I'm ready."

A conflicted look passed through Eve's expression.

"It's not about that," she sighed.

"What is it about, then?"

"I don't wish to put you in danger."

Helene scoffed before she could think not to.

"You didn't seem to be thinking too hard about that when you agreed to train me for a mission, Eve."

"That was before."

"Before what?"

"Before...whatever this is between us."

The words were spoken with unusual fragility, in a voice made of glass that threatened to shatter against any sort of pushback. A long stretch of silence endured. In one sense, Helene relished in the knowledge that she wasn't the only one who had recognized the shift in their relationship. It meant she wasn't the only one with feelings she couldn't control. On the other hand, seeing Eve full to the brim with such doubt felt wrong to Helene. There were things she wanted to say, reassurance she desperately wanted to give, but she chose to bite her tongue in favor of letting Eve continue.

It took several long moments before Eve finally shifted her gaze— eyes full of unshed tears that proved rather startling to see. Helene had never seen her cry before.

"Sometimes I wonder if it's worth it," she murmured, almost whimsically, as if lost in her thoughts.

"What? All this?"

"Yes," Eve played anxiously with the ring on her index finger, " Is the gain worth the loss at the end of the day?"

Helene didn't like this kind of talk. She told Eve so.

"This doesn't sound like you."

"Sorry to disappoint."

"Has something happened?"

Another moment of brief silence.

"Did you hear about Lidice?"

Ah, yes. Realization washed over Helene.

"Of course I did."

"An entire village wiped out of existence. Do you know why? Resistance efforts. Hundreds of people executed because of the chance–no proof at all–that someone there had helped the resistance effort in some way. Those two Chekh boys who killed Reinhard Heydrich; they could have easily been two of our operatives."

"But they weren't."

"Wilheim wants to send you into the field. He wants to send Arthur, too. Both of you would be under my direction, and whatever I decided you should do, you'd do."

"I don't see a problem with that; you are more than capable of it."

Eve wrung her hands together and shook her head disbelievingly.

"What if I gave an order that caused something horrible to happen? What if you were killed? What if Hitler decided some small French town would be the next Lidice? What if hundreds more innocent people die because I wanted one Nazi official taken care of? That's not the aim of this—we're supposed to be saving people."

A tear escaped its confinement and made its treacherous way down Eve's face. She wiped it away hastily before hiding her face in her hands, as if she was embarrassed to be showing emotion at all.

Helene wouldn't stand for that.

Cautiously, she closed the gap between them, gently lifting trembling hands away so Helene could rest her own against Eve's cheeks. Touching her like this, however tenderly, made Helene's stomach do summersaults. The feeling didn't stop her from wiping tears away with her thumbs as she endeavored to reassure her friend.

"Hey, listen to me. We are saving people. That's the whole point of this, like you said."

Eve, who at this point had melted into Helene's touch almost involuntarily, answered in a small voice.

"And yet it seems like more people are dying than living."

"Change doesn't happen overnight; it takes time."

Helene continued, now feeling more confident in her words.

"The day I joined, do you remember what you said to me? You asked me why I wanted to join at all."

"You said it was because you hated Hitler."

"I did, and you told me that wasn't a good enough reason. And you know what? You were right, it wasn't. The best kind of resistance doesn't put so much emphasis on hate. That doesn't really do anything but perpetuate more of it in turn. Lidice is the perfect example of that."

"Where are you going with this?"

"Someone very important to me once said that real resistance is composed of small deeds that have a large impact—actions focused on helping the victim more than getting back at the enemy."

"That person sounds very wise."

"I don't know anyone wiser."

She continued, choosing her words carefully.

"When I'm installed in France, my goal won't be to search out and kill every SS officer I find. That wouldn't be practical. My intent will be to uncover information that will help protect innocent people. So don't think about my assignment as a death trap because it's not. The opposite, actually."

"You're helping people keep on living."

"Yes, that's right," Helene couldn't help the smile that snuck across her face, "I'm helping people live. We are helping people— you and I."

Genevieve contemplated for several moments. She must have come to some kind of decisive thought, because she sighed with an air of finality.

"You will be careful, though, right? In France?"

"Of course I will."

"Do you promise me?"

"I promise."

It was then that Helene remembered herself and removed her hands from Eve's face. They didn't move far though, and she smiled as Eve interlocked their fingers.

"I wish we could communicate while you're there."

"You'll just have to be patient, I suppose. It'll make the reunion all the sweeter."

Eve blushed fiercely.

Some imperceptible force caused Helene to bring their foreheads together. A sound not unlike a whimper escaped Eve's lips unbidden as her nose brushed against Helene's ever so gently. The action was so brief–so magical– that later, she would question if it even happened at all.

I hope, by now, that it's rather obvious to you that the unseen force bringing them together was, indeed, me. Sometimes, the wisest thing to do is make one's feelings known.

In the next several moments dozens of thoughts passed between them without either of them speaking at all. It wasn't until several minutes had gone by that Eve endeavored to break their intimate silence.

"How is it," her eyes shone tenderly, "That you say all the right things at all the right times?"

Helene wished she could verbalize what she knew to be true about words–about how to wield them just right, about how to make them shine. But she was much too distracted by the smell of Eve's perfume and the fluttery feeling in her stomach to explain it correctly, so instead, she simply said,

"You'd have to ask my mother; she taught me."

The ghost of a smile flashed across Eve's face.

"I'd like to meet her someday. Your father, too."

"Mmm," Helene intonated, "Perhaps that could be arranged."

"I'm sorry I called you all the way here for this," Eve mumbled, "On a Saturday, too."

"No, it's nothing to be sorry for. I like being around you."

That coaxed Eve's dimples out of hiding.

"I like being around you, too."

Helene stayed for a while after that—her and Eve reading out loud to each other as they sipped on bitter tea and ate stale biscuits. It was heartwarming to watch them interact like that, all soft laughter and gentle touches. I am glad—even after all these years—that they were able to find bright moments hiding in the midst of the darkness that surrounded them. In a way, it felt like looking at what the future could hold once the war ended. It was a picture I wish I could have looked at for longer than I did.

INTERLUDE
Athens, 2022

"It's funny," Amphitrite exclaims, "How Helene is constantly under the impression that Anna could never understand her, when really they're so similar."

"Helene is all the best parts of her mother," Athena replies with a smile.

"What Anna said to her, it was pretty wise, huh?" Apollo surmises, "She's giving you a run for your money, sister."

"She impresses me. Not many do."

"Helene does realize that in helping the victim, she might be forced to kill people, right?" Ares asks, "I mean, there are people in the world who wouldn't hesitate to kill her."

"Right, but those are bad people. Being good is half the battle. Helene will kill if she must, but if she can help it, her efforts moving forward will be sustaining life rather than welcoming death."

"Well then, I am interested to see if she succeeds with those efforts," Ares sneers.

Athena doesn't deem an answer necessary.

ATHENA
November 9th, 1942

I t wasn't until the beginning of November that Helene finally found herself called to France. Since the school term had commenced, she'd been staying at the family apartment in the city with her mother and her siblings. She'd allowed herself to get re-settled into her academic routine—attending classes in the mornings and then meeting Eve to train in the afternoons. She'd written several more pamphlets since her first triumphant one—all of which had stayed up for longer than any of Arthur's. If he wasn't away in Poland, she certainly would have rubbed it in his face. She'd just have to wait to brag until he came back, she supposed.

The notice she'd been anticipating for months came by telephone at four o'clock in the morning. Her mother, who happened to be awake with a fussy Werner, answered the phone herself before waking Helene and dragging her—half-asleep still—to the receiver. She'd hoped it would be Eve on the other end of the call, but it was

Wilheim's deep voice that informed her of her assignment—told her to pack her bags and start moving as soon as possible. She had a train to catch.

There was hardly any fanfare at her departure. She didn't see the point in waking her siblings, and her father was out on the river. She did allow her mother to envelope her in a tight hug—both of their hearts beating much too quickly at the prospect of Helene going to another country on her own. The smell of Anna's freshly washed nightgown threatened to bring tears to Helene's eyes as she attempted to prolong the embrace for as long as she could.

"Just promise me that you'll be careful," Anna whispered against her daughter's hair.

"I will, Mutti. I'll be okay." Her voice sounded shakier than she wanted it to.

"Remember your purpose, my love. It is your greatest strength,"

"I know."

"You remind me so much of her," Anna murmured as she pulled back from their hug.

"Who?"

"Marta. You're named after her."

"Who is she?"

"She was my twin sister. She and my father died in a train wreck just before I found out I was pregnant with you."

"Oh, I...I never knew that."

"You have her smile, and her wit. You would've loved her."

"I'm sorry you had to lose her like that."

"Me too."

Before Helene could respond, her mother planted a long, hard kiss on her forehead.

"I love you," she smiled gently as warm palms cupped Helene's cheeks, "Now go before I decide to lock you in your bedroom so you cannot leave me."

✳✳✳

Thirty minutes later, Helene stood in the nearly empty Altona train station, her passport in one hand and her suitcase in the other. According to Wilheim's very specific directions, she was to board the five o'clock train headed to Geneva. Since Switzerland had chosen to remain a neutral country, Hitler had decreed that German citizens could travel there publicly without worrying about being fined or detained. She wasn't sure why he'd never moved to invade it, but she guessed he must be hiding treasures in the Alps or something preposterous like that.

Ha, if only Helene knew how not-so-preposterous that theory was.

The train ride to Geneva would take twelve hours, much to Helene's chagrin. Once arrived, she was to meet her designated contact in the Swiss station, who would take her by small aircraft into the south of France, called the *zone libre* because the Führer hadn't marched past Bourges.

Helene had no idea what to expect upon her arrival, seeing as she'd never left Germany. Her knowledge of France extended to the books she'd read about it. She'd dreamed for many years about standing in front of the Eiffel Tower or the Arc de Triomphe. She knew this particular trip wouldn't include marveling at either, but she told herself that after this dreadful war finally ended, she'd make a point to travel the whole continent and see every interesting monument there was. Maybe she'd even convince Eve to go with her.

I smiled at the thought of the two of them exploring the world together.

The train screeched up to the platform right on schedule. It reminded Helene of some sort of metal monster, with its roaring engine and sturdy exterior. Since the country–the whole world, really–had switched to electric railway systems, trains felt more powerful to Helene–more capable. She felt a sort of thrill in her chest as she climbed aboard. There were maybe ten other people at most heading to Switzerland with her, and it wasn't hard for her to find a row of seats all for herself.

The conductor, a short and staunch man who smelled of cigarettes and aftershave, came by to check her passport within a minute of her sitting down. His voice sounded sleep-deprived but still stern as he questioned her presence on the train. Helene did her best to keep a calm demeanor as she recited to him the story Wilheim had coached her through.

"What is your purpose for leaving the country, miss?"

"I'm headed to Geneva to meet up with my fiancé, sir."

"Is he a soldier?"

"Yes. Stationed in France, near Dijon. He's just gone on leave and we decided to go on a holiday together. I'm not sure when we'd have another good chance."

She tried her best to look like a smitten girl–meek and oh, so innocent. The expression on her face must have done the trick because the conductor stamped her passport before handing it back to her with a smile that didn't quite reach his eyes. Helene wondered if he knew someone out on the front lines–someone he couldn't meet on a holiday.

"You're all set, Fraulein Reinholdt. I hope you enjoy your time with your beau."

"Thank you, sir."

She let out a long sigh as he moved past her, already addressing the man seated several rows behind her. It was a rather good lie, when she thought about it. He hadn't asked for any soldier's name, but if he did later on, she would give him the name of her brother's best friend. She wasn't sure where he was stationed, but she knew he was serving in the German Army in any case. She wouldn't be staying in Geneva very long anyway. If her predictions were correct, the train would make it to the city by five o'clock that evening. As long as finding her contact went smoothly once she got there, she'd be out of Switzerland within an hour and would make it to the city of Toulouse by seven, maybe eight o'clock. It was all very pragmatic, albeit time-consuming. The thought of all the hours of traveling ahead of her felt utterly exhausting and it hadn't even begun.

As the train pulled out of the station, the steady vibration of the wheels against the rails proved rather lulling, and Helene couldn't seem to help the way her eyelids fluttered shut. After several failed attempts at distracting herself enough to stay awake, she decided a small nap wouldn't hurt. Everything blurred in an agreeable way as she slumped sideways, her suddenly too-heavy head lolling against the window as she finally succumbed to sleep.

✷✷✷

By the time Helene woke up, the darkness had faded, replaced with bright sunlight that made her squint as her eyes opened. Her neck felt stiff, thanks to the way she'd been leaning against the window. She groggily looked around before glancing down at the watch on her wrist. The tiny clock hands informed her it was very nearly nine o'clock–how she'd managed to sleep for four hours straight was beyond her, but she was grateful for the rest. Even harder to believe was the fact that she still had eight more hours of sitting on this bloody train before it reached Geneva. She'd wondered aloud to Eve several weeks ago why she wouldn't be flying straight into France from Hamburg, to which the reply had been that it was much harder to travel inconspicuously by plane. Helene had been skeptical, but Eve had refused to inquire about a switch in transportation. Apparently, she wasn't willing to risk Helene's life before she even started her assignment.

She spent the next hour gazing out the window at the passing scenery. She knew they were still in Germany, but the sights were still so interesting. She'd never been this far south before. There was a part of her that wished she could call up her family and tell them about all the new things she was seeing as she passed them—she was sure her mother would have loved to hear. She chastised herself as a knot formed in her stomach at the thought of Anna—now wasn't the time to be dwelling on things she couldn't control. She was here, racing towards France, and her family was back in Hamburg. There wasn't anything to be done about it. She was happy they were safe at home. She imagined that by this time in the morning, most of her siblings had gone off to school. Kitty and Werner were still too young for school, and while Ingrid had attempted Kindergarten, wearing her hip brace had proved detrimental to the effort. She currently sat somewhere on a long waiting list for a private clinic in the suburbs, and until she could have another surgery, Anna was doing her best to homeschool the girl. Helene felt horrible for Ingrid, especially because she knew how sad and defeated her sister had felt when she'd been forced to stop attending school with the other children. Perhaps she'd be able to find Inga some kind of souvenir from France to bring back with her. Helene knew she'd be positively enamored by it.

Around ten o'clock, a stewardess came around with a dining cart.

"I figured you might be hungry, fraulein," the woman said in an exceedingly pleasant voice. "You were sound asleep when I came around earlier."

"Oh yes, thank you," Helene smiled gently. Her own voice sounded rough from not using it for so long, "I'll have coffee if you have it, and perhaps some fruit."

The apple she was gifted in response proved just filling enough–she was cautious of upsetting her already fluttering stomach with too much food. She hadn't realized how much she needed the coffee until a steaming cup was placed in front of her a few minutes later. She sipped it slowly, letting the wonderful bittersweet taste wake her up. The smell of it all reminded her almost heartachingly of her father. She hated that she hadn't been able to say goodbye to him before she left. She would make it up to him once she returned. When would that be? She had no idea.

The conductor announced a stop in Frankfurt another hour and a half later. Helene presumed that meant some people would be disembarking. It didn't occur to her that new passengers would be boarding as well until a German officer took a seat directly across the aisle from her. After a small moment of white-hot panic followed by several minutes of forcing herself to calm down, she pulled her journal out of her purse with the intent to write for a bit. It proved to be a wonderful distraction, and she let herself get lost in composing her thoughts for a while.

They passed through Stuttgart in another two hours, and Helene deduced there were roughly four more hours left before they arrived in Geneva. The land had started to change significantly– she could see vineyards sprawling across the hills beyond the city, and if she squinted, she could make out mountainous terrain in the distance. She remembered from a map of Europe she and Eve had studied that Geneva was nestled between France's eastern border and the Swiss Alps. She'd studied the mountain range in school, and a part of her felt dismayed that the sun would be already below the horizon by the time she arrived. She would have loved to see them.

She had planned to read for a good portion of the ride, but with an officer sitting so close to her, Helene wasn't sure if she should. She'd grabbed the closest books to her when she'd packed everything up this morning, not even looking to see what titles they were at the time. Now, she saw that she'd picked *Orlando* by Virginia Woolf and *The Hobbit* by Tolkien. Both were surely considered offensive and possibly even heretical by the government, but she'd seen the official list of banned writers Hitler had created, and she knew that while Tolkien was certainly on it, Woolf was not.

Even I am unsure how Woolf stayed off that list. She was on another list of Hitler's, though, and a much more sinister one at that. Make no mistake, Adolf hated Virginia.

Helene settled on *Orlando*, seeing as it had a dust jacket that could be removed, ensuring the title and author were not present on the cover if the officer were to glance over. Luckily for her, the man seemed to be distracted by the newspaper.

Did she expect to read for the rest of the ride? Well, no, considering there were four hours left. But of course, she did read for all of that time. In fact, she finished over half the book, which only left her one more (plus the second half of the current read) for the extent of her stay in France. She'd have to find a bookstore if she planned to stay for longer than a week.

As the train pulled into the Gare de Genève in the center of the city, Helene looked out the window with analytical eyes. According to the instructions told to her before she left, a Blackthorn contact would be waiting for her next to the ticket stand in the main lobby of the station. He would be holding a sign with Helene's alias written across it (she'd picked the name Jeanne), and wearing a watch on his left wrist. As she approached him, she had a very specific phrase to say in greeting that would let him know who she was.

She ran through the directions in her head several times as she and the other passengers stepped off the train and onto the bustling platform. She couldn't help feeling like she stood out like a sore thumb, even though she knew she more than likely didn't. She'd purposely chosen nondescript clothes to wear throughout the entire assignment, hoping to direct as little attention to herself as possible. She lost count of the number of people she accidentally bumped into as she made her way towards the ticket stand, and she exhaled a sigh of relief when she made it past the platform and the crowd thinned out enough for her to see her surroundings clearer. As she scanned the sights in front of her, she noticed the large poster with "Billets" written in bright letters across it. Her heart suddenly started beating too fast as her eyes met those of a middle-aged man standing under the sign. He looked to be in his 30s–with a medium build and dark hair. The presence of a watch on his wrist, along with the handwritten sign featuring the name pretending to be her own confirmed this man was, in fact, the one she was looking for. She approached him at a pace that suggested purpose, but wasn't rushed. As she closed the distance between them, she cleared her throat.

"*Aujourd'hui c'est une belle journée, n'est ce pas monsieur?* It's a lovely day, don't you think?" She questioned in shaky French.

The man regarded her placidly.

"*Oui,*" came the short reply. She continued.

"I do fear a storm may be coming through the mountains, though."

At the sound of the agreed-upon phrase, the man cracked a smile in her direction and abruptly switched to fluent German.

"That has yet to be seen, I suppose," he extended a hand in her direction, "My name is Fabien. You must be Helene, or would you prefer I call you by your alias?"

"Helene is fine." she answered, "It's nice to meet you."

"The pleasure is mine. I have the plane waiting just a short car ride away to take us into France," he paused for a moment, contemplating something, "Are you hungry after such a long ride? We can stop for food if needed."

The offer proved very tempting, and after a quick stop at a boulangerie next to the station, Helene and her newfound companion stepped into a taxi. Fabien provided the driver with directions, and after several minutes of awkward silence, they arrived at a small airfield. Helene could see their plane in the near distance and also noted the absence of any other aircraft. Was that normal? Fabien seemed to be reading her thoughts as he assuaged her concern.

"This airfield was used quite extensively years ago, but has fallen out of favor ever since the construction of a newer, bigger one," he explained, "It is still used on occasion in the summer months."

"Won't it seem rather odd that we're using it then? Since it's November?"

"I'm not worried," Fabien shrugged, "Switzerland is a neutral country. The bad guys have their hands full in other, more important places—one of which we're about to fly into. To focus on what goes on in a neutral place? It's a waste of their resources and their time."

"I suppose that makes sense."

As the two of them exited the taxi, Fabien spoke to the driver once again before tipping him handsomely. She wondered if they'd just bought his silence. She didn't dwell on it long, due to the way the sight of the plane fluttered her stomach. She'd never flown in a plane before, and while a part of her wanted desperately to know what the experience was like, she was also cognizant of the anxiety that had settled in her stomach like lead. She was thankful it was dark outside already, and she wouldn't be able to see everything on the ground from so high in the air.

She crawled into the small cockpit next to Fabien, hesitantly taking the headset in his outstretched hand while simultaneously marveling at all the buttons and switches in front of her. Fabien chuckled at her fascination.

"Don't be alarmed, you won't have to touch any of those. Just sit back and relax; I'll take care of the flying part."

And take care of it, he did. Helene was amazed at how well he could maneuver such a large vehicle, although she presumed he'd probably done this before, perhaps many times. She wasn't prepared for the feeling of taking off—she heard a faint snort of amusement from her companion as she stifled a gasp and clutched the armrest as if her life depended on it. Luckily, once they were in the air the ride became much more pleasant, albeit loud.

The entire flight took around an hour. Helene tried her best to relax, but the occasional turbulence from the wind made sure she didn't even get the chance to doze, and once they began their descent into the darkness of the French countryside, the feeling of her stomach bottoming out forced any sort of calm thought out of her brain very quickly.

The plane connected with the ground hard and fast, propelling both Helene and Fabien forward and then back again as it rolled across the bumpy terrain. Once they'd come to a complete stop, Fabien turned to Helene.

"Are you alright? I'm sorry about the rough landing; it tends to happen when there isn't a runway to make things smoother."

"I'm okay," she replied. It wasn't a complete lie, "Where are we, exactly?"

"We're in a field surrounded by a small wooded area just outside the city limits."

"So, once you hand me off to the next contact, he or she will take me into Toulouse?"

"By car, yes. He should be waiting not too far from here. I'll walk you."

So the two of them exited the plane. Helene tried to be as quiet and efficient as possible, although her legs felt somewhat shaky. Fabien's compass directed them north, and they began walking in comfortable silence towards the meeting place. Fabien offered to carry Helene's belongings, but she remembered Eve telling her to always carry her own things as a precaution, so she politely declined the offer. She didn't mind the slight weight anyway.t helped in distracting her from the anxious thoughts in her head.

Fabien must have planned the route out weeks in advance, because even in the dark, he didn't need any kind of map, although he did regard the compass several times to make sure they were still on track. Eventually, a small car came into view. Helene felt relief flood through her. All she wanted was to make it to her destination.

As they moved closer, though, something in the air shifted.

Maybe it was actually something within Helene that shifted, but either way the surroundings very suddenly felt off. She couldn't seem to pinpoint why exactly, but a warning bell began chiming through her mind over and over and over.

That was me. I was the warning bell. Something was very much afoot.

Fabien noticed something physically wrong before she did, because his arm came out in front of her to halt her step. She risked a glance in his direction, only to find him staring into the near distance with a look of alarm in his expression. Upon following his line of sight, Helene felt bile in her throat immediately.

A man lay very still on the ground a few feet from the car with a bullet hole in the middle of his forehead.

The next several moments happened very quickly. A rustling sound came from behind them, and before either of them could react, a massive weight barreled straight into Helene. The force knocked her completely off her feet, and before a scream could make its way out of her mouth, she'd been thrown to the ground. Her head collided hard with the forest floor, and her ears started ringing as she tasted dirt in her mouth. The person—because it was obvious to Helene by this point that she'd been ambushed by a person—pinned her to the ground with a strength that far exceeded her own. She tried to struggle free, which turned out to be the wrong thing to do. Her assailant responded by slamming his body into her once again, this time landing directly on her arm. There was a sickening snap followed immediately by a kind of pain Helene had never felt before. It made her lightheaded, and the bile already stuck in her throat proceeded to exit her mouth in violent, breathless heaves. Despite this, she realized that staying on the ground would very likely mean the end of her life. Her mind flashed back to the training session with Eve when they'd simulated an attack just like this one, and she moved to recreate the movements the second she felt her assailant's weight shift off of her. She heard herself scream in pain as she twisted around to attack–poised to use her legs to kick a weapon out of her attacker's grip to at least make it an even fight. There was a split second where her eyes appraised the figure standing over her with a gun pointed at her skull before there were suddenly two short bursts of sound in rapid succession. She saw a flash of panic in the man's eyes, but the light extinguished just as fast as it came, and Helene watched as he fell sideways next to her, three bullets lodged deep in his chest. She snapped her gaze upwards to find Fabien kneeling not even a foot away from her, his own gun still in his right hand.

They stared at each other for a small eternity, chests heaving, until Helene's senses returned to her. Pain bloomed through her entire upper body once again as she tried to grapple with what had just occurred moments ago. The man lying dead next to her wore khaki pants, a buttoned shirt, and a dark blue jacket. A badge of some kind gleamed in the moonlight from his belt. She didn't have the slightest clue what to make of it, and before she could endeavor to wrap her head around it further, Fabien was crouched above her.

"Helene, look at me," she felt his palms against her face, "Are you alright?"

"I'm...I'm okay, I think," she replied through gritted teeth.

"You're injured," he observed with concern, "I saw you hit your head pretty hard."

"My arm..." The pain prevented her from finishing her thought for a moment, "I think it's broken. I heard it snap."

"Let me help you sit up."

She acquiesced as Fabien dragged her to the nearest tree and sat her upright with her back against the trunk. He inspected her head and her arm in silence.

"The arm is most certainly broken, and you probably have a concussion as well. Do you have a headache?"

"Yes, a horrible one."

Before he could say anything, she continued.

"Who was that man? He had a badge."

Fabien glanced back at the dead figure before responding.

"Most likely a member of the French police. They are often sent to intercept resistance agents if news of their whereabouts is leaked."

"But aren't we in the *zone libre*? I didn't think Hitler had marched this far yet."

"He hasn't, but he brokered an alliance with Pétain–the leader of Vichy France–that still ensures Jews are persecuted here, and any resistance efforts that can be averted, are."

"How convenient."

"Mm yes, very," Fabien mumbled sarcastically, "Come, we must keep moving. I know you are in pain, but there isn't much that can be done until you are safely at your destination."

"I don't know where I'm going."

"No worries, I will accompany you as far as I can in the car. It will be a short journey after that, but you'll be okay."

Helene was very unsure she would, in fact, be anywhere close to okay. But, she allowed Fabien to help her stand, and then help her into the front seat of the little car. She tried her best not to think too hard about the pain radiating in waves from her arm, or the numbness slowly spreading across her forehead as Fabien drove towards the faint collection of lights in the distance. She was thankful he didn't use the headlights. She was sure they would have made her headache worse and would have possibly drawn unwanted attention. She found herself thankful that Eve wasn't with her— even though she would have loved her company at the moment. A part of her was embarrassed that she'd been slightly compromised before the assignment had officially commenced. Luckily for her, the only person who would've been able to rat her out was lying on the ground dead.

✳✳✳

Fabien kept his word and drove her into Toulouse's city limits. He apologized profusely for not being able to drive her directly to the address on the slip of paper in her hand, but it would be safer if she made the rest of the journey by herself, injured or not. He provided her with vague directions that she forgot the second they entered her brain, and then drove off the way they'd come. Helene knew she'd never see him again.

If she'd had an arm that worked and a head that wasn't concussed, she would have willingly walked the distance between her and the residence listed on the note in her hand. But upon reflection, she knew she wouldn't be able to do it—not in a cold city she was unfamiliar with, and certainly not injured in the dark.

So, after some internal debate, she hailed a cab.

The streets of Toulouse were alive with people, seeing as it wasn't even seven o'clock yet. It did not take long at all before she'd caught the attention of a taxi driver. As the car pulled up to the curb, she concocted a false story to explain her haggard appearance. It was one she knew the driver would probably buy.

Sure enough, he did.

"I hate to be rude mademoiselle," he said through the cigar hanging off his lips, "But you don't look too good."

"I'm sorry monsieur, it's just that I'm trying to get away," she seamlessly lied.

"Away? From who?"

"My beau, he has an awful temper."

The man's eyes widened in understanding.

"He hurt you?"

Helene didn't verbally reply, only nodded her head quickly as if it was too painful to say it out loud. It was enough. The man sighed and shook his head.

"You can't even find a decent man around here nowadays," he turned his gaze back to the road ahead of him, "Where do you need to go? I'll get you there without a problem."

"27 Rue de Chaussas, monsieur. Thank you."

He did not speak to her for the duration of the ride, to Helene's immense pleasure. Just the sound of his voice earlier had been too much–her head still felt like it might explode at any given moment. She wanted nothing more than to sleep for three days straight, and she found herself pinching the skin of her thigh to keep from closing her eyes.

Eventually, the cab stopped in front of a house, and it certainly wasn't just any house. It was quite large, with arches flanking the entryway and a gate stationed against the sidewalk. Helene tried to hand the cab driver money as she slid out the door, but he staunchly refused it–saying she should use her money to get away from her abusive partner. She watched him as he drove back down the street, not taking her eyes off the car until it had passed out of sight.

She then turned to the home in front of her.

She didn't know if she'd ever felt so exhausted in her life. Everything felt slightly hazy and dream-like as if there was a possibility none of her surroundings were real. She knew it was just her mind trying to shut itself down, and the knowledge made her open the gate and make her way, trembling, up a stone pathway to the front door.

The door in question, Helene saw upon reaching it, was made of a dark and heavy wood. Whoever lived here was surely rich to be able to afford such a beautiful door of all things. She mustered up the very little strength she had left to rap the knuckles of her good arm against the wood as assertively as she could in the distinct pattern Eve had coached her through. One knock, a brief pause, and then two more knocks in rapid succession.

Her arrival must surely have been anticipated, because the door flew open to reveal a bespeckled man with very little hair and a kind demeanor about him. His eyes seemed very gentle, even as they nearly doubled in size upon inspection of Helene's appearance. He seemed very hesitant as he spoke in soft French to her.

"Vous êtes l'agent de résistance? The woman sent from Germany to help us?"

She couldn't bring herself to form words any longer but managed to nod in confirmation.

"You are hurt."

Another nod, followed by a weak gesture towards first her arm, and then her forehead.

"Come, I am a doctor."

He moved to let her through the doorway and she began moving towards him in turn, but it seemed her body had had quite enough movement for the day—because she managed to take one incredibly shaky step and then not a single one more. She was helpless to the way her legs buckled as her vision went completely black. She felt the man catch her before she hit the ground, and she thought she might have heard him shout something in French, but before she could think about what it could possibly mean, everything went silent, and she slipped out of consciousness completely.

ATHENA
November 10th-11th, 1942

The sound of traffic slowly pulled Helene out of her deep sleep much, much later. Her eyelids felt too heavy as she opened them reluctantly, moving into a sort of groggy, half-awake state. Sunlight filtered prettily through a window to her left—indicating that she'd more than likely slept through last evening and then the entire night, too. She regarded her surroundings warily. She'd been laid out across a bed, her body neatly tucked under a rose-colored quilt. Her attention turned to the makeshift sling wrapped around her broken arm. She vaguely recalled the man who she'd met briefly last night, mentioning he was a doctor. He must have patched her up. Her other arm dangled off the edge of the bed, her fingers still suspended limply in mid-air. She could see dirt and blood stained across her palms as she curled and then uncurled each finger. She was happy to see all of them worked how they were supposed to.

She then remembered the real reason for her less-than-graceful black out the night before: the concussion. She wondered if her head had been bleeding when she'd arrived—she hadn't thought about it before. She gingerly moved her hand upwards towards her hairline, and felt the thin cotton of gauze wrapped completely around her head. The saliva trailing lazily down her cheek led to the discovery that she'd been drooling copiously onto the pillow. The small, corked bottle of liquid on the nightstand suggested someone had poured medicine down her throat at some point during the night.

After several minutes of working herself up to the task, she got out of bed carefully. There were several bruises across her stomach that she hadn't noticed the night before, but she seemed to be fine otherwise. She found a small bathroom in the hallway just next to her bedroom, and she relieved herself before washing her face. Her reflection in the mirror looked like another human being altogether—surely that couldn't be her, with such matted hair, dried blood on her temple, and dark circles under her eyes. Luckily, she found a hairbrush waiting on the counter and spent the next several moments detangling her curls before taking a washcloth and carefully dabbing at the wound on her head.

A clock hanging in the hallway chimed loudly as she exited the bathroom, signaling the passing of the hour. It was now nine o'clock in the morning, which meant she'd slept for over fourteen hours. Her stomach groaned in hunger at the thought. She returned to the bedroom she'd come from to find her bag placed neatly on the window seat, all of her belongings folded neatly just as she'd packed them. She fished out a gray sweater and blue cotton skirt, changing out of the clothes she'd now been wearing for almost a day and a half straight.

With clean clothes on, Helene felt much more refreshed, and she decided it was time to go in search of the man who had so kindly taken care of her all night. She found the staircase leading downstairs easily and upon her arrival on the first floor of the house, she was shocked by its size. A well-to-do family certainly lived here. She paused at the landing, not quite sure where to go, when an unexpected voice from behind made her jump.

"*Tu es l'espionne?* Are you the spy? Papa said I wasn't allowed to bother you, but I've never met a spy before."

A flash of movement in Helene's peripheral line of sight became a small, fire-haired girl standing directly in front of her. Helene hadn't realized there were children living at this residence.

"*Non*, I am not a spy," Helene blurted, "And you aren't bothering me, so there's nothing to worry about."

The girl's bright eyes crinkled at the edges as she smiled in response.

"I don't think you'd be here right now if you weren't a spy," the girl explained mischievously, "But we don't have to talk about it if you don't want to."

I liked this pint-sized hurricane immediately.

"Does your arm hurt?" the girl continued before Helene could. Papa said he fixed it."

"I think he did; it doesn't hurt at the moment."

A look of pride flashed across the child's face.

"When I grow up, I'm going to be a doctor just like he is."

"I'm sure you will," Helene replied, "Do you know where your papa is now?"

"Probably in the kitchen, I'll take you there."

With that, the girl was off, skipping down the hallway as she hummed to herself. She reminded Helene of her sisters, which sent a pang to her heart. She followed her tiny new acquaintance through the house until they reached the kitchen—a sunny room that smelled like breakfast. The man from the night before sat at the table reading the newspaper and sipping a cup of coffee. He glanced up somewhat warily as his daughter bounded into the room like a bull in a china shop.

"Ma chérie, please slow down," he gently reprimanded, "I do not want you breaking anything, including yourself."

"But Papa, she's awake! The spy is awake, and she's so pretty and nice! You didn't tell me that before."

The man's gaze moved to appraise Helene's form standing in the doorway, his expression now shifting to one of immense relief. He addressed her with kindness.

"I am glad to see you awake mademoiselle," he smiled, "Hopefully you're feeling better than you were last night? That arm of yours is badly broken."

"Yes monsieur," she replied shyly, "I am grateful for your help. The circumstances that led to my arm breaking were...unexpected."

"I can imagine," the doctor's eyes darkened slightly, "These are dangerous times."

He looked off into the distance briefly, as if he was remembering something. He swung his gaze back to Helene as his daughter ran back out of the room in a whirlwind of movement.

"Please, sit down," he gestured to the chair next to his own. "I haven't even introduced myself properly yet. I am Henri Cadieux. Pleased to meet you."

"The pleasure is mine," she said as she slowly lowered herself into the seat, "I'm Helene."

"Would you like coffee, Helene? I stocked up on loads of it last year, and I like to make it for visitors. The chicory substitute lacks in its effect."

"That would be wonderful, thank you."

As he poured the steaming liquid into a mug for her, the doctor kept up the conversation.

"So, I see you've met my daughter, Théa. I am sorry for her theatrics."

"Oh no, she seems wonderful. She reminds me of my little sister."

"She's a good girl,"

"How old is she?"

"She turned seven in June."

Silence stretched between the two of them as Henri moved towards the counter. He placed a small plate with bread and jam in front of Helene when he sat back down.

"*Une tartine pour vous.* A former patient of mine runs a farm in the country, and he sends me jam through the post...although I am not sure how much longer he'll be able to keep that up. Everything seems to be illegal these days."

"Even jam?"

"Up in the occupied territory, everyone's been forced into rationing. It doesn't bode well for us farther south."

Helene chose not to respond, mostly because they were veering into a subject she didn't like thinking about. She'd always worried about food too much back at home–if there was enough to feed all of them, what would happen if they ran out of it. She hated the idea of eating this jam when Théa could be eating it instead, but she didn't want to be rude, either. Sweetness filled her senses as she took a hesitant bite. Henri stared out the window, seemingly preoccupied with something, as she ate quietly. She wondered if he often got lost in his thoughts.

If you were forced to live the kind of uncertain life he does, you would retreat inward to get away from it all sometimes, too.

The reminder from me pushed Helene onto matters of business.

"Monsieur Cadieux, my superiors...they've told me some things about why I'm here, but not everything," she took a small sip of coffee before continuing, "I'd love it if you could tell me."

"Oh yes, of course," he shifted to face her fully, "and please, call me Henri."

"You must call me Helene, then."

"If you wish. Now, where to begin? You are aware that we are Jewish, yes?"

"I am."

Henri's expression turned haggard as he sighed and continued.

"It is the reason I am unemployed, and have been for over a year. I was a doctor here in Toulouse for a long time. I had a good patient base and a satisfactory reputation. None of that mattered in the end."

Helene refrained from comment. There wasn't anything she could say that felt worthy, when Henri's livelihood had been stripped from him so basely. It felt horrible. It felt despicable. This was supposed to be the free part of France, the *zone libre*, and yet Pétain had agreed to be a Nazi puppet and take away people's freedom because Hitler wanted him to.

"The point is that my religious beliefs put a target on my back, on my family's back," he glanced towards the hallway with regret in his eyes, "There are very few of us living here anymore, I have avoided being arrested successfully, but now I have somehow gotten myself too far into a mess I would very much like to be out of. That is why I was in contact with the *Blagnac Résistance*, who contacted your superiors."

"Right, and what is this mess, exactly?"

"As I mentioned, over a year ago, I and several of my colleagues lost our jobs due to our lifestyles," Henri cleared his throat, "One of these colleagues, a friend of many years, took up the very illegal hobby of intercepting code in his newfound free time. Messages from the Allies."

Helene felt a thrill in her chest.

"They approached him to do this?" she inquired.

"Yes," came the quick reply, "He was British-born, you see, but had been living in Toulouse for a while. They must have thought he'd be the perfect candidate for the job. They weren't wrong, either. He was a great asset…until he wasn't anymore."

"What do you mean? What happened?"

"I have no idea how, but the government discovered that he'd been communicating with Britain for months, and a warrant for his arrest went out. I received a call from him maybe an hour before they came for him, begging me to take his coding machine and all the messages so the police wouldn't find it and the operation wouldn't be for nothing."

"And did you? Take it, I mean."

"I did, although I don't know why exactly. I think there was a part of me—there still is a part of me—that wanted to not only honor my friend, but honor the work he'd chosen to do."

"What he did, what you did, was very brave. Not many people would have agreed to do such a thing."

"As hard as this life can be sometimes, I recognized that I was still in a position where I could choose how I went about living it," Henri took a shaky breath, "That reminded me of all the Jewish people across the continent who had that choice completely stripped from them. I wanted to do it for them."

"I sense a misgiving."

"I've been sending and receiving code through the portable Typex machine for months now, but there have been rumors floating around that have pushed me to pass on the job to the resistance."

"Tell me about these rumors, Henri."

"There is talk that Hitler plans to take the south of France as soon as possible."

"But he signed an agreement, did he not?"

"Do you think Hitler cares about agreements? If he wants something, he takes it."

Helene couldn't argue with that.

"If the Nazi Occupation moved south," continued Henri, "My primary focus would have to be on my child's safety, even more so than it already is. I cannot, in good faith, keep an illegal coding machine in my home while my daughter lives in it. If it was ever found, they'd surely kill me. What would happen to my girl then? She already doesn't have a mother. I don't want her to live without me, either."

It hurt me deeply to know that most people could never bring themselves to believe just how far Hitler was willing to go to get what he wanted. Henri Cadieux believed he would die if he was caught doing something illegal. He would soon find out that for people like him, it wasn't a matter of criminal behavior. In Hitler's world, he could be sentenced to death for no reason at all. Worse, he believed the government would spare his daughter because of her age. He couldn't imagine that someone would kill a child for something out of her control–would potentially put a little girl to death because of a single word on her identification card.

Helene, of course, knew the truth of the matter. She understood the significance of Hitler moving south even clearer than Henri did. She thought again about her sister Ingrid–about all of her siblings back home–and vowed that as long as she was alive on this earth, she wouldn't let Hitler take Théa Cadieux away.

"These rumors are still only rumors," she said assuredly, as she tried to assuage the man's fears. "We will not think about such things unless we need to. Where is the Typex machine now?"

"Hidden in the floorboards of my bedroom. When I contacted the Blagnac people, they told me they'd spoken with your organization, Blackthorn, about taking the machine. Apparently, you will be able to make the best use of it from within Germany."

Helene's curiosity peaked at the same time my own did.

"Did they say in what ways, specifically?"

"They did not mention anything, but I might have a good example," Henri took a moment to clean his glasses, "One of the encoded messages I received last week mentioned the construction of a massive heavy water plant somewhere in rural Germany. You, of course, know why Hitler requires heavy water."

"Atomic weapons manufacturing."

"Correct. The water plays a vital role in creating weapons-grade plutonium out of uranium."

"Sounds like something Hitler of all people should not be allowed access to."

"You could say that. I would assume that if Blackthorn had that kind of information at their disposal, they could do any number of things to ensure the plant did not produce the heavy water needed for the creation of such weapons."

Henri's words implied that Blackthorn agents could destroy the power plant completely if they knew its location and size. Eve was going to have a heyday. Helene could already imagine her dressed in all black, placing explosives around the plant and then laughing as she watched it blow to pieces from a safe distance.

"I suppose then," Helene surmised, "That the Typex would be especially helpful to Blackthorn's efforts. I'll take it back with me. That way, you won't have to worry about getting caught with it."

"Thank you," Henri's eyes flooded with relief. "Speaking as a doctor, I would advise you to wait at least a day or two more before traveling again. In the meantime, my home is open to you until you are well enough."

Helene expressed her gratitude for the invitation sincerely. She would've been lying if she told him she felt well enough to make the journey back to Germany so soon—especially now that the trip would have to involve the illegal possession of an enemy country's coding machine.

She spent the remainder of the day getting to know the two occupants of 27 Rue de Chaussas. Although Théa was only seven years old, she had a kind of intelligence about her that Helene found she loved. She was incredibly precocious, and Helene loved the way Henri always answered every insistent question with thoughtfulness and patience. It was clear that father and daughter were very close—they sometimes even finished each other's sentences.

When she wasn't visiting, Helene occupied herself with finishing *Orlando*, although she took a nap in the middle of the endeavor. The medicine Henri had insisted she take left her feeling drowsy.

Supper was another rationed affair, and Helene felt incredibly guilty for taking food away from Henri and Théa, even though the doctor told her not to concern herself with it. Théa didn't seem to realize she had less food on her plate than usual—she was so busy talking Helene's ears off that when she did remember to take a bite, she shoved it into her mouth and chewed it in record time so she could continue her thought.

Little Théa made me smile. I could recall Aphrodite's stories from visiting the Reinholdt family when Helene was a child, and if my memory serves me correctly, Helene used to talk straight through supper, too—although with so many other children present at the table, it was harder for her parents to be as patient as Henri when it came to giving their daughter the attention she sought. As she grew older, Helene found it better to be quiet than to have her thoughts ignored or dismissed. Of course, she knew just as Aphrodite and I did that Anna and Otto never purposely ignored her, nor did they scorn her curiosity. As my sister has mentioned previously, Anna had every intention of answering every question Helene would ever have, back when she was a small girl. Helene's parents became, put simply, exhausted and distracted. It is a somewhat inevitable part of destiny for the eldest child of many siblings, especially an eldest daughter.

But alas, I digress.

Helene retired to her bedroom for the night earlier than she usually would have back home, but her headache had returned, and she hoped that another good night's sleep would somehow help it heal faster. As she turned off the bedside lamp and got comfortable under the pink quilt once more, she decided she would leave the next day. Henri had mentioned it would not be hard to find a member of the French Resistance to fly her back to Geneva or possibly even all the way to Hamburg. A train ride was not in the cards for the return trip, considering the cargo she'd be towing along with her. Either way, she felt good about it all—she was confident she'd be able to successfully get the Typex back into Germany and then into Eve's arms. Perhaps the coding machine wouldn't be the only thing in Eve's arms, if Helene had her way.

I watched Helene as she drifted off, dreaming about seeing Eve and her family soon. I wish I could've told her the truth of it—that she wouldn't be going home the next day, or the day after that, or even the day after that.

Something sinister was on the horizon, no pun intended.

✳✳✳

The next morning proved much less sunny than the day before, and it seemed to Helene that the overcast skies had painted the entire city gray. The locals often referred to Toulouse as *La Ville Rose* thanks to the way the sun bounced off the pinkish bricks that made up the entire city—at the right time of day, everything glowed. When Helene experienced it the night previous, she had stood in the middle of the street in awe of such a magical phenomenon. The city seemed alive as if the sun's rays had breathed light into the city until it came to life.

One of Apollo's many masterpieces, and one of my favorites.

Today felt very different. The gray seemed to permeate into the landscape outside Helene's window—there was a lack of vibrancy, a lack of love and life, that threw her off balance. She hastily threw her robe on and made her way downstairs. It was eerily quiet—no excited sounds from Théa and no clanking of pots or pans to indicate either member of the Cadieux family were going about business like normal.

That's because nothing about this day is normal. Toulouse will not be normal again for some time. Not after what has occurred.

Helene found the kitchen empty and so journeyed to the living room. Upon arriving, she found Henri sitting in an armchair next to the fire. There was a sense of melancholy that greeted Helene upon entering the room completely, and she felt it settle in her bones like lead as she met Henri's gaze. She found many emotions reflected in his eyes, but the one that shined the brightest was fear. It radiated off of him. Something was very wrong. Her voice sounded more afraid than she wanted it to as she sent an obvious question in his direction.

"What is it, what's happened?"

Henri did not answer her for a long moment. When he finally did, his hands shook at his own words.

"The Germans have crossed the demarcation line," he whispered. "They now have control of France in its entirety. They have control of Toulouse."

The confession forced Helene onto the settee opposite him, as a white-hot feeling of panic flooded her body from head to toe. The implications of Henri's words made her dizzy.

"How? They had no reason to."

"Oh, but they did," Henri conceded, "The Allies apparently took North Africa a few days ago. Hitler has called this march into the south a form of retribution, although he would've eventually taken it without the Allies' prompting. This was inevitable."

Silence descended between them as Helene processed what he'd said. Eventually, she found her voice again.

"Where is Théa?"

"In her bedroom," Henri gestured down the hallway before running his hands through his hair, "I did not tell her what happened, but she knows I am upset. I cannot keep it from her for long."

"What is your plan?"

"I do not have one," he huffed out a laugh that didn't reach his eyes, "Surely, though, you should leave now—while you still can."

She knew he was right. She should jump up, collect her things, and escape. But she found herself rooted to her seat. She couldn't go.

She *wouldn't* go. Not when she knew what Hitler's invasion meant. Henri might think that as long as he kept his mouth shut, the Nazis would leave him alone. Helene knew better. She refused to leave if it meant abandoning this man and his daughter–a little girl who could've been her sister. She would stay and help them–help them hide, help them leave.

"I'm not going anywhere," she answered with resolve. "Toulouse is one of the biggest cities in the south. There are surely German officers already within the city limits. It would only rouse suspicion."

"I am sure we could find someone to help you."

"I am afraid the risk might be too great," she persisted, "And I will not leave you to deal with them alone. Let me help you figure out what to do."

The gleam in his eyes shifted slightly at Helene's words–they shone with a little less fear and a little more gratitude.

"It would be foolish to stay, you know?"

A solemn smile flashed across her face at that.

"I'd rather be a fool than a coward, Henri."

My brother Ares would have loved to hear her say that. Sometimes, the foolish act is also the wise one.

"Alright," he acquiesced, "I think the smart thing to do would be to take a trip to the market–see if we can find anything before we're all forced into rations."

"That's a good idea."

"It does not make sense to go all together. You should go and take Théa with you. The fresh air would do her good, and I think you would prove to be a nice distraction for her."

"Are you sure?"

"Yes, quite. It will give me time to make sure paperwork is in order, and everything is how it should be."

Helene decided not to argue with him—he seemed distressed enough. Instead, she excused herself to change. She took a dark green dress out of her luggage and after struggling for a few moments, managed to get it on despite the obstacle of her slinged arm. The question of what she would potentially tell a German officer if asked about her arm flitted through her mind briefly, but she shoved it out as quickly as it came. She didn't have the time to be thinking about that. This was very much a situation that required her to think presently.

After grabbing her brown tweed coat from where it hung on the bedpost, she hastened back downstairs. Henri had Théa dressed and waiting at the bottom of the stairs. She looked more confused than anything. Helene couldn't blame her—a stranger arrived at her house one day, and the next, her father was acting abnormally. Helene wanted to do her best to reassure the girl, especially because she didn't know what they'd encounter at the market. She offered her hand to the child with a warm smile.

"*Bonjour*, Théa. Would you like to take a walk to the market with me?"

"Papa says I must go, but don't worry," There was a glint in her eye as she smirked, "I would've come even if he didn't want me to."

"Of course," Helene's smile widened, "You'll have to lead the way. I'm afraid I'm not as familiar with this place as you are."

"How do you expect to be a good spy if you don't know how to get around?"

"Mmm, very funny. Let's go."

They exited the property and turned right, heading down Rue de Chaussas.

"The market is next to the *Canal du Midi*," Théa explained as she grabbed Helene's hand and swung their arms back and forth between them, "It's only two blocks away."

Helene nodded her assent. She remembered Eve mentioning the Canal during one of their training lectures. A few minutes later, she could confirm that it was indeed beautiful, just as Eve had said it would be. It seemed that the news of German occupation hadn't stopped the citizens of Toulouse from going about their daily business—at least not yet, anyway. Several vendors were stationed along the canal, selling a variety of fruits and vegetables. Helene and Théa made their way to each stand, buying plums, radishes, carrots, apples, and figs.

Théa asked—no, begged—to stop at the *boulangerie* after they finished at the market. Helene was in a hurry to get back to the house, but Henri had been adamant about not telling Théa anything was wrong yet. There was no believable way to explain her desire to hurry back without giving away to the girl that something wasn't quite right. So, she agreed to a stop at the bakery. It would be nice to get some more bread, anyway.

While the area immediately surrounding the canal had been devoid of any sort of unusual activity, the same could not be said for other Toulousain streets. There was a noticeable presence of German officers—two of them—going about their business, although it wasn't clear what that business was. Helene watched them closely as she and Théa moved closer. They seemed to be talking about something urgently—they were huddled close to each other with expressions of grave seriousness. After a few moments, both officers looked up at the address in front of them before approaching the door and knocking. They didn't even wait for a response upon finding it unlocked. Both officers entered the residence, shouting the names of the people who lived there.

Helene could hardly think as she watched one of the officers exit the house with an elderly gentleman holding onto his arm. There was a kind of resignation written on the old man's face, like he'd been waiting for this exact moment and had chosen not to fight it. Where the officer was taking this man, Helene couldn't say for certain, but the sinking feeling in her stomach told her it wouldn't be anywhere good.

Théa, who had been watching the scene unfold in front of her, grabbed Helene's hand once more as her steps slowed significantly in hesitation.

"Miss Helene, who are those men in the uniforms?"

Helene sighed. She refused to lie to the little girl. That wouldn't do her any good, even if she was only seven. She'd apologize to Henri later.

"They are German soldiers. They came from the north in the middle of the night."

"I heard Papa talking about German soldiers once, when I was supposed to be sleeping," Théa confessed, "Why are they here?"

"Do you know who Adolf Hitler is?"

"Oh yes," the girl's eyes widened, "My teachers have talked about him. He's not a very nice man."

"No, he isn't," Helene took a steadying breath, "These soldiers work for him."

"Oh," Helene could see the gears in Théa's brain working hard to understand the implication of such information. "Why are they taking that man away? Did he do something bad?"

"I don't know," she replied.

Truly, she was at a loss of adequate words to explain to Théa where that man was probably being taken. More than likely, he was

Jewish, which meant he was being arrested. They'd take him to the police station first, but he wouldn't stay there long. They'd ship him off to someplace much, much worse.

The smell of fresh bread brought Helene away from that horrible thought as they entered the bakery. A tiny, middle-aged woman stood behind the counter—a smile she was obviously struggling to keep intact plastered across her face.

"Bonjour, Madame," Helene greeted, "Do you have any bread left? I'd like to get some before it's gone."

That word, gone, was said with a certain weight that implied Helene knew it was entirely possible that bread would soon be rationed and barely available. The woman understood immediately, of course she did, and Helene watched as her smile faltered.

"I have one small loaf left that you can have, but there are no more baguettes. The soldiers have already cleared me out."

Helene decided to attempt to push for information. Anything she could glean about the current situation would be helpful.

"We just passed two of them escorting a man from his home," she started carefully, "It seems they must want to speak with him about something urgent."

The woman's face darkened.

"Have you not heard, mademoiselle? That horrible excuse of a leader has ordered another roundup. I expect all the Jews remaining in the city will be arrested by the end of the day. *C'est horrible, n'est ce pas?*"

The woman's words seeped through Helene's consciousness like a cold frost crawling up a window. The soldiers had been ordered to round up all the remaining Jews in the city. By the end of the day, they'd be arrested and most likely transferred to who knows where. She felt as though she might get sick if she wasn't careful.

She paid for the loaf of bread in a half-daze—she found it rather hard to focus on the present moment when her brain kept trying to decide how the next several hours would play out. Since the bakery owner's confession, Théa had commenced squeezing Helene's hand so tight that Helene thought she might be bruised. The girl was trying to put on a brave face for Helene, but it was clear that the thought of Jews being taken away scared her. She was Jewish, after all. Helene felt the need to provide some sort of comfort as they exited the store and started walking in the direction of the house.

"Théa, look at me, please."

Big eyes met her own hesitantly.

"I won't let anyone take you away, okay?"

Théa's voice came out no louder than a whisper.

"Do you promise?"

"I promise. Nobody is going to hurt you."

They walked the rest of the way back in silence. Helene strained her brain, trying to come up with several possible routes to take now that she knew the Germans would be looking for the Cadieux's. They surely had the records that confirmed Henri and Théa lived at 27 Rue de Chaussas, which meant she'd have to work with Henri to get them out of that address—help them hide somewhere. She had no idea where that somewhere was, but she hoped Henri had a better inkling of an idea than she did.

Helene and Théa were three houses from the Cadieux's front gate when two things happened in rapid succession.

First: A car pulled away from the curb before speeding down the road. Had it been parked in front of the house?

Second: An officer with a swastika stitched onto his sleeve stepped out onto the sidewalk, a cigarette hanging from his mouth.

Helene inhaled sharply, suppressing a gasp. She felt Théa stiffen next to her. This was not good at all. Her mind blanked in pure fear as the man started towards them.

Breathe, darling. If you are anything, you are a storyteller. That is what you must do now. Tell this soldier a story, and make it a good one.

Thinking fast, Helene whispered to Théa.

"Do not say a single word, alright? I will take care of this."

The girl nodded almost imperceptibly as they stopped in front of the German officer. This close, Helene could see he was very young—not much older than she was.

That will work to your advantage. With youth comes naïveté. If you can confuse him, he will most likely choose not to confront you further.

Before he could speak, Helene dove into the conversation, making sure her voice sounded sweeter than sugar itself.

"Good morning, sir. Is everything alright?"

The officer regarded her with something akin to hatred. It sent a shiver down her back.

"Do you live here?"

It was delivered quite bluntly, with no room for anything other than a black-and-white answer. Or so he thought. Helene switched from French to German as she answered him.

"Well, I wouldn't say *live*," she began, "We just arrived last night."

The almost-hatred in the man's eyes turned to confusion. If she wasn't so afraid of being shot, she'd think this was rather funny.

"I do not understand," the man replied, "Are you related to Henri Cadieux?"

"Is that the man who lives here? He is a gracious host but I cannot say I even knew his name until you just said it to me. We came into town rather late last night, and I went straight to bed."

"So, you are...traveling?"

"I'm sorry, I suppose I haven't explained myself very well," Helene faked a laugh, "My student and I are staying here for a few days, but we do not live here, and we do not know the man who does. I was given his name as someone who would be willing to host us for the duration of our trip."

The officer's piercing eyes found Théa then. Helene prayed she wouldn't say anything and would hopefully not cry.

"This," the man pointed accusingly, "Is not Henri Cadieux's daughter?"

"Certainly not. I didn't know he had a daughter. As I mentioned, this is my student. We are German, from Stuttgart."

The officer's expression seemed to relax slightly. Good, that meant it was working.

"You are not Jewish, then?"

"No, sir. We're here on an educational trip," Helene continued the lie, "We started in Paris and we're moving around France. Little Ingrid here is homeschooled, you see. Her father works for the government."

Helene gave Théa her own sister's name on a whim, but she knew the German roots of it would help bolster the fake story she'd weaved in her head.

"I'm assuming you did not know the man who lived in this house was Jewish?"

Helene cringed internally at the use of the past tense. It did not bode well. Her stomach roiled as she forced her expression to one of cool indifference.

"Was he? No, I had no idea. Is that what all of this is about, then?"

"Yes. We're...collecting them around the city. I'm sure you understand."

"Mm, yes," Helene choked out as calmly as she could, "You have to do your job, of course."

He flashed her a sadistic grin that absolutely terrified her before making his decision.

"I suppose there's no harm in a good German woman and child staying in this house," he started, "Perhaps it will cleanse the walls of all that Jewish filth. It's such a nice house, after all."

She nodded, unable to make her lips move in response to such a heinous statement. He continued.

"I hope you enjoy your stay in France, fraulein. Please, do let an officer know if you are in need of anything. We help our own, after all."

"Yes, thank you, officer. Have a wonderful day."

Helene watched him walk off down the road, his figure getting smaller and smaller until he rounded a corner and was gone from her line of sight. She practically heaved a sigh as she ran shaky fingers through her hair. That had cut things a bit too close. It had not escaped her notice that the officer had forgotten to ask for any identification papers. He must have assumed that because Théa's hair was red and Helene's eyes weren't brown that their story was true. Truly, it was incredibly stupid to think one had to look a certain way in order to be Jewish, but then again, Hitler's entire platform was built around that idea.

See, I told you. Knowledge of someone else's ignorance will always help you.

She turned at the sound of Théa's footsteps running through the gate and up the path to the house. The relief flooding through her body soured into horror as she remembered: Henri. She ran after Théa, her heart splitting apart upon noticing the front door already wide open from the intrusion of the soldiers. The sound of Théa's voice bounced off the walls as she careened through the hallways, shouting for her father in a tone growing more desperate by the second.

"*Papa!*" Her words splintered as she halted at the bottom of the staircase to catch her breath, "*Papa, où t'es? Tu peux sortir maintenant.* Where are you? You don't have to hide!"

Helene felt tears trail down her face as nothing but absolute silence answered. Because Henri wasn't there. She realized that he must have known—must have recognized the speed with which officers would arrive at the house—and had convinced Helene to take Théa with her to the market so she wouldn't be at home when they came. He'd wanted to ensure his daughter had the opportunity to escape, even if it meant forfeiting his own chance. Helene had only known Henri Cadieux for a day, and yet she was certain he didn't care about his own odds, and hadn't for a while. All that mattered to him was his child, and he'd left her in Helene's company in hopes she'd be safe.

Helene very much intended to keep Théa safe. She'd made a promise, after all.

She sank to her knees as the girl turned to face her. There was a wild and terrified look in Théa's expression, like she was coming loose at the seams and didn't know how to stop it. Helene's tear-stained face did not help in reassuring her—her own eyes turned immediately glassy. She looked so little, so vulnerable. Helene hated that the conversation ahead of them had to happen at all. She brought her hands up so her palms rested gently against Théa's face, her thumbs brushing against tiny cheekbones in an attempt to rid them of tears.

"Miss Helene…" Théa murmured, "W-where is…where is Papa?"

It took a lot of effort to keep her voice level.

"He's not here, darling."

"D-did the soldiers…take him away?"

"Yes," Helene swallowed hard, "They did."

"When will he be allowed to come back?"

She didn't have it in her to tell this scared little girl the entire truth.

"I don't know. I wish I did."

Helene did know. Henri was likely never coming back. She thought back to months ago when she and Eve had discussed the not-so-false allegations surrounding Hitler's "Final Solution" plan. Eve had mentioned the rumors about a new kind of work camp being established in several locations around Europe. Members of the French Resistance had passed on intel that all French Jews were first being sent to a detention camp in Drancy before eventually being deported to the Auschwitz-Birkenau extermination camp in Poland. Just the name of that place sent a chill through Helene. According to the rumors, nobody—*nobody*—came back from Auschwitz. Someone had overheard a soldier talking about how prisoners were either killed in toxic gas chambers immediately upon arrival, or they were put to heavy labor until they succumbed. Helene guessed many probably died from illness, too.

She couldn't tell Théa any of that. She refused. There was a chance, however slim, that Henri would survive whatever ordeal lay ahead of him, and she would encourage Théa's hope of seeing her father again until she keeled over and died herself. If the child in front of her lost her reason to go on, what would she be? What would her life look like?

Throughout my many centuries, so many have claimed that Hope is the ultimate blinder, the supreme deceiver. I think those people must have lived shallow and sad lives indeed. Hope does not blind; it enlightens. It does not deceive it guides. The mighty poetess Emily Dickinson said it best: *Hope is the thing with feathers that perches in the soul, and sings the tune without the words, and never stops at all.* We are nothing without Hope. If there was anything I wished for little Théa, it was that she learned to find light in the darkest of places—Wisdom in the throes of chaos and folly. Helene was right to answer the girl's question with a half-truth. She wasn't ready for the whole truth just yet.

As it was, Théa could barely comprehend how she was to go on without her father.

"What..." her tiny voice broke through Helene's train of thought, "What happens now that Papa isn't here? Do I have to leave too?"

"No, darling," Helene reassured gently, "You and I are going to stay right here."

"But Miss Helene, don't you have to take the machine away? The one that makes messages?"

In truth, Helene completely forgot about the Typex until that moment. Obviously, Théa had been partaking in some eavesdropping the day before.

"Hush, no more talk of that machine," Helene hurriedly replied. It wouldn't do to have a child accidentally speak of such a thing in front of the wrong people. "I will have to do something about it eventually, but that isn't my concern at the moment."

"What is your concern, then?"

"You. The only thing that matters right now is you, Théa."

Fresh tears filled the girl's eyes as Helene tucked a loose lock of auburn hair behind her ear before stroking her cheek once again. She continued, choosing her words carefully to avoid upsetting Théa even more.

"You and I are going to lay low until I decide what to do next, okay?"

"Okay," Théa sniffed, "You told that soldier that I was you student, but that wasn't the truth."

"No, it wasn't, but I knew he would believe it."

"Would he have taken us away if you hadn't said that?"

"Don't think about that, it doesn't matter now. If we have to go outside, we'll pretend that what I said was true."

Théa didn't respond, but Helene got the sense that she understood how the next several days would have to go. They'd stay cooped up inside as much as possible, but Helene figured the Germans probably had eyes on the house, considering they thought Théa was missing. They'd have to leave at some point. No teacher and student on a field trip to France would stay inside the whole time.

If Helene was being honest with herself, she was just as scared as Théa about the current situation, possibly even more so. Surely, nobody in Blackthorn would have sent her on this assignment had they known an invasion was imminent. She was now stuck for an unknown amount of time in a very dangerous environment—not to mention she was technically hiding a Jewish child from the very people making the environment dangerous. To leave too soon would arouse suspicion and would put both her and Théa's safety in jeopardy, but the same thing would be true if they stayed for too long. She had no idea what to do, and it was starting to paralyze her. This child was counting on her to be brave, and she wasn't sure she could.

I sent a little Wisdom her way in hopes of snapping her out of that headspace.

Remember, Bravery does not mean you are unafraid. Bravery is recognizing that you are very afraid and choosing to lead through that fear—in spite of it. The fact that you've made it this far proves your ability to wear the armor of courage, even if to you, it feels like it doesn't quite fit. You can do this.

If only she could talk to Eve. She'd know what to do, surely. In her absence, Helene decided the best thing to do was to think like her. What would Eve do if she was stuck in a foreign country with a girl whose existence had been deemed illegal? She would probably try to get that child out of said foreign country. But where could Théa go where she'd be safe?

The solution came to her rather quickly: England.

She could send Théa to England.

How she'd go about doing that would have to be determined in the next several days, but it was an idea. A start. She was sure England had probably already received children who'd been sent to escape the war; what was one more child? They were now the closest Allied nation by a long shot, and thus far, Hitler hadn't been able to invade the island. She'd have to figure out where the nearest port city was that ferried children across the channel. If she could find a French resistance member here in Toulouse, they might be able to give her a credible answer. Once she ensured Théa was safe, she could figure out how to get back to Germany with the Typex.

Luckily, the coding machine was still hidden beneath the floorboards—a miracle, considering practically every inch of the house had been ransacked. In Henri's bedroom, Helene found a shattered picture frame next to the bed—glass shards embedded into the rug. She picked up the frame to find the picture still inside. It portrayed Henri sitting on a bench with his arm wrapped around the shoulders of a young woman. This, Helene presumed, must be Théa's mother. On the back, in delicate cursive, the words *Henri et Daphné* were inscribed. Helene wondered what had happened to Madame Cadieux. Henri had implied that she'd died, but hadn't mentioned the cause. She guessed that Théa didn't remember her, considering the girl hadn't mentioned her mother once.

Helene and Théa didn't leave the house again for the rest of the day. Helene was hesitant to even look out the window, in fear there would be a police officer on the other side of the pane. After she'd cleaned up some of the mess around the house, Helene had found Théa hiding in her bedroom—curled on top of her bed with her stuffed bunny clutched to her chest and tears still very much present on her face. Helene desperately wanted to reassure her that everything would be okay, but she was at a loss as to how to do such a thing. Théa was seven, but she wasn't stupid. Her father had been taken away with no explanation by soldiers who had invaded the city she lived in. She was now confined inside with someone she barely knew but had to trust to keep her out of harm's way. Had it been Helene in Théa's place, she knew with certainty that she'd be handling the situation the same way—probably even worse.

Eventually, she was able to coax the girl downstairs with the promise of supper. The girl had nearly forgotten her hunger in the midst of her panic, and it made Helene smile ever so slightly to see her eat a tartine and apple slices in record time. Her attempts to distract Théa with games were not as successful, and Helene gave up eventually. It wasn't until later in the evening that Helene discovered the only activity Théa would tolerate: reading, or more specifically, listening while Helene read to her. As it turned out, there were quite a few books in the house. Helene supposed there hadn't been nearly as many book bans and confiscations outside of Germany. Théa seemed most enthusiastic about a novel already placed next to her bed: *Little Women* by Louisa May Alcott (*Les Quatres Filles du Docteur March* in French).

"I've been reading this every night with Papa," Théa explained as she handed the book to Helene, "Can we read it together?"

"Of course we can," Helene replied. "I'll tell you what, why don't you get your nightgown on and then we can read until bedtime."

"Maybe we could..." Théa let her voice fizzle out before finishing her sentence.

"Maybe we could what?"

"Nothing, it's silly."

"No, you can tell me," Helene knelt to meet Théa's gaze, "I'm sure it's not silly."

Théa looked unsure for a moment longer before deciding in Helene's favor.

"I was wondering if we could read it...in my bed?"

Helene's heart threatened to melt at the confession. It wasn't surprising that Théa would request such a thing—she was sure the child was scared to be alone. Her father had been alone when he'd been taken, after all. There was no universe where she wouldn't give Théa the comfort she so innocently sought.

"Sure, we can do that," she smiled in a way that was hopefully reassuring, "Once you're changed, get warm under the covers, and

I'll be back as soon as I wash up."

Théa followed those directions to the nose, because Helene walked into the girl's bedroom to find her snuggled like a tabby cat under the blankets with the book open to the page she left off on the night before. As Helene joined her under the covers, Théa moved so her head rested in the crook of Helene's neck.

"Are you ready?" Helene inquired softly, "Comfortable enough?"

Théa's hair tickled her chin as she nodded. Helene's ability to speak French was not nearly as proficient as this kind of novel really required, but she didn't get the sense it bothered her companion very much. It didn't take long for Théa's breathing to even out, and Helene looked up from the words to find her little kitten had fallen asleep against her, face tucked snugly against the fabric of Helene's nightgown. She smiled as she accepted that she wouldn't be sleeping alone tonight. She didn't mind. The steadiness of Théa's heartbeat against her chest was enough to help her relax from the fight-or-flight mindset she'd been forced to harbor all day. As she set the book aside and turned out the light, Helene swore she would find someone who would help her—help both of them—tomorrow, danger be damned.

ATHENA
November 12th-13th, 1942

The next day proved sunnier than the previous one, although it didn't lift the heaviness in Helene's heart quite like it usually did. Part of her hoped the events of the day before had been some kind of twisted nightmare, and in reality, Henri would be in the kitchen preparing breakfast when she woke up— Théa skipping through the corridors happily.

But alas, no coffee smell wafted up the stairs when Helene opened her eyes, and Théa slept still curled against her. The clock on the nightstand told her it was only six in the morning. Her heart ached as she brushed the girl's hair away before extracting herself carefully from the bed. She pulled the covers more snugly around Théa's sleeping form. She hoped she'd stay asleep for a bit longer so Helene could have some time for herself—she needed to get to work on formulating a plan for the next several days.

She half stumbled downstairs as she suppressed a yawn. She'd been plagued with strange dreams all night—ones that involved running, and chasing, and the smell of blood. A particularly memorable one had included her mother dressed as a surgeon looking down at her and telling her it was alright to leave—as if she hadn't been strapped to an operation table at her mercy. After the last forty-eight hours, she supposed it made sense that she'd had nightmares. She just hoped Théa wasn't experiencing them, too.

Although Helene had initially thought it best for them to pretend to go about business as usual to give credibility to the lie she'd told the German officer, she had since changed her mind. She didn't like the idea of putting Théa in such a vulnerable position—it was best if the two of them stayed close to the house. Helene had opted for the "if they can't see you, you must not be there" philosophy—she'd been silently hoping that they'd been forgotten by the authorities altogether.

"That would make everything much more manageable, wouldn't it?" she said out loud to herself.

Almost as soon as the words were out of her mouth, a noise resonated throughout the house that made the hair on Helene's good arm stand straight up.

Several knocks at the front door.

She froze in the middle of the kitchen, her mind concluding at once that the only explanation for such a noise this early in the morning was that a police officer had come to arrest them—had come to ship them off to their deaths. Helene thought her heart might pound right out of her chest as she debated what to do. Really, she knew there was only one option that might end well for her, and it was something she'd hoped she wouldn't have to do. She certainly didn't want to do it with Théa in the house, but it seemed she didn't have a choice.

The knocking persisted as she silently opened a drawer next to the stove and pulled out the pistol she'd hidden there. It felt clunky in her hands, but she remembered how to use it. She clicked the safety off, stomach churning with anxiety, and stepped into the hallway. The thought of dying while still in her nightgown flitted through her mind. Arthur would've had some remark to make had he been there with her, surely. She almost wished he was there.

With the adrenaline coursing through her body came heightened senses—she could feel the smooth coolness of the polished wood under her bare feet and could smell the coffee grounds she'd left behind in the kitchen. The *tick tick tick* of the old grandfather clock replaced her own heartbeat as she tried her best to be more machine than woman. A machine would be able to approach the door, open it, and bury a few bullets straight into the chest of the piece of shit waiting on the other side. A machine would be able to take the body and hide it in the brush behind the house. A machine would do all of this because it had to— was programmed to—and it would do so without crying, without second-guessing, without anything but the mechanical movements of arms, legs, and firearms.

While I applauded Helene for this tactic—as it resembled one I had seen many times in battle—it didn't suit her nature. She wasn't a machine; she was a human, and doing scary things is not as easy as we tell ourselves it will be in our heads. Helene didn't want to kill anyone, but she would if it meant the child sleeping upstairs would remain that way. That conviction—and the emotions behind it—are not things machines are capable of.

The knocking at the door continued, this time a bit louder than before, as Helene approached it. Despite her best efforts, the gun in her grip shook as the hands holding it trembled, and she willed herself to focus on the task at hand and not the terror bubbling up inside of her. She needed to do this—she couldn't let anyone get to Théa. She wouldn't let anybody touch her. All she had to do was open the door and shoot whoever it was before they had a chance–

"Helene? Are you in there?"

Her mind, body, and soul froze in place as a voice cut through the pounding in her ears. She knew that voice–would recognize that voice anywhere.

"If you're inside, please open the door," There was a kind of desperation hidden within the plea. "It's me, it's Eve. Nobody is here to hurt you, I swear."

Perhaps she still should have followed some sort of protocol. Maybe she should have preserved a modicum of apprehension, considering she'd been prepared to kill someone only a moment prior. She knew she should have, but as the gun fell to the floor and her hand fumbled the lock on the door, all forms of common sense evaporated from Helene's imagination–replaced by one thought and one thought only. The only thought that mattered.

The door swung open, and Genevieve Harrison stood before her, utterly flustered and impossibly beautiful.

She was here, in France. In Toulouse. How, Helene wasn't sure, but that hardly mattered.

My girl, she would've climbed through the Alps if that's what it took to get here.

They stood in silence for several moments, Helene trying in vain to tame her raging heartbeat as Eve stared at her bemusedly. The morning sun had wrapped a halo of gold around her head and spilled warmth into her eyes in such a way that she seemed more goddess than woman. Standing in front of Helene on the porch with nothing but a coat and small valise, Eve's presence engulfed her in a warmth she'd been dreaming about for days. Was it all a dream?

Us goddesses do, in fact, glow in our purest form, so comparing Eve to me wasn't all that far off. Although, of course, my glow is so bright it literally blinds humans, hence the disguises.

Eve was the first to speak, after what felt like an eternity.

"Judging by the weapon at your feet, I've escaped within an inch of my life."

Oh, right. The gun. Helene glanced down at the discarded pistol briefly before meeting Eve's gaze again.

"Yes, well, I wasn't expecting it to be you," she explained as she found her voice, "The people aren't exactly *friendly* here these days."

Eve's expression shifted to one Helene wasn't used to seeing on her face. Was that concern written in the way her brows furrowed? Fear? She opened the door farther so Eve could step inside the house.

"Please come in out of the cold," she continued before Eve could, "I'll get a fire going—"

Before she could finish her sentence, Helene found herself engulfed in a tight embrace. Arms wrapped themselves protectively around her shoulders, and for a split second, she tensed at the way the contact overwhelmed her, although that didn't last long. Her own arm reciprocated the hug as she realized that this couldn't possibly be a dream, not if she could feel and touch Eve this strongly. She buried her face in her companion's coat before she could stop herself. It smelled like perfume and engine oil and cold air.

Eve's nose pressed gently against her hair and stayed there as she steadied herself as if she was remembering the way Helene looked, smelled, felt. Her voice was no more than a whisper against Helene's ear as she started to explain herself.

"When I heard they invaded the south, it felt like someone had doused me in ice water," her breathing almost seemed to shorten with every word she spoke, "I panicked. I knew you were here, and I panicked. One minute I was sitting at my kitchen table and the next minute I was flying out the door. I couldn't stand the thought of you stuck in France surrounded by those monsters."

She sighed shakily as her voice splintered.

"I found someone willing to fly me here overnight. I was hardly thinking, really. There was this image in my mind of you laying on the ground in a pool of your own blood that just wouldn't leave no matter what, and I just...I can't...."

"Hey, none of that," Helene pulled out of the embrace to look at Eve's half-crumpled face, "I'm okay."

She was starting to understand that the expression dancing across Eve's features moments ago hadn't been concern or fear, as she'd assumed. It was relief–burning, barely contained relief that Helene was alive. She reached for Eve's hand with her good arm and interlocked their fingers. The gentle squeeze she received in response made her smile.

"I'm glad you came," she murmured. "I've been wondering how to get out of this mess."

"Tell me what happened," Eve demanded, her confidence returning to her now that she knew Helene needed her for something, "Hopefully Henri has been a good host?"

"Do you know him?"

"He is the son of a man my father knew years ago when we lived in France."

Helene hadn't realized Eve had a personal connection to all of this. The knowledge caused a lump to form in Helene's throat at the thought of having to tell her what had occurred.

"He's not here, Eve," she couldn't make her voice come out louder than a whisper, "He was, but he's not anymore."

"What do you mean?" Eve's brow furrowed again, this time in confusion.

"The soldiers took him away. Yesterday morning. I was at the market with Théa when it happened, or I would've done something."

Helene watched in dismay as Eve's face fell. She opened her mouth to say something, but nothing seemed able to come out right away.

"If they took him," she spoke slowly, "He's headed for Auschwitz."

"Most likely."

"He won't come back from Auschwitz. No one does."

"Yes," Helene mourned, "I know."

The silence that descended between them was ripe with emotions neither of them acknowledged, at least not out loud. Eventually, a thoughtful look passed through Eve's eyes.

"Who is Théa?"

"Henri's daughter. She's seven."

"Is she in the house?"

"Yes, that's why I'm glad you're here. I need to get her somewhere safe, preferably England. She'll be better off there, but I haven't the first clue of how to go about sending her."

"We'll talk to someone about it later."

Relief flooded Helene at the confirmation that her plan for Théa was indeed possible.

She moved out of Eve's proximity to close the curtains on the window—heavens forbid someone saw them from the street. She heard Eve suck in her breath sharply as she struggled to slide the curtain over gracefully. She whirled around.

"What is it?"

Eve's skin looked paler as she regarded Helene with wide eyes.

"You said you were okay."

"I am."

"Your arm wouldn't be in a sling if you were okay, Helene."

Right. She'd forgotten about that small detail.

Best to play it off as more of an annoyance than anything.

"Oh, this happened on the trip here," she said, trying to sound as nonchalant as possible. "Some piece of shit working for Pétain ambushed me just outside the city limits. I have a concussion and a broken arm, but it's fine."

"That doesn't sound fine," Eve was reaching for her again, "I never wanted you to get hurt."

Firm hands gripped her upper arms as Eve regarded her with a look of sadness that threatened to melt Helene into a puddle of feelings. Eve's fears about Helene's well-being were not new, but this willingness to show those fears so sincerely was almost dizzying. The fact that Eve wanted to be this close to her at all sent shivers down Helene's spine.

"I promise you, Eve, I'm alright. I'm not going anywhere."

She felt soft hands frame her face in response, and Eve came even closer until their foreheads met. Helene thought back to the summer, the last time they'd been this close, and felt butterflies in her stomach immediately as longing filled her from head to toe. Eve was the only one who could make her feel this way. She didn't want it to ever be anyone else.

"I'm going to get us out of this," Eve replied in a low voice as her thumbs stroked the skin behind Helene's ear methodically, "I want to help you get the girl to England, too. We'll figure it out."

"I know," Helene breathed.

A beat passed where Eve seemed unsure of herself before her already low voice turned husky with what Helene could only hope was desire.

"It's not the only thing I'd like to figure out."

"What do you mean?"

"Ever since this past summer, I haven't been able to so much as look at you without feeling like I was losing control of everything I had, everything I was," she started, "You make me want to drop my guard, and nobody has ever been able to do that before."

Helene wouldn't have been able to reply even if she wanted to. She was too busy waiting in suspense for Eve to snap back behind her defenses. But she continued instead.

"I don't know much when it comes to whatever this is between us," there was a long pause, "But I think, by now, I do know one thing for certain."

Eve's eyes were nearly black with yearning as Helene regarded her. Gone was the restraint she'd seen in them moments ago, replaced by something possessive, something hungry.

"Tell me," Helene choked out. The butterflies had migrated from her stomach into her throat as she swallowed hard.

"There are other things I'd like to do with you," Another pause, "To you."

Well, it's about time. I was starting to wonder if she'd ever say it.

Helene very nearly exploded at the sound of those words, directed at her nonetheless. There was nothing she wanted more than Eve, nothing else she could conjure in her mind besides the feeling of Eve all over her.

For the first time in her life, she realized with a start, she wanted to be seen by someone. She wanted to feel hands exploring her, wanted to feel lips marking her.

She wanted to be Eve's rhyme and Eve's reason—the song on her voice and the knowledge in her head. The poetry and the mathematical equation. Eve was already all of those things to her. It was time she reciprocated.

"I'm going to close the rest of this distance," she heard herself command in a murmur, "And there's not much you can do to stop me."

Before any sort of reply could be vocalized, Helene's lips collided with Eve's in a tentative kiss.

It was gentle, at first. Helene barely knew what she was doing, and Eve was too stunned to remember anything at all. Neither of them dared to move an inch for a long while.

That is, until Eve hummed against her mouth in satisfaction, a delicate answer to the question sitting on Helene's tongue. She heard herself gasp as Eve deepened the kiss instantaneously. Her hand found purchase on slender hips as she pressed herself against Eve's chest in a manner that felt rushed but necessary. Her lips were so warm and soft, just as she always hoped they would be, and her hands felt deft and curious as they roamed all over her body. This was both too much and not enough. Helene had dreamed of being consumed by everything Eve was for some time now, and truly had thought she understood what it would be like. As it turned out, she'd been wrong in that assumption. It was predicable, until it wasn't anymore. Everything, until it was more than that.

It can be rather fun, every once in a while, to be wrong.

Eve moaned in protest as Helene broke away to catch her breath but simply decided to leave quick, hot kisses all along her neck instead, causing Helene's lips to part with desire. The kisses continued like flames down her shoulders as Eve removed her robe and let it fall to the floor. She was very aware that now the only thing between Eve and her naked body was a flimsy nightgown, and judging by the look on Eve's face, it wouldn't be on her for much longer. She felt her feet lose contact with the ground as Eve picked her up and straddled her against the wall so forcefully the picture frames shook.

"We need to be quiet," Helene gasped into Eve's ear, "I don't want to wake Théa."

"Where is she?" Eve answered distractedly.

"In her bedroom, we could go to mine."

Eve didn't verbally respond, just nodded fiercely before carrying her up the stairs bridal style, lips of fire continuing to leave marks everywhere she could reach the whole way. As she laid her down against the cool cotton of the quilt, Helene was positive that Eve would devour her whole if given the permission.

Permission granted.

✳ ✳ ✳

As the clock struck 7:30, the two of them laid in each other's arms in the bed, loose-limbed and love drunk. Helene seemed to have completely exhausted herself during their *performance*. She was deeply asleep against Eve's chest, snoring gently with her mouth open. Eve planted gentle, repeated kisses against her jawline as she slept, occasionally letting her fingers play with the hair at Helene's temple before caressing down her cheek. She just loved the feeling of having Helene so close—she didn't know if she could ever live without this proximity now that she knew what it felt like. Never in her wildest dreams had she imagined that Helene would feel the same way she did. It wasn't any small thing—what they now had together. Some people might say it was just as illegal as being Jewish was. Hitler would certainly say such a thing. Not that she cared what anyone thought at the end of the day—she just didn't want their feelings for each other to put them in more danger than they already were in. Helene didn't need to bear anything else on her shoulders, least of all the worry that their relationship could hurt them.

And yet, in spite of all of that, Eve wanted her desperately. In the worst way. In the best way. In any way at all. She'd been surprised at the way Helene brought her possessive side out. It felt like a wild and innate part of her that she couldn't control—a hunger to have, to hold, to keep, to protect.

Her thoughts were interrupted by a timid knock on the door. She made sure both she and Helene were sufficiently wrapped in the sheets before calling out to the girl she knew was behind the door.

"Come in."

A very freckled face awash with confusion greeted her hesitantly. So this was Théa Cadieux. She reminded Eve of a baby fox—she looked like she could be up to no good at a moment's notice. Her voice was laden with curiosity as she glanced from Helene's sleeping form back to her.

"Who are *you*?"

"I'm Eve. Helene's...friend."

The girl gave her a dubious look.

"Something tells me you aren't just her friend."

"How old are you again?"

"I'm seven, but Papa always said I was smarter than all the other seven-year-olds."

Her expression turned solemn at the mention of her father, which made Eve feel immensely sorry for her. She seemed to set her sadness aside as she continued her appraisal of the scene in front of her.

"You're very pretty, Miss Eve."

"Thank you. I think you're pretty too."

"When did you get here?"

"Earlier this morning, I came to help Helene...and you, too."

"That's good," Théa smiled in a strangely serious way, "I don't want anything bad to happen to Miss Helene. She's so nice and brave."

"You're right, she is," Eve stole a glance at her sleeping companion, "I won't let anything happen to her, don't worry."

"Do you love her, Miss Eve?"

"I...care about her a lot."

"So you do love her," Théa laughed, "I don't know why grown-ups are so afraid to say that. It's not that scary."

I've said it before, and I'll say it again: children are the wisest of us all.

"I suppose you're right," Eve conceded before endeavoring to change the subject, "Why don't you go get yourself dressed? We have work to do today."

Théa snapped to attention at the confidence in Eve's ask. She scampered away, her footsteps bordering on erratic as she ran back to her room. Eve turned her attention back to Helene's peaceful face. She wished they could stay in bed like this all day, but there were important things to be done. She stroked Helene's curls as she whispered gentle words in her ear.

"It's time to wake up, lovely."

Helene groaned weakly in protest, but opened her eyes anyway. Eve would never get sick of those eyes—green like sea glass on the ocean floor.

"Good morning, although it's the same morning as before you fell asleep," she murmured as she leaned to plant a chaste kiss on Helene's forehead.

"Hi," came the shy reply.

"I met Théa."

"She didn't see anything inappropriate, did she?"

"No," Eve smiled, "Only I'm allowed to see those things."

That turned Helene's cheeks bright red, and she moved out of Eve's arms reluctantly. She collected her nightgown and folded it neatly before donning a burgundy collared dress. She thought perhaps pants might be better suited for a resistance operative, but she didn't want to stand out among the other French women. She moved to the bathroom then, where she washed her face, brushed her teeth, and braided her hair into a loose plait. Théa came bursting out of her bedroom as Helene made her way back into the hallway, encircling her arms around Helene's torso tightly.

"Hello, sweet girl," she brushed a hand over the girl's hair, "Did you sleep well?"

"Yes, Miss Helene," Théa squeaked, "And I met your friend Eve."

"So I've heard. Did you like her?"

"Yes, she said we had lots of work to do."

"She's right," Helene agreed as they moved down the stairs, "Which reminds me that I must speak with you about something very important."

They'd made it to the sitting room, and Théa perched herself on the floor next to the fire as Helene took a seat in the armchair. She looked so attentive and interested, and Helene hated that what she was about to tell her would most likely scare her to pieces.

"I've been thinking about what needs to be done to make sure you are safe, Théa," she started slowly, "And I've decided that we—you—cannot stay here in Toulouse. It's too dangerous."

A flicker of confusion lighted through the girl's eyes.

"But Miss Helene, where would we go?"

"I must go back to Germany, darling."

"With the coding machine, right? I can go with you!"

Helene braced herself.

"I wish you could, but I'm afraid you cannot."

"What?" Théa's little voice went up an octave as she started to panic, "Why can't I?"

"Germany is more dangerous than France is, for a girl like you."

"You shouldn't go there either, if it's so scary there!"

"You are Jewish, Théa."

"So what?"

"Do you remember when I told you about Adolf Hitler?"

"Yes, he is the leader of Germany."

"He doesn't like Jewish people. Théa. If he ever found you, he would take you away."

"Like how he took Papa away?"

"Yes, darling," She reached to hold Théa's hand, running her thumb across the girl's knuckles in a feeble attempt to reassure her, "I don't ever want that to happen, so you must go someplace very far away from him."

"Like where?"

Helene hated how young she sounded when she asked that kind of question.

"Eve and I are arranging for you to go to England for a while. It won't be too long, just until the war is over."

Théa was silent for several moments, digesting what she'd been told.

"I've never been there before," she mused. "Are English people nice?"

Eve interrupted from behind her before Helene could respond. She hadn't realized she'd come downstairs.

"I should think so; that's where I'm from."

"Is that why you talk kind of funny?"

That made Eve laugh out loud. Helene loved hearing it—it broke up the somberness of the conversation and made a smile return to Théa's face.

"I reached out to a French contact just now," Eve looked to Helene, "He says if we can get to Calais by tomorrow, he can arrange for someone to take Théa across the channel to London."

"That's great," Helene proclaimed, feeling slightly reassured, "But how will we get to Calais so quickly? It's so far north."

"We'll go by plane. At night," Eve replied quickly, "We'll have to be vigilant, but it's doable."

The rest of the day was spent preparing for the trip. Théa's two small bags were packed first with as many clothes, shoes, books, and stuffed animals as they could find. Helene wasn't optimistic about the girl ever seeing this house again, and she wanted to make sure she could bring as many reminders of it as possible. When Théa wasn't looking, Helene stuffed the photograph of her parents into the pocket of one of her coats. She didn't want Théa to ever forget them.

The next task was to take the Typex machine from beneath the floorboards and prep it for travel. Henri had organized all the decoded messages into a file folder that Helene placed at the bottom of her suitcase so it would be hidden underneath her clothes should they be stopped and searched at any point. The machine itself was rather bulky, and Eve feared that taking it apart would be easier than putting it back together. They decided it would have to sit in one of their laps for the plane ride to Calais, as well as the subsequent one back into Germany. Everything about the next twelve hours left Helene's stomach in knots—especially sending Théa into an unknown country by herself—but she knew it was the only way out of this mess for both of them. Théa might be a bit afraid and uncomfortable for the foreseeable future, but she'd be protected and cared for. Helene's promise to Henri echoed through her mind.

She refused to let his sacrifice be in vain.

✳✳✳

The three of them left the city limits well past dusk, close to eight o'clock. Eve had suggested they wait until Théa fell asleep, and Helene agreed only because she didn't want to see the hurt in the girl's expression as she stared at the only home she'd ever known for the last time. It was best that Théa went to sleep in one place and woke up in another.

The newly instated curfew rendered the streets of Toulouse eerily silent. The only discernable sound was the occasional tap of military boots on the cobblestones as an unlucky soldier on night watch patrolled the area. Eve led them through alleys and down side streets in order to avoid confronting one of them. It seemed like she'd walked these roads before—in some other lifetime. Helene would ask about it later. For now she was trying her best not to focus on the way her arms were beginning to burn from holding Théa. She wished they'd been able to call a cab to drive them a little bit of the way, at least.

After what felt like an eternity, the city lights began to fade, and Helene could make out the tree line that served as the natural border to the countryside. Waiting for them next to a very old auto, to Helene's surprise and delight, was Fabien. He flashed her a smile as they approached.

"Helene, it's a pleasure to see you again. I hope you're in better shape than when I last saw you."

"I certainly am," Helene replied, "Thank you again for helping me that night. I might not have made it into the city without you."

She noticed Eve tense out of the corner of her eye, and Helene knew she was berating herself for not being there, too. She wished Eve would simply forget about her near fatal run-in at the checkpoint, but she knew that was unlikely to happen any time soon.

Fabien opened the car door for her as he brought them up to speed on what they could expect in the next twelve hours.

"We have to take a short drive to the plane, and then we'll fly into Calais," he began, "It will take roughly four hours to get there."

Once they were settled in the backseat, he climbed into the driver's side, turning the ignition until the car started with a low hum.

"I'll wait in the plane while the two of you take the girl to your contact, and once you come back we'll head straight towards Germany. It should take about two and a half hours, so you can expect to be back in Hamburg by four o'clock tomorrow morning at the latest."

If Fabien's calculations were correct, they'd make it to Calais around midnight, Helene thought to herself as they pulled up next to the plane. Looking at its size, it was clear that Théa would have to remain in her lap for the duration of the flight, especially if Eve held the Typex.

This was about to be the longest night of her life.

✳✳✳

She jolted out of a doze as her stomach did a flip. As her eyes readjusted to her darkened surroundings, she noticed they had started their descent into Calais, which explained why it felt like her heart was in her throat. Théa shifted in her lap, and a glance at the girl told Helene the landing would surely wake her if it was anything like the last one she'd experienced.

As it turned out, the ground was much smoother here than in Toulouse. Either that or Fabien's landing skills had improved in the short time since she'd last seen him. She moved to wake Théa gently, stroking her hair as she whispered against her temple.

"Théa, wake up, sweetheart."

The girl took in her surroundings warily, but acquiesced when Helene encouraged her to step off the plane and into the grass. In the very near distance, Helene could make out the harbor and if she squinted, she could make out the lights on the other side of the channel. That was where Théa was headed, she thought as she swallowed a lump of apprehension. She hoped with everything she had that this was the right thing to do.

Do not worry, my dear. What you are doing for the girl is going to save her, literally. She will live a long and happy life because of your actions tonight.

Following Fabien's instructions, Helene and Eve started towards the harbor with Théa in tow. Luckily, he'd offered to watch over the Typex for the short while they'd be gone. Finding their French contact turned out to be much easier than Helene had initially expected, and he seemed to have bargained with a fisherman to take Théa across the water. Eve had been concerned about Théa arriving in England with no idea what to do or where to go—which in turn made Helene's head spin with worry—but the Frenchman assured them that he'd gotten in touch with an older English woman who often took in refugee children. She'd offered to wait for Théa at the docks and take her to her farm in the countryside—the Germans had been bombing London for some time now, and it would be safer.

Hearing there was someone waiting for her on the other side made Théa's grip on Helene's hand relax. She bent down in front of the girl so they were eye level with each other. This was the part she'd been dreading all day, the goodbye. She was leaving this child all alone, abandoning her when she had nobody left. Knowing that it was all to keep her alive and well should have made her feel less guilty, less horrible, but it didn't. She tried her best not to let Théa see that guilt as she took her small hands in her own.

"It's time, sweet girl."

"I know, Miss Helene, but, um," Théa's eyes immediately filled with unshed tears, "I-I'm really scared."

There seemed to be an invisible knife twisting itself through Helene's stomach at the sound of those words.

"That's okay," she said as she fought to keep her voice level, "It's alright to be scared. It means you're about to do something very brave."

Ah, so my words have made a difference.

"Will you come get me? When the war is over?"

"Of course I will. The minute it ends, I'll catch a plane."

"What if you don't know where I am?"

"Doesn't matter, I'll find you."

Before Théa could say anything else, Helene brought her close for one last hug. They knelt there for several long moments, Helene's lips pressed against the girl's forehead until Eve said it was time to leave. Helene watched Théa try to put on a brave face as she marched away towards the boat, which only made Helene feel worse. She summoned up the courage to wave as the boat moved away from the shoreline, but she was sure Théa probably couldn't see her in the dark.

Now that she was alone with Eve, she didn't try to stop the tears as they made their treacherous way down her face. Eve held her hand and rubbed her arm lovingly as they walked back towards the plane.

"It was the right thing to do, Helene."

"It doesn't feel like it."

"We just gave that little girl a new life, a better life. Remember what you told me back in June? Resistance is about helping people. You did that, and I'm proud of you."

Of all the words that Eve had ever said to Helene, none made her feel so happy and so sad at the same time. Eve was proud of her, for doing what she knew was right despite not wanting to do it at all. Mostly, she was proud of her for keeping her promise to Henri Cadieux and getting his daughter to safety.

Eve was proud of her.

And so was I.

ATHENA
November 12th-13th, 1942

thena's throat feels so incredibly dry as she realizes that she's been talking for quite a long time. Her siblings seem to have also recognized how long it's been since she last took a break, judging by their faces. She can't blame them, really. They're all used to her rationing her speech, only talking when it's necessary.

"Well," Ares starts, "It's good to know you have feelings after all, Athena."

"You thought I didn't? Everyone has them."

"You are not *everyone*, dearest sister."

Well, obviously. But he doesn't have to make it sound like an insult.

"Helene means a lot to me, that's all."

She takes a swig of her drink to hide the blush creeping up her neck. She hates all this talk of emotions. They make her feel vulnerable. It's something Aphrodite has told her she needs to work on, and she's trying. Agreeing to tell this story is proof enough of that. But it's not easy by any means.

"You aren't the only one Helene means a lot to, it seems," Amphitrite teases in a way that changes the subject, to Athena's relief, "I was starting to think Eve would never tell her how she felt about her, and now that their mission is complete, they can enjoy each other's company."

"Perhaps, yes," Athena considers, "You'll just have to wait and see."

ATHENA
March 30th, 1943

A harsh winter had come and gone since Helene and Eve arrived home from their trip abroad. Now it was March, and the last traces of snow had finally melted back into the ground to nourish the roots of the trees. The third month of the year was a time of transformation—an adieu to the bitter sting of the cold, and a preparation for the return of the flowers.

On the morning of her 22nd birthday, I found Helene sitting primly at the desk in her bedroom, writing a letter in near-perfect cursive. I knew the letter was addressed to Théa. I also knew it would never be sent, just like the many missives that had come before it. I got the sense that Helene wrote them more for herself than for the little girl—detailing the ins and outs of her daily life in order to distract from the heaviness in her heart. But she told herself that someday, when she saw Théa again, she'd give her every letter so she could read them to herself and know how much Helene had thought of her in the stretch of unbearable time when they'd been forced apart. The war still raged ferociously, and with no sign of stopping in the near future. She was painfully aware that with each passing day, Hitler came closer and closer to invading England. She wasn't sure what she'd do if that happened. Her mother told her not to think about it. But how could she not? The world seemed so bleak to Helene, so devoid of light and color. Even today, on her birthday, she didn't feel the thrill in her chest at being another year older. She'd felt it every year for as long as she could remember, but it didn't feel right to celebrate herself when so many people around her were dying.

Despite this, there was one particularly bright spot in Helene's life that couldn't be discredited: her growing relationship with Eve. They both knew they could never actually be together in the traditional sense of the word—to even imagine they might someday felt so dangerous it often sent Helene into a tailspin. But Eve seemed determined to love her in secret anyway. These days, their meetings often involved very little training. Most of the time they just sat and talked, but sometimes they found themselves quite caught up in each other, and in those cases, they barely spoke. Any thought in Helene's mind could be easier communicated with touch than with speech. The passion she received in response took her breath away every time.

She smiled as she thought about getting to see her beloved later. Eve had called on the telephone the night prior, telling her to meet her at their usual spot for a birthday surprise. Helene couldn't fathom what this surprise could possibly be, but all she really cared about was getting the chance to spend her birthday with the person she loved. Eve had mentioned that Arthur would also be in attendance, which excited her as well. She hadn't had much of a chance to really talk to him since she'd come home from France—he'd been in Poland on his own assignment when she left, and then he'd taken some time away from Blackthorn for the holidays.

Her morning had started with Ingrid and Kitty rushing into her bedroom, waking her up to the tune of *"Zum Geburtstag viel Glück."* The commotion caused Margarethe to groan and hide under her covers, but Helene couldn't help but laugh at the sound of their little voices cracking on the higher notes. She'd barely been out of bed for ten minutes before presents were laid in front of her—a beautiful new dress that her siblings had pooled their money to buy and a new leather journal from her parents. She smiled at the way Ingrid exclaimed that she was about to be the most stylish person at school, and she promised all of them that she'd wear the dress to visit her friends later in the day, so they could see how beautiful she looked in it.

✳✳✳

When she finally got the chance to go visit her "friends," it was late afternoon. Arthur stood leaning against the back door as she arrived at the old restaurant, his legs crossed at the ankles and a cigarette hanging from his teeth. He'd grown some facial hair since she last saw him, but everything else seemed the same. Smoke encircled his head as he took the cigarette out of his mouth to speak to her.

"Look who it is! Thought you'd never show up, rookie."

"Well I had to spend the designated time with family, I'm sure you can imagine."

"Whatever you say," he winked in her direction, "How was France?"

"Successful, although it proved to be a bit touch and go at times."

"I'm sure you handled it just fine," a genuine smile lit up his features, "You're quite resourceful after all. Eve gave you a glowing review when Wilheim asked how it went."

That made her blush. Arthur's smile widened at the sight. I got the sense they were thinking two very different trains of thought. It hadn't escaped my notice that almost every word Arthur directed at Helene was flirtatious in nature to some degree. It had been that way for years. Helene didn't see it, of course. She was too busy fawning over someone else.

"I got you something," Arthur mentioned as he reached into his pocket, "Since it is your birthday."

He tossed a small rectangular box in her direction. Inside was a pen, engraved with her initials: *H.R.*

"Since you're so good at writing," he continued nervously, "I thought you could use something nice to do it with."

"Thank you, Arthur," Helene said with genuine gratitude, "It's wonderful, really."

The silence that ensued was more than a little awkward, and eventually, Arthur broke it for the sake of preserving whatever was left of the moment.

"Perhaps we should go inside? Eve is waiting."

Yes, Helene did very much want to see Eve. As Arthur followed her through the door and down the hallway towards the parlor, Helene wondered how she should interact with Eve in front of him. Surely, he did not know about their situation. No one did, and Helene intended to keep it that way. She decided that since Eve had a gift for her, that a professional interaction was most likely out of the cards.

Friendly but not too touchy it was, then.

Eve's face seemed to blossom like a daisy in springtime as she spotted Helene, and she sprung up from lounging on the armchair with a squeal.

"Oh, I'm so glad you're here!"

Helene was engulfed in a hug that lasted longer than she

thought it would, considering the company in the room with them.

So much for not too touchy, huh?

As they broke apart, Eve held her at arm's length as she inspected her from head to toe.

"Happy birthday, Helene."

"Thank you."

"Is this a new dress? The color suits you."

"Yes, a present from my brothers and sisters."

"How sweet," her smile made the cutest crinkles appear at the corners of her eyes, "It will go very nicely with my own present."

She reached for a tiny velvet bag on the desk, and deftly lifted its contents out for Helene to see: it was a necklace, with a crimson pendant in the shape of a rose. Her breath caught looking at how elegant but simple it was.

"Do you like it? It reminded me of you," Eve asked somewhat dismissively.

As Helene met her gaze, she saw feelings hidden in Eve's stare that didn't match the tone of her voice—her eyes gleamed softly as if to say, *You are my love, my courage, my rose.* Helene swallowed the lump forming in her throat and instead answered in as proper a way as she could muster.

"Of course I like it, thank you. You know how I love flowers."

"I do," Eve chuckled as she moved towards the desk again, "Would you like something to drink? Arthur and I are having whiskey, but there's tea here, too."

"Tea would be lovely," Helene replied, "Hopefully you have sugar, this time?"

Eve shot her an exasperated look, but before she could say anything, Arthur cleared his throat loudly.

"Just pour yourself a whiskey, Genevieve. I've got to get going."

"What?" Helene exclaimed, "But I just got here!"

"I know, and I'm sorry," he mumbled, "I've got some things to take care of for my mother, you know how it goes. But I wanted to give you your present."

There was a strange look across his face that Helene didn't remember having ever seen in his expression before. She couldn't for the life of her decide what it meant. It was as if he was suddenly uncomfortable standing so close to her, or was that confusion? Sadness? Helene couldn't tell. Perhaps there was something going on at home? Was he being sent on another mission?

"Thank you again for the thoughtful gift," she replied, "I'll try it out tonight."

Arthur nodded quickly before turning back towards the hallway with a haphazard wave in Eve's direction. Then, he was gone.

"Well, that was strange," Eve observed with slight amusement as she placed a steaming teacup in Helene's waiting hands.

"He seemed distracted, like something was bothering him."

"Whatever it is, I'm sure he'll straighten it out," Eve said as she came closer, "I'm not horribly offended he decided to leave, anyway."

"Why do you say that?" Helene wondered as perfume filled her nose.

"Because now we're alone, and I don't have to pretend I'm not dying to touch you everywhere all at once."

The comment was promptly followed first by a chaste kiss on Helene's cheek and then another on the lips that lasted a bit longer. The bitterness of the whiskey that still sat on Eve's tongue only made Helene want her more.

"Let me set my tea down, or we'll be dealing with a mess," she spoke as she moved towards the nearest flat surface.

"Better hurry; I already miss the way you taste."

It didn't take long, a few seconds perhaps, for Helene to set the cup down and Eve to guide her until she sat on top of the desk with her feet swinging like a child on a swing. Eve held her face firmly in warm hands and, for a few moments, simply stared at Helene lovingly.

"Has anyone ever told you that you are so incredibly beautiful?"

"Someone might've mentioned it, once or twice."

They both laughed before Helene brought their lips together once more.

Little did the two of them know, amidst their affectionate moment, that something wasn't quite right. I didn't even notice it at first, and if it hadn't been for my desire to give the two of them privacy, I don't know if I would've. When I did see it, there was instantly a dreadful sensation in my stomach, heavy as lead. I didn't know what the implications of it all might be—and I desperately hoped it wouldn't end up amounting to anything serious—but it forced me into a spiral of overthinking that I hadn't succumbed to in centuries.

Pressed against the wall in the hallway, hidden by shadows and silence, a young man stood with clenched fists and a bruised heart.

What exactly had he seen? Well, everything.

INTERLUDE
Athens, 2022

Athena is interrupted by a low whistle from Ares and something reminiscent of a surprised choke from Amphitrite.

"There's nothing as frustrating as an unrequited crush, huh?" Her brother chuckles, "Things are finally getting interesting."

"If only Helene and Eve had waited to make sure he was really gone," Amphitrite laments, "He never would have known. Oh, I'm sure the poor boy is heartbroken."

"I don't feel sorry for him," Apollo sighs, "Rejection is as necessary as air. He'll be fine."

Athena hums in response as she glances at Aphrodite. Her sister sits very straight in her seat, her nails tapping a nervous rhythm on the tabletop as she stares out the window over Apollo's shoulder. Athena knows she doesn't particularly like how the story unfolds from here.

"I suppose all of you will just have to wait and see if Arthur tells Helene about his feelings for her," Athena surmises, "I'll admit they're both about to have much bigger problems on their minds in the next bit of the story."

"What do you mean?" Amphitrite's eyes widen, "What happens?"

"Destruction," Ares answers ominously.

ATHENA
July 24th, 1943

You need to wake up, Helene.

Her eyes flew open as the siren went off. At first, she was confused as to what it was, but she could hear her father as his footsteps flew through the hallway, knocking open all the doors.

Get out of bed, now.

As Otto's shouts carried through every cabin, she detected a fear in his voice that she'd never associated with him before now. Her blood ran cold. She suddenly knew exactly what she was hearing.

You must hurry, there isn't much time.

The radio had been broadcasting about the possibility of this since the war started. They'd all practiced what to do if it ever happened, over and over. Somehow, it was still hard to believe it was actually happening. Helene glanced at the clock as she jumped out of bed—12:57 am. The middle of the night! She didn't know why she felt surprised; it was the perfect time to do it, really.

Wars are often won not because of a show of physical strength, but with strategic surprise.

She could barely think as she stumbled into the hallway. Her mother shoved Werner into her arms as she raced around, trying to collect the rest of the children. The sirens were scaring him, it seemed, because he was sobbing. Helene held him close to her chest as she ran somewhat haphazardly through the apartment, trying to find what needed to be grabbed and brought with them to the bomb shelter across the street.

In record time, Otto had woken the rest of the children, each of them clad in pajamas and shoes, their pillowcases stuffed hastily with what Helene assumed were clothes. It appeared that Margarethe had prepared a knapsack for her, as well. She wanted to smile in thanks and probably would have if everything hadn't felt so chaotic in the moment.

Her mother seemed to be spinning every which way, depositing younger siblings into the arms of older ones to save time. Werner was still sobbing into Helene's nightgown, and one look at Ingrid and Kitty confirmed they were also scared out of their minds. What child wouldn't be, in a situation like this? She was terrified, and she wasn't a child by any stretch of the word.

It is always the children who suffer the most in war.

Helene didn't want to think about what could happen as a result of an air raid—to her home, especially. Before she could think too hard about it, her father pushed her forcefully out the door.

She knew—with all her heart—that this would be the last time she stood in this apartment.

Remember that when all is said and done, home is not composed of places, but people.

The realization reminded Helene of the severity of the situation. The sirens that threatened to make her ears bleed indicated that the city was being attacked from the sky, and it was quite possible that bombs would start falling from planes at any moment. One could fall right on her head, for all she knew—her siblings' heads. An intensely protective feeling took over every inch of her in a single instant. The thought of a bomb exploding on her brothers and sisters–on her parents–and killing them was enough to completely knock the air out of her, and it suddenly felt like she could barely breathe. It wasn't supposed to be like this. She was the one who'd signed up to willingly participate in dangerous situations, not them. They weren't meant to wake up in terror to the threat of bombs raining down on them. It wasn't fair. It wasn't right.

In that moment Helene could think of nothing, *nothing*, but the safety of her family. She needed to get to the shelter. It seemed like the best option, although at the moment, not even a shelter felt truly safe to her.

The street outside the apartment looked like a scene from a film, or a nightmare. Children were screaming, mothers were wailing, sirens were screeching. It was utter chaos. Helene followed the crowd surging towards the shelter, silently hoping with everything she had that there would be enough space for them all inside of it, when her mother was suddenly next to her, shouting over the noise:

"Take the children with you into the shelter; your father and I will come back for you once the raid is over!"

Helene could've fainted right there on the street corner.

"*What?* Where—where are you going? You can't leave; they're dropping bombs from the sky! *Bombs*, Mutti!"

355

"We're going to the boat—we have to make sure it's protected! If we lose that boat, we lose everything, Helene. Everything!"

"And if I lose you, *I lose everything*!" She was screaming now, hot tears falling down her cheeks and her arms clutching baby Werner like he'd disappear if she didn't, "Please don't go, please..."

"Do you trust me?"

There was a flicker in Anna's eyes, a spark of stubborn determination that she seemed to reserve for dangerous occasions. It crossed Helene's mind that her father's face was painted with the same expression. Of all the possible moments for her mother to act like her father, was this truly the right time?

Of course it was the right time. People like Anna understood the art of stepping up to the plate. She repeated her question to her bewildered daughter.

"Do you have faith in your father and I, Helene?"

"Faith in—of course, Mutti!"

"Then I need you to trust me right now—put every ounce of faith you have left in me when I say that I promise, *on my sister's grave*, that I will come back for you."

Before Helene could find any kind of word to say, her mother smiled reassuringly before kissing her forehead long and hard. As she and Otto turned to run towards the docks, Helene heard her shout:

"I love you, meine Hummel."

Anna hadn't called her that since she was a child. She tried to watch them go, but they disappeared from view so quickly. Now they were gone, and the white-hot feeling of panic Helene felt deep in her gut threatened to buckle her knees.

There comes a time in everyone's life when they must come face to face with the kind of chaos that bends and breaks things. It is essential in this moment, whenever it may manifest, to choose Bravery over everything else. It is the only way to survive. Helene had been tested before–had been forced to wear Bravery's armor on multiple occasions–but nothing compared to this moment. It required the kind of courage she had yet to become acquainted with–this wasn't about conquering fear. This required looking fear in the face and agreeing to dance instead of fight. This meant that Helene had to first face the fact that people she loved might die–that she might die–and then she had to sit with that fear in silence because it meant protecting the people she loved. In France, she'd been able to put her fear of being arrested into action. She'd been able to formulate a plan and take the necessary steps to complete it.

But she wasn't hiding from the police in Toulouse. She was hiding from bombs in Hamburg, and she could not in good conscience decide to stop hiding now, no matter how much it scared her to remain.

When every fiber of your being tells you to run, but you choose to stay? That's the kind of courage that keeps you alive. Helene felt terrified, of course she did, but she needed to keep her siblings safe.

Truly, it didn't really matter if Helene had wanted to run after her parents because the crowd seemed to be pushing everyone along like cattle being herded into a pasture. She nearly collapsed onto the hard stone floor of the shelter before looking around frantically for all the other children. She flew through their names in her head: *Margarethe, Ernst, Anneliese, Ingrid, Kitty, Werner.* They are all here with her, all safe from the bombs. She sighed in relief. A knot had formed in her stomach and a lump in her throat that made her want to break down and cry until there weren't any tears left, but she refused. She couldn't, not in front of her little brothers and sisters. She needed to be strong for them.

See? That's the kind of courage I'm talking about.

She heard Ingrid's small voice ask Margarethe where their parents were. Helene felt sick thinking about Otto and Anna out there, amid all that dust and fire. All she could do now was hope the raid wouldn't last too long and pray the bombers weren't aiming for anything on the river.

A part of her mind—a rather big part—also found itself consumed with thoughts of Eve. Was she alright? Had she made it to a shelter? Was she afraid, too? Helene wished with everything she believed in that if Eve was anything, she was safe.

✳✳✳

The raid lasted for an hour—sixty whole minutes of nothing but the constant sound of bombs falling above their heads. Helene lost count after the first hundred booms. She couldn't even begin to imagine what it looked like up there on the streets. Surely, the entire block had been decimated. Somehow, Werner had fallen asleep against her; something about the consistency of the bombs must've proved lulling. She took a moment to look around the room at everyone else—some she knew, like the Stiner family from next door, and the couple who ran the pharmacy down the block. There were also people she knew but did not see, like sweet, old Mrs. Fischer from the bakery. Her stomach churned once again, thinking about what she didn't want to be true, but probably was. Anyone who did not make it into some sort of shelter was probably dead by now. It made her even more nervous for her parents, although she was sure the water would provide some last-second protection from anything with a flame.

Finally, the sirens stopped. Everyone looked at each other with nervous expressions, as if they knew that no sirens signified the raid was over, but they were all still afraid it was not. Eventually, a few young men decided to leave the shelter. Everyone else heard them yell down from above moments later, saying there weren't any more planes flying over the city, and that the raid was over for the time being. So, everyone filed out one by one, the nighttime air still singed with sparks and smoke. Helene had been expecting destruction, but she was still utterly floored at the scene spread out in front of her. When she brought the children into the shelter, they'd left a city street complete with apartment buildings, businesses, and cobblestone sidewalks. What they were returning to was...nothing but a shell of that. Piles of rubble surround them—the dozen or so buildings that once stood mighty and tall were now structural skeletons. It felt nothing short of haunting. Was this really what must be sacrificed when war was waged? Was this the unfair price they had to pay? She wondered, bitterly, what the Führer would say if he were standing next to her. Would he mourn the loss of a beautiful city and its beautiful people? Would he even care?

I'd wager the answer is no, he wouldn't have. He might've pretended otherwise, but psychopaths don't tend to care about anything but themselves.

Helene was pushed out of her spiraling thoughts as little Ingrid touched her hand, pulling at her fingers and pointing upwards. She looked up to see the sky had cleared itself of smoke just enough so one could see the stars if they looked close enough. She couldn't help but think the stars looked as beautiful as ever—burning just as bright as they had been yesterday and would burn tomorrow.

The scene made me think of human (and, I suppose, godly) connection and the ways in which the ones we love can serve as our own personal stars. They give one a reason to go on in the midst of war, death, and anger.

At that moment, it seemed the stars agreed with Helene very much and had decided to give her what she really needed. A particular voice seemed to float above all the others in the crowd, like the talented soloist in an out-of-tune chorus:

"Helene!"

A flash of raven hair. A click from polished heels.

And then Eve was moving towards her, dirty and exhausted, but *alive*.

Helene found herself shouting her name back louder than she thought possible after not speaking at all for so long, and as she came closer, Helene automatically passed Werner off to one of her sisters just as her feet involuntarily carried her across the pavement without her even consciously willing them to do so. The two of them collided despite knowing how many people might see them do so—Helene's arms wrapped around Eve's neck while her friend wrapped her own around Helene's torso. Eve reeked of smoke and fire, but Helene supposed she did too. She felt a gentle hand against the back of her head as she buried her face in Eve's shoulder. She pressed one, then two kisses, swift and secretive, against her lover's exposed neck—relishing in the goosebumps they caused. She'd never been so happy to see Eve—living and breathing just as she should be. They stayed rooted to each other for several more blissful seconds before breaking apart reluctantly. Eve's eyes widened, and her hands found Helene's as she took in the landscape around her.

"There's nothing left."

"I'm afraid not."

"Are you alright?" Eve's eyes scanned the length of Helene's torso, looking for injuries and other anomalies, "Are you hurt?"

"I should be asking you that question."

"I'm dirty, but otherwise fine. Your parents gave me shelter, thankfully."

"You saw my parents?" Helene immediately scanned the crowd, "Where? Are they okay?"

"They're fine, Helene," Eve reassured as she placed gentle hands on her shoulders, "They should be coming shortly. I ran ahead to see if I could find you."

"What were you doing near the docks?"

"Looking for you, obviously. I didn't realize you had an apartment in the city...well I suppose it's gone now."

Before Helene could think too hard about the fact that Eve's priority during an air raid had been her safety, Ingrid spotted Anna in the crowd, and any sort of embarrassed reaction was temporarily forgotten by the sheer feeling of relief at knowing her parents hadn't perished on the boat. As Anna went around and kissed every one of her children silly, Otto strode up to Helene and Eve—that same look of determination still plastered across his face. Helene wrung her hands together anxiously.

"Vati, what are we going to do now? The apartment is gone."

"Well, first thing's first, we're going to go to the boat," He explained as he kissed her forehead. "Luckily, no bombs came near it, so it's still in top-notch working condition."

"And once we get to the boat, what will we do?"

"We'll be leaving the city right away. We cannot stay," His expression turned solemn, "This was the first raid; it will not be the only one. As sure as I know my children's names, I know there will be another raid once the sun is up, and another, and another. The leaders of this country have crossed many lines and angered many other countries. I reckon this is revenge."

Before she could think not to, words she hadn't expected to

say came tumbling out of her mouth.

"Perhaps there is room on board for Eve, too? I hear you've been acquainted."

"Oh yes," her father's eyes glinted mischievously, "We've met. A firecracker, this one is. I didn't know you had a friend like this, darling. She is welcome aboard."

"Thank you, sir," Eve said as she smiled back at him.

And so, they traipsed through the war-torn streets of what used to be Hamburg—older children carrying younger ones—until they made it to the boat. Helene had never been more grateful to be standing on the deck again. By the time she'd helped her mother get all the children back to bed, they'd left the dock. The city was still lit up in shades of orange—its receding outline flickering like a dying ember. Otto sat silently at the wheel, his mind set on getting out of Hamburg's vicinity by daylight. As she went to stand next to Eve at the bow, she turned to ask him what she'd been wondering for a while:

"When do you think it will be safe to go back?"

"I don't know."

His answer made her grab Eve's hand and squeeze.

INTERLUDE
Athens, 2022

T his is where, Athena decides, she needs to cease speaking, at least for a brief time. Aphrodite had allowed Apollo the chance to narrate—it only seems fair that she'd be allowed to pick someone to recount a small bit of the next part.

Ares sits across from her, his arms crossed (when are they not?) and an expression across his features that lets her know he's really starting to enjoy the story. It makes sense, considering his taste for war and acts of aggression. She isn't too sure how good of a storyteller he is, truthfully, but she supposes everyone needs practice before they can master anything. She'll make a wordsmith out of him in no time.

"Ares? I'm wondering if you could do me a favor, just this once?"

He looks delightfully confused as he answers her.

"What do you want?"

"I'd like to take a break from being the sole narrator. You are quite familiar with the next installment of the tale," she concentrates on sending the metal images through the door of his mind, "Aren't you?"

A sinister smile creeps across his face, and Athena is sure he knows exactly what she's talking about. Her brother has always taken an interest in watching humans inflict pain on each other, for no other reason than that it proves they are fallible and oh, so mortal.

ARES
August 27th, 1943

Well, this is unexpected, isn't it? I'm not a fan of anything too *cerebral*; that's Athena's job, and it has been for... well for as long as I can remember. And I have a good memory. I'm supposed to be the brawn, not the brains. But alas, my sister has a way of making it nearly impossible to tell her no. Besides, I simply can't resist taking over for her just this once, considering the circumstances. I have always enjoyed watching those puny little humans do three things above all else: battle, betray, and bleed. This next bit includes all of that. Can you feel the way I'm practically vibrating with excitement? No, of course, you can't. I don't do *that*.

When my sister left her dear Helene last, the family was high-tailing it out of Hamburg after the Allies started blowing it to smithereens. In the month between that recounting and this one, the Reinholdt's had arrived in Berlin with the intent of staying for a few months, but possibly longer if the bombings continued in

Hamburg. Otto and Anna decided that everyone would remain on the boat together—seeing as it was summer—and there would be one designated day per week that the children would be allowed to explore the city if they so chose, as long as they were back on the boat by supper. So far, Helene hadn't ventured far from the boat due to the near-paralyzing fear that things would start blowing up around her if she did so.

The date was August 27th. It was a Friday, and the sky had erupted with rain. Honestly, that should've been a sign. But who am I to draw attention to such things? It ruins the fun when the humans are prepared. Helene had been feeling rather restless as of late—being stuck on a tugboat with her many siblings and all. Her one saving grace was, of course, Eve. She loved having her on board, and every time Eve caught her in some forgotten corner devoid of prying eyes and curious ears, she kissed her deeply until Helene panted for air. They did not have much time to themselves, and the secrecy of their relationship left Helene feeling frustrated in more ways than one. Both of them were also eager to make the most of their time in Berlin—seeing as it was the city of Blackthorn's origin—and Eve had started making plans to contact local agents about meeting to discuss something to help with. She'd already sent Arthur a telegram telling him where they were and where to find them if he decided to leave Hamburg. They hadn't received a reply from him, which worried Helene endlessly. She hoped he was well, and that his family had survived the attack on the city.

Thinking too much about the destruction in Hamburg left her with a suffocating feeling in her chest as if she was back in that crowded shelter and not safe and sound on Poseidon. The boat felt more claustrophobic to her now, but the thought of leaving it made her nervous, too. If Eve hadn't been there every day to encourage her to explore with her one day, she probably never would have.

Eve finally did convince her, on the fourth Friday in August. As she handed Helene an umbrella, she proclaimed in her no-nonsense voice that it didn't matter if they got wet from the rain, they were getting off the boat.

If only they realized how dangerous it was for them to leave such safety. A pity.

Neither Helene or Eve knew Berlin very well, but after questioning several local women crowded together smoking on a street corner, they found a small park only a few blocks from the harbor. A single, lonely flower booth stood along the meandering walkway, and as they approached it, the vendor shouted the names of three, maybe four different flowers. Noticing Helene's interest in the dahlias in particular, Eve stopped to buy a bouquet. Once they were out of immediate sight, she handed the flowers to Helene with a bow.

"For you, my most honored lady."

Helene felt the blush on her cheeks as she accepted the bundle and brought it to her nose.

"They're beautiful, thank you."

"It only seemed fitting for such a beautiful person."

I don't care what Aphrodite says; Love is almost too cliché to handle.

The two women linked arms—that seemed plausible enough for *friends*—as they continued down a quaint side street. Helene couldn't help but imagine what it might look like if the Allies bombed the city. So many people lived here, even more than in Hamburg, and the loss of life that would be the sure consequence of a raid would be nothing short of devastating. She hoped when it did happen—because it wasn't really an "if" anymore—she and her family were nowhere near it. Perhaps she could convince her parents to stick out the rest of the war in a small country town. It would be so much safer for the children and would certainly make her feel more at ease.

The street ended as they approached a large, impressive building—the Märkisches Museum, according to the sign. Helene marveled at the architecture of it.

"Eve, isn't this wonderful? We should walk through it. I'm sure there are lots of interesting things inside it."

When her companion gave no answer, Helene drew her gaze away from the museum. She must've been mumbling—she sometimes did that when she wasn't speaking directly to someone's face.

But once Helene was facing her again, she noticed the way Eve wasn't focused on what she was saying. She wasn't focused on Helene at all. As Helene followed her gaze, she saw two things that forced her heart into her stomach.

A black car sat idling against the curb, as if waiting for someone.

An SS officer stood leaning against it.

When the man saw that he'd attracted their attention, he started walking directly towards them. Every fiber of Helene's being told her to find a way out of the imminent situation as the *click, click, click* of his polished shoes grew closer, and she probably would've tried had Eve not latched onto her arm with a grip of iron.

"Don't run, that won't do any good."

"Eve, do you think—"

"I don't know what I think, yet. Let me handle this. I'm sure he just thinks we're pretty."

Sure, that thought may have passed through his mind. That's not why he's there.

Before Eve could think of anything to say, the officer beat her to it.

"Well, if it isn't Genevieve Harrison and Helene Reinholdt. If I didn't know better, I'd think you were waiting for us to find you."

The sound of both of their names on this man's lips sent an icicle of panic down Helene's back, and it froze her on the spot. She couldn't have run away even if she wanted to. Something was very, very wrong.

"How do you know who we are?" Eve nearly snarled.

A sadistic smile answered her.

"I make a point to round up as many Blackthorn agents as I can. I'm sure you know the Führer isn't exactly a fan of your... efforts."

Holy shit. This was not happening. It could not be happening, not here, not now.

Oh, poor, unassuming Helene. Of course this is happening.

Eve opened her mouth to speak, but the officer cut her off with a wave of his hand.

"Don't think you can deny your involvement in the group. My informant has lots of intel, and you especially," He leveled Eve with a spiteful stare, "Are a person of great interest."

His informant? Intel? Helene's head was spinning, half in dread and half in confusion. He continued speaking, a level of nonchalance in his voice that didn't fit the occasion.

"So what's going to happen now, you might be wondering? Well, we're going to get inside of that car over there and head to an undisclosed location, where my colleagues and I will question you," his black eyes met Helene's then, "And if you're thinking about trying to run or fight, just know that I have eyes and ears all over this city, several of which are watching a particular boat as we speak. Those children are so precious; I'd hate to see something happen to them."

The remaining air fled her lungs completely at the implications of his threat. This could not be real. There was no way he'd hurt innocent children.

As soon as she thought it, Helene knew it wasn't true. He would hurt them, easily.

"You fucking piece of shit," Eve growled as her hold on Helene's arm tightened.

"Call me what you like," he replied, "It won't change the facts of the matter."

The look on Eve's face implied she was weighing the outcomes of the two choices placed in front of her. For Helene, though, there was only one choice. Her voice seemed altogether too fragile as she spoke before Eve could.

"If I go with you now, do you promise me you won't touch a hair on their heads?"

"Helene—" Eve started.

"Of course," the officer cut her off, "They are not the ones who have committed treason. Unless, of course, they know of your involvement."

"They don't," she lied through her teeth.

"I didn't think so," he moved to the side with his hand gesturing towards the waiting car, "After you, ladies. Don't make this hard on yourselves."

Helene forced herself to take a step in the direction of the car, then another, and another. She felt Eve next to her, although her field of vision had narrowed, so she could only truly focus on what was directly in front of her. It felt like one strong gust of wind would knock her clean over as she shakily climbed into the backseat and allowed another officer—who had been waiting in the passenger seat—to snap handcuffs onto her wrists. As Eve was practically shoved into the car next to her, their gazes met—Helene's eyes rendered glassy while her companions were full to the brim with fury. She tried to smile, and although she failed miserably, she hoped she'd conveyed to Eve that they'd be alright. They'd get through this and be back on the boat by sundown. It was just questioning, after all.

It's funny how the smartest people can be so incredibly stupid.

The smell of chemicals roused Helene from the depths of unconsciousness. She detected a wet rag held against her nose and assumed it had been soaked in ammonia purposely to wake her up. She was still sitting up in the chair they'd strapped her to, her chin against her chest and her hands tied behind her. As her awareness returned, so did the pain—the excruciating pain that seemed to have seeped into her bones and settled there. She tried to flex her hands from within their confines only to remember several of her fingers had been broken. She was sure that if a mirror was placed in front of her, she'd find bruises across her abdomen. It hurt to breathe. It hurt to think. She felt naïve for having taken the idea of "questioning" so literally. It had been more than a professional inquiry, more than an interrogation—and she sensed they weren't done.

Of course they aren't done. They don't have what they want.

It took significant effort, but she managed to peel her eyes open—if for no other reason than to find out what they'd done to

Eve. She had still been awake when Helene's vision had blacked. A groggy glance around the cinder block cell they'd been placed in led Helene's eyes to land on the limp form of her companion—now also unresponsive. She didn't want to think about what they might've done to her before she finally passed out. Now, her head was tilted back towards the ceiling, and blood leaked from several places, including her mouth, her nose, and the deep gash that decorated the entire left side of her face. If Helene's own injuries were any indication, Eve had probably sustained a broken rib, as well.

Her eyes refocused on the cause of her abrupt waking. The officer who had found them on the street was crouching in front of her with a relaxed composure. It made Helene sick to look at him, because she knew he was enjoying this.

"Welcome back," his voice was so terrifyingly calm, "I'm glad you could join us again. I think that, perhaps, we got off on the wrong foot earlier. I'm going to wake up our friend over there, and then we can have another chat, hopefully with a better outcome."

Helene didn't think she had enough strength to respond, but she didn't get the sense the officer wanted her to. She watched as he approached Eve and held the ammonia under her nose until she gasped and sputtered and coughed herself awake. By the time her body relaxed again, her chin was covered in bloody saliva. The man repeated to her what he'd spoken to Helene only moments ago, although Eve didn't really seem to be listening to him. Her half-open eyes kept focusing and refocusing on Helene from across the room as if trying to gauge how badly she was hurt. Helene tried to send a reassuring look back, one that told her she was okay, but she wasn't sure how successful she was.

"Now, where were we?" the officer asked before answering his own question, "I believe I was inquiring about the future plans of your little treasonous faction."

When he was met with silence, he continued.

"While I have a feeling that one of you," he spat in Eve's direction, "Won't cave to anything short of extreme violence, I do think the other might be open to reason."

His gaze shifted until his eyes met Helene's. They were black as night. She would've shuddered had she been able to find the strength to. She braced herself for a punch to the stomach or some other form of physical abuse.

It never came. Instead, the officer moved briskly to the door before disappearing through it. The only sound Helene could detect was Eve's jagged breathing and the sound of the wind blowing haphazardly outside. The moment of reprieve gave her time to think. How had they been caught? Someone must have ratted them out, but she couldn't for the life of her think who that might be. Hardly anyone even knew they were in Berlin.

Exactly, use that brain my sister is always talking about. There's really only one person with the ability or desire to give the Nazis your location.

As the only possible name appeared in Helene's mind, her eyes filled with tears. How? Why? Had she done something? Had hands been forced?

Helene, please. This is not the time to be a sniveling baby about this. It's not about what you did; it's about what you didn't do. What you didn't choose.

Before she could ruminate on my comment, the door creaked open once again, only this time, it wasn't the man from before who entered the cell, ready for another round of torture.

Rather, it was the betrayer himself.

This one was not an SS officer—far from it in all reality,

although there was nothing he wanted more than to prove himself worthy enough to be one someday. It was the very thing that pushed him, motivated him, damned him. The desire to be important. It was too bad, really, that it had gotten to the point where it didn't matter if the attention he so desperately sought came from power-hungry villains. It was intoxicating to him either way. So intoxicating, in fact, that he'd agreed to a dangerously long con—an undercover mission—to get more of it.

My sister was very correct when she said that children are the most affected by war. This young man hadn't been roaming the Earth long enough to know what it felt like to truly be a man. Deep down, he was still very much a boy, and Hitler had taken advantage of that.

As he stepped farther into the room, Helene heard a breath hitch in genuine surprise to her right. She knew how much this betrayal would hurt Eve—how she'd blame herself for not seeing him for what he was all along. Thinking about that guilt sitting on her beloved's shoulders was enough for Helene's sadness to simmer into blinding anger. The only person who should feel guilty was him, yet looking at his face now, she knew he felt none. How dare he do this to someone she loved?

It's precisely because you love her that he did it. It means you don't love him.

The realization dawned on her all at once, and it did nothing to quell her fury as words finally dislodged themselves from her throat.

"Arthur. You fucking asshole."

"Wow," he feigned surprise, "I didn't think you knew those words, Helene."

"I reserve them for special occasions."

"I'm honored."

Helene glanced in Eve's direction if only to not have to look at him for a moment. Her eyes seemed to have glazed over, almost as if she was in a trance. Helene had never seen her look like that before, and to say it scared her would be an understatement. Eve couldn't shut down. Not yet. Not now. Not ever. She needed to do something—needed to rouse her enough that she'd help her fight back.

It seemed Arthur had other plans for her. Before Helene comprehended what he was doing, he closed the distance between himself and Eve. His fist connected with her jaw in one impressive, impassioned swing that sent her flying, chair and all, to the ground. Helene heard herself scream for her as though she might hear it.

She did not, in fact, hear it or anything else. Arthur had sent Eve back into the depths of unconsciousness as easily as one might kick a ball into a net.

Helene stared at him in horror.

"Why did you do that?"

"I've been wanting to for a long time," he said as he pulled a vacant chair in front of her, "But I also wanted to have you to myself for a while, to try and convince you."

"Convince me of what?"

"The benefit that would come with taking a deal when it's offered to you."

A deal? What could he possibly mean?

"Perhaps you could enlighten me about what the fuck you mean," Helene sneered through gritted teeth.

"Eve's turned you feisty," Arthur clicked his tongue in disapproval, "We'll have to work on that."

He continued before she could comment.

"Let me give you some context, first. My father was a member of the Reichstag, and after Hitler rose to power ten years ago, he climbed the ranks, too. He approached me several years ago with a way for me to make a name for myself within the Party. The Führer needed someone to infiltrate a newly created rebel group called Blackthorn to gain information and learn how to take down the operation. It was quite the involved job—I would have to be undercover for years—but I agreed to it gladly."

"So this whole time," Helene felt positively sick, "You never actually cared about making the world a better place. You never wanted to help people."

"It's not that I didn't care, Helene. It's that we have different definitions of 'better.'"

"You believe killing innocent people is the solution? To what, exactly?"

"I believe the Führer wants to make Germany strong again."

"You're fucking disgusting."

A dangerous look flashed through Arthur's eyes, and Helene thought he was about to hit her, but he restrained himself at the last second. His fists clenched into balls instead as he moved the conversation along.

"You are in a bit of a predicament, wouldn't you say?" He questioned sarcastically, "There is a way out of it, luckily. All you have to do is agree to my terms."

"I didn't know your people liked making deals."

"Oh, they don't. But they owed me a favor."

Helene hated where this was headed.

"You see, the man who was in here before, Oscar, he wanted to send you to a camp hours ago. I convinced him to let me talk to you instead."

"How kind," Helene spat.

"I can get you out of those handcuffs and back on that boat in less than an hour."

"Where does the blackmail come in? What's the caveat?"

"Don't call it that—I would make sure you were happy."

"What's the damn catch, Arthur?"

Oh, here it comes.

"I'm sure you are aware that homosexuality is illegal and immoral?"

Helene's mouth instantly dried up. How did he know about that?

"Yes," he said, smiling at the panic in her eyes, "I caught the two of you. On your birthday. Perhaps you should've checked to see if I was truly gone before letting loose."

What fools they were. He continued.

"I will get you out of here and keep your little secret if you agree to never act on any sinful thoughts again."

"And, what? I know there's more than that."

"You would also, of course, become my wife."

Imagine being this delusional. What a psycho.

Something in Helene snapped at such a ludicrous proposition. Surely, he wasn't serious. He couldn't be. *His wife?* Before she could think to stop it, a chuckle formed on her lips, followed by another, and another, and another until laughter spilled into the tense silence of the moment uncontrolled. Even as the seriousness in Arthur's eyes turned to hatred, Helene found herself unable to move past the absolute ridiculousness of the idea. Did he really think she'd agree to that? After what he's done? After a moment, she'd calmed enough to respond to him.

"Are you actually insane? Your wife?"

"Would it really be such a bad thing, Helene?"

"Such a bad—" She cut herself off, "Arthur, you've just told me that the only way I get to see my family again is if I marry you."

"It's an offer many wouldn't hesitate to take."

She was getting irritated now.

"I think you *are* insane. I am in love with a wonderful, beautiful, intelligent woman who is lying unconscious on the floor mere feet away. Why on Earth, Arthur, would I ever consider abandoning her for the bastard who put her there?"

Fury flashed white hot in Arthur's expression.

"Your freedom is looking you in the face, and you want to deny it?"

"You and I both know I would never be free if I became your wife. There might have been a time years ago, had you played your cards right, when I would have given you a chance, Arthur. But this mess you've caused? The people you've hurt? The betrayal? It's not something I want to ever forgive you for."

"You don't need to forgive me," he was practically pleading now, "You are all I think about, the only thing on my mind. You belong with me—to me. Just let me love you, please."

"I don't belong to anyone," she seethed, "Least of all you. I will not marry you, and there's nothing you can do or say that will change my mind. I don't negotiate with people like you, and certainly not at the cost of my body or my choice."

My sister has trained her well.

The rage pulsing through Arthur's bloodstream threatened to seep out of him as he took a long breath. He tried to collect himself and only half-succeeded.

"Fine, have it your way. I hope Auschwitz isn't too hard on you."

And with that, he was gone.

✳✳✳

The officer from before, Oscar, came back after Arthur left. He spent the next several hours attempting to glean more information about Blackthorn, and Helene spent that time floating in and out of lucidity. By the time he grew bored enough to stop, she was pretty sure she was missing a tooth, and one of her eyes was swollen shut.

"I think it's about time," Oscar huffed, "That the two of you were loaded onto the truck."

There was too much blood in her mouth to answer. He seemed to revel in that knowledge as his voice trailed on.

"You'll be joined by more of your comrades in about a day, thanks to the extra intel Arthur so graciously provided us with."

The look on her face was enough to get her question across: *What do you mean?*

"There happens to be a Blackthorn checkpoint en route to our destination," he explained with a grin. "Arthur has informed us that if we were to ambush said checkpoint, we would find several agents as well as the Jews they are illegally transporting. Luckily, we'll be able to round them all up now."

Helene very nearly threw up at the implication. Of course Arthur would rat out those agents; what did he have to lose? She'd gone and pissed him off, and now he wanted to use that anger against other people. Would he have provided that intel if she hadn't refused him? Was she the reason why so many innocent people were about to die?

If Oscar noticed how vehemently she reacted to the news, he didn't let on. He unlocked her handcuffs briefly to get her out of the chair before clamping them back on again. She watched as he did the same to Eve. Looking at her caused a lump to form in Helene's throat, but she didn't want to cry—she wouldn't give these vile humans the satisfaction of seeing her break down. Eve's shoulder bumped her own as they were led out of the cinder block cell towards a caravan of cargo trucks, and as their eyes met, she could see that Eve's hope was dangerously close to being snuffed out completely. Helene hated seeing her like that—hated that anyone had dared to try and steal her light.

Try as they might, Helene wouldn't let them succeed.

She was going to fix this.

Well, that's a daring proposition, not to mention an unlikely one.

INTERLUDE
Athens, 2022

Apollo claps his hands together obnoxiously as Ares finishes, making Athena chuckle.

"What a twist!" he exclaims, "I had a feeling Arthur would confront Helene about the issue of his unrequited love for her, but I did not expect him to be such a traitor."

"I can't believe I felt bad for him before," Amphitrite mumbles.

Even Athena hadn't realized Arthur's true intentions until after he revealed himself. It isn't something she's proud of, although she recognizes that even if she had known, there isn't really anything she could have done. As much as she wishes it could be, Fate cannot be deterred.

"That was quite enough storytelling for me," Ares says, breaking through her thoughts, "Athena, you can continue from here. I wouldn't want to take Helene away from you for too long."

She nods at him once before glancing briefly in Aphrodite's direction. Discomfort can be found in the way her arms are crossed over her torso, as if she's trying to comfort herself. Athena reaches out and telepathically squeezes her sister's hand. She knows Aphrodite can't feel fingers interlocking with her own, but she can feel the reassurance such a feeling would accompany.

"Alright," Athena straightens in her seat, "Onward we go."

ATHENA
August 28th, 1943

I t was hours later, after being thrown into the back of a military truck and immediately falling asleep, that Helene felt a gentle hand against her face—the first non-violent physical touch in days. She relished in the feeling as she woke further: soft fingers stroking her cheek in a way that only one person ever had before. Sure enough, as her eyes opened, Helene found herself lying with her head in Eve's lap, the two of them swaying gently with the movement of the truck. Sunlight peeked through the canvas flaps on either side of the vehicle. She must have slept through the rest of the night, which meant it was the twenty-eighth now.

She noticed with a start that her handcuffs were missing. She reached for her wrists and slowly ran her fingers over the irritated skin she found. She then glanced upwards with questions in her expression.

"I took the cuffs off," Eve smiled, "It'll be easier to figure out an escape route without them on, don't you think?"

Well, it seemed Eve had gotten some strength back. It made me happy.

"How? The officers have the key."

"I picked the lock, silly. Used one of my hairpins."

Helene shouldn't have been surprised that Eve knew how to pick locks.

"Oh, of course. Why didn't I think of that?" She mumbled as she struggled to sit up. The muscles in her midsection felt terribly tense, and one look proved her entire abdomen was a mottled mix of blues and purples. "Do you have any ideas for getting out of here?"

"Well, the obvious one is to jump."

"That plan isn't your soundest," Helene snorted. "There's too many of them, we'd most likely be caught immediately."

"It's the best plan we've got."

"We have to find a way to divert the convoy away from the Blackthorn checkpoint. I don't see a way for us to get away, but if we can warn—"

"Helene, no," Eve interrupted her with a resigned look, "It's too late to warn anybody. We've been driving for hours; we're probably almost there. We have to fend for ourselves now. That means finding a way out of this damn truck."

Helene stared at Eve for a long moment after she finished. The resolution in her voice left Helene with no doubt that she was dead serious in her belief that there was nothing more they could do. But that wasn't true, was it?

There was always a choice.

Helene had vowed to fix this. For Eve. For Théa. For the innocent people who were about to suffer needlessly. She could not, in good faith, plan her own escape, knowing that if she did, others would still be sent to Auschwitz anyway. No, she needed a better plan than simply jumping out of the truck.

It was in the exact moment that Eve stood up to investigate the door that Helene's eyes landed on the solution: a wooden box sat in the corner of the truck bed. A cartoonish flame was drawn boldly across the slats: *flammable*. Helene looked towards her companion. Eve had her back to her, focused intently on breaking through the door. Good, she was distracted. Helene knew she'd hate this idea.

She stood shakily, against her body's ultimate wish, and shuffled in the direction of the box. It was difficult to move around when the ground you stood on was also moving, but she managed in spite of her rather sorry state. The box was medium-sized, and based on the way it wasn't bolted shut, Helene assumed their captors hadn't originally planned on using this specific truck to transport them anywhere. The lid moved easily to reveal what was surely hundreds of sticks of dynamite.

More than enough to cause a scene.

As a burst of adrenaline rushed through her bloodstream, Helene picked up the nearest bundle of explosives with shaky hands. This was certainly something she could work with. If she could only find a way to light one, the rest would blow with it. This entire box could easily take out the entire convoy.

She heard Eve approach from behind before she could think to close the lid.

"Is that what I think it is?"

Helene turned to find Eve staring wide-eyed at the box.

"It's dynamite, yes."

"Maybe we'll take a bundle with us when we jump; it might be useful later."

"I think it would be rather useful now, don't you think?"

"It would just cause a mess. Not to mention, one of us might get hurt if we jump from a truck as it blows up."

Helene realized then, as Eve spoke, what detonating these explosives would mean. There was no way both of them would have enough time to light the fuse and get a safe enough distance away before everything exploded, and Helene had already decided that everything must explode—in order to save the people waiting at that checkpoint, every vehicle in this damn convoy had to be blown to pieces.

One of them would have to stay in the truck. It was the only way to put a stop to this.

Eve had continued talking excitedly as Helene ruminated on the thought, and she was now pointing at the back door of the truck with a proud look on her face.

"I figured out how to unlock this door, it really was quite simple. All we'll have to do is open it and jump out. But we'll have to be quick, or else the car behind this one will be able to catch us."

Helene found all she could do was stare at Eve wordlessly. There was no doubt in her mind, now, which one of them should stay behind. She was surprised by the sense of deep conviction the realization gave her.

The world desperately needed people like Eve—fierce, quick-witted, kind souls who made it their mission to seek out the goodness in humanity and use it to combat the evil. This war was far from over. It wouldn't be right for Eve to die now, not when she had so much life to give—*to save*—still.

Eve would survive this, even if it meant Helene wouldn't.

She wasn't stupid, though. She understood that in order for her plan to work, she couldn't tell Eve anything.

"If we're really going to do this," Helene declared, "I need to calm myself down a bit. I can barely think right now. You wouldn't happen to have a cigarette on you, somehow?"

A sly smile formed on Eve's lips, "Of course I do; you think I'd hide a cigarette somewhere where some Nazi asshole could find it and smoke it for me? I even have the lighter, still."

She pulled a singular cigarette and a small lighter from her bra and held both out in front of her. Helene almost caved right then, as she stared at the blind innocence on her lover's face. Guilt filled her from head to toe as her hand brushed gently against Eve's in the exchange, but somehow she managed to stay silent.

"I didn't think you liked to smoke," Eve remarked as she moved closer to the door again.

"I usually don't, but I thought it might give me some courage."

You could say that.

"You have all the courage you need; never forget that."

The brilliant, understated look of adoration Eve sent in Helene's direction as she said that brought tears to Helene's eyes. She hadn't known she was even capable of being courageous before she'd met Eve. It was because of her that Helene understood what it meant to help others. It was because of her that Helene knew what it felt like to believe in herself. This woman was her first love, and now, she supposed, her last one, too.

She moved almost mechanically until she stood directly in front of Eve. The broken door latch was visible just behind her shoulder.

"Darling," she nearly whispered, "I need you to promise you'll do something for me, when all of this is over."

"You know I'd do anything for you," Eve replied quickly, a softness in her expression that nearly forced Helene to look away.

"If I don't get the chance to, I need you to go back to England and find Théa. Promise me you will, Eve."

Confusion swept between them as Eve's brows furrowed.

"Alright, I promise. But you're going to get the chance to, of course. Once we're off this bloody, truck we'll find our way back there together."

Oh, how my heart ached for both of them. There was nothing I wanted more than to see them stay together.

"Théa needs someone good and kind to take care of her."

"I agree," Eve lifted a lock of hair behind Helene's ear affectionately.

Helene rushed on before she could force herself to stop.

"I know," she began as she trembled, "That whatever this is, whatever we have, isn't something that would ever work out the way we wish it could, but for what it's worth, you are the best thing I've ever known—"

"Helene, we're going to be fine. It's not too far of a jump, and we can run fast."

"You are the sound of the ocean in the morning and the smell of hot, black tea at night. You are my light and my love in a sea of darkness—an anchor for this world and an anchor for me."

"Helene, stop."

"I love you, Genevieve. I wanted you to know. I used to tell myself that I would never fall in love with anybody, but I guess the universe knew something I never did."

Oh, my sweet girl.

Eve moved to embrace her, and Helene took her chance.

"I hope you can find it in yourself to forgive me someday," she murmured as she planted one last searing kiss to Eve's lips. As she started to pull back in apprehension, Helene reached past her and flung the latch up and over the catch. The hot, late summer air blasted her in the face as she studied Eve for one last beautiful second. She was so heartbreakingly beautiful when the sunlight reached out to touch her like this.

Helene used all the strength she had left to shove her sideways out of the truck.

"*Helene, no!*" Eve let out a horrified scream that shattered every defense she had left, and she fell to her knees as a sob flew from her mouth. She watched as Eve met the ground hard before rolling down the grassy hill bordering the road, just as Helene hoped she would. It meant she'd be safe from what was about to happen next.

Moving as quickly as she could, considering the officers in the car behind her had begun signaling for everyone to stop, she crossed to the other end of the truck bed with the lighter in one hand. She grabbed a stick of dynamite with the other.

It was here that she finally hesitated. Her hands shook so forcefully I wondered if she'd even be able to start a flame. She looked so young and so scared in that moment that, against my better judgement, I decided to do something I very rarely did, something that I knew could easily get me in trouble with my father. It didn't matter, truly. I wouldn't let my girl down now.

As Helene Reinholdt froze in fear, I froze time and stepped from behind my invisible curtain.

I showed myself to her.

At first, neither of us said anything. I'm sure she didn't know exactly what to say—it's not every day that one finds herself in the presence of a goddess and knows it. She looked as if she'd seen a ghost. I spoke before she could faint or do anything else inconvenient.

"It's okay to be scared, Helene."

Recognition flashed through her expression as she relaxed slightly.

"You're the voice in my head. The one that's always been there."

"Yes, I've been guiding you since your first breath," I confirmed, "And now I'm here to help you through your last one."

"I don't want to die."

"I know."

"But I will if it means those people get to live."

"Do you realize how brave that is? How selfless?"

"I guess. I just want to do something good, and I want it to mean something."

"Mmm," I hummed in agreement, "You've always wanted that, haven't you?"

When Helene didn't respond, I continued.

"When you were born, I could see so clearly the way Wisdom favored you. It surrounded you like a mist, and it showed you that knowledge is the highest form of power," I paused in surprise as my breath hitched with emotion I wasn't expecting, but I soldiered on, "But as you grew up—as I watched you learn to harness words and devour books—I noticed there was something else about you that I couldn't quite pinpoint. It took me years, but I understand what it is, now. You get it from your mother, if I had to take a guess."

"What is it?"

"Wisdom chose you in the seconds after you came into the world, but so did Love. You are the perfect combination of the two, Helene Reinholdt—Reason reflected in Love, and Love shaped by Reason. It is your essence and your greatest strength. It will see you through this."

Helene contemplated my words for a moment before replying.

"Will you stay with me? Until the end?"

"I cannot think of a higher honor."

I mustered up my brightest smile for my girl, my Helene, as my parting words floated past my lips.

"If you need any last reassurance, know this: you do mean something, darling. To the woman you love, to the little French girl, to the mother who birthed you. But especially, you mean something to me. You always will."

With that, I unfroze time.

She grinned in a way I knew I'd never see from any other human again, and before she could think about all the reasons not to, Helene lit the wick, which detonated the blasting cap in turn. There was a flash of immense heat before the darkness came and took her away.

But there was something about it—the feeling of burning—that felt triumphant, felt right.

When you burn for others, you burn for love.

My girl left the world exactly the same way she came into it.

Mighty.

Fierce.

Glowing.

✳✳✳

It would take Eve several hours to find what Helene left for her. After her screams and tears had morphed into grief-stricken silence, she remembered her predicament and searched her pockets frantically for food, a weapon, anything to help her until she made it to the nearest town. She didn't find any of those things.

She did find something, though, and it was enough to bring her to her knees in the grass. It glinted as she held it up to the sky.

A ruby-studded necklace in the shape of a rose. The only thing Eve had left of her.

She'd given it to her at the last moment—a final reminder of everything she'd been, and everything she would continue to be. Her love, her courage, her rose.

INTERLUDE
Athens, 2022

Silence greeted Athena as she finished the tale, at least the part she could tell. The story wasn't quite over, but she hadn't started it, and she didn't think it was her job to end it either.

"Aphrodite," she said quietly, "It's time."

Her sister's eyes brimmed with tears as she nodded once.

APHRODITE
September 1st, 1943

I t took me several days to find it within myself to do what had to be done. I didn't want to do it—didn't want to face the pain that would inevitably come with it—but Athena convinced me. Anna deserved to know what happened to her daughter, she said. She deserved closure. I knew better than anyone that closure wouldn't make the pain go away, but I also knew my sister was right.

I'd expected storms to trample the Earth the moment I finally stepped onto *Poseidon* again. But there was no rain in sight. Sunlight soaked the deck boards in warmth. Apollo must have sensed I needed a boost of confidence in however small a way. I'd deliberated on how to break the news to Anna for some time, but with Athena's help, I had come up with something that didn't feel completely unworthy.

I found Anna alone on the foredeck, staring off into the sunrise. It was still quite early, and I was glad nobody else but Anna would be privy to this conversation. A look of concern flashed through Anna's eyes as I moved closer to her as if she had already sensed my presence.

I lifted my shield of invisibility as my hand reached for Anna's shoulder and squeezed.

For a moment, we simply stared at each other. Anna's gaze shifted as she regarded me, and it was clear that there was something about me that she recognized on a soul-deep level. Another moment passed before she endeavored to speak.

"I've always wondered if I would ever meet you in the flesh, and here you are," she murmured, "I suppose...well, I suppose it can only mean one thing."

I couldn't bring myself to answer. The words stuck to the tip of my tongue as a tear escaped down my face. Sadness filled Anna's features at the sight.

"She's gone, isn't she?"

I nearly choked at the resignation in her voice.

"Yes, she is."

I watched as Anna squeezed her eyes tightly shut at the confirmation in an attempt to keep her tears at bay. Her and I both knew it wouldn't help.

I held her as she cried.

We ended up crouched on the floor, Anna clutching at my dress as I carded my fingers through her hair. I wasn't usually this affected by the plights of humans, but this was so very different. I knew this feeling, this pain. I'd felt it over and over, every day and every night. Because my daughter had been taken from me, too. I also had an unrepairable hole in my heart, and would forevermore.

I knew how, from this day forward, Anna would feel her child's absence like a bullet to the chest. There was no getting over this kind of thing—the death of a daughter. To get over it would surely mean to forget.

Anna lifted her head and stared at me with red, puffy eyes.

"Did she feel the pain of it?"

"No, I don't think so."

"I suppose," her voice sounded so fragile, "That I ought to be thankful, hmm?"

"No. It's not fair, and it never will be. Mothers shouldn't have to live without their daughters."

"All I mean is that I'm thankful I got to live with her, when all is said and done."

"What do you mean?" I wondered. There wasn't anything to be thankful for, was there?

"Better to have loved and lost, than never have loved at all, right?"

The question sent shockwaves through me as Love leaped and bounded across my bones. Was she right? Of course she was.

"Do I wish I had more time with her?" Anna continued, "Of course I do. But I have all of the memories of her, and those are so much better than nothing."

It is not often that humans outsmart goddesses, but this was one of the few times. How had I never been able to feel that way myself? After Zeus took Harmonia from me, I'd been so blinded by grief and the sense of loss that came with it that I hadn't been able to function correctly. I'd gotten so caught up in the panic that came with thinking about a future without Harmonia in it that I failed to remember the beautiful, wonderful, precious moments I had already spent with my daughter. That wasn't wasted time—

quite the opposite. It was everything. The pain I felt was the price I had to pay for loving Harmonia. It was the price Anna had to pay for loving Helene.

It didn't matter, either, that Helene had been beaten by the very people that she sought to beat herself. There is a cost to everything, especially when it comes to war, and war is never fair. But the bad circumstances that Helene lived, loved, and died within don't negate the good memories, do they? No, certainly not.

Because hearts of war are, after all, still hearts. They beat, and they bleed, and they spend every second of every day fighting for Love. The lack of it. The abundance of it. The magic of it.

FINALE
Athens, 2022

"So, the story comes to an end," Aphrodite concludes, "And with it, this challenge."

"I've lost then, haven't I?" Ares moans.

"I wouldn't call it a loss, brother," Athena muses, "Think of it as more of a lesson. While this night started with the notion that either Pain or Love had to be superior to the other, it is now rather obvious that neither one is more powerful, per se. They are equally powerful–inextricably intertwined. To suffer is to love, and to love is to suffer. Great pain does not exist without great love. It exists because of it, in compliance with it. Truly, it's the greatest wisdom of all, isn't it?"

"Yes," Aphrodite can't help but grin, "It is."

"I need to know what became of Eve," Amphitrite demands, "Did she escape?"

"Of course she did," Athena assured, "And she abided by Helene's ultimate wish, too."

"She found Théa?"

"She did, and then she took the girl back to the house in Sussex where she'd grown up," Aphrodite chimes in, "She took care of her until Théa was old enough to go off on her own."

"Did she forgive Helene eventually?"

"I don't think there was really anything to forgive in the first place. Eve spent the rest of her life hurting from Helene's decision and missing her to pieces, but she knew there wouldn't have been a chance at changing Helene's mind. She was proud to have known and loved someone brave enough to sacrifice so much."

The tavern comes alive as her brothers start talking at the same time, Ares grumbling and Apollo cheering for everything and nothing all at once. Amphitrite claps fervently, as if joining Apollo in celebrating Aphrodite's victory. She can't bring herself to do anything but smile. She can't believe she actually did it—she can't believe she proved Ares wrong and won the bet. She wouldn't have been able to do it without Athena.

Amidst the chaos that's erupted around them, her sister has stayed rooted to her seat, just staring at her in silence.

Aphrodite knows she should meet her gaze, but for some reason, she can't bring herself to. Perhaps it's because everything feels different between them now that their tale is told. She thinks it's a good kind of different, but she's spent her entire existence knowing Athena is everything she isn't—her dichotomy, her competition. They've never been equals—kindred spirits—before. Has reminiscing about Anna and Helene been enough to change that?

Aph.

The sound of her sister's voice in her head cuts through both the silence and her thoughts. It's jarring how kind and soft it sounds, and she's only breathed a syllable. Aphrodite finds it almost overwhelming to know Athena wants to speak in such a way to her, of all people. She doesn't know how to articulate that, though, so in the mental space where a response should come from, there is only the slight hum of magic.

Athena acknowledges the lack of an answer and immediately knows everything she needs to. Of course she does. Her lips lift slightly like they do when she's about to say something vaguely contemptuous, and Aphrodite braces for a comment about being so easy to read, or so silly for thinking–

I love you.

Aphrodite's mind blanks as the words filter into her consciousness.

Even if no man or god ever truly does, know that I do. You are my sister, and I love you.

The confession is instantly met with teary eyes as she struggles to keep a calm demeanor. Never in her wildest dreams has she ever thought Athena would explicitly express her love for anything beyond a superficial level. To hear the sentiment in her sister's regal voice is astounding in itself, but to have those words–the three most powerful words in any language–directed at her? Referring to her? No form of wealth or material desire could ever elicit the warm and addictive feeling blooming in her chest–something she has always accepted as non-viable, uncreatable, unsustainable in the vessel of her being.

The Goddess of Love has always known what it means to adore others.

Now, she knows what it means to be adored in return.

THE END

"I have hated words and I have loved them,
and I hope I have made them right."
-Markus Zusak

ACKNOWLEDGEMENTS

To say this book has been a long time coming would be a mighty understatement. For the past two and a half years, I've worked to tell this story in the best way I could. To finally be able to say I've written a novel feels surreal.

The inception of this book started, funnily enough, with the creation of a different one. In the summer of 2019, I was introduced to the story of a very special family by my boss (and family friend), Al Ulsrud. His wife's grandparents, I discovered, had plied the German rivers before and during World War II on their tugboat named Poseidon. Ten children were born to Karl and Emma Kluge from 1921-1941. My fascination with the family led me to write a non-published, fictionalized account of their life for their descendants to enjoy. The bones for this story were created from that one. Otto and Anna Reinholdt are based in part on Karl and Emma, and I would be remiss to leave them out of my acknowledgements. I had a wonderful time learning about the Kluge family, and it was truly an honor to spend so much time getting to know them.

I'd like to thank my family and friends for unflinchingly believing in my ability to succeed as a writer—specifically my parents, Ryan and Lisa, my best friend Ashley, and my aforementioned friend and patron Al Ulsrud. Without your encouragement and support, this book would not exist.

Thank you also to the many teachers I've had the pleasure of learning from over the years. It is because of you that I found my confidence as both a writer and a fellow teacher.

Last but certainly not least, thank you to the writers who have come before me. Your ability to convey Love and Wisdom through words will inspire me forevermore.

Printed in the USA
CPSIA information can be obtained
at www.ICGtesting.com
LVHW090433281024
794800LV00001B/1